30119 026   D0550613

ALL THE DAUGHTERS

ALL THE DAUGHTERS

PENNY FREEDMAN

Copyright © 2012 Penny Freedman

The moral right of the author has been asserted.

Apart from any fair dealing for the purposes of research or private study,
or criticism or review, as permitted under the Copyright, Designs and Patents
Act 1988, this publication may only be reproduced, stored or transmitted, in
any form or by any means, with the prior permission in writing of the
publishers, or in the case of reprographic reproduction in accordance with
the terms of licences issued by the Copyright Licensing Agency. Enquiries
concerning reproduction outside those terms should be sent to the publishers.

Matador
9 Priory Business Park
Kibworth Beauchamp
Leicestershire LE8 0RX, UK
Tel: (+44) 116 279 2299
Fax: (+44) 116 279 2277
Email: books@troubador.co.uk
Web: www.troubador.co.uk/matador

ISBN 978 1780882 772

British Library Cataloguing in Publication Data.
A catalogue record for this book is available from the British Library.

Typeset in Aldine by Troubador Publishing Ltd
Printed and bound in the UK by TJ

Matador is an imprint of T

For Zoë Emmeline
and Genevieve Joy,
who are and are not
the daughters of this book,
and for Robert
with all my love

FOREWORD

I lived very happily for thirty years in the city which was the inspiration for Marlbury and I have many good friends there. I would not want anyone to think that Gina's jaundiced view of the city is mine. The characters who appear in these pages bear no relation to any of that city's inhabitants, and the places of learning and entertainment have only the most superficial resemblance to prototypes there.

I am all the daughters of my father's house
And all the brothers too, and yet I know not.

Twelfth Night, Act 2, Scene 4

1

TUESDAY 21st SEPTEMBER

'And what's her history?'

'So what's your policy on farting in class, Eve?' Ellie asks.
Eve gives a hoot of laughter. 'Well, I try not to do it as far as
possible,' she says. 'It helps if you don't eat gipsy tart for
lunch.'

'You know what I mean,' Ellie protests, waving her wine
glass with dangerous vigour. 'They drove me mad this
afternoon. You just get them settled and working on something
and then one of the boys farts – or the others say he has – and
they all start flapping their arms and holding their noses and
making a big production. Next thing, they want to open the
windows to clear the air and then they start dropping things
out – not their own things, other people's – all sorts – pencil
cases, books – there was even a shoe this afternoon – and then
the owners want to go down and collect them, and the whole
lesson collapses. And all the teachers in the rooms below know
you've lost control when all these things start hurtling past
their windows.'

She ends with a comic wail, but I can see she's perilously
close to tears. Poor Ellie: my twenty-two-year-old daughter,
fresh out of university and in her first term of teaching at The
William Roper Academy, Marlbury. Now Marlbury isn't your

crumbling post-industrial city. On the surface, it's a prosperous and charming town – quite a tourist attraction, in fact, with its fine abbey and gardens and little half-timbered houses – but it has its areas of social deprivation and William Roper is creamed several times over by three grammar schools and a bunch of private schools. Middle class parents have numerous ways of avoiding William Roper and avoid it they do. I taught there myself for fifteen years, give or take a few terms of maternity leave. It wasn't an academy then but I doubt the change has been anything more than cosmetic: a lick of paint, a smart uniform and a shiny logo. That unpleasant American expression comes to mind; Ellie is discovering that, even with lipstick on, The William Roper School is a pig.

'There are extra problems to teaching drama,' I say to Ellie. 'It's a bit easier if you've got them pinned down in desks.'

'That's why I asked Eve. They all mill about in the art room, don't they? How do you keep them focussed?'

'Well, I don't have the farting problem, for a start,' Eve says. 'My room stinks so much of paint and turps nothing else gets a look-in. But the real secret is being relaxed. If they know you're rattled, then they know they've got you. You start by pretending – you should be good at that, you being an actress and all – and then you find you're doing it for real. Of course, it's hard jumping in the deep end like you're doing...'

Eve's voice, with its soft Irish consonants, is like warm honey and her sitting room is an improbable feast of colours and textures. There are rugs, covers, cushions, curtains, all made by her over the years, in a palette of blues, greens and yellows; there are ebullient arrangements of dried flowers and grasses; there are vigorous sketches of her four gorgeous daughters and her growing brood of grandchildren. As she talks on, though, soothing Ellie, and I sit back on my sofa and sip my wine, I find I can superimpose on all this the sights, sounds and smells of William Roper as I met it when I was only a year older than Ellie is now. Sights and sounds are easy: gum-smeared windows, graffiti-gouged desks, leprous paint and the clattering, shattering soundtrack of a thousand teenage voices ricocheting between hard surfaces. What surprises me is the way the smell comes up to meet me, compounded of many simples, that unmistakeable blend of spearmint gum, cheese and onion crisps, cheap floor cleaner and teenage sweat.

I did my time there at the coal face and then, as I was coming up to forty, I got out. Eve stayed, but then Eve is a better woman than I am. Eve is the woman I would like to be if I could somehow be wiser, calmer, sweeter and kinder. If I were quite unlike myself, in fact. But still I aspire. Misguided, neurotic, sour and judgemental as I am, I still believe that I could be that warm, consoling earth-mother if only – if only what? If only the world were a different place, I suppose. Anyway, I didn't stick it out at William Roper; I escaped to teach English for academic purposes to foreign students at Marlbury University College, where the ambience is superior, the students are, for the most part, well-motivated and the classroom smell is different: garlic mainly, with sheepy overtones of damp wool between October and March, when students from warmer climes – Greeks in particular – don't like to take their coats off.

Enough of this. I snap back into the conversation. 'I've remembered,' I say, 'what I used to do about the farting issue.'

Ellie and Eve turn to look at me. I sense that their conversation has moved on in my absence.

'I told them that in polite society it wasn't done to comment on other people's bodily functions and I made anyone who mentioned farting come in at lunch time and write rhyming couplets on the subject of polite behaviour.'

Ellie objects, 'But we're not supposed to punish kids by giving them extra work to do. We're supposed to engage them in the work, not make it a chore.'

'Well, I never made them write rhyming couplets at any other time. I hate rhyming couplets – they make everything sound trite and trivial, like Pope.'

'The Pope?' Ellie asks, startled. 'He doesn't speak in rhyming couplets, does he?'

Eve shouts with laughter and I splutter on my wine as I say, 'Not *the* Pope, Pope – Alexander – 18th century poet, so-called. What an ignoramus you are, Ellie. I told your father he was wasting his money on your expensive education.'

'Ah yes,' says Eve. 'That will be a bit of a handicap in coping with the William Roper kids – you having been to Lady Margaret College for Girls, all posh and civilised and well-behaved.'

'Not as well-behaved as all that.'

We turn to look at Colin Fletcher. I'd almost forgotten he was here. He's withdrawn himself a bit from our female circle and is mulling over a crossword, I think.

'Lady M has a bit of a drugs problem at the moment, I hear.'

'There always were drugs around,' says Ellie. 'We got them from the boys at The Abbey.'

'This isn't just the odd bit of cannabis or ecstasy,' Colin says. 'It's serious stuff.'

'Wow,' says Ellie. 'That'll be getting Mrs Mayfield in a flap. I wonder if they're coming from The Abbey too.'

Colin smiles. 'As we're the school doctors for Marlbury Abbey, I couldn't possibly comment. Professional confidentiality.'

Colin is a GP – our GP, in fact – and if he were an actor you'd be bound to cast him as the old-fashioned family doctor. He's tall and broad-shouldered, with a lot of springy grey hair and a rather military moustache. Like my ex-husband, Andrew, he is an alumnus of The Abbey School, Marlbury's finest and most ancient public school, but he has surprisingly left-wing

4

views and I bumped into him on several demos during the Thatcher years. I saw him on the march against the Iraq war in 2003 too – though you didn't have to be left-wing to join that – just in possession of a couple of brain cells. He is gentle, humorous and charming, and if I'm never quite comfortable with him, it's simply because he's been familiar with the most intimate bits of me and that feels rather odd.

'Talking of drugs,' I say, 'did you know I'd given up smoking?'

'How long since your last cigarette?' Colin demands with professional scepticism.

'Six weeks.'

Eve gives me a round of applause and I bow graciously.

'I'd like to say it was your influence, Colin,' I tell him, 'but actually it was because of Freda.'

Freda is the fifth member of our party this evening. She hasn't joined in the conversation yet, although Ellie and I are proud of her extensive vocabulary. She is Ellie's three-year-old daughter, born at the end of her first year at university and the reason, I'm afraid, that Ellie is facing the rigours of William Roper at the moment. It's a sensible career decision for a single mother but it's not what Ellie envisaged, I'm sure, when she went off to study drama at university, and I'm sorry she has to be sensible. I am also furious with Freda's father, who has never been named and has never, as far as I know, contributed anything to her life. Since Ellie has a huge student loan to pay off – day nurseries don't come cheap – she and Freda are living in my house. I've always claimed that I was looking forward to an empty nest once Ellie's sister, Annie, took herself off and left me in peace, but the nesting habit is hard to break, I find, and I think I may have been ruined for living alone.

Aware that we've all turned to look at her, Freda gives us a wide, gummy smile. She is exploring a basket of toys (property of Eve's grandchildren) and with a performer's instinct, she demonstrates her ability to create a tower of beakers in descending order of size. We watch and admire, but Ellie is preoccupied.

'Eve,' she says, 'do you teach Marina Carson?'

'Do I teach her! She practically lives in the art room. If she's not painting, she's tidying my cupboards. They've never been so immaculate. I'm her refuge from the world, I think.'

'Is she any good?'

'Oh yes, she's quite talented.'

'Marina Carson?' I say, 'That's not a William Roper name. She sounds like the heroine of a romantic novel.'

'She's a puzzle,' Ellie says. 'She's in my tutor group.'

'9X?' asks Eve.

'What does "X" stand for?' I chip in.

'Extra,' Ellie and Eve tell me simultaneously.

'And is that Extra Bright or Extra Dim?'

'Extra maths and English. They don't do a language or physics and chemistry.'

'So Extra Dim. What we called remedial in my day.'

'Ach, you're so out of date, Gina,' Eve reproves me.

'So what's the puzzle?' I ask.

'When I first met her,' Ellie says, 'I wondered if she'd got into the wrong class by mistake. You can see at a glance that the others have problems – there's that "nobody at home" look – but she seems different. And she's not bad at drama. Then I got her first piece of written work in and I was really shocked: it was like primary school work.' She takes a swig of her wine and carries on. 'I was intrigued so I went and looked up her record in the year nine tutors' office, and it's really weird. It looks like she was abroad somewhere for eighteen months and only came back here a year ago. The weird thing is, before she went away she had a good VRQ – and an above average reading age – but when she came to William Roper

6

last year, her VRQ was only 84 and her reading age was way down too. How can she have gone backwards?'

'Where was she at school before she left?' I ask her.

'St Ursula's in Upper Shepton. I wonder why they didn't send her back there. It's just the place for nice, dim little girls.'

I notice Colin Fletcher shift in his chair and Eve says, 'Colin, I'm going to gossip about the Carsons and you won't like it, especially with them being your patients. So, why don't you go out and start cooking the stir-fry. It's all cut up ready and you always complain I overcook it anyway.'

Colin gets up. 'OK,' he says. Then he puts a hand on Eve's shoulder. 'Just try not to say anything libellous, darling, that's all.'

As he goes out, we all hunch forward over the coffee table. 'So Eve,' I say, 'give us the dirt.'

'Well, I'm surprised you don't know – Marina's mother is Glenys Summers.'

'Glenys Summers? I haven't heard of her for years. She used to be a name to conjure with, though.'

Ellie is looking blank. 'She was a child star,' I tell her. 'A few years younger than me. She specialised in appealing waifs. "Elfin" was the word they used to use about her. Then she grew up and didn't quite make the transition. I do remember her playing ditsy Dora in a film musical of *David Copperfield*, though. She could sing. She made a few records, I think. She was a bit of a *Hello!* favourite for a while, wasn't she, Eve? There was some sort of scandal – drugs and a breakdown?'

'Drink mainly, I think, though there were probably some drugs as well – and wild nights and crap men and not turning up on set and all the rest of it.'

'But she wasn't living here in Marlbury then was she?'

'Oh no. You'd be hard put to find a *Hello!* night here. Hector, her husband, brought her down here in the end to try and get her away from all that. Bought Charter Hall out at Lower

Shepton, a few hens and a horse and hoped country life would do the trick. And there were the two children by then.'

'Did it work?'

'Not at all – except that the paparazzi left them alone – too lazy to shift their arses far out of London. After a couple of years, Hector rented out the house, booked her into a very exclusive clinic in Switzerland and uprooted the whole family. That's how our Marina went missing.'

'For eighteen months?' Ellie asks. 'Her mother can't have been in a clinic all that time, surely?'

'Well, I suppose she wasn't in the clinic all the time, but I guess she was having treatment. Or maybe Hector was afraid to bring her back.'

The penny drops. 'Hector?' I ask. 'Hector Carson? The *Trilogy of Corisande* man?'

'The very same. He's a lot older than Glenys, of course. Married her when she was at her craziest. He was going to be her rock, and I must say he's stuck it out. There were some pretty hairy times. Colin was at his wits' end with her – always some panic or other. The Swiss clinic was his idea.'

I turn to Ellie. '*The Trilogy of Corisande* was a vogue thing in the seventies. It's *Lord of the Rings* meets *Morte d'Arthur*, with some fake Chaucerian language thrown in. I couldn't stand it but a lot of people loved it. There was a year when I was in the sixth form, when everyone was going round calling each other "a goodly wight" and that sort of thing. Really annoying.'

'You said they had two children, Eve,' Ellie says. 'So Marina has a brother or sister?'

'Oh yes. She hasn't told you about Edmund? She will, I guarantee. He's four years older than her and I've not seen him but he's apparently handsome, brilliant, talented and the apple of everyone's eye.'

'Where's he at school?'

'The Abbey, I believe.'

'That's pretty weird, isn't it? One child at The Abbey and one at William Roper?'

'I think he got some sort of scholarship. But there's no money for school fees for Marina, I guess. Switzerland will have been expensive and Hector's royalties must be drying up. They'll be doing better now, though, if Glenys's show keeps running.'

'Oh, that's where I've heard the name,' Ellie says. 'She's in that musical – *Amy* – isn't she?'

'The thing about Amy Robsart?' I ask.

'Yes. Sort of Elizabethan murder mystery. She – Glenys Summers – plays Amy. It's supposed to be really good.'

'She's a bit old, isn't she? She must be forty at least, and Amy Robsart was only in her twenties, surely?'

'The magic of theatre, my love.' Eve gets up. 'I'd better go and see how Colin's doing. And remember, Ellie, it's up to you and me to look after our little Marina. We'll see she's all right.'

2

WEDNESDAY 22ⁿᵈ SEPTEMBER

'He was a bachelor then.'

We banned any further school talk last evening and with good food and another couple of glasses of wine I watched Ellie's tight little knot of anxiety untwist itself under Colin and Eve's benign influence, but as we walked home I could feel the weight of William Roper descend on her again and she started to agitate anew about Marina Carson. 'I'm her form tutor,' she fretted. 'I ought to know what's happened to her. I ought to understand. What Eve told us helps but it doesn't explain the underachieving. Who can I ask about that? Who would know?'

'Well I don't', I said, 'but I know a woman who might.'

And so, when we'd got home and settled Freda, and I'd sent Ellie off to a relaxing bath, I e-mailed my friend, Hannah. Like Eve, she is a good woman. I choose them as my friends to compensate for my own shortcomings. Hannah is a paediatrician, specialising in trauma. She works for Médecins sans Frontières and I never know quite where she is, but she is able, surprisingly often, to answer e-mails, so I fired one off, summarising the Marina Carson case and asking for a diagnosis. 'Why would a child's VRQ and reading scores go backwards?' I asked. 'Enlighten us, please'. Then I went to bed.

This morning I am amazed to find, when I log onto my e-mails at work, that I have a reply. Does the woman never sleep?

From: "Hannah Walton" hannah.walton@freenet.com
To: "Virginia Gray" gina.gray@marlbury.ac.uk
Sent: 22nd September 2010 09.05
Subject: re a mystery

Dear Miss Marple (see – I can do literary references too)

I'm sending this to your work e-mail because I'm assuming that's where you are and I know your impatience of old. These are my first thoughts about your mystery girl. I'll let you know if anything else occurs to me.

She may have had a serious illness or trauma of some kind. Severe meningitis, for instance, could have that effect, or epilepsy, or a brain injury from a car accident or something of that sort. From what you say, she hasn't made rapid progress since starting at Ellie's school, so it does look like some permanent damage has been done.

An emotional trauma could have set her back too, but you would expect her to make up lost ground eventually (unless the trauma is on-going, of course).

We don't know what kind if life she was leading while she was in Switzerland. If she was away from her parents for some reason and not speaking or hearing any English, then I imagine she could have begun to lose her English and that would affect a VRQ test as well as a reading age test. But again you would expect her to make up ground rapidly once she was back in an English-speaking environment. (Do you know if she speaks French or German, by the way?)

Does she have any siblings? It might help to find out how they're doing.

I do remember Glenys Summers, mainly in musicals. She was the new Julie Andrews for a while and then faded away. You got me intrigued so I googled her – web page www.glensfans.com. It looks as though her daughter wasn't the only one who went backwards for a while. This is the official fans' website and pretty sanitised, I imagine. We need back copies of *Hello!*

Happy sleuthing. Love to Annie, Ellie and Freda.

Yours truly,

Dr Watson

I sit and look at this for a while. I can't spend long as I have to teach, so I don't click onto the web page, but I text Ellie, reckoning it ought to be break time at WR about now.

R u free 4 lunch?
Walk 'n' sarnies?
Have some ideas
from dr hannah
. re marina. How's
yr day so far?
Xx ma

I get a reply just as I'm walking downstairs to give a class on the stylistic possibilities of relative clauses. You know the kind of thing. My opening example for this morning is, "The Chancellor of the Exchequer, who has a multi-million-pound inherited fortune, said in Parliament that we must all be prepared to tighten our belts". I read Ellie's message:

Lunch ace. Crap
day. Run in with
Doug Fraser who
is A TURD. C u
1ish
Xx El

I get on my bike after my class, buy two superior sandwiches, two cartons of tropical juice and a bar of fruit and nut chocolate at M&S Food and cycle on to William Roper.

When I get there, I go in through the side entrance out of old habit but find there are no bike blocks there any more – too low-tech for this shiny new academy, I suppose – so I wheel my bike round to the front and pause to admire the impressive glass and chrome façade, the bold "WR" logo in red and black and the completely undefaced sign declaring this to be The William Roper Academy *Pursuing Excellence*. I padlock my bike to a bench which sits beside a glossy shrub to the right of the entrance and go to push my way in through one of the logo-enhanced glass doors. The door, however, won't budge, and as I put my shoulder to it to give it a shove a startling electronic voice addresses me from a shiny box on the wall: 'This is a security door. Do not attempt to open it until you have swiped your card'. I scan the wall, locate the card-swipe affair and gaze at it in wild surmise. Is this a test? What kind of card am I supposed to use? Surely not my credit card? I could, at this point, give up and go and sit on the bench with my bike to wait for Ellie, but I don't see why I should, so I press my face to the glass door and gesticulate at a woman I can see sitting behind a reception desk. I open my arms and raise my shoulders in a *What the hell am I supposed to do?* gesture and she reciprocates with a poking gesture of her index finger which seems to me to be just rude. Eventually, though, the speaking box addresses me again. 'If you are a visitor, please press the intercom button'. Intercom button. Yes, I suppose I should have noticed that but I'm not in the right mindset; this is just a school door for God's sake.

I press and a different voice (the receptionist's, actually – I can see her lips moving) asks me if I have an appointment.

'Yes,' I say firmly.

'And you are?'

'Sorry?'

'Who are you?'

'Well,' I say, 'it's a bit early in the day for existential questions. Who am I? That's a question most of us struggle to answer, isn't it?'

There is a silence. Then, 'Your name?' the voice enquires icily.

There is threat in her tone and I'm afraid she may call security. There was no such thing here in my day – any trouble and you called the biggest available member of the PE department to deal with it – but there will be security now, I'm sure; burly men in uniforms, possibly with truncheons. I cave in.

'My name is Gina Gray,' I say crisply. 'I'm a former member of staff here and my daughter is on the staff now. I have an arrangement to meet her for lunch.'

There is an electronic buzz and the door swings open before me. The receptionist regards me balefully and says nothing. I retreat to the Welcome Area, a corner of soft chairs and a coffee table bearing a potted plant and lifestyle magazines. A girl in William Roper uniform is leaning against one of the chairs but she stands up guiltily as I sit down.

'Don't worry about me,' I say. 'I shan't be here long. I'm meeting my daughter. We're going out for lunch.'

'Oh,' she says, 'that's nice.' She is tall and skinny but flat-chested, a pre-adolescent with a pale, freckled, unformed child's face and colourless fair hair cut in a rather old-fashioned bob.

She sounds so wistful when she says "That's nice" that I think she may have misunderstood and imagined a fellow pupil being whisked off for a treat in the middle of a school day. 'She's not a pupil,' I explain. 'She's a teacher. Miss Gray.'

Her face brightens. 'She's my Drama teacher,' she says, sitting down on the arm of a chair. 'She's really nice.'

'Good.' My heart gives a warm little flutter of maternal pride.

'She's my form tutor too,' she adds, and I can really claim no credit for acuity when I tell you that now, of course, I know who she is. It's not just that she's in the remedial class but doesn't have what Ellie calls "the nobody at home look", but that her accent entirely lacks the pungent, nasal Estuarine force that has always been the William Roper style. She speaks barely above a whisper and with precision, like a child who has had old-fashioned elocution lessons. I'm not going to spook her by telling her I know who she is and there is a silence until she says, 'Actually, I'm waiting for her too. I need to see her about something really important.'

I take it that "really important" is by way of an apology for delaying our lunch date but I say nothing to let her off the hook because actually Ellie needs her lunch break. 'Shouldn't you be in class?' I ask.

She flushes. 'I couldn't do games. Someone's taken my PE kit.'

'That's bad luck.'

'Yes. I got a detention.'

'That's not very fair, if someone stole it.'

'Yes,' she says casually, as though it's a triviality. 'Well, you're supposed to have your name embroidered on your stuff so no-one can take it, but mine hasn't...' She trails off. 'Anyway, it doesn't matter.'

We sit in silence while I contemplate the consequences of having a mother who can't or won't embroider names on a PE kit. Then she says, 'I need to see Miss Gray because I have to go home.'

'Aren't you feeling very well?' I ask, looking again at her pallor and weediness. She is like a plant that has been grown in a cupboard.

'Oh no, I'm all right. It's my mother who isn't well. I have to go home to be with her.'

'Poor you. Is she very poorly?'

'Well, no. It's just – ' she stops and looks away from me for a long moment, then turns earnest eyes back to me. 'People don't understand but I'm sort of tuned in to her. If she's not all right I always know.'

'Oh, mothers and daughters,' I say cheerily. 'And she always knows when you're not all right, I expect.'

I don't get an answering smile. She gives a little frown of puzzlement, then lifts her head and sticks out her chin. 'Oh, I'm always all right,' she says.

I'm at a loss for an answer to this but I don't need one as the shriek of an electronic bell interrupts us and I feel the building around us erupt into life. Feet pound, a thousand voices rend the air and the doors to the interior of the school fly open to admit a stream of children, who charge past us towards the dining hall, flattening me to the back of my chair by their centrifugal force. I can't believe that I lived with this daily for years and thought nothing of it. *Gone soft, Gina* I tell myself as I cower in my seat.

Eventually Ellie appears. She looks startled to see the two of us together and shoots me an anxious, questioning look.

'By coincidence,' I say blandly, 'we found that we were both waiting for you. This young lady has something she needs to talk to you about, so I'll go on up to the park and see you there.'

Ellie looks around at the streaming hordes and says, 'We'd better go outside to talk, Marina.' She ushers her out and I follow.

As I turn out of the front gates I look back to glance at Ellie and Marina sitting on the bench to which I've padlocked my bike. Marina is talking, quietly and intensely, fixing Ellie with those earnest eyes. Ellie is uncomfortable, I can tell: she's biting a thumbnail, twisting a lock of hair. She looks terribly young.

"The park" is a little green patch just down the road from the school, in my day a favourite hang-out for truants and smokers. I find a reasonably salubrious bench and sit quietly, waiting for Ellie, turning my face up to the September sunshine.

'So that was Marina Carson,' I say when she arrives.

'It was.'

'And I gather she wants to go home.'

'Her and me both,' she says, plonking herself down beside me. 'Did you bring some lunch? I'm starving.'

I hand her a sandwich and as she's fighting with its plastic casing she says, 'You shouldn't have left your bike outside school. There's an epidemic of thieving going on.'

'It's insured,' I say, 'and I could do with a new one.'

We munch for a bit and then I say, 'I remember Doug Fraser. He was always a bastard. What happened?'

'Ohhh,' she groans. 'That was about Marina too. I'm getting so much grief about her today.' She starts in on the second half of her sandwich before she carries on. 'I was barely in the door this morning and there he was looming over me in that really threatening way – wanted to know why "the Carson girl" wasn't in class yesterday afternoon. Well I didn't know she wasn't in class so he had me completely wrong-footed. He'd checked my register, he said, and it wasn't marked yesterday afternoon. Why was that? And then I remembered I had a rehearsal of *Twelfth Night* yesterday lunchtime and was late back for registration, so most of them had gone off to class already. And then he was so horrible, so sarcastic. I said I thought Marina seemed a reliable girl and there must be a good reason and he just sneered at me, "And that's speaking from your vast experience of children is it, Miss Gray? Well, let me give you a tip about that young lady. She's quite the little actress – runs in the family." Dickhead.'

'So did you ask Marina about it?'

'Yes.' She breaks off a couple of squares of chocolate, puts

17

them in her mouth, and then says indistinctly, 'She was worried about her mother.'

'Oh yes, she told me.'

'What?' She looks accusing, as though I've been caught trespassing.

'She said she always knows when something's wrong with her mother – she's "tuned in" she told me."

'Well, I think she probably is. It's happened a couple of times recently. She's gone home knowing something was wrong and she's found her mother "in a state" as she calls it. I don't know what she means exactly, and I didn't think I should probe too much.'

'But surely Hector Carson must work at home, doesn't he? Where's he in all this? Did you ask her?'

'He works in a sort of summer house, apparently, somewhere in the garden. "He's a creative person," Marina says. "He doesn't always know what's going on. He likes us all to be happy." They don't like to worry him, I gather.'

I start in on the chocolate. 'Great,' I say. 'A mother who's not actually off the bottle, I would say, and a father who's in cloud cuckoo land. Poor child.'

'That was the weird thing, when I was talking to her. She said her mother was frightened and then she said something like, "I don't want her to be frightened. It's horrible being frightened and being all on your own." It sounded so strange – like she was the parent and her mother was the child.'

'It sounds like she knows about being frightened, too. And where was her mother, I wonder, the times when Marina was frightened and all alone? You know, I asked Marina if her mother always knew if there was something wrong with her too, and she just said, "Oh I'm always all right" as though that just didn't come into the equation.' I dig my straw into my carton of apple and passion fruit juice and take a slurp. 'Have you thought that she might be being bullied?' I ask.

She lets out a weary breath. 'I have. I don't think she's being beaten up or anything, but her stuff keeps going missing and there's been graffiti on some of her books. I've talked to the year head and it happened last year as well, apparently, but Marina won't talk about it – says it's not a problem.'

'Has anyone talked to her parents?'

'They've tried, but they didn't get anywhere. They don't even turn up to parents' evenings.'

I drain my juice carton. 'I e-mailed Hannah about the regression in her scores and she thinks Marina could be suffering from emotional trauma – possibly ongoing. I'll show you her e-mail tonight.'

'What kind of trauma?'

'I don't know. Abuse, I suppose, is one possibility.'

'But who?'

'I don't know.'

We're silent for a bit, each coping with our own mental images. Then I say, 'So, was her mother *in a state* when she bunked off yesterday?'

'She'd fallen downstairs and broken her ankle.'

'Blimey! Does that mean she can't do her show?'

'The understudy's doing it. That's the point. She'd normally be doing a matinee today, but she's at home.'

'I suppose they're all busy denying that she's drinking again?'

'She claims someone had spread grease on the stairs, apparently. She says someone's trying to kill her.'

'Oh please! She's suffering from alcoholic paranoia, more like.'

'Well, nobody's saying that. Hector Carson says the grease on the stairs was probably some butter from her breakfast tray and she'll see things more calmly when she gets over the shock, but Marina says she's afraid of being left alone.'

'And I suppose there are no neighbours out at Charter Hall?'

'Apparently not. I did ask if there are friends who could call in, but she said her mother only knew theatre people really – as if it was understood that you couldn't expect them to do anything useful.'

'So what did you tell her?'

'About going home? I said she could go. What would you have said?'

'That her mother is a grown up woman and not her responsibility.'

'No, you wouldn't.' Ellie stands up and brushes the sandwich crumbs off her skirt. 'You talk tough, but you're as soft as anything when it comes to your students, you know you are.'

I get up too. 'That,' I say, 'is a terrible slander. But I can see that Marina's hard to say no to. If ever there was a child you just want put your arms round, it's her. Fragile and brave at the same time. It's enough to break your heart.'

As we walk back to the road Ellie says, 'Well, she's only missing double art with Eve this afternoon, so it shouldn't be a problem.'

'Was Doug Fraser the only thing that was crap about your morning?'

'God no. There was the massacre of the Incas too.'

'The what?'

'Year eight integrated humanities. They're doing voyages of exploration and I'm supposed to do drama improvisations to help it come to life. Last week we went into the gym and they all climbed the wallbars to be Columbus's sailors spotting land. It worked really well, but this week I did the arrival of Pizzaro among the Incas and it was nearly a massacre for real. It was supposed to be slow-motion, symbolic, but it turned into a free-for-all and Atahualpa had a nosebleed.'

I do feel sorry for her but I'm shaking with laughter. 'The massacre of the Incas! Oh Ellie, what a daft idea!'

She stops walking, about to protest, and then she starts to laugh too. We stand there giggling helplessly, leaning on each other for support, two women – one old, one young, one small and plump, one tall and slim – legless with mirth in the public street. We pull ourselves together, though, and we're sober by the time we part in the school drive. As Ellie turns to go inside, she says, 'She looked so old, Ma. So grey and tired and – adult, somehow.'

'Don't get in too deep,' I say. 'You can't love them all.'

As she swipes her card and goes in through the double doors, a man comes out, a man in his early forties with crisply-cut brown hair, a good suit and a watchful expression. Detective Chief Inspector David Scott, a man with whom I have a certain amount of history. For a start, I knew him when he was a mere spotty youth – taught him A-level English, in fact, at this very school, when I was a very new, very green teacher. Then a couple of years ago we bumped into each other again when there was an incident on our campus and the police were involved. We were, briefly, quite close and I think we both hoped more would come of it but things got complicated and I called it off. Well, I just stopped calling him, actually. I was sorry to drop him like that and I've always felt a bit guilty about it but it couldn't be helped. I've managed to avoid seeing him since, but now here he is, walking towards me, so I shall just have to be brazen.

'Hello, David. Has there been a crime? They don't get chief inspectors to investigate bike thefts, do they?'

He blinks for a moment, and the colour rises in his face. I remember it's one of the things I liked about him, how easily he blushed. His voice is cool, though. 'Gina. Hello. I've been talking to the A-level people about careers in the police. Tom Urquhart gets me in to do it every year.'

'Of course, you're a distinguished old boy of William Roper.'

'Something like that.'

We stand and look at each other. I can think only of stupid, jokey things to say and I don't want to say them. Eventually, he says, 'And you?'

'What am I doing here? My daughter teaches here. We've just been having lunch.'

'Not Annie?'

'No, no. Annie's off to Oxford next week. Ellie, my elder daughter. You never met her.'

'I met Freda once, though. In the supermarket.'

'Of course you did.'

He remembers everything: the names of my daughter and granddaughter, the details of every meeting. Has he puzzled over them, wondering where he made a mistake? Well, I remember everything too: every conversation, every look, every clever-clogs remark I made, everything.

'Well, nice to see you, David,' I say inanely. 'I must get back to work.'

He says nothing – just gives an odd little wave – and I go and retrieve my bike, which has, disappointingly, not been stolen.

3

THURSDAY 23rd SEPTEMBER

09.05. INTERVIEW ONE: THE TEACHER

'This is Marina's form tutor, Miss Gray – Eleanor Gray.' Tom Urquhart, the headmaster, ushered a young woman into the room – his room, in fact, since Scott was sitting in the headmaster's study, at his desk, with Paula Powell beside him.

'Have a seat, Miss Gray,' Scott said. 'I'm DCI Scott, and this is DS Powell.'

He knew who she was, of course. *My daughter's teaching here – Ellie, my elder daughter. You never met her.* He had seen her yesterday, in fact, coming into the school as he left it, but he hadn't paid attention, had just an impression of height, blondeness and youth. He had been too pole-axed by the unexpected sight of Gina standing there to notice much else.

Tom Urquhart, he saw, had settled himself watchfully in the corner. He and Gina had taught together, he knew, so presumably he'd known Gina's daughter since she was a child. Scott would have liked to talk to Eleanor Gray on her own but it was difficult to turn Tom Urquhart out of his own office and he didn't want to make an issue of it.

He looked at her. Not much of her mother there, he thought, no hint of the mocking smile, the air of finding the world infinitely absurd. Would she turn out to be as mocking, or as spiky, as her mother? At the moment, she had the familiar puzzled look that the basically law-abiding always have when they find themselves confronted unexpectedly by the police. You had to catch them while they were still dazed, before they'd got it together and started editing their story. You got closest to the truth in those early moments.

'I'd like to ask you some questions about Marina Carson.' She opened her mouth to ask something, but he put up a restraining hand. 'What can you tell us about her movements yesterday?'

Her voice wobbled a bit as she said, 'I gave her permission to go home at the end of the morning. Her mother had had an accident the day before and she was worried about her.'

'And what time would that have been?'

'About one o'clock. That was when I spoke to her, anyway. Has something happened to her? She's not missing, is she?'

'No, she's not missing,' Scott said. 'You didn't see her leave school, then?'

'No, I – look if you'd just tell me what's happened, then I can concentrate on answering your questions. You may think it's clever to keep me in the dark but it really isn't going to help.'

Oh yes, her mother's daughter, Scott thought. That hadn't taken long.

'Has she had an accident?' Eleanor Gray asked. 'Is that it?'

Paula Powell shot a questioning look at him and he nodded. 'I'm sorry to tell you that she's dead,' Powell said. 'The family GP found her dead at her home yesterday afternoon.'

Eleanor Gray made an odd sound, something between a gasp and a cry, and the colour drained dramatically from her face. Scott thought she was going to faint, but she slumped forward and said, indistinctly, with her head between her knees, 'Sorry. It's all right. Be all right in a minute.'

Paula Powell got up and knelt beside her; Tom Urquhart called to his secretary to bring her a glass of water. By the time the water arrived, she was upright again, awkwardly brushing aside their concern, but still white and beginning to shake. Sandra Sheldon, Tom Urquhart's secretary, cast a professional glance over her and brought in a blanket from the sick room, which she draped around her shoulders. As Eleanor sipped the water, Scott could hear her teeth rattling against the glass. Wrapped in the blanket, she looked, incongruously, like someone who had just been rescued from drowning.

'What happened to her?' she asked.

'She fell down the stairs and broke her neck,' Powell said.

'But how? How could she have?'

Scott interrupted. 'It's been a shock for you, of course, and you'll be able to take in the details later. At the moment, though, we really need to know as much as we can about the circumstances in which she was sent home yesterday.'

'She asked if she could go home and I said she could. That was all there was to it.'

'Did you phone her home at all, either before she left the school or when she might be expected to have arrived home?'

'No.'

'Wasn't that – unusual?'

'Unusual?'

Paula Powell pushed some stapled pages across the desk towards her. 'We've got a document here which the headmaster gave us. *Procedures to be followed in sending a pupil home*. Have you read it?'

He watched the colour rush back into her face. 'I – don't know. I may have done. I've only been here a couple of weeks. I was given a lot of stuff at the beginning of term but there's a lot to absorb in a school this size.' She glanced over at Tom Urquhart, who was looking at the floor, avoiding her eye, Scott thought.

'So you can't tell me what's in it?' Powell persisted.

'Not exactly, no.'

'Then I'll remind you. There are various categories – suspension, temporary suspension for uniform infringements and so on – but this is the relevant section: *Sick Pupils*.'

'Marina wasn't sick,' Eleanor Gray protested. 'I sent her home because she was worried about her mother.'

'That doesn't seem to come under any of the sections here,' Powell said, pushing the document further towards her. 'You see if you can find it.'

Eleanor Gray slammed her glass down on the desk so that the water splashed over onto the polished leather. 'It's quite possible that it's not in there – it was a fairly unusual situation,' she said. 'But that was no reason to make her stay in school. She was upset and worried. There was no point in keeping her here – she wouldn't have been able to concentrate anyway.'

She was squaring up to Powell but Scott could see tears threatening.

'So, as she wasn't fit to stay in school, you treated her as being sick?'

'If you like.'

Her tone, and the shrug that went with it, made her seem suddenly no more than a teenager. *Whatever*, they said.

'So, let's look at the procedure.' Powell pulled the document back towards her and opened it. '*One: Ensure that there is someone at home to look after the child.* Did you do that?'

Eleanor Gray gave a shaky laugh. 'This is unreal! She didn't need anyone to look after her. SHE went home to look after her MOTHER!'

Powell said nothing and Scott glanced at her. He wondered where she was going with this line of questioning – wondered too whether it was necessary to be so hard on the girl. As if sensing some sympathy, Eleanor turned to him.

'There's – there was – an odd dynamic in that family. I

thought so when I was talking to Marina yesterday. It was like she was the adult and her parents were the children.' She paused. 'Anyway,' she said, still addressing him, 'her mother was at home of course.'

'Was she?' he asked.

'Well, yes, she –'

'As a matter of fact, she wasn't. If Marina left school at the time you say she did, she'll have caught the 13.02 bus to Lower Shepton from outside the school. She won't have got home until one thirty, and her mother had already left to catch the train to London.'

'To London?'

'Yes.'

'But she can't have done. She fell downstairs and broke her ankle – ' She stopped. 'Oh, that's weird, isn't it?'

'Weird?'

'That she fell downstairs too.'

'It's certainly a coincidence.' He paused. 'In fact, it turns out she didn't break her ankle – only sprained it. She still couldn't do the show, which is quite strenuous, I gather, but she decided to go and watch her understudy.'

Wasn't that an odd thing to do, he asked himself. Why would she do that? To check that her understudy wasn't better than her, he supposed. No fun for the understudy, though. He knew what happened in a theatre audience when people opened their programmes and those little white slips fluttered out: *Owing to the indisposition of Glenys Summers the part of Amy will be played by…* Had the star enjoyed the little waves of disappointment as she sat incognito in the audience? Or was that unkind?

He watched Eleanor Gray. She was struggling out of the folds of the blanket and rummaging in her handbag. She found a tissue and wiped her eyes. 'Sorry,' she said. 'It just hit me again that she's dead. I can't believe it. I suppose people always say that, don't they?'

27

'Quite often.'

Paula Powell cleared her throat as a preliminary to going back onto the attack. She'd have a few caustic comments to make to him later about his going soft on a witness because she was young and blonde and in tears. 'So, if you'd followed procedure and rung Marina's home, you would have realised that she actually had no reason to go home – or at least not the reason she gave you.'

'I don't believe she was lying to me. I'm sure she was worried about her mother.'

Powell gave her a long sceptical stare. 'Well,' she said eventually, 'let's return to this document. *Two: The child or parent should phone the school as soon as possible to confirm his/her safe arrival home.* I checked with the office and there was no phone call from Marina yesterday. Did you tell her to ring?'

'No.'

'Even though it's standard procedure?'

'I didn't know it was standard procedure. I haven't read that thing. It's a black mark against me at school, I'm sure, but it's not a crime, is it? Anyway, if you send a sick child home I can see that you want to check they haven't collapsed on the way or something. But I keep telling you Marina wasn't sick.'

'A pity, though,' Powell said. 'It would help us if we could pinpoint the time she arrived home.'

'Why?'

'It might help us find out who was in the house.'

'I thought you said no-one was there.'

'We said her mother wasn't there, but that doesn't rule out other people. It's pretty unusual for a healthy young girl to fall like that for no reason. We have to establish exactly what happened.' Powell paused to let this sink in before she said, 'We spoke to the deputy head earlier. She said you had raised concerns about Marina being bullied. Can you tell us about that?'

'You think someone pushed her down the stairs?'

Powell said nothing. Tom Urquhart was watching Eleanor keenly now, and she glanced at him before she took a long breath and said, 'There were – incidents which I thought amounted to bullying. Her PE stuff was taken, and other things, and someone scribbled stuff on her drama folder. She'd tried to cover it by colouring over it with a marker pen, so I couldn't read it, but it wasn't something she'd have done herself. She took a lot of care with that folder. So I reported it to the deputy head and I gathered that there were problems last year too, though she always denied it. But I never thought that she was being bullied physically. I really can't believe –'

'What you believe really isn't relevant, is it? Something or someone caused her to go from top to bottom and break her neck. It may have been a game that got out of hand. We don't know, but I'm sure you can see why it's important to us to know just what she was doing yesterday afternoon, and who knew what she was doing. And your failure to follow through and check on what happened to her after you sent her home doesn't help us.'

Scott intervened, turning to Tom Urquhart. 'We'll need the names of any pupils who were out of school yesterday afternoon, obviously. I assume you can let us have those?'

'Oh yes.' Tom Urquhart smiled for the first time. 'Our card swipe system doesn't just keep the school premises secure – it gives us an electronic record of when every pupil enters and leaves the school.'

Scott saw Eleanor Gray's head go up sharply and she opened her mouth as if to comment but closed it again and looked away. He thought he knew what she had been tempted to say. The kids would have found a dozen ways to evade the electronic system; there was nothing to stop several from exiting on one card and there would be a brisk market in stolen and exchanged cards. The system would be no help to the police at all.

'One more question,' he said, turning to Eleanor. 'Could Marina have kept a mobile phone anywhere in the school?'

Again she glanced uncomfortably at Tom Urquhart. 'The pupils aren't allowed to use mobiles in school. They can keep them in their bags but they have to be switched off and they get confiscated if a teacher sees one.'

'Could she have left one in a desk or a locker?'

She shook her head and Tom Urquhart said, colouring slightly, 'There is a theft culture in the school, I'm sorry to say, which we're addressing but we haven't cracked it yet. The older pupils have lockers with keys, which are reasonably secure, but the younger ones simply have to carry everything around with them, I'm afraid. If Marina didn't have a phone in her bag, then I imagine she didn't own one.'

Scott and Powell drove back to the station in silence until, finally, Scott said, 'You were pretty tough on her. You don't actually hold her responsible, do you?'

'She sent the child into harm's way, didn't she? A child she knew was being bullied. I'd like to know what she thought she was playing at. A child died and someone has to take responsibility. And by the way, if this was just an accident, why does it need a DCI leading the case? Why couldn't I have dealt with it?'

He shrugged an apology. 'The public interest,' he said. 'Or rather, the interest of the public. Her mother's a name. The media are homing in on us as we speak. The chief super thought it needed big guns, but I'm happy for you to handle it your way. I can do moral support and the media as needed.'

'Well OK. But I warn you, you may go mushy at the sight of big blue eyes full of tears, but I don't.'

4

THURSDAY 23rd SEPTEMBER

Youth's a stuff will not endure

My mother is in hospital. I learn this when my office phone rings at 9.55, just as I'm about to go and teach. Gillian in the department office says, 'There's a Dr Sidwell to speak to you, Gina,' and then there is my mother's voice, crisp as ever.

'Virginia? I won't keep you, I'm sure you're busy. I'm just letting you know I'm in hospital. Fractured femur. Slipped on the front step. Very stupid. All done and dusted now, though. Jim Samson's made quite a neat job of it as far as I can tell. I should be out of here in a day or two.'

'So, when did you have the fall?' I ask, bewildered.

'Oh, a couple of days ago. Tuesday.'

I am furious. Furious. I am a dutiful only daughter: I ring my mother twice a week without fail, I take an interest in her well-being, I worry about her. I know her determination to be independent is a good thing; I know she was a doctor and doesn't react to illness and injury quite like the rest of the population does, but all the same – to wait for two whole days before she thinks to let me know? Keeping my voice admirably even, I say, 'I wish you'd let me know sooner, Mother.'

'Why?'

'Because I could have been with you.'

'And what use would you have been? You weren't planning to insert the intramedullary nail for me, were you?'

I breathe deeply. 'No,' I say carefully, 'but I could have brought you grapes and books and a clean nightdress, just like other daughters do.'

'Well, that's why I'm calling now. I could do with some things from my flat.'

I perform a rapid mental scroll through my timetable for the day and say, 'I'll come up this afternoon. I haven't any teaching after twelve. I've got tutorials this afternoon but I'll rearrange them. Where are you?'

'The Nuffield, Dulwich.'

'Private?'

'Yes.'

'Good Lord!'

There is a silence. Then she says, 'Ring me when you get to the flat and I'll tell you what I need,' and rings off.

As I'm leaving my office just after midday, I pick up my mobile and realise that I have two missed calls – both, it turns out, from Ellie. I hope she's not having another bad day. I decide I'll ring her from the train during her lunch break and set off for the station.

It's fifty miles from Marlbury to London and the train takes a good hour. It's dirty and smelly but the view from the window is good: September sunlight spreading its blessing on fields and trees. I get out my phone to ring Ellie but am alerted by disapproving looks to the sign that tells me this is a quiet carriage, so I send her a cheery text, switch my phone to silent and abandon myself to thought. I think about my mother. The truth is, she has never been able to see the point of me really. Her job was all-absorbing to her and all she expected of me was that I should be as little trouble as possible. If I'd wanted to follow in her footsteps and become a doctor myself, I suppose she might have been pleased and proud. As it is, I don't think she has ever been proud of me. But this is all old stuff and I have dealt with it, as the therapists say. What really worries me, the thought that lodges in me like severe indigestion, is that she won't be able to go back to her flat when she gets out of hospital and I shall have to ask her to come and stay with me. Neither of us will want this – my mother will fight it furiously – but I suspect that there is no alternative. Four generations of Sidwell females living under the same roof; the prospect terrifies.

I grew up in South London and during my early married life in Marlbury I used to play the city slicker, mocking Marlbury's provincialism. I'm not a Londoner any more, though. I feel a complete bumpkin as I step off the train into the clamour, the vigour, the sheer force of London. I steel myself to take the underground to get to my mother's flat in Clapham and follow her instructions about what to bring: clean nightie, reading glasses, sudoku puzzles, garden diary, chocolate digestive biscuits. Then, because I have no idea where to find The Nuffield Hospital in Dulwich, I take a cab.

The cab driver wants to talk about immigrants. Don't they always? The only surprising thing this time is that he's black. He wants to have a go about the Muslims, of course. I'm usually up for a good argument but I haven't the heart for it today, and even if I had the heart, I'd have difficulty engaging with the soggy incoherence of my driver's discourse. His target is "Them" – that much is clear –and They seem to encompass anything from al-Qaeda to kebab shop owners. Even President Obama gets a look in. I gaze fixedly out of the window, volunteering ambiguous murmurs only when challenged with a direct question. I am delighted when we draw up outside the Nuffield Hospital.

The hospital has an imposing stuccoed front and a flight of white steps up to glossy doors. The reception area inside is like a hotel foyer, and a smiling receptionist welcomes me in. I feel a sharp pang of regret for those snappy women who man the reception desks in NHS hospitals. They are neither helpful nor friendly, but I like their air of irritation, the implication that you are probably wasting everyone's time and they have really sick people to worry about. It has always comforted me; all the time they treat me and mine as malingerers, I reason, we can't really be ill, can we? The woman facing me now, though, is only too eager to help, so I approach and say, 'I'm here to see Dr Sidwell.'

A frown forms between her nicely plucked eyebrows.

'Dr Sidwell? No, I'm afraid we don't –'

I spot the problem. 'She's a patient,' I say.

Relief irons out the frown and she gives me directions. As I trail off down a corridor, I'm struck by the absence of that all-pervading hospital disinfectant smell. They must keep the place clean, obviously. Is there some special, expensive, odourless disinfectant designed for exclusive use in places like this? When I find my mother's room, with its little card saying *Dr Jean Sidwell*, I tap lightly on the door and go in. My mother is sitting in a chair by the bed, listening to the radio and looking out of the window at the little courtyard outside, so I'm able to take a look at her before she sees me. She looks small and old and her face, unguarded as it is, is yellowish and etched with pain. What did I expect? Was I actually taken in by her brisk tones on the phone? She's eighty-seven years old, for God's sake, and she's just suffered a serious injury. All my life people have told me that my mother is a wonder, but she is not, after all, indestructible.

I should say something warm and kind and comforting, but instead I hear myself say, 'This is very posh. What made you give up on the NHS after all these years?'

I see her mouth purse itself into an irritated little smile before she says, 'Have you seen the MRSA and *C difficile* stats for London hospitals? I decided that's not the death I'd choose. Do you think I should have risked it?'

34

Good start, Gina. Thirty seconds in the room and you've already started a row. 'Sorry, sorry!' I say, hands up in surrender, and I unload onto the bed the things I have brought from her flat. 'I've brought you some grapes, too,' I say, and go through to her en suite bathroom to wash them, giving myself a moment to recover.

'How very conventional,' she calls through to me. 'Not like you at all.'

'There's a time for conventions,' I retort. 'Cards at Christmas, cakes on birthdays, champagne at weddings, grapes in hospital.'

At this point a nurse appears with a tray of tea and runs off to get another cup for me. As we sip, I ask, 'So, how are you? Give me the latest bulletin.'

'As well as can be expected,' she says. 'Temperature normal, BP up slightly, pain manageable, appetite good. And I walked a few steps with a frame this morning.'

'That's a bit soon, isn't it?'

'Not if I want to avoid a thrombosis.'

We drink our tea in silence until I gird my loins for the fray and ask, 'Have you any idea when you'll be able to leave?'

'Early next week. I've booked myself a few days at Hapworth Hall – it's a convalescent place in Surrey – just to get back on my feet, and then I shall be ready to go home.'

I take the plunge. 'Come and stay with us,' I offer, with all the conviction I can muster. 'You shouldn't be on your own when you're still wobbly on your feet. We'd love to have you.'

She snorts. 'Don't be ridiculous, Virginia. You've got a house full as it is. Annie, Ellie, Freda. Where are you going to put me?'

'Annie will be off to Oxford the weekend after next. The timing's perfect. As she goes, you arrive.'

'Well, it's no good putting me in Annie's room. I shan't be up to stairs. I'll be much better off in my flat.'

'I have thought of that, Mother. I'm not completely stupid. I can make the dining room into very comfortable room for you. Since the girls stopped learning the piano and I stopped giving dinner parties, it only gets used at Christmas. It's got French doors to the garden and it's near the downstairs loo. Couldn't be better.'

I am almost convincing myself but she is mustering counter-arguments. 'What am I going to do all day? You'll all be out at work.'

'You can do whatever you do at home.'

'I can't garden.'

'You wouldn't be able to garden anyway! And you'll have company in the evenings.'

'That would be a mixed blessing. We don't have the same taste in television. I can't share your devotion to fiction.'

'You can see Freda, though. You'll like that.'

I have caught her unawares and her face changes before my eyes: all its hard edges dissolve into a smile that can only be called beatific. 'Yes,' she says, 'I'd like that.'

She was an indifferent mother and a half-hearted grandmother, but her devotion to her great-granddaughter never ceases to astonish me. *I've got her then*, I think miserably. *She'll come. I've won.* A pyrrhic victory if ever there was one.

I know better than to press home my advantage now and I'm casting around for a new topic when I'm rescued by a nurse, who bustles in to check her blood pressure and temperature, write things on a chart, give her a couple of pills and tell her she's doing very well but it's time to hop back into bed in a tone more patronising than I would ever dare to use to her. My mother accepts all these attentions graciously, however, and settles back into bed with evident relief.

'Would you like me to go?' I ask. 'Do you want to sleep?'

She rouses herself. 'No, no. Tell me about the girls. How is Annie feeling about going up to Oxford?'

'It's hard to say. I hardly see her. She's on a non-stop round of farewell parties in the evenings and goes shopping for clothes during the day. Andrew is so cock-a-hoop about her going to Oxford – and not just going to Oxford but doing law at Oriel, just like him – he seems to have handed over his credit card to her.'

Andrew, I should explain, is my long-divorced husband: human rights lawyer, scourge of the over-mighty state around the world, dysfunctional husband and father. He was never what you'd call a hands-on parent when we were married and his attentions to his daughters were sporadic at best after we parted, but since Annie got a place at Oriel, they've become inseparable. And I'm as sour as hell about it.

'And you're out of the loop, as they say,' my mother comments wryly.

'Oh, completely. I'm the doubting Thomas, the one who didn't think she could get in and didn't think she'd be happy there if she did. Mind you, I could still be proved right about that,' I mutter darkly.

'And Ellie? How is she finding teaching?'

'*Challenging*, I would say, but I think she'll survive.'

'And Freda?'

'Freda's fine. She loves the day nursery and is talking her head off. You'll notice a big difference since the last time you saw her.'

She doesn't argue. It's a *fait accompli*. I take my leave.

I hit the rush hour on my homeward train and spend the journey pinned into a corner by the obese man who shares my seat. I rummage in my bag for my phone as we're leaving London, intending to let the girls know where I am, and find I have missed five calls while the phone has been set to silent. When I ring home, Annie's outraged tones assault my ear.

'Where are you? Where have you been all day? Ellie's kept

ringing you and so have I. When are you going to be home? I'm having to cope with everything here.'

'Why? What's happened? Where's Ellie? Is Freda all right?'

'Freda's all right. I've given her tea and everything. It's Ellie. It's horrendous, Ma. A girl from her class has been killed and the police think it's Ellie's fault.'

'Annie, for God's sake. Stop over-dramatising and tell me what's happened. Better still, put me on to Ellie.'

I hear a muffled conversation and Annie is back on the line. 'She doesn't feel up to talking now. She says she'll tell you everything when you get home. How long will you be? Why aren't you at work?'

'I'm on a train back from London. Granny's in hospital.'

'Oh God!' Annie's voice is a dramatic wail. 'What's happened? She's not going to die is she? I can't cope with all this!'

'Annie,' I say through gritted teeth, uncomfortably aware that about twelve people are now taking an unashamed interest in the drama of my family life, 'get a grip. Granny is fine. She had a fall, that's all. Now cut the drama queen act and tell me, calmly, what happened to this girl at school and how it involves Ellie. Was it an accident in a drama class?'

'No. She fell down the stairs.'

'At school?'

'No, at home. Yesterday.'

I draw breath in a huge gulp of relief. At home, yesterday. Nothing to do with Ellie then. Now I'm furious. 'So why the hell did you tell me the police think it's Ellie's fault? Honestly, Annie, why do you have to talk such nonsense? You'll say anything for dramatic effect, won't you? You're so irresponsible. Why don't you grow up?'

My fellow-passengers are riveted by this, of course, but I don't care. There is a silence at Annie's end and then I hear her voice again, quite changed: she is no longer the hysterical

38

teenager but the fledgling lawyer. 'I think you'll find, Mother,' she says, 'that I'm not talking nonsense. Ellie was questioned for an hour by two police officers this morning and they say they'll want to talk to her again. And the headmaster's sent her home. She tried to ring you but you weren't answering, so I've been taking care of her. Now, perhaps you wouldn't mind answering my question and telling me what time you expect to be home.'

I get home at six-thirty, taking a taxi from the station to hasten my arrival. Annie is hovering on the doorstep with Freda in her arms as the taxi draws up. 'I have to go,' she hisses. 'I'm late. I should have been at Monks half an hour ago.' Monks is the smart wine bar in town and it's not a place you can go to with toddler dribble on your cashmere jumper. I receive Freda and dismiss Annie to her pleasures.

In the sitting room, Ellie is lying on the sofa looking flushed and swollen-eyed. A bottle of rather good whisky is sitting on the coffee table alongside two empty glasses – Annie's remedy for shock, presumably. Freda struggles to climb on top of her mother, so I distract her by giving her my briefcase to empty while I kneel down by the sofa to talk to Ellie.

'Oh, Ma,' she whispers, 'It's Marina.'

'Marina?'

'She's dead.'

'No!' We stare at each other and I can feel the tears welling up in my eyes, mirroring hers.

'How? Annie said a fall down the stairs. Was that it?'

She nods, a picture of misery. 'Yesterday, when she got home. Her mother wasn't there after all and it's my fault because I let her go home. You're supposed to ring before you send them home and I didn't read the thing and I'll never forgive myself.'

I give her a hug and let her weep and tell her it's not her fault and she's not to blame herself, and that I'm sure it will turn out to have been just a terrible accident, but she struggles out of my arms and shouts, 'No! It won't. It won't, Ma. They told me – the police – they told me they think someone pushed her down the stairs. They think it was kids from school – the ones who were bullying her – and I knew she was being bullied and all I did was pass the buck.'

I stare at her. 'Oh, Ellie,' I whisper.

She stares back at me. 'It's the worst thing,' she says.

'Yes, it is. Tell me everything,' I say.

She knows no more about the death itself than she has already told me, but I hear about the sarky woman detective who went on and on at her about the regulations; I hear about DCI Scott, who was nicer but very serious; I hear about Tom Urquhart, who sat in on the police interview but didn't stick up for her and then, she thinks but isn't sure, suspended her.

'So what did he say, exactly?

'He just told me to go home.'

'What were his exact words?'

'Oh Ma, you always ask that!'

'I'm an English teacher, Ellie. Words are my thing. It makes a difference what words people use.'

'Well, I don't remember exactly what he said. I think he said something like, "In the circumstances, I think you'd better have some time off. I'll arrange for someone to take over your classes."

Well, that doesn't sound good, and my encouraging words sound feeble even to my own ears. 'Maybe he could see that you were in no fit state for a day's teaching and needed time to recover. Perhaps he was being kind.'

'No, he wasn't. You do words, I do tone of voice. His was a pissed-off,you've-screwed-up-big-time-and-don't-think-because-I've-known-you-since-you-were-a-little-girl-you-can-expect-special-treatment tone.'

'It still doesn't mean he was suspending you.'

'I don't know *what* it means. I don't know whether I'm supposed to go into work tomorrow or not.'

'Well, I don't think you'll be in a fit state to go in tomorrow anyway. Look at you. You've had a terrible shock. A day off wouldn't hurt.'

'But I have to know what's happening.'

'Well, there's a simple answer to that. I've got Tom's home number. Give him a ring and find out.'

'I *can't*,' she wails, tears spurting again. She wipes them away with the soggy ball of tissues in her hand. 'I just can't. I shall start blubbing, I know I will.'

'Do you want me to ring him?'

'Oh would you, Ma?'

It appears I would. 'But I'm just going to find out what the situation is,' I say. 'I can't try to influence Tom – it's not fair. He has to do what he thinks is best for the school.'

I retrieve the address book from under a pile of stuff in the dining room – I'd forgotten, when I offered it to my mother, that I'd let this room become such a dump – and I go into the kitchen to phone. Tom sounds less than delighted to hear from me and I am placatory. 'I'm sorry to bother you, Tom. You must have had a terrible day. What a tragedy. I'm so sorry.'

'What exactly can I do for you, Gina?'

'Well, it's about Ellie, Tom.'

'I thought it might be.'

I know what Ellie means about his tone. 'She's very upset, of course, and she seems to have got it into her head that you've sacked her, or suspended her or something.'

There is a silence.

'Well I haven't sacked her,' he says finally. 'You know as well as I do that I don't have the power to sack a teacher on the spot. But I don't want her in school for the time being, until we see what direction the police investigation is taking.'

'But Ellie's not a suspect, is she? They can't think –'

41

'I can't second guess what they think, Gina, but Ellie was the only person who knew that Marina was going home. There is a question about responsibility. And duty of care.'

'Don't suspend her, Tom, please. She's just starting out and it'll look terrible on her record. I know she didn't follow procedure, but you know she can't have had anything to do with the girl's death. She just let her go home because she was so worried about her mother.'

'So she said. But her mother wasn't even at home. It may be much more complicated. Ellie knew she was vulnerable. She should have been more careful.'

'Vulnerable?'

'She'd reported concerns about her being bullied. All the more reason not to let her out of school at a time when she was supposed to be in our care.'

'But Marina was worried about her mother, Tom. She told me so.'

'What do you mean, told you?'

'I met her yesterday while I was waiting to go out for lunch with Ellie. I had a conversation with her. Have you ever had a conversation with her?'

'I don't –'

'No, I thought not. Well, I can tell you she certainly is vulnerable, but more because of parents who don't care about her than because of anything in school, I would say. If we're talking duty of care, the police ought to be looking there first.'

I can't try to influence Tom, a mocking voice in my head sneers at me. There is a pause so long that I wonder if he has walked away from the phone. When he speaks, I can hear the dead weariness in his voice. 'Look, Gina, today's Thursday. Tell Ellie to stay at home tomorrow. Call it sick leave. Tell her to come in to see me early on Monday morning. I should have more idea of where the police are on this by then.'

He is a nice man and I have taken advantage of his niceness, but I am desperate and unscrupulous. 'I'd be terribly grateful if you could keep me posted in the meantime, Tom. If the police get in touch.'

He sighs. 'I really don't think that would be appropriate, do you? But you know, I assume, that David Scott is heading the investigation. You two know each other, don't you? If you want the news from the horse's mouth, I suggest you speak to him.'

As he rings off, I stand with the receiver in my hand for quite a long time. Then I go in search of my mobile. I retrieve from its address book a number which I once knew by heart, and I make the call.

5

THURSDAY 23rd SEPTEMBER

11.15. INTERVIEW TWO: THE FATHER

Hector Carson was one of those men whose physical size and strength seem to be an unfortunate accident. Well over six feet, broad-shouldered and barrel-chested, with a heavy grey beard and longish grey hair, he was the type often described as "a bear of a man", except that in his case he most resembled an oversized and very battered teddy bear. It was difficult to tell how old he was: the hair and beard put him well into his fifties but his face was surprisingly unlined, his complexion, even today, clear and rosy, though his eyes were dull and red-rimmed and his hair in mad disarray.

'He's in his writing room, sir,' the PC on duty at the front door of Charter Hall had told Scott and Powell. 'Round the back and follow the path through the garden and you'll see it.'

They had skirted the assorted outhouses behind the house and found themselves only twenty feet or so from water. The River Mar flowed past, shallow and weedy, and a small boat with an outboard motor was moored by a wooden jetty. The shiny little boat was in almost comic contrast to the unkempt garden, the disintegrating jetty and the scabby hulls of two upturned rowing boats lying in the long grass. They had followed the path, which ran parallel to the river, past a rusty climbing frame and a rotting swing, round deserted rabbit hutches and handsome stone urns full of vigorous weeds to an ancient wooden summerhouse, rotten to the point of imminent collapse.

'Come into my den,' Hector Carson had invited them, and for once the word seemed truly appropriate. The room had a fetid smell (damp wool, mildew, pipe tobacco and very old sweat, Powell told Scott afterwards) and the appearance of having been filled, layer by layer, from the outside in. Ancient, rotting rugs, ingrained with dirt, lay overlapping on the floor; books obscured the walls – haphazardly on shelves, crammed into stacks of boxes, piled in tottering towers. More books lay in smaller heaps around an old kitchen table in the centre of the room, from which papers flowed in wild abandon. Among them lurked a manual typewriter, its ribbon lying in inky coils beside it. Scott wondered if there was actually any power in the room. There were candles stuck into bottles on the bookshelves and a kettle stood on a camping stove. How was it possible that Carson hadn't yet set fire to himself?

Their host pulled a heap of rugs off a lumpy studio couch at the end of the room and invited them to sit down, which they did cautiously, settling themselves among the springs. He brought a large leather chair over from the table and sat down opposite them. Then he waited, eyes wide and trusting, like a child's.

Scott spoke. 'Let me first express our condolences again, Mr Carson. We understand that this is a very painful time for you and we don't want to distress you further, but I believe the family liaison officer – PC Shepherd – has told you that we aren't yet sure whether Marina's death was simply an accident and we have to establish how it happened and who, if anyone, was responsible. That has meant that we've had to ask you to vacate the house for the present. We have to keep it secure for forensic investigations. We'll try to complete those as soon as possible.' As Carson continued to gaze at him, he went on, 'I gather your wife has gone to stay at The County Hotel in Marlbury. Are you planning to join her?'

Carson shook his head. 'No. We both stayed there last night, but I don't like hotels. Now I think I shall just stay here.' He looked round the chaotic room. 'Your officers did whatever they needed to do in here and they said they wouldn't need to come back. I'd sooner be at home.'

Scott asked, 'Can you tell me where you were yesterday afternoon? Were you here?'

Carson shook his shaggy head. 'I wasn't, as a matter of fact. I'm working on a new saga, you know, set in a mediaeval monastery, so I work in the abbey library a great deal these days, where the materials for background research are to hand.'

And where there's warmth and electric light Scott thought.

Paula Powell said, 'We gathered from Marina's form teacher that Marina asked to go home early yesterday because she was worried about her mother being left alone. She thought she was still shaken from her fall the day before. Were you worried about leaving her alone?'

Her question seemed to cause him extreme discomfort. He shifted his great bulk, ran ink-stained fingers through his wild hair, spread his hands out on his lap, as if to study them, and then said, 'My wife was frightened by her fall, and I should have taken it more seriously. I let her down, I'm afraid, and I let my daughter down.' Here his voice broke and he blew his nose on a dirty handkerchief, then put it away and looked from one to the other. 'I feel as if I'm in the middle of a nightmare, you know, and I really don't know how to explain it all to you. I don't know how much you've heard about the show my wife is in – *Amy*, it's called. It's a historical story – very inaccurately told, of course – about Amy Robsart, who was the wife of Robert Dudley, the Earl of Leicester.'

'The one who was supposed to be Elizabeth I's lover?'

Paula Powell asked. 'Jeremy Irons played him on TV – with Helen Mirren.'

'There was a lot of rumour to that effect – and rumours that the Queen wanted to marry him. But he was married already, to Amy. And then Amy died under suspicious circumstances and the rumours were that Dudley had had her murdered, or the Queen had, or the two of them had plotted it together.'

'What were the suspicious circumstances?' Scott asked.

'She was found dead – at the bottom of the stairs – at her home in Cumnor.' Carson looked at him. 'Now, do you begin to see?'

'See what, exactly?' Scott asked. He had some inkling of where this was going but he wasn't willing to tell Carson's story for him. Carson sighed, a mild, weary sigh of disappointment.

'You must see that it's rather extraordinary in the circumstances – all these falls. When my wife had her fall – whenever it was – Tuesday, was it? – she was convinced, you see, that someone had put something on the stairs to make her slip. I didn't believe it. I didn't believe it and I blame myself now for not taking it more seriously, but it seemed so – improbable, you know, and my wife does tend to...' He petered out. 'Well, she's an actress,' he finished lamely.

'Did you look to see if there was anything on the stairs?'

'I did, and there was a smear of something, perhaps. I thought maybe some butter from my wife's breakfast tray. The stairs are uncarpeted, of course – but you'll have seen that when you – when you were here yesterday. They're beautiful oak, three hundred years old. It would be a sin to carpet them.'

'But they are quite uneven, aren't they?' Paula Powell commented. 'It would be quite easy to slip.'

He looked at her vaguely, pursuing some private thought. 'Do you know,' he asked, 'how Amy Robsart came to be alone at Cumnor Place on the day she died?'

'No?'

'Her husband was away at court in London and she had given all her servants the day off, to go to a fair in Oxford. She insisted that they went, which gave support to those who wanted to argue that she'd committed suicide.'

'I don't quite see where –'

'Bear with me, please. Now, we don't have a large domestic staff here at Charter Hall – but we have a very reliable cleaning lady – well housekeeper, really – Mrs Deakin – who comes in several days a week. I'm not sure which days exactly, but yesterday was one of her days. Yesterday morning, she had a phone call from my wife – or so she thought – giving her the day off. The caller, whoever she was, suggested that she might like to take advantage of her day off to go to the Wednesday market in Marlbury, as she didn't usually get the chance.'

'Are you saying the call wasn't from your wife?' Scott asked.

'It was not, but it was from someone well acquainted with our domestic arrangements and familiar enough with my wife's voice to imitate it.'

'Your wife's an actress, Mr Carson,' Paula Powell objected. 'A lot of people have heard it. And it's unusual. It wouldn't be very difficult to imitate.'

Scott intervened. 'How did you learn that Mrs Deakin had had this call?'

'From my wife. When Mrs Deakin didn't turn up for work, my wife rang her. Mrs Deakin was terribly apologetic, apparently, and explained that she'd had this call.'

'Do you know if the caller gave any reason why she didn't want Mrs Deakin to come that day?'

'Yes, I believe she said she had a heavy cold, on top of her broken ankle, and she was intending to sleep for most of the day, so she didn't want to be disturbed by vacuuming and the like.'

'And the heavy cold would explain why her voice might have sounded different. Clever,' Paula Powell said.

Scott said, 'My scene-of-crime officers found no sign of an attempted burglary. There was no break-in but, as you know, we found the kitchen door unlocked yesterday afternoon.'

'Yes, yes. We are rather slack about locking up out here, I'm afraid. And Glenys was anxious to catch her train, you know.'

'My officers found no sign that anyone had been going through the house for things to steal, but I shall be asking you later to look round the house to see if there is anything missing. We need to establish whether Marina interrupted an attempted burglary.'

Carson stared at him in alarm, running a frantic hand through his hair

'I understand that it will be difficult for you to go back into the house,' Scott said gently, 'but –'

'No, no,' Carson interrupted. 'Well – it will be difficult of course, but the problem is I don't notice things, you know. I'm not sure if I could tell you if anything was missing. My wife might – or Mrs Deakin would be better. Mrs Deakin knows where everything belongs.'

'We'll talk to her,' Scott said. 'She lives in Willow Close. That's in the village, is it?'

'Yes, it'll be on the new estate. It's all Willow and Ash and Sycamore down there.' He spoke with the gentle disdain of a man who couldn't understand why everyone didn't choose to live in a three-hundred-year-old house.

'Even if nothing is missing,' Paula Powell said, 'it could be that Marina interrupted them before they had a chance to take anything. Or that they were looking for something in particular. Do you have anything of special value in the house, Mr Carson?'

'Nothing. We sold a good deal, for my wife's medical

treatment, you know. We have things that are precious to us, of course – my wife's Emmy award, for example, but nothing worth stealing, I think.'

'Are you sure that the call to Mrs Deakin mentioned your wife's injured ankle?' Paula Powell asked.

'I think so, yes. It worried my wife – that the caller seemed to know everything that was going on here.'

Scott stood up and Powell joined him. 'Thank you, Mr Carson,' he said. 'You've been very helpful. We will need to talk to you again, but that's all for the moment.'

They moved towards the door, and Paula Powell asked, 'Did Marina have a mobile phone, Mr Carson? We haven't come across one among her things.'

Hector Carson frowned in puzzlement for a moment and then said, 'Oh no. She had no need of one. My wife has one, for emergencies – coming back late from London and so on – but not the rest of us.'

'Right. And had Marina behaved at all oddly in recent days? Did she seem worried or frightened at all in the past few days or weeks?'

He looked surprised and a little frightened, Scott thought. 'Behaved oddly? I don't think – she was always very quiet, you know – very biddable. And I didn't see her much, really – always working – you know how it is with a new project. Frightened? What would she have been frightened of?'

Scott could feel Powell beside him suppressing a snort of fury. She ignored the question as rhetorical and merely said, 'Our WPC Shepherd will be available for as long as she's needed, Mr Carson. Do talk to her if you feel it will help.'

'Yes. Thank you,' he said, and his face was as blank as a mask.

6

THURSDAY 23rd SEPTEMBER

13.00. INTERVIEW THREE: THE MOTHER

Scott and Powell walked back towards the house in silence at first, each mulling over possibilities. There was something strange about this set-up, Scott thought. You never forgot the violent deaths of children and he couldn't remember one where the parents hadn't clung together. Even divorced parents hung on to each other like drowning swimmers. Later they might be pulled apart, by guilt, by blame or just by the intrinsic loneliness of grief, but for the first forty-eight hours, at least, they couldn't be prised apart.

'What did you think of him?' he asked.

'He's away with the fairies, isn't he?' Powell said dismissively. 'Useless father and useless husband, I'd say. Why isn't he with his wife, instead of lurking down there in all that *mess.*' The last word came out as a hiss.

'That was more or less what I was thinking. To be fair, it's difficult for them, not being able to be in the house, but you would expect them to want to be together. I wonder how she's coping.'

'I guess she'll be our next port of call, won't she?' she asked.

'We'll just call in at the house first and see how the SOCOs are doing. And then, Paula, why don't you go and see Renée Deakin, since she lives here in the village, and I'll go on into Marlbury. The family liaison officer can sit in on my interview with Mrs Carson. I assume she's with her.'

As they rounded the corner of the house, Scott thought about the SOCOs at their work. It was a difficult crime scene, Scott knew: a preliminary tour of the place the previous evening had shown him a jumble of rooms, large and small, all sparsely furnished but crammed with a clutter of miscellaneous objects from broken rocking horses to collections of butterflies. There were cellars and attics, nooks and crannies, cupboards and pantries. It had obviously been a handsome house but there were signs of decay everywhere: brown rings of damp on ceilings, flaking rot in window frames, peeling wallpaper and sagging furniture. He thought Mrs Deakin must be working heroically to prevent the place from sinking into chaos.

The moment they stepped into the house, he sensed that there had been a development in the search. The SOCOs were going quietly about their work but there was a vibrating excitement in the air. The officer in charge approached him.

'Found something?' Scott asked.

'Golf club, sir. In the bag of clubs over there at the bottom of the stairs. Do you want to see?'

Scott and Powell watched as he drew from a worn leather golf bag a sharp-bladed club with a crust of blood at its rim. 'Didn't even bother to wipe it,' he said.

The body had been removed but Scott remembered how he had seen it the previous afternoon, sprawled on the stone slabs at the foot of the stairs, a bleeding gash clearly visible on the white forehead. He looked at the great staircase which rose straight from the middle of the hall, ran up for a dozen steps and then branched off from a small half-landing into two wings, each going up a further six steps to either end of a gallery. Even in the middle of the day, there was very little natural light – only that which came in through a glass panel on the front door, and the empty space beside it where the doctor, who had seen the body from outside, had smashed the glass to get in. In that gloom, it wouldn't be difficult to lurk on the stairs to the side, waiting for a girl or woman to come down to the half-landing from the other side and then use the impetus of the run down those six treads to push her with deadly force down onto the stone floor. So why a blow on the head as well?

'Get that club to forensics as a priority,' he said, 'and the area at the top of the stairs is crucial as well as the area at the bottom here. I need anything at all you can find.'

Back in the car, they drove out through a handful of reporters who had not been there when they arrived. They were locals only as yet, he thought. The death was probably on the mid-day news, though, and would be in the national press tomorrow. Glenys Summers' name was bound to bring the news hounds baying and a media scrum would just be a hindrance in this case; he didn't believe a call for information from the public would bring them anything useful.

As they stopped outside Renée Deakin's smart little house in Willow Close, Paula Powell said, 'You know what I'm thinking?'

'That we're barking up the wrong tree with bullying?'

'Well yes, it's all looking too carefully planned for kids' bullying. But more than that. A lot hangs on Renée Deakin's story, doesn't it? Because if her caller did mention Glenys's injured ankle then they weren't trying to clear the house for a burglary because they would expect that she would be at home and not at the theatre.'

'In which case the call was designed to make sure that Glenys would be alone in the house.'

'But they didn't find Glenys, they found Marina.'

'And if that's a murder weapon we just saw, they deliberately killed her. Why?'

'And would they have killed Glenys if they'd found her there?'

'Get the story about this phone message,' he said, 'then ring for a car to come and pick you up. I'll see you back at the station.'

As he drove into Marlbury he called Lynne McAndrew, the pathologist. 'How busy are you?' he asked.

'Are you asking me out to lunch?'

'Sadly not. The young girl who was brought in yesterday – it's beginning to look more like murder than accident. How quickly can you do the autopsy?'

'I can do it this afternoon. You're going to tell me you've found a weapon, aren't you?'

'A golf club.'

'That figures.'

'Meaning?'

'The head wound. When I examined the body yesterday, it looked too deep a cut to have been made by striking the floor, and I couldn't see a sharp edge on the stairs that could have caused it.'

'Do you think the head wound killed her?'

'I'd say not. Her neck was broken. But I'll be able to tell you more when I've done the autopsy. What kind of golf club, by the way?'

'I can't tell you. I don't play. But the SOCOs are bringing it in.'

In Marlbury, he parked in the car park at the County Hotel, went in through the back, where a couple more reporters were hanging about, and enquired at the reception desk for Mrs Carson. Drawing a blank there, he asked for Miss Summers and the flustered receptionist glanced at the front doors, where two uniformed porters stood on guard, and said Miss Summers had left instructions that she was not to be disturbed.

'She's not ready to talk to anyone yet,' she said in an earnest whisper.

'I'm afraid she'll have to talk to us,' Scott said firmly.

The woman eyed him for a moment, weighing up her conflicting fears of upsetting Glenys Summers and annoying a police inspector, and picked up the phone. It rang for a long time and when it was eventually answered it was a long time before the receptionist spoke. Scott watched as she flushed with the impact of what he assumed was an outpouring of abuse. 'I am very sorry, Miss Summers, really,' she said at last, 'but I have a police chief inspector here and he says he needs to speak to you.' There followed more from the other end of the line. 'She'll be down,' she said as she put down the receiver. 'She doesn't want you to go up there.'

As Scott waited, he wandered round the reception area. He was familiar enough with the hotel: its position on the High Street in the centre of Marlbury, its host of meeting rooms and its banqueting hall made it the premier venue for conferences, civic events and gatherings of the great and the good in general. There would be an empty meeting room somewhere where he could interview Glenys Summers. He could do with some lunch at some point, he thought, and glanced into the coffee shop which led off the reception hall. It was pretty full but his eye was caught immediately by a uniformed WPC sitting in the corner. She saw him at the same moment and jumped up. 'I'm sorry, sir. I didn't know you were here. WPC Sarah Shepherd, family liaison. I was asked to stay with Mrs Carson – Miss Summers – but she wants to be on her own for the moment and I thought –'

'That's all right. It's useful you're here. You can sit in on my interview with her. She's coming down in a moment.'

The young woman hesitated. 'I should warn you, sir. I don't think I got off to a very good start with her.'

'Oh?'

He looked at her. She was a large young woman with a round face that retained a child-like pudginess. He doubted there was anything naïve about her, though. Family liaison was a difficult job and she had a reputation for being good at it.

'I haven't come across a reaction quite like hers before,' she said. 'She just seems so angry.'

'Grief can make people angry, though, can't it?'

'Oh yes, but it isn't usually the first emotion. Usually it comes later, when people feel the investigation has stalled and they start to get angry that we're not doing enough.'

'Is she angry with you?'

'She seemed to be.'

'Well, here she comes.'

A woman of forty or so was limping down the stairs towards them, recognisable in the way people are who are known only from print or celluloid – familiar but different. Small and slight, her face pale inside her trademark blond bob, she was wearing a calf-length black jersey dress and a startlingly white bandage on her right ankle. He went forward to wait for her at the foot of the stairs. As she reached the bottom and released the handrail she put out two hands to him. 'The chief inspector, I presume?' she said, and her voice had the breathy, child-like quality he remembered from her films.

'Chief Inspector David Scott,' he said, releasing a hand to fish out his warrant card.

'I'm Glenys,' she said.

'Of course you are,' he said, and felt foolish. 'You know WPC Sarah Shepherd already, I think,' he added. She gave a dismissive nod and he said, 'She'll be sitting in on our interview. I hope you'll find that she'll be helpful to you in the next few days.' Getting no response, he said, 'I'm sure we can find an empty meeting room down here, where we can talk in private,' and turned to lead the way into the interior of the hotel.

She clutched his arm, however, and looked up into his face. 'Do you mind if I lean on you? It's still difficult to walk on this wretched ankle.' And so they set off arm in arm down the wide corridor with Sarah Shepherd falling in behind like an awkward, serge-clad bridesmaid.

Scott spotted an empty room off to the left, with no signs that it had been prepared for a meeting, and they settled down at one end of a long conference table. 'Would you like a drink or anything?' he asked. 'I'm sure Sarah would –'

'Oh, a glass of water perhaps,' she said, turning to Sarah Shepherd, 'with ice.'

'Can I get anything for you, sir?' the WPC asked.

'A cup of coffee would be wonderful, Sarah.'

'No problem.' Swapping bridesmaid for waitress, she left the room.

'Mrs Carson,' Scott said, 'Let me –'

'Oh please,' she interrupted, 'do call me Glenys. Everyone does.' And that was really awkward, Scott thought. He couldn't call her Glenys – it was inappropriate – but he couldn't call her Mrs Carson now either, and "Miss Summers" felt odd when he was talking to her as Marina Carson's mother. He'd have to avoid calling her anything, and that was uncomfortable.

'I just wanted to say,' he went on, 'how sorry I am for your loss. This is just a preliminary interview and I hope not to distress you too much. We just need to establish some facts about events yesterday afternoon.'

'Don't worry about me, Chief Inspector,' she said, brushing a hand across her eyes (she was wearing no make-up as far as he could see). 'I'm tougher than I look. If there's anything I can tell you that will help you find out what happened, I will.'

Sarah Shepherd reappeared with the drinks and Scott asked, 'Can you tell me what happened about the phone call to Renée Deakin yesterday morning? You definitely didn't make it?'

'Definitely! I don't do mornings, Chief Inspector. I keep theatre hours – late nights and late mornings. I certainly don't make phone calls at 9 a.m.'

'And when did you realise that the hoax call had been made?'

'Well, when Renée didn't turn up. She comes from twelve till three. As I told you, I don't like to be disturbed in the morning. Coming in at midday, she makes my lunch among other things, and then she goes off at three to pick up her boys. I didn't notice that she hadn't arrived until about twenty past twelve, I suppose, and then I rang and she told me about the phone call.'

'What was your reaction when she told you?' Scott asked.

She took a sip of her water, put the glass down and folded her hands together. 'I was terrified, Chief Inspector. I realised immediately that someone was ensuring that I would be alone in the house, incapacitated and vulnerable. That someone knew everything that was going on in the house – Renée's hours, my accident, everything.' She gave a little laugh and sipped some more water. 'I don't want to sound like a heroine in a Hitchcock film but I have no doubt that someone was trying to kill me. My slip on the stairs the day before was no accident – someone had spread grease there while I was still sleeping. It wasn't there when my husband and Marina went down earlier – they didn't slip. And there have been other times, too, though nobody would take me seriously about them.'

'Can you tell me about the other times?'

'Oh, you'll probably say I'm imagining things, just like my husband does, but the other day there was definitely someone creeping around the house.'

'When was that?'

'Last week. Tuesday? Yes, Tuesday.'

'Did you see anyone?'

'No, but I heard him, upstairs, going from room to room, opening drawers.'

'What made you think it was a man? Did it sound like a man's tread?'

'Well, I don't know.' She looked at him, startled, her composure shaken for the first time. 'I assumed – a woman alone – an intruder – you assume it's a man, don't you?'

'What did you do when you realised someone was there?'

'I slipped out of the back door and went and hid in Hector's writing room in the garden. It's got windows on three sides so I could see anyone coming, and I armed myself with a paper knife. Pathetic really.'

'And did anyone come?'

'No. Eventually Marina got home from school and came looking for me. We went in together and he'd obviously gone.'

'Who did you tell about this?'

'Only my husband – and Marina knew, of course.'

'And your son?'

'Oh Edmund boards at Marlbury Abbey. He's a weekly boarder – home at weekends – which suits us all perfectly. He was missing out on the extras – school plays and so on – as a day boy, but we didn't want to lose him altogether. He wasn't here so I didn't bother him with it.'

'You said no-one would take you seriously. That was only your husband and daughter then?'

'And Dr Fletcher. My husband told him.' She paused and looked directly at Scott. The look was so unwavering and disturbing that he had to look away. 'The thing you have to understand,' she said, 'is that I used to be a drunk – and, quite frankly, I still am sometimes. Now the people who run my life – my husband and my agent – didn't want the world to know that sweet little Glenys was a lush, so they put it about that I was "fragile" and "delicate". When Colin and Hector concocted the plan of carrying me off to Switzerland, the story was not that I was going to be dried out but that I was "in very precarious health" and "in need of complete rest". Well that's all very well, but what people thought was that I was off my chump.' As she grew more animated, Scott thought, you could hear her original Welshness bubbling through under her clipped English accent. 'Trouble was,' she went on, 'Hector's started to believe his own fiction – acts as if I'm half barmy. Which I most definitely am not.'

'Yesterday,' Scott said, 'you decided to go to London. Was that because you were afraid to stay in the house?'

'Of course it was. It seemed the only thing to do.'

'Did you ring Marina at any time – or text her – to let her know where you were?'

'Well she doesn't have a mobile. And I forgot to take mine with me, I was in such a rush to leave. So –' She shrugged.

'You didn't think she might be worried about you, given the fact that she knew that you felt you were in danger?'

She looked at him. 'I really didn't. I'm afraid I panicked,' she said.

'And it didn't occur to you that if there was an intruder, Marina might encounter them?'

She put her hand to her mouth and shook her head. 'I just didn't think. I'll never be able to forgive myself. I just didn't think. I knew they were after me. It didn't occur to me that anyone else could be in danger.'

Scott allowed her a moment and then asked, 'You've thought for some time that you were in danger. Who did you think was trying to harm you?'

The blue eyes took on a misty vagueness. 'Celebrities attract all kinds of madmen, don't they? I assumed it was someone who'd seen the show and got an obsession. Someone with a sick mind. It's not uncommon for actresses to be threatened by stalkers, as I'm sure you know.'

'So you think it was a single individual?'

'I suppose so.'

'The phone call to Mrs Deakin suggests that it's a woman.'

She raised her eyebrows. 'I suppose a woman might find me attractive too,' she said.

'Do you think it is at all possible that someone could have mistaken Marina for you – if they saw her only from the back?'

She gave a little shrug. 'Well, I think of her as just a little girl, of course, but she shot up recently and Hector commented the other day that she was as tall as me. And she's always insisted on wearing her hair in a bob like mine – very sweet, really. And I'm very slight, of course. That's how I get away with playing young.'

'Given your fear of intruders,' Scott said, 'I'm surprised that we found the kitchen door unlocked. Do you really think that you could have gone out and left it unlocked?'

'I think it was probably locked, but I didn't take the key out of the lock. There's a cat flap, you see, and you can reach in and get the key. We leave it in the lock when we're at home but we try to remember to take it out when we go out. Yesterday, I was in such a panic, I didn't do it.'

'If it's any comfort,' Sarah Shepherd put in quietly, 'it won't have made any real difference. In our experience, if an intruder's determined to get in, he will anyway.'

Uncomforted, Glenys Summers gave her a look of cold dislike.

'Could you just tell me which train you caught?' Scott asked.

'It was the train that leaves Shepton Halt at one thirty-three. It meant I was a bit late for the show but they weren't going to refuse to let me in.'

Scott closed his notebook. 'I think that's all for now, thank you. I won't distress you any more.' He helped her to her feet and as they proceeded back down the aisle he asked, 'There's just one thing. If someone wanted to find you alone, why didn't they go into the house before Mrs Deakin was due to arrive and save themselves the trouble of the phone call?'

'Hector,' she said. 'Hector's around in the morning. He's not an early starter either. He potters about, reads the paper, goes for a walk. Then he goes into Marlbury to work in the abbey library. He likes to have his lunch in the café in the crypt there.'

As he left her at the lift doors, he said, 'WPC Shepherd is here to support you and keep you informed of any developments. I'm sure –'

He got no further. She raised both hands to her head in an extravagant gesture of impatience. 'Oh please!' she hissed. 'Spare me her mooning around. I don't need *support*. I'll deal with my grief in my own way. Take her away and give her some real work to do.' She stepped into the lift and the doors closed smoothly behind her.

Scott looked at Sarah Shepherd. 'Have you had lunch?' he asked. 'If not, I'll buy you a sandwich.' They ate more or less in silence. Scott could see that Sarah was mortified by her failure with Glenys Summers but he didn't know how to reassure her and his mind was on his next interview, with Dr Fletcher. He had read the statement that Colin Fletcher had given the previous evening and there were things in it that didn't add up. He needed some answers.

The clutch of reporters at the back of hotel had grown in size by the time they left. No longer anonymous, with Sarah in her uniform beside him, he had to push through the mob issuing a curt 'No comment at this stage' as he went.

Colin Fletcher's surgery was in a row of well-proportioned regency houses not far from the back gate of the abbey. At two o'clock in the afternoon there was nothing going on except, it appeared, a baby clinic, judging from the scrum of mothers, push-chairs, fractious toddlers and wailing infants that occupied the downstairs waiting room. Directed upstairs, Scott and Sarah found Colin Fletcher sitting at his desk in a high-ceilinged room with a view of the abbey tower. In fact, it was that view that seemed to be occupying him, Scott noticed, rather than his computer screen or his heaped in-tray. He had called 'Come in' to their knock but was turned away from them as they entered and only swivelled his chair round when Scott spoke.

'I hope this isn't an inconvenient time, Dr Fletcher? I'm DCI David Scott. And this is PC Sarah Shepherd. She is acting as liaison officer with the Carson family.'

'Ah, yes.'

He looked terrible, Scott thought. He was a big man with a strong face and a head of vigorous greying hair but his eyes, under their bushy brows, seemed to have sunk into his head and his face had a yellow pallor. He was still capable of mustering his professional manner though. He stood up and reached across to shake hands, his grip firm. 'Do sit down,' he said.

'I have the statement you made yesterday, Dr Fletcher,' Scott said, 'but I would just like to run through it with you again.'

'Of course.'

'It must have been quite a shock for you, finding Marina Carson as you did and we don't always remember things clearly in those circumstances.'

'I suppose not.'

'You say in your statement that Mrs Carson phoned you just before one o'clock and asked you to come out to her house.'

'Yes.'

'And this was connected with the fall that she had suffered the day before?'

'Not directly. She –' He gave a sigh. 'She was in a highly

63

anxious state. Experiencing a panic attack, in fact. I could hear that she was having difficulty breathing.'

'And it's usual, is it, for you to go out to a patient under those circumstances?'

'With some patients, yes.'

'What sort of patients are those?'

'Particularly vulnerable patients. The very elderly.'

'Which Glenys isn't.'

'Isn't what?'

'Very elderly.'

'No.'

Colin Fletcher looked at him for a moment, his expression unreadable, then abruptly pushed back his chair and stood up. 'Look,' he said, slapping a hand on his desk, 'you're here because you want to find out how Marina died, and we all want to know that, of course we do, but I fail to see how that's helped by questioning my professional ethics.'

'I wasn't –'

'Oh I think you were. I think it bothers you that Glenys seemed to get preferential treatment. Well Glenys and Hector are old friends of ours. We've seen them through some difficult times. And Glenys called me for help. It was lunch time. I wasn't on duty. No other patients suffered from my going out to Lower Shepton. It wasn't a professional visit. I went because Glenys was alone and frightened.'

'Well thank you for clarifying that,' Scott said, as Colin Fletcher sat down again, heavily, and leaned back in his chair. 'We're just trying to build as complete a picture as possible of the events of that afternoon. Did Mrs Carson tell you what exactly she was frightened of?'

Colin Fletcher rubbed his eyes for a moment. 'Yes. She believed she was being – stalked, if you like. She believed that someone had been getting into the house. She thought that her fall down the stairs had been deliberately engineered.'

'And do you think she was right?'

'I – don't know what to think.'

Scott thought he had rarely heard a man sound so utterly weary.

'Perhaps you could tell us what you found when you got to Charter Hall,' he said. 'What time was that, by the way?'

'Twenty past one. I was there only for a few moments. Glenys was desperate to get out of the house and wanted me to drive her to the station, so we got straight into the car and I drove her there.'

'Yes. We are investigating some tyre tracks at Charter Hall. My forensics officers will need to take a look at your car.'

'Of course.'

'There's something in your statement that I'd like you to clarify, if you would. You say that on the way to the station Mrs Carson remembered that she ought to leave a message telling Marina where she had gone, and that was why you returned to the house.'

'Yes.'

'But you didn't return to the house till three o'clock. Why didn't you go straight back, since you were only a few minutes away?'

Colin Fletcher gazed back at him for moment, then got up again and walked over to the window. 'I was embarrassed,' he said eventually, turned away from them, looking out of the window. 'Embarrassed for Glenys. She's just lost her daughter under terrible circumstances and I didn't want you – the police – to think she was a neglectful mother.' He turned. 'The truth is, Glenys didn't ask me to leave a message. She didn't think of it. She was preoccupied with getting the train. It was only later, when I was at my desk dealing with paperwork, that I thought of it. I realised that Hector and Marina would have no idea where Glenys was, and given the state she was in they would be terribly worried. I had no way of contacting either of them. So I went back to leave a note for them.'

'I see.'

'I apologise if I wasn't strictly accurate in my statement.'

'Yes. And can you tell me again what happened when you returned to Charter Hall – at just before three, is that right?'

'Yes. I rang the doorbell in case someone was there – Hector, for instance – and as I was standing there I looked in through the glass panel of the door and could see someone – I couldn't tell who – lying at the foot of the stairs. I rang the bell again and hammered on the door but there was no response, so I used my shoe to break the glass and reached through to open the door.'

'Did you realise immediately that she was dead?'

'I thought so from the angle she was lying at. I checked for vital signs but there were none.'

'What did you do then?'

'I phoned the police.'

'Was that because you didn't think her fall had been accidental?'

'It was a sudden death. That's all.'

As they left the surgery Sarah Shepherd said, 'He seems more traumatised that the parents, don't you think? I might be better employed looking after him.'

7

FRIDAY 24th SEPTEMBER

Bring your hand to the buttery bar and let it drink

David Scott refused to talk to me yesterday when I rang him. I rang twice. Both times I heard the phone ring and I heard it click off. I understand that I hurt his feelings but that was more than two years ago and I think it's unmanly of him to sulk.

Anyway, I have to talk to him and, if he's in charge of this case, then he's going to have to talk to me. I have to talk to him because I heard Ellie crying in the night and because, no matter how wrong she was to let Marina go home without checking that her mother was there and no matter how much she blames herself, and probably always will, there are plenty of other people who have more to answer for than Ellie. There are Marina's parents, for a start, who seem to have made her responsible for them rather than sheltering her from the cruel world, and then there's the school. It would suit Tom Urquhart to load all the blame onto Ellie but he's bloody well not going to. If he tries, I shall threaten to go public on staffing practices that put an unqualified novice teacher in charge of a difficult tutor group and left her to sink or swim without any kind of mentoring arrangements. And there are the wretched children who were bullying Marina and who may or may not have

67

literally pushed her too far. It's that fall that haunts me. The image is there at the corner of my vision, it seems, all the time: the spindly child, all arms and legs, turning and twisting in the air. My stomach churns each time with the panic of it – the terrified, screaming step into space.

If someone pushed her or made her fall then I passionately want the police to find out who it was, but they're not going to achieve anything by bullying Ellie and I need David to acknowledge that. He's not much of a morning person, as I recall; early morning calls take him unawares. It's now half past seven and I think it's time. I dial and it rings for some time, but then I hear him.

'David Scott.'

'David,' I say in the bracing tones of a PE teacher. 'Good morning! I hope you're not busy.'

There is a clunk and a clatter and he says nothing. Has he fainted? Or thrown the phone across the room? Then he speaks, his voice muffled. 'Gina?'

'Certainly.'

'Do you know what time it is?'

'7.32 a.m. and you're heading an inquiry into the suspicious death of a child, so I'm assuming you've been up for hours.'

'Gina, would you just tell me what you want?' He's not muffled any more; he's crystal clear and very cool.

I take a deep breath and go off the top board. 'I want you to tell me that my daughter isn't any kind of suspect. And I want you to tell Tom Urquhart that you're not interested in her. Tom isn't the man he once was and he's being a real jobsworth over this. Ellie didn't follow official procedure when she sent Marina Carson home from school and Tom's entitled to be pissed off with her about that, but he won't let her into school, for God's sake, because someone might accuse him of exposing the children to a suspected criminal. You must know she's not a criminal, so tell him she isn't.'

He says nothing for at least a minute, but I can hear odd sounds – a kettle going on, possibly. Finally, he says, 'I can't believe you're asking this, Gina. You know I can't let any personal feelings affect the way I handle an investigation. I can't assume Eleanor's in the clear just because she's your daughter and you say she's innocent. What kind of police officer would that make me?'

Personal feelings: a little nugget of warmth settles in my chest. I pitch my voice lower, I speak more slowly. 'I'm not asking you to do anything unprofessional, David, of course I'm not. I'm just saying if you do decide that Ellie's sin of omission isn't a police matter, then please will you tell Tom Urquhart so? Then Ellie can go back into school and I don't have to spend another night lying awake listening to her sobbing in the room next door.'

There is another silence, shorter this time, then a heavy sigh and he says, 'We're reviewing our evidence so far this morning. I have to tell you that it's very early days to be ruling anyone in or out, but if – *if* we decide that Eleanor is out of the frame then, yes, I'll tell Tom Urquhart.'

I want to shower him with verbal kisses, entwine him in a virtual embrace, but I merely say, 'Thank you. That's all I ask.' And I ring off.

I can hear Freda toddling about upstairs so I scoop her up and bring her down and we both eat toast and marmite at the kitchen table. Then I take Ellie a cup of tea, take Freda into Annie and tell her to look after both of them, ignore her protests and cycle off to my day job.

It's a full morning: a staff meeting followed by a two-hour class on the language of business negotiation with a group of Chinese students taking MBAs. In their exam, they will have to role play a negotiation and it's my job to provide them with handy phrases and useful linguistic strategies. I'm hardly the person to be teaching this course – I have never participated in a business negotiation of any kind, since it was Andrew who bludgeoned a bargain price out of the vendor when we bought our house, and I won't demean myself by haggling even in an Istanbul market. I am an expert in what is known as cross-cultural pragmatic competence, however – the ability to give and understand subtle social signals in another language or another culture. So, armed with this knowledge and a good text book – *The World of Business* – I do my best.

This morning we concentrate first on preliminary pleasantries. They find these extraordinarily difficult. I can't believe that in China they just plunge straight into the hard bargaining, so I think the problem is that this bit really seems like "acting" and makes them self-conscious, whereas the negotiation itself has a goal and they forget that they're acting. After the pleasantries we move on to co-operative language and I press on them such useful expressions as "I take your point", "I understand the problem", "if you were in my shoes", "what would you do in my place?", "our mutual advantage" et cetera. (From personal prejudice, I try to discourage "a win-win situation" but they're awfully keen to use it). Sadly, I act as the internal examiner when it comes to the final test and I have to sit and witness their wilful abuse of my careful instruction. A couple of years ago, a sweet Thai woman, in the throes of salvaging her end of a deal, cried beseechingly to the large Greek she was partnered with, 'Please put your shoes in my place!' then turned to me and mouthed, 'Sorry!' before carrying on. Viewed as surrealist theatre, it works rather well.

By the end of this I am starving, but I've also got a load of e-mails to answer, I want to ring and see how Ellie is and I'm teaching again at two. I need to eat a sandwich at my desk, but this is not as easy as it sounds. The sandwiches in the senior common room come not in cellophane packs but arranged on plates with a tasteful garnish of parsley and what not, and a covering of clingfilm, and there has been a directive that staff should not take plates, cups and glasses away to their offices. We can't be trusted, you see. Slobs and slatterns as we academics are, we don't return them; instead we abandon them in our rooms, where they grow mould and are dug out weeks later from under a snowfall of paper.

Well, today I'm prepared to brazen it out. I sweep into the SCR, scoop up a plate, pay for it and head for the door signalling, I hope, life-and-death matters to attend to. Before I get there – head down, purposeful stride – I run slap into Diane, who is clearing tables. Caught red-handed, I stop and gaze guiltily at my criminal cheese and coleslaw sandwich. Then I smile. 'Diane!' I cry. 'I'm a sinner, I know, but I've got such a heap of work I'm going to take this away, but I promise I'll wash it up and return it, good as new.'

She purses her lips in exaggerated disapproval then she smiles too. 'That's all right, Gina. I know you're well trained.' She lowers her voice. 'It's the men who are the problem.'

'Tell me about it, Diane,' I say and make to move on.

She follows me to the door, adjusting her tray of dirty crockery. 'I was hoping I'd see you, Gina,' she says. 'Didn't you say your daughter was teaching at William Roper?'

Did I say that? Probably. I chat to the ground staff and the domestic staff more than common courtesy requires. I don't want to seem snooty and I overcompensate, I suppose. Diane cleans the English language building and you can't sit in silence while someone empties your bin and spritzes antibacterial stuff into your handset. Children are useful common ground and it's possible that Diane knows more than she needs to about Ellie and Annie by now.

'Yes, she is,' I say, mentally touching wood that this is, in fact, still the case.

'So, did she know that poor little girl – Glenys Summers' daughter?'

'How did you –'

'It's in the local paper today. Front page. Haven't you seen it? But I knew anyway. My sister-in-law, Renée, she cleans for the family. She's been interviewed by the police and everything. She's terribly upset. She thinks she could have stopped it happening.'

'Why?'

She looks at her laden tray and glances round the room. 'Hold on a minute,' she says, 'and I'll tell you about it. Just let me get rid of this tray.'

It's a quarter past one and my lunch hour is rapidly disappearing, but I have to hear this story. I sit at an empty table near the door and start to eat my sandwich. Diane joins me.

'We're not busy,' she says, sitting down. 'I can take five minutes. The thing is, Renée got a hoax phone call.'

'When?' I ask through a mouthful of coleslaw.

'The day it happened. When was it? Wednesday. In the morning, a woman rang – sounded just like Glenys Summers, she said – and told her not to come in to work. Said she'd got a bad cold and wanted a quiet day in bed.'

'And it wasn't her?'

'No, it wasn't. So Renée thinks the police think it was the killer, or a – you know – accomplice wanting to make sure the coast was clear.'

'Clear to kill Marina?'

'No. I don't suppose they were going to kill anyone. They wanted to burgle the place, didn't they? And the poor child came home while they were there.'

'But why would they kill her?'

'Panicked, I suppose.'

Oh God. And if Ellie hadn't sent her home, she wouldn't have been killed.

'Diane,' I say. 'Ellie's really upset about this too. Marina was in her class. I'd really like to know more. Do you think Renée would talk to me?'

'I should think so. It'd save her going over it all again with me at least. She's coming here this afternoon, actually. She's going to pick me up when I finish here. My car's in the garage so she's giving me a lift home.'

'What time do you finish?'

'Half past four.'

'Do you think you could ask her to get here a bit early and talk to me? Would she mind? I'd be really grateful.'

'I can give her a call. Her boys stay for football on Fridays and their dad'll pick them up.'

'That would be really kind.'

I manage the urgent e-mails and a quick call to Ellie and then run off to take my literature class. We are studying Pinter's *The Caretaker*, which is fun and they like the idea that they are studying a play by a Nobel laureate, but I do worry about sending our foreign students home all talking in repetitions and non sequiturs – not to mention the pauses, of course.

At four o'clock I go across to the SCR, where Diane is dispensing tea at the buttery hatch. She makes conspiratorial signals at me and I slip in through the door into the kitchen, where a woman who looks nothing like the cleaning lady of the popular imagination is sitting drinking black tea. Renée Deakin is about ten years younger than me, slim, dark and polished; she is wearing trim black trousers and a v-neck red sweater, with matching mouth and nails. I am momentarily intimidated, as I always am by this degree of gloss, but I accept a cup of tea from Diane and go and join her.

'I'm Gina Gray,' I say. 'You must be Renée. I do hope you don't mind talking to me.'

She gives me a wan smile. 'That's all right. I don't seem to be able to talk about anything else at the moment anyway. Diane says your daughter taught Marina. Well, I expect she'll have told you, she was a lovely girl. A bit strange – old fashioned – but a real sweetheart. She was the one that kept that family going. I don't know how they're going to manage without her.'

'Really?' I am genuinely surprised.

'Oh, don't get me wrong. I think Glenys is a wonderful actress, and Mr Carson, he's a very clever writer, I'm sure, but they're not practical people, you know what I mean? Nothing would ever get mended in that house if I didn't get my husband to go in and see to it. I don't think either of them knows how to work the washing machine. I'm not sure they know where the supermarket is.'

'But Marina can't have done all the washing and shopping, can she?'

'Oh no.' She laughs. 'I wouldn't want you to run off with the idea that she was Cinderella. No, I do the washing on a Monday, ironing Wednesday, supermarket shop on Friday. To tell you the truth, there's not that much cleaning to do, with Mr Carson out in his shed most of the time and Edmund away at school, so I don't mind. But Marina, she used to make a breakfast tray for her mum every morning before she went off to school. She'd leave it outside her room for when she woke up. Sometimes she'd pick a little bunch of flowers to put on the tray. There's not many kids would do that. And then in the evening she'd cook her dad's supper.'

'She did all the cooking?'

'Well, I make a good lunch for Glenys on the days I'm in and then she just has a snack in her dressing room before the show, but Marina cooks – cooked for her dad. It seemed hard, so sometimes I'd make something she could just heat in the oven. She'd always leave me a nice little note, thanking me. And when she was home in the school holidays, she'd follow me around. "You always make the house look so nice, Renée," she'd say.'

'Have you worked for the family long?'

'About a year. Since they came back from abroad. My mum

74

used to clean for them before, but she didn't feel up to it when they got back. I was looking for something to do. My youngest was just starting school and I wanted something part-time, so I'd be free to pick them up and so on. I was a dentist's receptionist before I had the boys, but I didn't want to go back to it – long hours and no school holidays – so I thought I'd try this. I've always been a bit stage-struck, to tell you the truth – I do quite a bit with Marlbury Operatic – and I quite fancied working for Glenys Summers.'

'What's she like to work for?'

'Oh ever so nice. Said to me on the first day, "Do call me Glenys." Never criticises or anything. "That's lovely, Renée," she says, that's all. I don't think she notices really. Well, her life's in the theatre, isn't it?'

'Diane told me about the call you had on Wednesday morning. You really didn't suspect that it wasn't Glenys Summers?'

She shakes her head.

'It's so stupid, isn't it? It sounded just like her – except with a cold. It wasn't so much her voice but the way she talked. "Oh Renée," she said, "I'm utterly miserable." That's the way she is – theatrical. Then she said she'd broken her ankle and she'd got a bad cold and her understudy could do the show and she was staying in bed. "I love you dearly Renée," she said, "but I really don't want you and the monster hoover battering at my peace today. Why don't you take yourself off to the Wednesday market and look for bargains. You don't usually get the chance." I'm sorry.' Her face crumples and she pulls a wad of tissues out of her bag and blows her nose. 'I just feel so guilty about it, you see. When she rang at half past twelve and said, "Renée where on earth are you?" I was so flustered. I said I'd come in right away, of course, but she said not to bother. Well, I was having a bit of a clear out in my kitchen – stuff all over the place – so I was glad not to go in. But I should have insisted, and then I'd have been there and – well –'

And you might have got pushed down the stairs, I think, but I say, 'I suppose her mother must feel the same. If she'd been there it would all have been different.'

'I'd no idea she was going to go off to London,' she says. 'I stopped off at the Hall on my way to pick up the boys – just to see if I could get her anything – but I saw a car there and I thought if she's got visitors I'd better not intrude. It's usually people from the theatre – the Aphra Behn – who call there. She lets them keep scenery – flats and stage cloths and that – in the old stables. So I just drove off. I realise now –' she rummages for a dry tissue '- it was probably Dr Fletcher's car. It must have been just about when he found her. If I'd gone in I'd have seen – well, I'd have seen her.' She looks up at me. 'I'd have seen her.'

I'd have seen her. That's the picture I've been working hard at keeping out of my head. It's enough that the fall is in there, playing itself in an endless loop; I can't allow myself to picture the dying. I get to my feet, thank Renée and Diane and go.

I have errands to do in town on my way home: a couple of books to pick up from Waterstones, shoes from the mender's, cash from the cash point. I'm not paying attention, though, and I have to retrace my steps twice. I'm thinking about that phone call. You could tell that Renée Deakin does a bit of acting because she got Glenys Summers' voice just right when she told me what her caller had said: "Oh Renée, I'm utterly miserable." She got that old-fashioned diction, that high, clear tone. But actually, it's the words, not the accent that jumped up and hit me: "I don't want you and the monster hoover battering at my peace today." It's a quote, "battering at my peace," and it's from *Macbeth*. When Macduff is down in England trying to stir the torpid Malcolm into action against Macbeth, he gets a visit from the Thane of Ross, hot from

Scotland to tell him that his wife and children have all been savagely slaughtered by Macbeth. Only Ross can't bring himself to spit it out, so Macduff keeps asking questions: "How does my wife? And all my children? The tyrant has not battered at their peace?" And poor old Ross, with terrible dramatic irony, tells him, "No, they were well at peace when I did leave them." It's not a run-of-the-mill expression, "battered at their peace," is it? Anyone who uses it has to have *Macbeth* in their head somewhere. And it's about the murder of innocents, that's the chilling thing. Surely the caller had to have that in her head somewhere, didn't she? Well, it's a pretty cultured class of burglar/burglar's accomplice we're looking for, which is interesting. I'd be surprised, in fact, if Glenys Summers herself quotes from *Macbeth* a lot, but that's because I'm snobbish about musicals. The people I'm really wondering about are these people from the theatre that Renée Deakin mentioned, the people who had regular access to Charter Hall and would know everything that was going on. They'd be likely to know *Macbeth*, wouldn't they? And it's when you've actually performed in plays that the words burrow into your brain and nest there on a permanent basis. They do the same if you've studied them for an exam. I'm pretty sure *Macbeth* was a set text when I taught David Scott A-level English twenty-five years ago. I wonder if he spotted the quote.

I'm having all these thoughts as I collect books, shoes and cash in an abstracted sort of way, and then I'm ready to cycle home, only I think I'll pop into The County Hotel to use the loo first. The powder room at The County Hotel is my convenience of choice when I'm out in town. It is warm and scented and offers little individual hand towels and hand cream as well as soap. If you walk confidently through reception and don't look too chavvy, no-one challenges you, so I stride in now and am heading off in a loo-ward direction when a lift door opens to the left of me and a woman steps out.

I recognise her immediately but can hardly believe it. It's Glenys Summers, in the flesh. I falter for a moment. I feel, ridiculously, that I should say something – how can you simply walk past a woman whose child has just been killed? – but of course I know I shouldn't, so I recover myself and walk on a bit faster. I'm impressed, from that brief glance, by how together she looks: pale, admittedly, and her face closed and wary, but on her feet, taking a lift, existing in the world. I can't begin to imagine how it must feel to lose a child, but I think if it were me, if I lost Ellie or Annie or Freda, I would just want some intravenous narcotic that would keep me out of the world forever. I can't imagine choosing what clothes to wear, washing my hair, eating, pressing lift buttons, talking, thinking.

I've almost reached the loos when I hear a disturbance behind me and I turn back to see that she is now being embraced: a boy in the uniform of Marlbury Abbey School has his arms round her and is hugging her tight. I can't tear myself away; I have to stand and gawp. He is taller than her and as he pulls out of the embrace, she gazes up at him. This must be Edmund, Marina's brother. I'd forgotten about him. This can't be the first time they've seen each other since Marina died, can it? And where is father? Upstairs perhaps, in their hotel room, on an intravenous narcotic.

Cycling home, I turn my mind to the most disturbing discovery from my conversation with Renée Deakin: Colin Fletcher found Marina dead. Why? What was he doing at Charter Hall? In the middle of the afternoon? When no-one was there? I have to talk to Eve. I shall ring her when I get home.

8

FRIDAY 24th SEPTEMBER

09.30: TEAM MEETING

Was the traffic worse than usual? Probably not. It was just his mood that was worse, and the cause of that, he knew, was a crack-of-dawn phone call from Gina Gray. What the hell did she think she was playing at? She'd walked out of his life, cut him off without a word, and now here she was, picking up the phone and asking favours – favours, for God's sake – as though nothing had happened. He ground the gears and swore. He'd been rattled by how hurt he'd been at getting dropped by her – he'd mooned about like a teenager for a while. Pathetic. It wasn't as though they'd ever actually got together, but he'd thought that there was a possibility and she obviously hadn't. And now she felt entitled to phone him at home at 7.30 in the morning and ask him to compromise a murder inquiry. Well, she wasn't getting any favours.

Paula Powell was in the incident room with a scattering of others. She was busy writing on a whiteboard; a photo of Marina Carson was up on display. Powell was his senior DS now after recent changes. He had a newcomer in the team: Andy Finnegan, newly promoted to DS – quiet at the moment but with a good track record. Steve Boxer had been with him for three years now – great with the IT stuff but without the all round qualities to go any further, probably. Powell, though, might go a long way if she didn't put too many backs up. She was learning, biding her time, only making a fuss about the force's ingrained male chauvinism when it really mattered. She was a good detective and he would have been happy to let her take the lead on this case if it hadn't turned into a murder inquiry. Anyway, he was glad to have her beside him.

'Do you want to do the update, Paula,' he asked, 'before we start considering options?'

'OK.' If she was surprised, she showed it only by the slightest flicker. 'Listen up, guys,' she called as the rest of the team started streaming in. 'No time to lose.' She pointed at the photo on the wall. 'New info since yesterday. We've got the PM results now and they confirm that Marina died between one and two on Wednesday afternoon. And she was murdered – that's definite – first pushed down the stairs and then hit over the head by a blow which fractured her skull.'

'Have we got the weapon?' a voice asked.

'A golf club. It came from a bag of clubs that was lying near the foot of the stairs. Marina's brother plays golf, apparently. The killer made no real attempt to hide it. It was put back in the bag.'

'Any sexual assault?' a voice asked.

'No.' She pointed to the white board. 'We know that she caught a bus from outside the William Roper School just after one o'clock and got off the bus in Lower Shepton at twenty past – we've talked to the bus driver, who remembers her and doesn't remember any other school kids being with her. Unless she diverted on the ten-minute walk home, she'll have got home at about half past. We've now got alibis for all the family. Father, Hector, is a writer and was doing some research in the abbey library. He's a regular there and several people saw him that afternoon. The seventeen-year-old brother, Edmund, is a weekly boarder at Marlbury Abbey School and was definitely in classes. The mother, Glenys, the actress, was in London. She caught the 13.33 train from Shepton Halt. The train manager saw her on the train – he's a fan apparently – and she went to The Duchess of York's Theatre. The ushers say she was definitely there. She's supposed to be in the show but she'd had an accident and sprained her ankle, so her understudy was doing her part.'

'What sort of accident?'

'She fell down the stairs.' Scott watched as she raised her hands and voice to quell the hubbub. 'Yeah, yeah, it looks like more than a coincidence. Now here's the thing. Marina's parents think the mother was the intended target. That whoever pushed Marina thought it was her mother. This show she's in – *Amy* – has anyone seen it? No? Well, apparently the character she plays is pushed down the stairs and killed. They think someone – some deranged fan – was trying to kill her in the same way.' She stopped and looked at Scott. 'Do you want to take over here, guv? I think we're into options now.'

'Yes. Thanks, Paula. OK. Now, on Wednesday morning, Renée Deakin, the Carson's cleaner, claims she got a phone call telling her not to go in and clean that day. Steve, do we have the number the call was made from?'

'It was made from a public phone box. The box outside the post office in Lower Shepton.'

'Must be the only unvandalised phone box in the county,' a voice commented.

Above the laughter, Scott said, 'We need to talk to the postmaster and anyone else who was in the shops there. See if they saw anyone using the box. It's a pretty unusual sight these days.'

'I've done it, sir.' Sarah Shepherd raised a hand, blushing. 'DS Finnegan asked me to look into it. The postmaster saw a woman go into the box at about that time. Not a local, he thought. Dark hair, wearing a tracksuit and sunglasses. He noticed the sunglasses. Unusual for nine o'clock on a September morning.'

'Any description of a car?'

'No car, he thought.'

'Renée Deakin's got dark hair,' Paula said, 'and she lives five minutes' walk away from the village shops.'

'You mean she could have made a call to her own number and invented the conversation?'

'But it wouldn't show up on the Deakins' phone record if it wasn't answered,' a voice objected.

'It would,' Steve Boxer returned, 'if it went to answerphone.'

'We need to talk to her neighbours. Find out about her movements. Do it carefully, though, Paula. We don't want to flag her up as a suspect when she may be perfectly innocent.' Scott picked up a board writer and moved to a white board. 'Obviously, a call like that could have been designed to make sure the house was empty so it could be burgled, but the Carsons don't think anything was stolen and if Renée Deakin's telling the truth, then it wasn't a burglary they had in mind. The caller mentioned the injured ankle, so she knew that Glenys Summers – Carson – wouldn't be performing that afternoon. So, it points to her – if the woman was working alone – or someone else wanting to find Glenys alone in the house – after Hector Carson left for Marlbury late morning, and before Marina got home from school. So let's consider this theory first – the Carsons' own theory. Can anyone see any flaws in it?'

'Do we know if the cleaner went in every day?' Steve Boxer asked. 'Wouldn't there have been another time when she'd have been alone in the house, without all the business of the phone call?'

'Three days a week she goes in,' Scott said, 'but there's a bit more to it. This show Glenys Summers is in, it's based on a true story – 16th century. I won't bore you with the history but her giving the staff the day off does fit the story.'

'So who killed the real woman?' Andy Finnegan asked. 'It'd help to know that, wouldn't it, if we're thinking it's some sort of copycat killing?'

'It remains a mystery, but the rumour was it was her husband.'

'So someone was setting up Hector Carson?'

'Possibly. Any other comments on this line of inquiry?'

'Could anyone really have mistaken a thirteen-year-old for a grown woman?' one of the DCs asked. 'Wasn't she in school uniform for a start?'

'The uniform's black trousers and a white shirt,' Paula said. 'She'd taken her blazer off. From the back it wouldn't look like a uniform.'

'But the killer would have seen her close to when he or she hit her with the club, surely?'

'Maybe they were afraid that she'd seen them – decided they couldn't risk leaving her alive.'

There was a silence as they pictured the scene. When he thought they'd had time enough, Scott said, 'It's not the only theory, of course. It's quite possible that Marina actually was the intended target. We know she was the target of some bullying at school – nothing violent as far as we've been told, but we're checking the school records to see what other pupils were out of school that afternoon.'

'I wanted to ask, sir,' the same persistent DC said, 'what she was doing leaving school at one o'clock. Was it a half day or something?'

'No, she went home early because she was concerned about her mother, who she thought would be at home with her sprained ankle. She did this quite often, apparently.'

'And the killer could have known that.'

'They could.' Now was the moment. He turned to Paula

Powell. 'Paula, you've got an issue about the teacher who gave her permission to go home, haven't you – Eleanor Gray?'

Powell coloured. 'I did wonder if she might have been involved. At first I thought she'd been just slack in sending Marina home without checking that there was anyone at home, but then we heard about the supposed phone call from René Deakin and I thought, well, she's a drama teacher and she might have put on the voice and made the phone call. She's got an alibi – she was teaching all afternoon – but she was the only person who knew that Marina would be home in the early afternoon, so I thought she could have let the killer know.'

'I sense a *but* coming, Paula.'

'Yep. She was speaking in school assembly at nine o'clock on Wednesday morning – when that phone call was made – seen by about fifteen hundred people, and her mobile phone record shows no calls made later that day, except one text.'

'Who to?'

'Her mother.'

There was a ripple of laughter, over which Scott said, 'She failed to follow guidelines in sending a child home to an empty house and the headmaster's got her on temporary suspension, but are you saying she's not in the frame as far as we're concerned, Paula?'

Powell looked him directly in the eye. 'I think we focus on finding the killer, don't we?' she said.

'Right,' he said briskly. 'Then this is how it stands. The theory that the mother was the intended victim sounds far-fetched but it makes more sense than a thirteen-year-old girl being the target. There's the timing for a start: no-one could predict that Marina would leave school early and be home at that time. And the caller expected Glenys Carson to be there that afternoon.'

'Except, sir,' Sarah Shepherd said, 'Glenys Carson said she

decided to go to London because of that phone call. When she spoke to Renée Deakin and realised it was a hoax, she thought someone was out to get her and left the house.'

'You're right, Sarah,' Scott said, 'and if the killer was someone close to the family, someone who knew them well and could guess how Glenys would react, they could probably guess, too, that Marina would stay at home or go home early because of her mother's accident. There's the access too. They seem to have got in through the back door – either it was left unlocked or they did the old arm through the cat flap trick. Again, it points to someone who knew they could get in that way. OK, so we're looking at people close to the family. We need to talk to relatives, neighbours, friends – including the children's friends. Edmund Carson's a weekly boarder at The Abbey. Paula, why don't you go and see him? Find out if he brings friends home with him at the weekends. Let's find out who comes to the house, if anyone else works there. And check on Renée Deakin's contacts. Find out if she gossips about life at Charter Hall. I need a picture. I need to know what went on in Marina Carson's life. Let's get into it.'

9

SATURDAY 25th SEPTEMBER

O had I but followed the arts!

Today being Saturday, I've arranged to meet Eve for coffee. We've agreed on The Pumpkin, the fair-trade, organic café where you can get dandelion tea and muesli biscuits if that's your inclination, but you can also get excellent coffee and whisky-soaked fruit cake, which is ours.

Eve is smaller and plumper than I am, which is always a comfort. She arrives today sporting a plaid cape, which she bought in Ireland, and vibrantly red hair. 'I thought it needed spicing up,' she says as she settles herself in a comfortable heap at a bamboo table in the window. We watch the Saturday shoppers for a bit before she asks, 'How's Ellie doing?'

'Not great. She's really upset about Marina, obviously, but then there's this other thing – suspension. I think Tom Urquhart's taken leave of his senses.'

'You have to understand all head teachers are running scared these days. Anything at all can bring parents down on them with a law suit. He's just watching his back.'

'I suppose. It's just not like the Tom I used to know.'

'The Tom you used to know didn't have a school to run, four teenage children with expensive tastes and a holiday home in the Algarve.'

'How's Colin?' I ask. When I suggested this meeting, it was on the pretext of wanting to talk about Ellie, but I need to work round to Colin.

'Oh, you know,' she says. 'He doesn't say much, but he's quite shaken up. He's not sleeping, which isn't like him.'

'It must have been awful finding her like that – even for a doctor.'

'Yes.'

We sit and munch our cake for a while, until Eve says, 'Come on, spit it out.'

For a moment I think she means the large bite of cake that's wrapping itself round my molars, but she doesn't. 'I've known you forever, Gina,' she says, laughing, 'and I've never known you this quiet. You've got something you want to say and you don't know how to say it, so come on – just spit it out.'

I finish my mouthful and take a swig of coffee. 'I just wondered,' I say tentatively, 'how Colin came to be there on Wednesday afternoon. I mean, I know it's none of my business and you'll think I'm just being nosey but –'

'You, nosey!' she hoots. 'Now why ever would I think that you were nosey, Gina Gray?'

'Well, all right, I know, but it just seems odd. I mean. I'm sure there's a perfectly sensible explanation, but...' I tail off because, quite honestly, I can't think of a sensible explanation.

'Colin is Glenys's GP, Gina. She rang him and asked him to call.'

'Why?'

'Because she was in a state.'

'She was lucky to get a house call, wasn't she, for "a state"? GPs don't do those any more unless you're dying.'

'Well, Glenys expects house calls and it's probably too late for Colin to try and retrain her now. She gets into states and she rings Colin.'

'What sort of states?'

'Anxiety, panic attacks, the screaming abdabs. You name it, she has it. Anyway, she rang on Wednesday and Colin went. After morning surgery. She told him she couldn't stay in the house and he drove her to the station so she could go up to London. On the way to the station, she remembered she hadn't left a message for Marina, telling her where she was, so Colin went back to the house to leave a message.

'Couldn't she have phoned her – or sent her a text?'

'Marina didn't have a mobile. OK?'

'OK.'

Only it's not OK actually, not at all. I sit with my coffee trying to swallow my objection, and then somehow the words are out of my mouth. 'But Eve, if she was going to see a matinee, she must have caught a train round about one o'clock. Renée Deakin said it was about three when Colin found Marina. Isn't that odd?'

'And who's Renée Deakin?'

'She's the cleaner at Charter Hall. I talked to her yesterday and she said –'

I wouldn't have believed that Eve's face could acquire hard edges; I've never seen it anything but soft and smiling. But now it's all angles. 'You have to leave this, Gina,' she says. 'Stop talking to people. Stop thinking you know better than the police. All you have to go on is hearsay, and I must tell you I resent being invited for coffee to be told that you think my husband is a murderer.'

'I don't think that,' I stammer. 'Of course I don't. I'm sorry Eve, it's just –'

'Just that you always have to know better than anyone else. Well, you don't. Colin's not a murderer, and I think you know that, but if you're in any doubt, then you'd better ask him yourself what he was doing on Wednesday afternoon. I think the coffee's your treat, don't you?' And she goes.

I beat myself up all the way to Sainsbury's. How could I have been so stupid? *Stupid, insensitive, blundering, thoughtless, arrogant, intrusive* I berate myself. Eve is the best friend I have and I may have lost her for good. I can't believe I sat there telling her, not that I thought her husband was a murderer – I never thought that – but that I didn't trust him, that I didn't believe his story. How could I have done that? *Because you don't believe his story* a small voice mutters in my head. *Because you are stupid, insensitive and all the rest of it, and you also think you're right.* But there's nowhere to go with my suspicions now. I can't talk to Colin himself – not now I've blown it with Eve – and I suppose I'll have to trust David Scott to get onto it. He's still holding me at arm's length at the moment but I'll keep working at it. I'm not easy to shake off.

I stumble round Sainsbury's, throwing the usual stuff into my trolley pretty randomly, and Annie picks me up. Annie now has a car, a Smart car – the kind everyone says you can park sideways. Her father bought it for her as a birthday present. The college authorities won't let her take it up to Oxford with her so it will sit outside my house unused for weeks at a time. Andrew will be happy though: Andrew thinks a house is not a home without a flashy vehicle sitting in front of it. In the meantime, before being parted from it, Annie is driving it on every possible occasion, today even condescending to drive the shopping home.

It's just as well I'm getting this lift because I have a plan for this afternoon. I'm going up to London to see *Amy*. I shall hate it, of course, but that's not the point. The trip is by way of research. All these falls downstairs at Charter Hall and Amy Robsart's death at Cumnor Place: there must surely be a connection, and the show seems the place to start. I got a ticket quite easily: people have been returning their tickets, apparently, because they don't want to see the understudy play the lead. The price was eye-watering – about as much as

I've just spent at Sainsbury's – but it gets me out of the house, away from Annie's frenzy and Ellie's gloom.

At The Duchess of York's Theatre, I pick up my very expensive ticket and present myself to be herded with a thousand other people up endless flights of stairs to the balcony, from which I gaze down on the tiny stage below and settle back to spend three hours looking at the tops of actors' heads. The show rises to meet all my worst expectations. The music is just unremarkable: trite, derivative, repetitive. I can bear that. I would like better but I can bear it. It's the words. Oh God, the words! The lyrics have not been so much composed as spewed out – banal chunks of language arbitrarily chopped up into lines and sung with inexplicable dramatic fervour. There's not an arresting image, a telling phrase, a clever epithet in the whole interminable show.

I would like to go home at half time but I need to be in at the death – that's what I've come for. I nod off in the second half, but I'm woken by the sudden cessation of noise, a moment of blessed silence. I survey the stage and find that we've reached the crucial moment. A vast sweeping staircase dominates the set and at the top of the stairs stands Amy, a tiny figure in scarlet silk. This is her moment, the show's great climax. She opens her mouth and sings. And what does she sing? Let me tell you. She sings

Why doesn't he love me?
Why is he never here?
Why is my young life blighted,
A life of grief and fear?

Once, I know, he loved me
How different it might have been,
But he gave his heart to another
And chose to love the Queen.

I know now he doesn't love me.
God give me strength, I pray,
To end this life of sadness.
Oh let me die today.

These are, quite truthfully, the words. I remember them because they are branded into my brain in all their awfulness and may never be excised. The poor girl does her best with them: she pumps and plumps the lines with throbbing, plaintive yearning. She is young, pretty and touching, and she is giving it her all. That's what I mind most, I decide – the way all these actors are driving themselves on, pushing themselves to the limit in the service of this garbage, as though the sheer power of their conviction can get the dead words to stand up and walk.

Well, I've seen what I came to see. The line the show takes is that, though Amy is contemplating suicide, it's the husband who actually does for her. He appears, Robert Dudley, gorgeous in black and gold, behind her. He raises his arms; she gives a terrible scream; there is a blackout; the music rises to a frenzy; the lights come up to reveal her spread-eagled in her scarlet dress at the foot of the stairs. Robert Dudley and the Queen (in matching black and gold) sing a duet from the top of the stairs and – curtain! Tumultuous applause, cheers and whoops, several curtain calls, exeunt.

On the way out, when I am finally disgorged into the street, I see that the theatre is making the best of the temporary loss of its big name. Two large photos of the understudy adorn the front of the theatre, and splashed across them are review quotes. "A star is born!" says the *Daily Mail* critic with startling originality; "genuine youth and freshness" says *The Telegraph*; "Move over Glenys" says *The Mirror*. If Glenys Summers has read these – and no doubt she has – I'd guess she'll be back on stage on Monday, come what may.

My rage at the sheer badness of the musical has evaporated, leaving space for a wave of sadness to come surging in and take me unawares. And I can't any longer avoid the image, which I've been at such pains to keep out, of the crumpled little body in its school uniform lying at the foot of the stairs. I've kept my busy mind on Ellie's problems, on Colin and Eve, on David Scott, on anything but that, but now it's in there like a virus, invasive and consuming, and I'm shaky and nauseous under its attack. So shaky, in fact, that as I'm walking past the stage door on my way to the tube, I almost miss a familiar back in the clutch of autograph-hunters. I know the line of the hair and the set of the shoulders really, but it's only as he turns to say something to the young woman following in his wake that I recognise David Scott. I raise a hand to wave but his gaze slides past me. He puts a protective arm round the young woman and elbows a path to the stage door. I take a few deep breaths and head for the tube and my solitary journey home.

10

SATURDAY 25th SEPTEMBER

17.45. INTERVIEW FOUR: THE UNDERSTUDY

Glancing through *The Independent* as he chomped his breakfast toast – why was it he could never organise fresh bread for Saturday mornings? – Scott noticed an article about the cast change in *Amy*. "Justine Todd," the reviewer wrote, "at half Glenys Summers' age, endows the part of Amy Robsart with a fervent, youthful passion that was missing from the older actress's portrayal. Where Summers' Amy was a victim from the start, a pale, timid, doomed creature, too easily swept aside by her husband's ambition, Todd, with her remarkable Piaf-like voice, goes down fighting all the way." He didn't read the rest but the old adage of CID training came into his head: *cui bono?* To whose advantage? If Glenys Summers was the intended victim (and he was veering in that direction) then you had to ask who would have benefited from her death. They hadn't asked yet about the contents of her will, if she had made one, but if everything would have gone to Hector, he would hardly have gained anything more than he enjoyed at the moment, unless the team came up with evidence of a double life for him; unless he wanted to get away and start again with someone else. It seemed improbable, but you learnt to expect the improbable, and quite often the impossible too.

One person who stood to benefit from Glenys's removal – who had benefited already from her fall – was Justine Todd; twenty-two years old, new out of Drama School, a complete unknown a week ago, now a hot property. She must have sat night after night watching the show on the monitor, seeing a woman old enough to be her mother playing the twenty-something Amy, ready to explode with the force of her own energy and ambition. Night after night, she saw that push from behind, saw the crumpled figure at the foot of the stairs.

'It sounds like something out of the ballet stories I used to read,' Paula Powell said, when he rang and told her why he wanted her to drive to London with him. 'There were always wicked girls in the corps de ballet booby-trapping the prima ballerina so they could dance Giselle or whoever it was.'

'All the same,' he said, 'I'd like you there. Have you talked to Edmund Carson yet?'

'I'm seeing him this morning. They have Saturday morning school at The Abbey, so I've arranged to see him when they finish. I'm taking Sarah with me.'

'I'll pick you up at two.'

Paula and Sarah waved their warrant cards and waited as the porter grudgingly raised the barrier to the staff car park, an oddly-shaped enclave between Marlbury Abbey school and the great abbey itself, which loomed above the school, baring its Reformation scars – its ancient, ruined choir – to the sky. Paula looked about her. 'I don't know about you,' she said, 'but my comp wasn't anything like this. This doesn't look like a school at all to me.'

'Me neither. Nothing the matter with Stoke High, but we didn't run to cloisters.'

Accosting a lad in a purple academic gown, they asked for directions to the office of the Head of Sixth Form and found him waiting for them, seated protectively on a sofa with

Edmund Carson beside him. He stood up to introduce himself as Marcus Bright, but returned to the sofa, directing them to armchairs some distance away. Paula looked at Edmund. When she had interviewed him briefly on the day of Marina's death, he had been intensely pale, the light spread of freckles standing out on his cheeks like coffee grounds. Today, he looked better but his face was still pale against his dark hair.

Marcus Bright put a hand on his shoulder for a moment. 'Well, if you have to be interrogated by the police, Edmund, these lovely ladies don't look too intimidating, do they?'

Paula glanced at Sarah and bit back a tart response. *Tread carefully*, she told herself.

'I don't know if you remember me, Edmund,' she said. 'I spoke to you the day your sister died.'

A smile of immense charm lit up his face. 'I remember you very well, DS Powell,' he said. 'You were very professional and very kind.'

Oddly flustered, Paula could think of no response to this. 'And Sarah Shepherd you know, of course,' she went on hastily.

'Of course.'

'I know Sarah has told you that we believe your sister's death was not accidental, and so we are trying to establish who had access to the house, who knew the family's habits and routines. And that's what I need to talk to you about. You're a weekly boarder here, right?'

'Yes.'

'And that means you go home every weekend?'

'Well, normally, yes.' He glanced at Marcus Bright. 'Not at the moment, obviously, because I don't have a home until you've finished with it.'

'Yes, quite. Do you ever invite friends home with you at the weekend?'

'Yes. When they could get exeats.'

'Exeats?'

'Permission from me,' Marcus Bright put in.

'Could you give me a list of the boys you've invited? I'd like all their names – even if they only came once.' She tore a page from her notebook and passed it across to him with a pen.

Marcus Bright seemed about to protest but she said firmly, 'We shall need to talk to all of them – with you present, of course, Mr Bright.'

As Edmund started to write, she went over to Sarah Shepherd and, after a murmured conversation, returned to her seat. 'Do you ever lend your golf clubs to friends, Edmund?' she asked.

He looked up. 'My golf clubs?'

'Yes. I'm sorry – this will be upsetting for you – but it is likely that one of your clubs was used to attack Marina.'

His head dropped and he gave a short groan, as though he had been punched. 'Hell,' he said.

'So we obviously want to check any fingerprints we find on them.'

'Yes.' He looked up. 'Well, up to last term I played golf on sports afternoon – Wednesdays – and no-one used them except me. Then last term I switched to fencing and I let a couple of guys borrow my clubs because they wanted to have a go at golf.'

'Could you write their names down too?'

Edmund glanced again at Marcus Bright, who nodded minimally.

'And has anyone used them since last term?' Paula asked.

'Well I played a bit during the summer vac, but I don't remember anyone else using them.'

'And you didn't bring them back to school at all this term?'

'No. I'm sticking with fencing. My mother regards it as an essential accomplishment.'

'Are you planning to go on the stage?'

'No.' Again the smile flashed for a moment. 'I'm planning to make a bit of money.'

He completed his list of half a dozen names and handed it to Marcus Bright, who glanced at it briefly and passed it on to Paula.

'Thanks,' she said. 'Can you tell us about anyone else who was a regular visitor to the house? Friends of your parents? Friends of Marina's?'

He shrugged. 'Well, I'm not there much, obviously. You'll know already about the wonderful Renée, who keeps the place afloat. Otherwise, the parents are pretty much recluses to be honest. Mamma has enough of the world when she's up in London, I think. At home she wants peace and quiet.'

'I understand she has some friends at the Aphra Behn Theatre?'

He looked vague for a moment. 'Oh, they just store some of their stuff in our stables. I don't think you'd call them friends.'

'But they are sometimes in the house?'

'Maybe. I've never seen them there.'

'And what about Marina? Did she invite friends home?'

He shook his head. 'Never when I was there. But she may have done, I suppose.'

'Did you notice any change in Marina in recent weeks? Did she seem worried about anything?'

'I didn't notice anything.'

'Would you say you and your sister were close, Edmund?'

He shrugged again. 'We were when we were younger. We went through some difficult times together. But now, you know, four years is a big age gap, and different sexes, different schools – we were very different people.' He looked at her and his blue eyes seem to darken as he said. 'That doesn't mean I won't miss her. She was my only sibling. I'm an only child now.'

When Scott picked her up in the afternoon she relayed the results of the interview to him. 'Not a lot really. The list of names of boys who went to he house might be useful – and the ones who used the clubs.'

'Except that it's pretty certain the killer used gloves,' Scott said.

'Yes. He seems a nice lad. Grown up for his age. I guess he's needed to be with parents like that.'

They drove in silence as Scott negotiated his way out of the town. Then, as they sat on the motorway, he said, 'I can't imagine you reading ballet stories,'

She laughed. 'I thought I wanted to be a dancer for a while.'

'What changed your mind?'

'I didn't have enough commitment. I didn't want ballet to take over my life.'

'So you became a police officer, because that doesn't mess up your life at all.'

'I discovered I liked commitment. Did you always want to be a cop?'

'I thought I wanted to be an archaeologist.'

'And why did you change your mind?'

'I thought I'd prefer live mysteries to dead ones.'

Paula said, 'She couldn't actually have done it – the understudy – you know that, don't you? She must have been at the theatre. She was playing Amy.'

'She'd have needed an accomplice, certainly, but she could have made the phone call. Who better to imitate Glenys Summers than her understudy? I'd like to show a photo of her to the guy in the post office at Lower Shepton. See if it resembles the woman in the phone box.'

'But isn't killing her a bit extreme? After all, the sprained ankle was enough to provide her moment of glory.'

'I know. Maybe she thought the ankle wouldn't keep her

off the stage for long enough. Maybe her accomplice had another go – trying for a more serious accident.'

'Then why hit Marina over the head?'

'Because she saw him – or her? Even maybe recognised them?'

'It's a bit off the wall, isn't it? I'm still happier with the interrupted burglary scenario. I know they expected that Glenys would be there, but they'd have thought they could deal with her – she was incapacitated with her ankle, after all. What they didn't want was two women there, one of them young and able-bodied.'

'I know this is a long shot, but let's just talk to her, see what kind of vibes we get.'

They parked the car and were approaching the theatre just as the audience started streaming out from the matinee. Heading for the stage door through a pressing throng of fans, Scott turned to make sure that Paula was still behind him and saw Gina Gray, of all people, staring at him from the edge of the crowd. What the hell was she doing here? She'd started waving but he was damned if he would acknowledge her. She had no business anywhere near this investigation and he wasn't giving her any leeway. Keeping his face a perfect blank, he pulled Paula towards him and pushed through to the stage door. As they followed the stage door keeper's directions to the star dressing room, he was thinking furiously. Gina wasn't stalking him, was she? No. She didn't drive so she couldn't have tailed him up the motorway. It was no coincidence though, her being here, today. She was trying to muscle in.

The dressing room, which still said *Miss Glenys Summers* on the door, was empty when they got there, which gave them a chance to look around. Justine Todd had obviously moved Glenys's personal belongings to one end of the mirrored bench that ran down one side of the room. They didn't amount to much: a few first night telegrams and congratulations cards, a make-up box, some bottles of mineral water. No photos of the family, he noticed, and no furry mascots. The things looked practical, workmanlike; they fitted the composed, clear-eyed woman he'd met better than her fragile, troubled, unpredictable public image.

Justine Todd appeared at the open door clutching an armful of bouquets, smiling and breathless. She stopped in the doorway, composing herself. 'You're the policeman who telephoned, I suppose,' she said.

'DCI David Scott.'

'DS Paula Powell.'

Scott wasn't a performer himself but he had stage managed a couple of shows at university and he knew the buzz actors felt after a performance. For this girl, the buzz must be immense, he realised, and he was sorry to put a damper on it. 'It's very good of you to see us,' he said. 'I'll try not to keep you long. I know you've got another performance to get ready for.'

She off-loaded her flowers into the basin in the corner, pulled off her wig to reveal short dark curls and said,
'Actually, would you mind going outside for a minute? I need to get out of this costume.'

As they were leaving the room, a middle-aged woman came bustling along the corridor. She threw them a disapproving glance and said, as she went in, 'I'll get you out of that dress, Justine. There's a bit of a tear near the hem. I'll take it and get it fixed.' She closed the door firmly and emerged five minutes later with an armful of scarlet silk.

Back in the dressing room, Justine Todd was wearing jeans and a blue t-shirt, and cleaning off her makeup. She watched them through the mirror. 'Do sit down,' she said, still with her back to them. 'I'm happy to help if I can, but I have to tell you I've never met Glenys's daughter – I didn't even know she had a daughter, actually – so I'm not sure how I can help.'

Scott sat and waited for her to turn round. 'How much do

you know about what happened to Marina Carson?' he asked.

'I know she fell down the stairs at home, and the papers are saying it may not have been an accident. That's about all.'

'You'll understand, then, that we're interested in the coincidence of that fall and Miss Summers' fall the day before, and what happens in this show.'

'Well, yes, I can see that but –'

She had picked up a pile of unopened cards and was shuffling them in her hands, looking at the envelopes as she spoke.

'We're pursuing a number of lines of inquiry, and one of them is the possibility that Marina Carson might have been attacked in mistake for her mother,' Scott said.

'You mean someone wanted to kill Glenys?' Her eyes were wide and ingenuous. He could hear no hint of falseness in her tone, but dealing with actors made life complicated.

'It's possible. A fan with an obsession, for example. We're trying to get a picture of her life here, doing the show, and we don't want to question her more than necessary, in the circumstances.'

'I honestly don't know if I can be much help. I really hardly saw her.'

'You didn't discuss the part together?' Powell asked. 'After all, you were her understudy.'

Justine Todd gave a hoot of laughter with a surprisingly hard edge to it. 'You must be joking! Glenys was very much the star and I was very much the nobody. She wasn't going to discuss the part with me.'

'You had to be at the theatre every night, presumably?' Scott asked. 'Where did you spend the time while the show was on?'

'Oh I usually play a walk-on – one of the Queen's ladies-in-waiting. I'm down in the dressing room with the others.'

'So you didn't see Glenys during the show?'

'No.'

'You must have watched her rehearsing,' Powell said. 'What's she like?'

Justine Todd stood up. 'Look, I really don't feel comfortable talking about her. I can't see that it's relevant and I –'

'Have you ever been to her home – near Marlbury?

'Once. She invited us all down soon after we opened – a Sunday barbecue in the garden. It was very nice.'

'You said you'd never met her daughter? Wasn't she there?'

'Well, I suppose she may have been, but I wasn't introduced to her. I think Glenys's son was there.'

'Can you tell me where you were at nine o'clock on Wednesday morning?' Scott asked.

'Wednesday? Yes, I can. I'd played Amy for the first time the night before and some friends came round and took me out to a champagne breakfast. Why?'

'Could you give DS Powell the names and addresses of those friends?'

'Why? What do you think I've done?'

'Nothing. We'd just like to eliminate you –'

'– from your inquiries. I watch murder mysteries on TV, Chief Inspector. I know what that means.'

She sat down and looked from one of them to the other. 'Look,' she said, 'I don't pretend I like Glenys – and I'm not sure anyone does – but we don't hate her and we feel terrible about what's happened to her daughter. I feel bad that it's given me my big break – I really do – but not that bad because that's how it is and you have to take your breaks where you can get them. And if I'd wanted to push Glenys down the stairs so I could have her part, I'd have done it right here on those nasty stone steps outside, all right?'

'What did you think of her?' Scott asked as they walked back to the car.

'I think she's straight,' Paula said. 'I should think Glenys is a cow to understudy and she wouldn't have minded sticking a foot out and tripping her up, but she doesn't look like someone who'd plan an elaborate scenario with hoax phone calls and accomplices, does she, honestly?'

Scott's instincts were the same but he was reluctant to abandon this line quite so easily. 'I don't know,' he said. 'Get those alibis for Wednesday morning checked out, and then we'll see.'

11

SUNDAY 26th SEPTEMBER

If she be so abandoned to her sorrow
As it is spoke, she never will admit me.

It's all coil at home this morning: Ellie has heard nothing from Tom Urquhart and is weepy and irritable; Freda is starting a cold and alternates grizzling and tantrums; Annie, deprived of the distraction of farewells now that all have departed but those waiting for the start of the outrageously short Oxbridge terms, has realised that she's scared as hell but is too proud to admit it and is sublimating her fears in biting sarcasm directed towards her nearest and dearest.

And me? How am I, you ask? Well, I intend to go out this afternoon, leaving them to the washing up and their own salvation. I was really interested, you see, to find David Scott at the back door of The Duchess of York's Theatre yesterday. He evidently thought the Amy Robsart connection was worth following up, but I'm not sure it will have got him anywhere. He's flailing about, it seems to me, and he has the advantage of all kinds of information I don't have. He's been to Charter Hall, for a start, and now I need to go there if I'm to be of any use.

I know what you're thinking: you're wondering why I have to be involved at all. Why aren't I leaving it to the professionals, you want to know. You remember Eve's words – "Stop talking to people. Stop thinking you know better than the police. You don't" – and you agree with them, but you have to admit that David and his team have got off to a spectacularly witless start, suspecting Ellie of all people of being involved in this horrible business. I can't be expected to sit here watching old films on the telly this afternoon while Ellie's job – her whole career in fact – hangs in the balance because of the idiocy of the boys in blue. So, I have to go to Charter Hall.

It won't be easy to get inside, I realise. The family have obviously been moved out but I remember from the time we had a violent death on the college campus that the scene was guarded and under wraps for weeks. I need an excuse for being there, and I have, in fact, found one. Earlier this morning, I came across Ellie weeping over a pile of school folders. I assumed that the tears were because she doesn't know whether she will ever be in a position to return these projects to their authors, but when I attempted reassurance she cut me off. 'This is Marina's,' she wailed.

I took the folder and looked at it. It had THE ELIZABETHAN THEATRE stencilled very carefully in gold pen across its blue cover and inside it was mainly pictures. I recognised their inspiration: they were sketches of the costumes worn in *Amy*.

'What am I going to do with it?' she snuffled.

It sat there limply in my hands, both poignant and pointless in the way the belongings of the dead are: freighted with significance and devoid of purpose both at the same time.

'Her parents might want it,' I suggested.

'No! That's really morbid, Ma.'

'No, it's not. If it had been you or Annie, I'd have wanted to have your books.'

'Are you sure?'

Am I sure? I really have no idea. My imagination refuses to stretch beyond the narcotic haze that I hope some medic would put me into.

Ellie looked at me for a moment, then said dismissively, 'Anyway, you're not normal, Ma. You can't expect other people to feel the same as you. '

'All the same, I think it's the best thing to do with them. Then they can decide if they want to keep them.'

I swear all this was said in perfect innocence, with no ulterior motive, but then I had a light bulb moment of sorts.

'Have you got any of her other books?'

'I took in their notebooks to look at last week. I've got that.'

'If you give them to me, I could take them out to Charter Hall this afternoon.'

'Why?'

'Because they're only upsetting you and I think her parents should have them. And I fancy a cycle out to Lower Shepton, anyway.'

'You have remembered you're looking after Freda this afternoon?'

'No. Why? Where are you going?'

'I'm seeing Ben Biaggi.'

'And who's Ben Biaggi?'

'He's the music guy at school. He's offered to do the music for *Twelfth Night*. He's going to show me his synthesiser.'

'Oh, that's what he calls it, does he?' I said, but my quip was lost on Ellie.

'And don't tell me it's not worth it because I'm probably about to be sacked,' she warned.

'I wasn't going to. Can't you take Freda with you?'

'No! I can't concentrate with her around, specially in the mood she's in today. He's going to try things out on his synthesiser so I can decide what I want. I need to be able to really listen.'

So Freda is going to have to come with me and having her in tow will blow something of a hole in my cover. I had pictured myself cycling airily up the drive at Charter Hall, explaining my mission to the chap on duty: *just out for an afternoon cycle – thought I'd drop these off – Marina's books – my daughter was her teacher – thought her parents should have them.* The copper would then take them indoors and I'd be able to do a bit of rubber necking. Depending on how things went, I might even get a guided tour, the absurd little optimist in my head told me. With Freda, though, this scenario looks improbable. I could cycle her the five miles there in the child seat but then I'll have no buggy to confine her in when we get there and she'll be all over the place. So, it'll have to be the bus, with the buggy, and arriving as granny-with-buggy more or less demolishes the plausibility of my story. I'm not to be stopped now, though. I'm going, come what may.

I hurry us all through lunch and leave the girls to argue over the washing up while I wrestle with Freda. We visit the loo, we gather toys and an emergency drink, we find my bag and phone. I put Marina's folder and book into a soft tote bag I got as a freebie at a recent conference. "English – it's global" the message on it reads, and just to push the point home, the 'g's in "English" and "global" are filled in with little worlds. I never use it – I'm more of a fair trade hessian woman really – so I'm happy to donate it. I don't know if Marina's things will actually find their way to her parents, but I'm not going to leave them in supermarket plastic, anyway. We're about to leave when I realise it's starting to rain, so I fix Freda's rain cover onto the buggy – a collapsible structure of metal struts covered with thick transparent plastic. From inside it, Freda gazes solemnly out at the world, making goldfish faces. I think this demonstrates an early sense of the absurd and I wonder if she takes after me.

It's only when we're settled on the bus and Freda is poring

over *Miffy Goes to the Zoo* that I realise, with a prickling of my spine, that we are retracing Marina's last ride out to Lower Shepton four days ago. The road we are travelling is obviously Roman – narrow but straight as a die. For the most part it's without pavements and fallen leaves are beginning to form dark heaps on either side. Ellie said that when the police first started asking questions about Marina's departure from school on Wednesday afternoon, she had a sudden vision. She saw, in a flash, the bus missed, Marina, desperate to get home to her mother, accepting a lift down the long empty road, then the unimaginable – terror, panic and death. But that wasn't how it happened, was it? She reached home quite safely, and found death there. I have my own vision: Marina wandering the house, looking for her mother, going upstairs and knocking on her mother's door, then standing at the top of the stairs, about to go down and look elsewhere. And then the violent shock of a push in the back, the sickening step into space, and oblivion. Perhaps, please God, there was no time for terror and panic.

We turn off the straight road and start to wind our way past big houses, secret behind immaculate hedges, until we hit a triangular village green with a squat, grey, stone church at one end and a smart pub and whitewashed post office facing one another across the hypotenuse. Lower Shepton; picture book village.

We stop outside the shop and get out into the rain. I have no idea where to find Charter Hall: it may be one of the houses we've just passed but the impression in my mind is that it's older than any of those. 'Chotlit,' Freda is saying hopefully, homing in on the display in the shop window, so I take this as my cue and we go inside. It's very upmarket as village shops go: farm eggs, air-freighted vegetables, Belgian chocolates, several types of olive oil, an assortment of tasteful toiletries and a couple of stands of "literary" paperbacks, not to mention a post office counter, a delicatessen counter and large stocks of liquor, What it lacks is the authentic village shop smell – the sad, sour aroma of food that has been there for a very long time. I select a bag of chocolate buttons and move towards the chap at the counter, smiling brightly.

'I'm looking for Charter Hall,' I say, as I hand over the cash. 'Can you tell me which way to go?'

Stupid! Stupid! I see instantly that this is a mistake. His mouth tightens and he slams my change into my hand. 'No,' he says, 'I can't.'

Why didn't I think? Our friends in the media must have been out here like flies round a turd. Of course he's not going to give out information. 'Oh, I'm not from the press or anything,' I say, even more stupidly. Of course I'm not from the press. Do I look like an ace newsperson, standing here in my anorak with Freda wiping her snotty nose on my sleeve? I look like what I am – a nosey middle-aged woman with nothing better to do on a Sunday afternoon than come snooping round a tragedy. Still, I'm reluctant to accept defeat. I seize my 'English – it's global' bag off the back of the buggy and offer it in evidence. I abandon the breezy tone and lower my voice. 'My daughter was Marina Carson's form teacher,' I say. 'She asked me to return these things of Marina's to her home. She thought her parents would like to have them.'

He looks pretty unmoved but a woman has emerged from a door behind the counter as I've been speaking and she says, 'Well, that's thoughtful, isn't it, Eric? I can't imagine what they must be feeling. And she was such a lovely girl. Came in here most days, when she got off the bus, for bits and pieces. Such a terrible shame. We're all stunned.'

This has the feeling of a rehearsed speech, honed by repetition over the past forty-eight hours. 'I saw Renée Deakin on Friday,' I say, seizing the moment. 'She's obviously very upset. Especially with that business over the phone call. '

'Oh, do you know Renée?' she asks.

'Oh yes,' I say in a tone implying years of acquaintance.

'Well,' she says, and I see, out of the corner of my eye, a silencing gesture from Eric, but he's too late: the stopper is out and the words are flowing. 'You know that call was made from outside here, don't you? Eric saw the woman who made it, didn't you, Eric?'

Eric has turned away and is tidying the shelves of cigarettes behind the counter. 'I saw someone, Linda. We shouldn't jump to conclusions.'

'A stranger,' Linda continues, unperturbed. 'We know everyone round here, but she was a stranger – young and dark-haired – wearing sunglasses on a cloudy morning. We should have realised.' She shoots a look at her husband as though by quick thinking he could have averted the tragedy. 'Do you know your way to Charter Hall?' she asks. 'No? It's quite easy. Follow the road along the side of the green and round the church. Round the back of the church, the road forks. Take the right-hand fork and it'll take you down towards the river. Charter Hall's the last house before the bridge.'

I fix up Freda's goldfish bowl rain cover, pull up my anorak hood and trudge off through the steady rain. I find Charter Hall without difficulty, helped by the subtle clues of yellow and white tape across the gates. A uniformed policeman comes to the gates in a studiedly unhurried way to greet me and as I'm waiting for him I glance to my right and notice, down by the bridge, a remarkable car: an old-fashioned, open-topped car that I would associate with the 1930's except that I was married to a classic car fanatic for several years and I know what this is. This is the kind of car that Andrew always craved; the classic MG that he drives now is but a pale shadow of this, the perfect form of the car. This is a Morgan, handmade in a small factory somewhere in the Midlands, I think. You have to put your name down for one years in advance, like entering a son for Eton, and you need the price of a medium-sized house available to spend on it. Andrew would have sold me and the girls into white slavery if he'd thought we'd fetch enough to buy a Morgan. Two men are sitting in this nonpareil of cars having a heated argument, and I'm surprised that they're not worried that the rain might be spoiling all that beautiful leather upholstery.

I repeat my farrago about the bag of books to the policeman and he gives me a narrow-eyed look but allows me in. I then tramp up the gravel drive towards the front door, watched impassively by a second policeman, who is guarding the door. As I go, I take in the slightly seedy grandeur of the house, its weathered grey stone and solid square front, its pock-marked Ionic columns flanking a panelled front door. When I get to the door, I do a third performance – I'm sure I'm less convincing each time – and the policeman gives me the narrow-eyed look, just like his colleague's. Presumably it's part of the basic training. I imagine a module at Hendon Police College called *Facial Expressions as a Tool of Policing*. He takes the bag, looks inside it with infinite slowness and says he'll let Mr Carson have it.

'Oh, is he here then?' I ask brightly, but Hendon Police College has prepared him for this too.

'I'll let him have the bag, madam. Was there anything else?'

I wish I felt more winsome. I want to be charming, but I've never felt less so, standing here with my anorak hood up and the rain trickling off my nose. I resort to Freda. 'Ducks, Freda,' I say.

'Quack, quack,' she cries, performance perfect.

'I promised her we could go to the river and look for ducks,' I tell the narrow-eyed policeman confidingly, 'but it's hard to get down to the river round here. Do you think we could just nip round the back for a moment?'

He looks at Freda, who dimples up and looks shy in a

perfect parody of little-girliness. 'Three minutes,' he says, 'and then I'm sending a squad car after you.'

We set off at speed round the side of the house. I feel honour bound to find the river, and we give it a quick look and donate a few chocolate buttons to a pair of moorhens before I turn to survey the back of the house. There is no grandeur here, even of the seedy variety. What confronts me is a jumble of run-down outhouses, originally stables or a coach house I assume vaguely. The closeness to the river makes me think of Toad Hall, but it's not spruce enough; it's more like Mariana's moated grange. To my left, a door is hanging open – an invitation to entry in my book.

I push the buggy inside and find myself in what were clearly stables – four stone stalls side by side. There is no horse and no smell of horse. Instead, what I find is that each stall is stacked with neatly piled cardboard boxes. Since the box on the top of one pile is open , its flaps hanging down, I take this as another invitation and stand on tiptoe to reach for the contents. What meets my hand is a sharp-edged plastic box, which reveals itself to be a DVD case. Inside, the legend superimposed on a vibrantly pink Tudor rose declares this to be a recording of *Amy* – "Now a West End Smash Hit". I dig into the box again and come out with an identical box. I look down the row of stalls and calculate that if all these boxes have the same contents there must be hundreds of these DVDs here. Why? What are they doing here? You'd expect these to be being sold in the foyer of the Duchess of York's theatre alongside souvenir programmes and t-shirts. I didn't see them yesterday, but then The Duchess of York's is one of those theatres where the plebs in the balcony go in through a separate entrance and don't get a sniff of the main foyer. But why are these stacked here? Is Glenys Summers planning to send them out as Christmas presents to friends and admirers? That presupposes a fairly monstrous vanity, doesn't it?

I turn over the case in my hand and find a large "4" stamped on the back and the message, "Recorded live at the Aphra Behn Theatre, Marlbury with the original cast starring Glenys Summers". So, the show had a pre-London try-out in Marlbury. I never noticed it but then, as Eve says, popular culture passes me by. I guess these were produced in Marlbury in an excess of enthusiasm on the part of the theatre management and that The Duchess of York's now wants nothing to do with them. So here they sit, remaindered, a sad comment on the transience of theatrical glory.

I put the DVDs back and I'm reflecting on this and wondering what other clutter from the Aphra Behn has been off-loaded into these outhouses as I push the buggy back out and the sky falls in on us. At least, that's what seems to be happening. I sense a movement above my head and I close my eyes and duck. There is a thud and then Freda starts screaming. I open my eyes to see Freda's rain cover lying buckled and twisted on the ground and Freda herself still in the buggy, screaming in terror. I snatch her up, hugging her to me, running my hands over her, feeling for broken bones, for blood, and all the time my mind is repeating the mantra, *if she can scream, it can't be too bad.* Miraculously, I find neither broken bones nor blood and Freda starts to quieten in my arms. It is only then that I turn round and see the woman who is standing in the entrance to the stables.

She is small, slight and very pale, and her blonde hair is flattened to her head by the rain; her hands are clenched round a heavy garden spade. It is Glenys Summers, of course. Up till now, the bit of my brain that was free to wonder what hit us has assumed that something fell from the roof. Now I realise that we've been attacked. 'What the fuck,' I say, 'do you think you're doing?'

'I might ask you the same question.'

And that would be a question I'd have some difficulty

answering, so I keep on the offensive. 'You could have killed her with that thing,' I shout.

'Well fortunately, I didn't.'

She's remarkably composed, I'll give her that, and her voice has that high, clear, child-like quality that I remember from twenty years ago. She tosses down the spade and says, 'I'd have thought you'd realise that we'd be on the lookout for intruders, after all we've been through. What are you – a journalist?'

I aim for being equally composed. 'No,' I say coldly, 'I'm not a journalist. I came here on an errand for my daughter. She was your daughter's teacher. I brought some books she thought you'd like to have. I gave them to the policeman at the front door.'

'And then you thought you'd have a snoop around, I suppose?'

'And then I brought Freda here to see the river, and,' I say in a moment of inspiration, 'we came in here because we thought there might be a horse.'

'Which there isn't,' she says, looking at me with her very light blue eyes.

'Which there isn't.'

A hint of pink comes into her pale face. 'I suppose I overreacted,' she says, 'but I heard you moving around and I was terrified. I simply snatched up the nearest thing to hand to protect myself. I'm sorry if I gave the little girl a fright.'

'And I'm sorry for your loss,' I say, and the formulaic words feel strange on my tongue.

She puts up a restraining hand, as if to ward off sympathy, and then says, 'I'm sorry not to be able to offer the little one a drink or anything, but I'm afraid I'm barred from my own house at the moment.' She stops and then smiles very sweetly. 'It's fortunate,' she says, 'that I don't have a very good aim.'

'Good enough,' I comment, looking at the ruined rain cover.

'I'll just leave this here, I think. It's no use now.' I take my anorak off and tuck it round Freda. I leave without farewells.

On the homeward journey I devote myself to keeping Freda happy. Or perhaps I'm keeping myself happy. I don't want to let go of her. I need her on my lap and in my arms: I need to feel her little heart beating and the soft snuffle of her breath against my neck. When we get home, the house is empty, so we have a bath together, which Freda loves, and then we eat boiled eggs and toast soldiers in the kitchen in our dressing gowns, and I tell myself repeatedly that there is no harm done. Will I tell Ellie what has happened? I'm not sure I can, not yet anyway. I put Freda in danger and I'm horribly ashamed.

When Freda is in bed, I sit down with pen and paper because, despite my fright, there are things I saw and heard this afternoon that interest me and I need to get them fixed. In random order, my questions are as follows:

What kind of criminal relies on a public phone box to make a call?

There were tyre marks along the grass verge at the side of the drive. Why, when the drive is wide enough for two cars to pass?

The policeman said he would make sure Mr Carson got the bag of books. Where was he?

Why Mr and not Mrs Carson, if he knew Glenys was there?

If she's nervous about being around Charter Hall, why was she there?

Who uses the motor boat that was moored at the jetty?

Who owns that Morgan?

David Scott will know the answers to some of these questions, but I haven't worked out how to prise the information out of him. I'm just pondering this when my mobile rings and I check the caller ID.

'David,' I say, 'I was just thinking about you.'

12

SUNDAY 26th SEPTEMBER

19.30. TWO PHONE CALLS

Sundays: what was the point of them? Once you'd done a supermarket trip and a session at the gym, work was the only real option, but you couldn't get on with it because no-one was there: no-one in forensics, no Steve on the computer, no-one to sit in on interviews. So, when he had idled away as much of the morning as he could bear to, Scott had gone into the station and trawled minutely through the interview transcripts and witness statements in the Carson case. Preliminary forensics found no DNA at the murder scene other than the expected: the parents', the doctor's, Renée Deakin's. Whoever killed Marina Carson took care to wear protective clothing. If you were looking for inconsistencies, he supposed there was one here. The killer, or killers, had been meticulous in their preparations: they had studied the pattern of life at Charter Hall, identified their point of access, thought about DNA evidence, prepared the ground with the hoax phone call, but the call itself, from a phone box, screamed *amateurs*. Even the smallest of small-time villains knew how to buy a mobile with a fake address and ditch it once it had served its purpose. The phone box business had been risky and no-one would have done it unless it was the only way they knew of calling anonymously. He needed to widen the pool of suspects. There was no-one here, among this lot whose statements he had in front of him, who looked like a villain. OK, so the Carsons were less than perfect parents but that didn't make them murderers and besides they both had cast iron alibis; Renée Deakin could, in theory, have been the dark woman in the phone box, but none of her neighbours had seen her go out that morning and the postmaster would surely have recognised her; the understudy had got a major career break out of Glenys's accident and Marina's death but she hadn't killed Marina and he was prepared to bet that her alibi for Wednesday morning would stack up; Ellie Gray had bent the rules a bit in sending the girl home, but even Paula acknowledged there was nothing to link her to the death, which reminded him that he'd promised Gina he'd phone Tom Urquhart about Ellie.

He picked up the phone and hung up three minutes later, hot with embarrassment. He had not been prepared for Tom's dry tone, the snide implication of his, "Well, I'm sure Gina will be very relieved to hear that. Very thoughtful of you to let me know, David, when you're so busy." Scott cursed. He'd been scrupulous, hadn't he? If Paula had said she still had questions about Ellie, he'd have told her to carry on. He wasn't in Gina's pocket. He had felt sorry for Ellie, he had to admit, because she was young and shocked and, he thought, patently innocent. Damn Tom and his insinuations. He'd made it impossible for him to phone Gina now. Well, he would phone but he would simply ask to speak to Ellie, he decided. That way Gina didn't come into the picture. He had interviewed Ellie, and now he was letting her know that they wouldn't need to talk to her again. That was all.

And then she answered, in that casual, teasing, familiar tone. 'Hello, David,' she said. 'I was just thinking about you.'

'Actually, I wanted to speak to Eleanor,' he said, stiff with embarrassment.

'Why?' Her voice was sharp, her hackles up. 'What's the matter? She's told you everything she knows.'

'No, I don't mean talk to her in that way. I mean – look, can I just talk to her, please.'

'Well, no, you can't. She's not here.'

'When will she be back?'

'I've no idea. She's a grown woman. She'll be back when she's back.'

'Then could you ask her to phone me when she gets in?'

'I could. Alternatively, I could give her a message. I can be trusted, you know.'

Oh, what the hell. This was juvenile. 'OK,' he said. 'Just tell her that I've informed Tom Urquhart that we have eliminated her from our inquiries.'

'You have? Oh David, that's fantastic. Thank you.'

This was just what he didn't want, the implication that this was personal, the whiff of special favours. 'There's absolutely no need to thank me,' he said flatly. 'It's just routine. We'd do the same for any witness whose job was put in question by their involvement with a case. We're always concerned to work with members of the community and we don't want anyone to suffer as a result of –'

'All right, all right!' She was laughing at him. 'I get the picture. When I said "Thank you," that wasn't actually code for, "Now I see you're a bent cop who's prepared to bend the rules for your friends." I just meant, "Thank you for letting us know." OK?'

'As I say, we would let anyone know in similar –'

'ALL RIGHT! And I hope anyone would say *thank you*! I'll let Ellie know, and I'll be sure to tell her not to thank you.'

'Fine.'

He was about to hang up but heard her say, 'On a related matter, David, I went out to Charter Hall today.'

A surge of fury made him briefly speechless.

'David?' she queried.

'And what the hell did you think you were doing there?'

'I was just doing an errand for Ellie – returning some of Marina's books.'

'Oh, really?'

She went on blithely, ignoring the irony of his tone, 'Yes, so your chaps let me into the grounds and I saw several really interesting things which I thought you might not know about and some things that puzzled me, that you might have the answer to, and I wondered if you'd like to meet and do a sort of information exchange – to our mutual advantage, so to speak.'

'Gina.' He was clenching his teeth so hard he could scarcely get the words out. 'This case is absolutely nothing to do with you. I've told you Ellie is out of the frame. You have no excuse for any further involvement. I have no intention of discussing it with you in any way, sh –'

'Shape or form? Oh David, do steer clear of clichés. I expect better from you.'

'I'm hanging up, Gina.'

'Well, I think that's no way to treat a concerned citizen. What was all that guff about working with members of the community if you won't listen to a member of the community who's trying to help you?'

Scott stood silent, the receiver in his hand.

'I can see you're not keen on a meeting,' she was saying, 'so let's just do it now. I'll be succinct – I'm good at that. I have four points. Number one, there were clear tyre tracks on the grass verge at the side of the drive and I wondered if you'd noticed them and if you had any theories about them.'

'Well no, Gina,' he said. 'We never noticed them because we're only police officers and we never look at things like tyre tracks.'

'So you did notice them?'

'Of course we bloody noticed them, and examined them, and took a cast of them, and identified the car and its owner.'

'And that is?'

'No-one you need to know about.'

'Only I wondered if you had any theory about why he or she was driving on the verge when the drive is as wide as it is. Do you think something might have been blocking the way?'

'Shall we move on to your next point?' he asked.

'OK. I bumped into Glenys Summers while I was there. Or rather she bumped into us. Tried to bump us on the head, actually.'

'What are you talking about, Gina? And who are *us*?'

'Freda and me. She attacked us with a garden spade. Did you know she was there? I'm not sure your chaps did. And that leads on to my third point. I wondered if she'd come up by river. There was a very smart little boat moored round the back, and that made me wonder whether the murderer could have come that way.'

He quite wanted to know about the attack with the spade but he was resolved not to ask questions. The only way was to freeze her out. 'Surprisingly,' he said, 'we had noticed that there's river access to Charter Hall. And your next point?'

'The hoax call from the phone box. It's in a very public place and I thought surely on the telly villains always have mobiles, don't they? And then they throw them away.'

'And your point is?'

'Seems as though your murderer is an amateur, and maybe an amateur sleuth stands a better chance of tracking him down.'

She hung up. Damn her. What malignant fortune had involved her in this case? And how did she have such pure bloody nerve? And why couldn't he slap her down? How did she manage always to wrong-foot him? He couldn't blame it all on the fact that she'd been his teacher twenty-odd years ago. There was just something about her that turned him into a clumsy, tongue-tied idiot.

He paced about the room. He needed a drink but he didn't keep anything but beer in the house. Drink was the downfall of too many good policemen: it offered the instant unwind you needed after a heavy day and it got a hold all too soon. He could go to a pub, but he hated drinking alone in pubs – it was lonelier than drinking alone at home. He didn't have friends here in Marlbury; he barely knew his neighbours; all he had was colleagues and he realised he had no idea of the patterns of their lives, couldn't imagine what they might be doing on a Sunday evening. Well, he couldn't stay here, pacing about, kicking the furniture. He found a number on his mobile and rang it.

'Paula?' he said. 'It's David. You don't fancy a drink, do you?'

13

MONDAY 27ᵗʰ SEPTEMBER

The rudeness that hath appeared in me have
I learnt from my entertainment

Have I mentioned that I'm doing the costumes for Ellie's production of *Twelfth Night*? No? Well, it turns out I am, and now that Ellie is reprieved and normal life continues, I'd better get on with them. Ellie was mortified to find that none of her colleagues was willing to take this on, but I had to tell her that teachers in general hate school plays. They hate the kids' overexcitement and general air of distraction; they hate the homework not done and the football practices missed; they hate the sense of threatening chaos in the last frantic week; they hate the fact that the most cussed kids are usually the stars; and most of all they hate the fact that the director gets to be hailed as a hero by kids, parents and governors alike. Why would they spend night after night working the lights or give up free periods to construct scenery or trail round gathering up props when they aren't going to be the ones to be called on stage to have a bunch of flowers thrust into their arms amidst a frenzy of whooping and clapping?

Anyway, Ellie has got some help. This keen young chap, Ben Biaggi, is doing the music for her and Eve has her GCSE class painting a wonderful backdrop of a neglected formal garden – all tangled ivy and lush, overblown roses. Eve has also offered to make the women's costumes. Ellie has decided to dress it 1920's, so Eve will do the flapper dresses and it's my job to get hold of striped blazers and boaters for the boys. When I get into my office I ring the Aphra Behn Theatre.

I should possibly explain a bit about the name of our local theatre. Aphra Behn isn't exactly a name to conjure with, I must admit, but she was the first English woman playwright (17th century). She was also an English spy in The Netherlands, which is rather distinguished, and she was almost certainly born near Marlbury. On their own, these facts would not have got her a theatre named after her – have you noticed how few theatres are named after women? – but the construction of a theatre in Marlbury, in the shell of an old cinema in the 1970's, happened to coincide with a period when a cabal of feminists formed a controlling faction on the town council. These half dozen or so (ever after known in Marlbury folk lore as The Bra Burners) beat down all opposition to build a women's refuge, establish a crèche in the town hall, organise a women's night bus and name the theatre after Aphra Behn. Before my time, of course, but they must have been heady days. The 80's swept away the crèche and the night bus but the refuge and the theatre remain.

The phone rings for a long time before a man's voice eventually says, 'Aphra Behn Theatre.'

'Good morning,' I say brightly. 'I'm after your costume hire department.'

'We don't have a costume hire department.'

'Really? Then I wonder why you advertise "Theatrical Costume Hire" on your website.'

'We hire out costumes but we don't have a costume hire department.'

His voice is light, nasal and extremely unfriendly. I resist the urge to tell him to piss off. 'I see. Well, perhaps you could tell me to whom I should talk to about hiring some costumes.'

'You may as well talk to me.'

'Good. I'm glad we've got that sorted out. Well, I'm dressing a production of *Twelfth Night* in early December. We're dressing it 1920's and I'm looking to hire twelve men's costumes – mainly striped blazers and flannels but one or two other suits as well – and a fat suit for Sir Toby, if possible.'

There is a pause, and then he says, 'This is an amateur group, is it?'

'It's a school.'

He laughs; I wait; he says nothing.

'So perhaps you could tell me,' I say, tight-lipped, 'whether it's worth my coming to see what you've got or whether I'd be wasting my time.'

'Anything we've got was made for adults. We don't do kids' stuff.'

'I've got measurements. These are quite big lads.'

'Well, if it's just for a school, we've probably got something that'll do.'

'Like your costumes for *The Boy Friend*, for example?' I ask, sweetly. 'When can I come in?'

'I've got a lot on this week. We go up with *Blithe Spirit* on Thursday.'

'Then it's best if I come in before you get really busy. How about this afternoon?'

'As I say, I am very –'

'About four fifteen?' I ask.

He sighs. 'Come in if you like. I shall probably be around.'

'And you are?'

'Alex Driver. Stage Manager.'

He doesn't ask my name but I tell him anyway. 'Gina Gray. On behalf of William Roper School. I'll come to the stage door, shall I?'

I thump down the receiver and steam out into the corridor.

On a reflex, I'm heading outside for a cigarette, only I forgot I don't smoke any more. As I stand there, toying with the idea of running over to the machine in the student union, my colleague Malcolm, he of the alcoholic tendency, comes out of his office.

'If you were a cat,' he says, 'your fur would be standing on end.'

'Supercilious sod,' I growl. 'They advertise themselves as hiring out costumes and then behave as though you're wasting their time when you actually want to hire something.'

I look at him and realise he doesn't look too good. He wants a drink as much as I want a cigarette. Well, there's still one drug we're allowed. 'Come on, Malcolm,' I say. 'Let's go to the SCR and I'll buy you a double espresso.'

It's a trying sort of morning: students slow on the uptake; colleagues faffing over trivialities; the rain streaming relentlessly down the windows; my boots letting in water. At lunch time, it gets a whole lot worse because I ring my ex-husband. Let me tell you how it goes.

I have concocted a plan. I want to go to Cumnor, you see. Cumnor is where Amy Robsart died. All right, I know. David is perfectly capable of finding out who killed Marina Carson and I've got no reason to get involved any further. In fact, I've got very good reasons not to, given that my efforts so far have already ruined a friendship and nearly got Freda killed – not to mention being shouted at by David. So I'm really not sleuthing any more. Really. I've just got interested in Amy Robsart. I tried googling Cumnor but all I got was tourist fodder, so I've been over to the library, where I found *The Oxford Literary Guide to the British Isles*, which contains quite a scholarly little account:

"Cumnor: Oxon village WSW of Oxford. The site of the mediaeval Cumnor Place where in 1560 Amy Dudley (née Robsart) was found dead 'at the foot of a paire of staires' is W of the church. The first written account of rumours of her murder, *The Secret Memoirs of Robert Dudley*, published on the continent, accused Dudley of poisoning not only her but his second wife's husband too."

Poisoned her? Where did that come from? Or rather, since this was the first account, where did the fall down the stairs come from? My own picture of her death comes from Walter Scott's account in *Kenilworth*. There, I remember, the two killers construct a trap – a sort of walkway across the stairwell with a trap door in it – and the most vivid bit is where they go back, like hunters, to see if their prey is in the trap. "Is the bird caught?" one of them asks, and you get the image of the young woman – hardly more than a girl – lying like a dead sparrow at the bottom of the stairwell. But let us continue with *The Literary Guide*:

"Ashmole told the story in *Antiquities of Berkshire*, where Scott saw it. Scott also read Kickle's ballad, *Cumnor Hall* (1784), the title he preferred for his novel but changed to *Kenilworth* (1821) at his publisher's wish.

The church has a small collection relating to Amy Dudley, and the ornate tomb of Anthony Foster, her host, who was suspected as her husband's agent in her murder. A few heavy stones in the churchyard wall are all that remain of the house."

OK, so I can't see the scene of the crime, but the collection in the church sounds interesting and I'd like to know more about Anthony Foster. I hadn't realised that Cumnor Place wasn't the Dudleys' own house. It's with all this in mind that, in my lunch hour, I phone Andrew, my erstwhile spouse.

'Andrew,' I say, skipping the conventional enquiries as to health etc., 'this trip we're doing up to Oxford to deliver Annie on Sunday, how do you fancy coming home by a scenic route?'

Silence. Oh they do silences, don't they, these men, while their slow brains process unexpected information? And I've learnt not to rush in to fill them, though it goes against the grain and I have to chew my tongue to ribbons to keep quiet.

Finally, he says, 'I didn't realise you were thinking of coming.'

'Well, Andrew, of course I'm – why would you think I wasn't coming?'

'Because Annie doesn't want you to.'

'What do you mean, she doesn't want me to?'

'Have you talked to her about it?'

'Yes. Well, no. Yes, in a general way – what she needs to take, which cases she's using – that sort of thing. I just assumed –'

'Well you shouldn't assume. Annie's worried you'll spoil the day.'

'Why? How? When have I ever spoilt anything?'

'You really don't understand her, Gina. She's nervous about going up. She knows how negative you are about the place and she's afraid you'll put a damper on things. If it's just her and me, it'll be more relaxed.'

Well, sod them then.

'Fine,' I say. 'That's absolutely fine. I'm terribly busy anyway, with my mother arriving on Monday. A hundred and one things to do. That's quite a relief, actually. Absolutely fine.'

I could work myself up into a lather of outrage and self-pity; I could bring tears to my own eyes by reminding myself of Andrew's years of neglect and my own heroic efforts as a single mother – my patience, my tolerance, my unstinting support in the unending drama of Annie's life, but I'll not weep. I have full cause of weeping, undeniably, but my heart's in no danger of breaking into a hundred thousand flaws, so I'll simply move on. I will just add, though, that when Annie gets the miseries, as she undoubtedly will, when the work is boring and the men are horrid and the strain of living in a world of high achievers begins to tell, I do hope it will be Andrew she rings for the tearful late-night heart to heart. Ha bloody ha! Fat chance.

At four o'clock, I don my cagoule and cycle round to the theatre. I have drunk too much coffee in the course of the day and I have an incipient migraine niggling behind my right eye. I am almost looking forward to a row with Alex Driver as a way of letting off steam.

The theatre is not far from the minster, in a group of buildings which overlook a rather unattractive stretch of river. At some point it was given a pseudo-Tudor front of stucco and beams, but it's strictly functional inside – this being where the council's interest in the arts, and its financial support, gave out. Unfortunately, the functionality isn't of the stripped wood and unplastered brick variety, but veers more towards sticky plastic and pock-marked chrome.

I find the stage door easily enough (I have fraught memories of taking the girls to perform in dance displays here – what was I thinking of?) but there is no sign of Alex Driver, nor of anyone else. I drop off my wet cagoule in the green Room and head cautiously upstairs to the dressing rooms, assuming that there must be a stage manager's office up here somewhere. On the first floor, I find only dressing rooms, their doors open, their interiors empty, waiting expectantly for their new inhabitants. On the second floor I bump into a girl, a diminutive girl with a lot of frizzy blonde hair and a huge bunch of keys hanging from the belt of her jeans. It turns out she's the ASM.

'Alex is on stage somewhere, I think,' she says, looking harassed. 'There's a problem with the tabs.'

Tabs are curtains, and they're of mainly antiquarian interest in theatres these days, but maybe *Blithe Spirit* calls for a curtain. I head back downstairs and through swing doors into the wings, where I encounter a stack of flats and that familiar stage smell of raw wood, paint and Leichner dusting powder. I move towards the sound of hammering and spot a man, half-way up a ladder, doing something to a curtain track. I have no doubt that this is Alex Driver: the designer jeans and spotless trainers tally exactly with the voice on the phone.

'Hello,' I call. 'I was told I'd find you here. I'm Gina Gray.'

He looks blank. Has he genuinely forgotten or is this just another refinement of the put-down?

'Costumes for William Roper School,' I say, a clipped edge entering my voice. 'We spoke on the phone this morning.'

He continues to stare at me, then light dawns, unpleasantly. 'Oh shit, I'd forgotten all about you.' He looks at his watch; I look at mine; it is 4.35. 'Well, I can't spend time on you now,' he says. 'I've got more important things to do.'

This is my cue to say I'm sorry for bothering him and I'll come back another time, but I don't take it. I remain resolutely silent, maintaining an expression of polite but detached interest.

'Well, you'll just have to find your own way round,' he mutters. 'I'll take you down there and leave you to it.' He leaps with ostentatious agility from his ladder and heads off across the stage. Through a door, down some steps, through another door, he switches on a light to reveal rack upon rack of costumes so closely packed together as to be unidentifiable at first glance.

'What play was it you said you were doing?' he asks.

'*Twelfth Night*,' I say, 'set 1920's.'

He sucks in his cheeks and gives me a long, sceptical stare. Then he opens his arms in a gesture which neatly combines an invitation to look around with a warning as to the hopelessness of my quest. He turns for the door. 'Let me know when you're leaving,' he says, and lets the door bang behind him.

I've missed my chance of the row I was looking forward

to; the man is so impossible he's taken my breath away. My head is pounding with unvented rage. On the other hand, I have this place to myself, the whole of the under-stage area crammed full of costumes and leisure to look around without Alex Driver's sneering assistance. For once, I count my blessings and I get looking.

It takes me a while to find what I'm looking for and I get diverted several times along the way. Hats are my weakness and I have to try on several. It's hats in the end that lead me to the *Boy Friend* costumes. Boaters are sitting in a tower, high up on a rack at the end of the room, and beneath them hang a row of striped blazers, which seem just right: light-hearted without being laughably gaudy; stylish enough to give the boys some swagger without being embarrassingly camp. There are loads of them – enough for a sizeable chorus, I suppose – so we should be able to accommodate most shapes and sizes. There's also something that looks like a Maitre D's outfit, which would do for Malvolio. There are some lovely women's dresses too, and I wonder if I should tell Eve about them and save her the trouble of making, but I'm not sure that Eve is actually speaking to me at the moment. I've been trying not to think about this since our *contretemps* on Saturday – that is to say I have thought about it a lot but haven't come up with a plan of action. Apologising would seem like a good idea, except I don't know what to say. "I do apologise for thinking your husband might be a child-murderer" hardly trips off the tongue, does it? So, I've done nothing and I'm rather relying on Eve's sweetness of nature to see us through. Only I'm afraid I may have gone too far even for that.

The *Boy Friend* costumes offer nothing brash enough for Sir Toby, and I wander further, in search of pantomime costumes. That's when I spot the *Toad of Toad Hall* rack and, beyond it, a couple of heaps of foam rubber that look as though they may be fat suits. I pick up one which turns out to be female shaped, all boobs and hips, but the other one offers a good beer belly. I pick it up and hold it against me to judge its size and it's when I go to put it back that I see that it has been lying on top of a couple of packing cases and that the contents of the cases are oddly familiar: vibrant Tudor roses in plastic cases – DVDs of *Amy* identical to those I saw at Charter Hall. I startle myself with my own laughter, which echoes suddenly in the silence. I can't help it; I hoot. Where else, I wonder, in what other odd corners are these pathetic things lying, embarrassingly unwanted on *Amy*'s triumphant voyage?

I'm still laughing when the door opens down the other end. I assume it's the charming stage manager returned but I find instead, as I fight my way through the racks, that it's another person altogether: a tall, distinguished-looking man with the flawless tan and silver-grey hair of a soap opera tycoon.

'What are you doing here?' he demands.

'The house style in this place leaves a lot to be desired,' I say. 'I'm doing what you might expect. I'm looking for some costumes to hire.'

'Is anyone else down here?'

'No.'

'Well you shouldn't have been left down here on your own.'

Since it doesn't seem to be the discourtesy to me that he's worried about, I make no reply.

'I'm Neil Cunningham, the theatre's director,' he says, without offering a handshake. 'Which company are you from?'

'Gina Gray,' I say, 'Marlbury College. I'm doing costumes for a production at William Roper School.'

'A school?' If lips curl, his curls. 'I don't believe we hire to schools. Some of these costumes are quite valuable. We don't want a lot of grubby oiks getting their mitts on them. Does Alex know you're from a school?'

'Yes. He seemed to think I could be trusted not to vandalise anything.'

'Well, I'm locking up down here now.' He jangles some keys.

'That's quite all right,' I say, moving past him to the door. 'I've found what I was looking for.' And then, because I hate him, and I want to wipe that sneer off his face, I turn at the door and say, 'You're having trouble shifting those DVDs of *Amy* aren't you? I noticed Glenys had a lot of them lying around the last time I was out at her place.'

The flush that spreads underneath his smooth tan makes his face a curious contrast with the immaculate silver hair. 'Are you a friend of Glenys's?' he asks.

Now, I know I'm inclined to bend the truth in a good cause, but I don't like to tell a direct lie if I can help it, so I offer him rueful smile. 'If Glenys can be said to have friends,' I say and go to sweep out of the door, only to collide with Alex Driver, entering at speed. He seems to take in the situation at a glance.

'Ah, Neil, I'm glad you came down. I had to leave er –'

'Gina,' I supply.

'– Gina down here to look around. Crisis on stage.' He turns to me. 'Found anything?' he asks.

Neil Cunningham interrupts. 'Gina was just telling me she'd seen some DVDs of *Amy* down here, Alex. I can't understand what they're doing here.'

The brick-red flush has subsided but there's a lot of rancour and it's directed not at me, but at Alex Driver. It's his turn to flush – a rather nasty salmon pink. 'Oh yes, they're just here temporarily. I thought we'd sell them while the panto's on. It's the sort of thing people might like around Christmas. I'll get rid of them, though, if you feel they're in the way.'

Neil Cunningham says nothing but his look is still venomous, so Alex Driver turns to me. 'Any luck?' he asks.

'Oh yes, the *Boy Friend* blazers will do fine and there are a couple of *Toad* costumes that'll be good too. Do you want me to show you?'

He glances at Neil Cunningham. 'Ah well, the *Toad* costumes,' he says. We like to keep those for professional productions – or reputable amateurs at least. I'm not really prepared –'

Neil Cunningham interrupts. 'It turns out that Gina is a friend of Glenys's, Alex.'

The two of them stand looking at each other and I know where I have seen them before. They're the two I saw arguing in a Morgan car outside Charter Hall on Saturday afternoon. I feel vindicated. My gut instinct told me they were theatrical, and they are. Alex Driver adopts a smile that is, if anything, more unattractive than his sneer.

'Well then, I'm sure you'll look after them, won't you, Gina?' He appears to swallow something rather large that's stuck in his throat – his pride, possibly? 'Let's go and have a look at them, shall we?'

Fifteen minutes later I'm out of there and I see, as I unlock my bike in the car park, something I didn't see on my way in – a splendid Morgan car parked in a reserved space which, presumably, says *Director*. As I cycle home, I wonder if the two men are discussing me. That will depend on what they were doing in Lower Shepton yesterday, of course. If they talked to Glenys, then she may well have told them about the nosey woman from William Roper who'd come prowling around, in which case it won't take them long to work out that I'm not a friend of Glenys's at all. Well, I've paid a deposit on the costumes now, so let's hope, I think, as I splash through the puddles, that we're home and dry.

14

WEDNESDAY 29th SEPTEMBER

09.30: TEAM MEETING

'So let's start with key points from the house to house and witness statements,' Scott said. 'Paula?'

'Renée Deakin. I went carefully with the neighbours – didn't want to suggest we suspected her of anything. I said whoever broke into Charter Hall seemed to have taken care to go in when they knew she wouldn't be there and then I asked them if someone keeping a watch on her would have been able to see what her work pattern was. Only two of them are at home during the day – a retired woman across the road and a woman with a baby two doors down. Oh yes, they said, Monday, Wednesday and Friday you'd see her go, round about quarter to twelve. And did she always take her car with her? Yes she did. Did she take her car if she was just going to the village shop? Like the rest of them, she'd generally stop off at the shop when she was out in her car anyway. No-one said, "Funnily enough I saw her go out on Wednesday morning just before nine, and I thought it was odd because she was wearing sunglasses."'

'OK. Thanks, Paula.'

'I did sound them out about whether she gossiped about life at Charter Hall. Never, they said. She was very loyal. "Like she worked for the royal family," one of them said.'

'Except they're all selling their stories to *The Sun* these days,' Andy Finnegan commented.

'Andy. How did you get on with the Carsons' friends and neighbours?'

'I started by asking Hector Carson for a list of people who visited the house, and he couldn't come up with anyone much. They don't seem to see family at all. He's got a brother living in France; she's got two sisters still living in Cardiff, where they grew up. We did contact them but they said they never saw her. I get the feeling there's no love lost there.'

'But not that they hated her enough to kill her?'

'I wouldn't think so. They had nothing to gain, did they? Everything goes to Hector.'

'Right. What about friends?'

'They don't seem to have any locally. Glenys has lots of friends in the acting world, apparently, but they don't come down to Marlbury. People from the Aphra Behn Theatre call in, though neither of the Carsons would call them friends. They let them use the outhouses at Charter Hall for storage on an informal basis – no money changes hands.'

'Did you talk to them?'

'I talked to the stage manager – Driver – Alex Driver. Nothing very useful, though. Said he was last up there a couple of weeks ago and saw nothing out of the ordinary. He did say Glenys seemed jumpy, though?'

'Did he know why?'

'Said he didn't. He wasn't exactly chatty, I must say.'

'And neighbours?'

'The Carsons say they don't know their neighbours, not even their names. It's believable. They're big houses there, down long drives. You wouldn't chat over the garden fence. We talked to the neighbours on both sides and they confirmed it. They know who Glenys is, of course, but they've never been invited to Charter Hall and they don't want to seem pushy, I

135

guess. One thing, though. The neighbour a couple of houses up river said he notices the Carsons' little blue motor boat going to and fro – up to Marlbury, he reckoned. Different people on it, he said, adults and children. He wondered if someone was running it as a business. Now, when I asked Hector Carson who used it, he said no-one much. Edmund and his friends messed about on it at weekends, he said. That was all.'

'Which doesn't sound convincing. For those of you who haven't seen it, it's a good boat, new-looking, well-maintained, seats up to six, I would say. So what do we think?'

'Could be a tax dodge,' Steve Boxer said. 'They're running a business doing trips up and down to Marlbury but keeping it a secret from the revenue.'

'But if they don't advertise, how does anyone know about the trips?' Paula queried.

'They'd let the B&Bs in Marlbury know about it, informally. If they're not paying tax, they can undercut the competition.'

'Well, it doesn't sound like a motive for murder,' Scott said, 'but see what you can find out, Andy. Send someone round the B&Bs. Sarah, what about the children's friends?'

'As we thought, Marina was very much a loner. No friends really. The kids in her class looked embarrassed when we asked about her. I'd say she was definitely being bullied. Teachers didn't have much to say about her. She was in what used to be called the remedial class when I was at school. It's officially called the extra class at William Roper, though the kids call it "the retard class", I discovered. The maths teacher said she was brighter than she pretended to be. Just lazy, he thought. Eleanor Gray, her form teacher, said she was articulate to talk to but had poor writing skills. The art teacher – who's Dr Fletcher's wife, by the way – said Marina spent a lot of time in the art room but never really talked about life at home. She suggested Marina was a bit neglected – parents preoccupied with their careers and so on – but I think we knew that already.

And she didn't really have any specific examples of neglect.'

'And the brother's friends, Paula?'

'Oh he's a pretty popular guy, it seems. Good academically and stars in school plays. He does invite friends home at weekends. We've got a list of boys who've been to the house and we've talked to them all. The headmaster insisted on being present, though, so I'm not sure they'd have told us any dark secrets about Charter Hall, even if they knew any.'

'There were some other fingerprints, besides Edmund's, on his golf clubs,' Andy Finnegan said. 'He says some friends borrowed them. We've only just got prints from the boys – we needed parental permission and some of the parents were hard to track down.'

'Anything else?'

'Justine Todd's friends confirm she was drinking champagne with them on Wednesday morning,' Paula said, 'so that rules her out as the hoax caller.'

'I was wondering about Dr Fletcher,' Boxer said. 'Does anyone confirm he was at the surgery that afternoon?'

'Yes, the practice manager. She confirms he arrived at about two, though she didn't see him leave.'

'So he could have left earlier, killed the girl and then 'discovered' the body?' Boxer persisted.

'Not really. Apart from the question of a motive, his 999 call saying he'd just found the body was logged at 15.02. We were out there within fifteen minutes and Dr McAndrew was with us. She thought Marina had been dead at least an hour – probably closer to two, which ties in with her being killed as soon as she went into the house.'

'It's a bit odd though, isn't it, the way he behaved? Beyond the call of duty?' Paula queried. 'He's only their GP, after all, and there he was being chauffeur and nanny.'

'I get the impression he's a lot more than just the GP,' Scott said. 'He seemed pretty shaken up by Marina's death. He's known her since she was small and he says he's seen the family through some difficult times. I know you say the Carsons don't seem to have any friends, Andy, but I think he's probably the nearest thing to a friend they've got.'

'It's odd they didn't mention him when we asked about friends, in that case.'

'I think,' Sarah Shepherd said, 'Glenys is one of those people who takes it for granted that people do things for her. They think they're doing it out of friendship, but she just takes it as her due.'

'Go Sarah with the psychology!' Steve Boxer said. 'You in training to be what's-her-name on *Waking the Dead*?'

'Piss off, Steve,' Paula said.

'OK,' Scott intervened. 'We've mostly closed off lines, but let's look at what we have got. The river. Let's get going on finding out about that boat. Talk to people with houses on the other side of the river – see what they've seen. Glenys got onto the property on Sunday without being seen by the uniforms on duty. It seems she came up by boat, and the killer or killers could have done too. The other thing is the caller from the phone box. If we can get a lead on her, we're home. DCs Sweet and Temple have been outside the post office in Lower Shepton since eight- thirty this morning – a week since the call was made. I'm hoping they may be able to jog some memories.'

He stopped and looked round at them all. 'I think that call is key in other ways, too. It must have struck you all how old-fashioned it is, how amateur. What villain can't get hold of an unregistered mobile? So, was it all amateur? A bungled burglary of a house with nothing valuable in it and a panicky killing of a witness? All cock-up? Yes, maybe, except, they did their homework, knew all about the house, left no DNA. So that's a puzzle, and I'll be glad to hear any theories you may have.'

Silence. Then Paula said, 'Maybe it's someone who watches old movies – that sort of thing.'

'It's a thought. If we run out of other leads, we'll take a look at people's DVD collections. The other point is – and it's bothered me from the start – why did they choose a day when Renée Deakin usually came to clean. She's not there on Tuesdays and Thursdays. Why go to all the trouble of the phone call when they could have done it the next day? Or early in the morning before she got there?'

'Perhaps they did try to do it on the Tuesday,' Paula said. 'That was when Glenys had her fall. Maybe they did booby-trap the stairs but it wasn't enough, so they went back for another go and made sure that time.'

'And they couldn't do it earlier in the morning,' Sarah Shepherd said, 'not if they wanted to push her down the stairs. By all accounts, she doesn't get up till about twelve, so they'd have had to kill her in her bed.'

'OK. And why not leave it till Thursday?' There was a silence and Scott answered his own question. 'Well, if we're talking about an obsessive fan, maybe the obsession had got too strong and he or she couldn't wait. On the other hand, if someone actually had a motive for getting rid of Glenys, then perhaps they couldn't afford to wait. It had become urgent to rid of her. Why? What was she going to do that they had to prevent?'

'Make a will?' Andy Finnegan suggested. 'Maybe she was going to leave everything to someone other than old Hector.'

'Except he's got a cast iron alibi,' Steve Boxer objected.

'I need to talk to her again,' Scott said. 'In the meantime, keep going on the slog. My instinct tells me we're not going to get a sudden breakthrough in this case. It's going to be inch by inch all the way.'

At lunch time, Scott picked up a sandwich from the canteen and headed out for a walk along the river. If he was honest with himself, he knew he was avoiding Paula. Things had changed between them since Sunday night. Nothing had happened: they'd had a couple of drinks and chatted, that was all, but Paula's manner to him had changed. It wasn't enough for anyone else to notice, he hoped, but he could feel that she seemed to be expecting something from him. He wished he hadn't rung her; it was never a good idea to socialise outside work, not when you were in charge. He regretted being so snappy with Gina too, really. Of course she had no business in the case, but she did make some good points. There had been no need to be so paranoid about her involvement.

His mobile rang.

'David?'

'Gina,' he said. 'Would you believe me if I said I was just thinking about you?'

'Were you really?' She sounded genuinely pleased. 'Well I've got a proposition for you. How would you fancy a trip into Oxfordshire at the weekend, to research Amy Robsart and Cumnor Place?'

'What are you talking about, Gina?'

'You think there's a connection between Marina's death and Amy Robsart's don't you? You wouldn't have been at *Amy* on Saturday otherwise.'

'Gina, I wasn't at the show, I was there to interview a witness.'

'Oh.' She sounded uncharacteristically dashed, but she rallied rapidly. 'Still there is the possibility of a copycat killing, isn't there? And anyway, it's going to be lovely weather and there won't be many more golden autumn days, so why don't we just think of it as an outing and if we find out anything interesting, that's a bonus?'

'Gina, I'm really not sure what you have in mind. You know you can't get involved in this case, don't you? It was different last time when it was one of your students who was killed, but –'

'It's all right. I understand. I promise not to mention the case – not a word. If we talk of murder at all, it will be about Amy Robsart's murder. If I utter a syllable about Marina you can turn me out of the car and leave me to hitch home.'

'All right.'

'You'll come?'

He was startled by her delight. 'Yes,' he said, and then, because that sounded pretty ungracious, he added, 'It'll be a pleasure.'

15

SATURDAY 2ⁿᵈ OCTOBER

For I myself am best
When least in company

For the past few weeks I have had an invitation lying on the hall table. It goes as follows:

> *Verity and Simon Maxwell*
> *At Home*
> *On Saturday 2ⁿᵈ October*
> *From 6.00 p.m.*
> *At 11 The Precincts, Marlbury*
> *RSVP to verity@freenet.com*
> *Verity's birthday but no prezzies please!*

I e-mailed some time ago, saying I would be delighted to come, though in truth delight is far from what I feel at the prospect, especially since Verity replied, reciprocating the delight and adding, "I should tell you, we have invited Andrew and Lavender."

I realise I haven't told you about Lavender. She is Andrew's new wife. She is barely older than Ellie (twenty-seven) and comes from a slightly county family – not titled but terribly *well-established*. She is rich, pretty, well-connected and appears to hold no opinions on anything. She is the woman Andrew should have married when he made the mistake of marrying me – except, of course, that she was only a year old at the time. She is always referred to by the girls and me as "The Fragrant Lavender". Her name isn't her fault, of course – her sisters are called Saffron and Bryony – but we like our little joke.

A few weeks ago, The Fragrant Lavender gave birth to Arthur. *Arthur Edwin Gray*! He sounds as though he should be editing dictionaries rather than lying on his back blowing milk bubbles. I thought the arrival of the baby, particularly when it turned out to be a boy, would put paid to Andrew's new-found interest in Annie, but it seems to have made him even more eager to be out of the house. That shouldn't surprise me (he was never much interested in our babies) but I suppose I imagined that if he was doing parenthood all over again, he would want to do it differently and be one of those doting older fathers. Well, obviously not. Perhaps Arthur is just a little present to keep Lavender amused.

Actually, I feel a bit guilty about Lavender. Knowing him to be a hopeless husband, should I really have let him loose to drive someone else round the bend? I'd like to think I'd broken him in a bit but really all I did was to give him plenty of practice at being impossible. Still, I suppose he came with a health warning of sorts – one marriage down the pan – but no doubt she thought I was the impossible one. Hard to believe, that.

I dither a bit about what to wear. I can't win in any sort of competition with T F L, so I'd like to go for *soignée* older woman, if only my wardrobe were up to it. In the end, I opt for a black skirt and top, both in fairly good nick, and a long black and white silk scarf I bought in Venice several years ago. I find some tights with ladders only at the top and a pair of rather smart but hideously uncomfortable black patent shoes and I'm quite pleased with the effect, though the scarf does slip about a bit and will probably end up in other people's canapés.

It's no surprise that Andrew will be there: Simon and Verity are his friends. Simon is a house master at Marlbury Abbey School and Verity occupies herself in managing her own brood and mothering Simon's boys. Everyone there will be from Andrew's world and I'm not sure why I'm going, except that it was kind of Verity to ask me and I won't have her thinking I can't face Andrew and Lavender.

Conversation and Pimms are flowing freely when I arrive at their elegant Georgian house in the abbey precincts. 'We're pretending it's still summer,' Verity chirps merrily as she hands me my Pimms, and I see that the French windows are open and some intrepid guests are out on the lawn. I feel I am altogether too autumnal in my black. She introduces me to a passing woman who, it turns out, runs pony clubs for the disabled, which is a worthy calling but doesn't give me many points of contact. I'm drinking my Pimms too fast and sympathising, on automatic pilot, over the prohibitive expense of keeping horses these days, when I'm conscious that several people seem to be looking at me. I check that my scarf hasn't run amok and then I glance round. They have arrived: Arthur, Lavender and Andrew, the holy family, and the crowd seems to part like the red sea to allow me access to them (yes, I know I'm mixing my testaments).

Noticing as I go that Lavender is looking impossibly slim and impeccable in a pale blue cashmere sweater and grey silk trousers, I perform my turn: I sweep towards them, all delight; I mwah mwah Lavender and Andrew; I exclaim at the beauty of Arthur. Then, as more seems to be expected, I tell Lavender how good it is of her to do without Andrew for the whole day tomorrow, when he's taking Annie up to Oxford. She looks puzzled. Is it possible he hasn't told her? *This is how it's going to be, Sunshine*, I think. *Start getting used to it*. And I look for a means of escape.

I turn to swap my empty glass for a full one from a passing tray and across the room a man catches my desperate eye, a man who is only vaguely familiar but is hastening across, smiling broadly. 'Ginny Sidwell,' he calls as he gets closer.

'Excuse me,' I say to Lavender. 'A man from a past even before Andrew.'

'I haven't been called Ginny for about twenty-five years,' I say to my rescuer. 'You're coming back to me, though. Marcus? Marcus Bright?'

'The same. And still Marcus. You and I spent May Morning in a punt together. What do you call yourself now?'

'Gina.'

'And still Sidwell?' he asks, glancing at my naked ring finger.

'I'm Gray these days,' I tell him, 'from a passing liaison with that man over there, the one with the baby.'

He looks across at the holy trio. 'Don't I recognise him?' he asks.

'Possibly. He was at Oriel – where our daughter starts tomorrow.'

Why do I say this? I pride myself on not boasting about my children. What's the matter with me? I blame the strength of the Pimms.

He smiles delightedly. 'Splendid,' he says. 'But why did you stop being Ginny?'

'Ginny sounds like a girl on a Thelwell pony,' I say, a little too loudly because it attracts the attention of the pony club woman, who bears down on us expectantly.

'Marcus,' I say, 'this is Frances –'

'Yes, yes,' he cries, shaking her hand vigorously. 'I know Mrs Felversham very well. Charles is doing splendidly this term,' he tells her confidentially. 'Worth his weight in gold on the rugby field.'

She beams and departs, saying she promised Verity she would go and have a look at her pelargoniums.

'So you're a teacher,' I say. 'Marlbury Abbey, presumably?'

'Head of sixth form. This is my second year. Can't imagine why we haven't bumped into one another before.'

'I paddle in these waters only very occasionally. It's not really my scene.'

'And what do you do with yourself?' he asks, as one might ask, *And do you prefer crochet or macramé?*

'I'm head of English language at Marlbury University College.'

'English as a foreign language?'

'No.' I start sounding tetchy, I know. 'EAP – English for academic purposes. We run degree courses for overseas students and prepare them for –'

He breaks in. 'But you've got qualifications in TEFL and all that?'

'I've got an MA in applied linguistics. What is this, Marcus? A job interview?'

'It might just be. You could be the answer to my prayers.'

'In my experience, that's usually a preliminary to being asked to do something for nothing.'

'Oh don't be cruel, Ginny. You never were. You were always a model of kindness and tact.'

'I was too scared to be anything else. I'm older and nastier now.'

'Nonsense. You don't look a day older.'

'What is it you want, Marcus?'

'Walk with me into the garden and I'll tell you.'

Outside, among what may possibly be pelargoniums, he launches into his tale. 'We have a link-up with Nepal,' he says. 'You may have heard about it – we get in *The Herald* quite a lot. A number of our boys – and the girls who join us in the sixth form – go out on their gap year to do VSO-type work. Some of them take part in development projects, but most of them help by teaching English. They do a four-week course in teaching

146

English as a Foreign Language but the feedback we had from last year was that they felt unprepared, and they struggled quite a bit at the beginning. I've been feeling that it would be much better if they could have a year-round course, as part of General Studies.'

'And I fit into this how?'

'You'd be the perfect person to teach the course.'

'But, as I think I mentioned, I have a job. A demanding job. I'm responsible for half a dozen staff and over three hundred students.'

'This would only be an hour a week.'

'Plus preparation and marking. And exams. This will be an examined course, presumably?'

'Those are details that can be ironed out later.'

'I'm sure they can, only not with me. I believe schools like Marlbury Abbey should be stripped of their charitable status and squeezed out of existence, Marcus. I'm not teaching for you.'

'Your principal writes in *The Herald* this week that he wants to see Marlbury College using its expertise to become more engaged in helping the community. I'm sure this is just the kind of thing he has in mind.'

Now draining my third Pimms, I laugh at him.

'Marlbury Abbey isn't "the community"! It's a little island of privilege devoted to nothing but its own self-perpetuation. Nothing would induce me.'

My dignified departure is marred only by my shuffling gait in my crippling shoes and the need to disengage the end of my scarf, which has found its way among the bits of cucumber and mint in the bottom of my Pimms glass.

16

SUNDAY 3rd OCTOBER

CUMNOR

He wondered if the jacket was a mistake. Bought in a hurry the day before, it had cost a lot more than he had meant to spend, and now he wondered if it was right. Did it look too obviously new? He could easily not wear it. After all, he hadn't bought it specifically for today, had he? In the end, he went with it; the golden autumn morning invited it.

Gina emerged from the house in a greenish-blue jacket which matched her eyes. She was carrying a picnic basket. 'My contribution,' she said. She was quiet in the car, which disconcerted him. In his mind, she was always talking, in full flow, hands waving – either that, or bending his ear down the phone.

'Does not talking about the Carson case mean you're not going to talk at all?' he asked after a while.

She looked startled. 'What? No. Sorry. It's just – Annie's going off to Oxford today and I'm – I don't know – not quite sure what I'm feeling.'

'Didn't you want to go with her?'

'Andrew's taking her.'

'Oh, I see,' he said, though he wasn't sure that he did.

'Anyway, this is lovely,' she said. 'And now I'm going to

tell you everything I know about Amy Robsart/Dudley and her mysterious death. I've been genning up on it.'

'Go ahead.'

'Stop me if I'm telling you things you know already. Amy Robsart was the only child of a Norfolk baronet and she was married to Lord Robert Dudley when they were both eighteen. A love match, apparently. William Cecil called it "carnal". It can't have been a very good match for the Duke of Northumberland's son, but perhaps the Robsarts were rich. Anyway, their early married life was difficult because Robert Dudley was involved in the plot to put Lady Jane Grey on the throne – his brother was married to her – and he was stripped of all his property, sent to the Tower and sentenced to death. He was reprieved, though, and eventually got his property back because he did good service in the war in the Netherlands. Then Elizabeth I came to the throne and things got really good for him because they'd known each other since childhood and she fancied him. He was made master of the horse, I think, and had the ear of the queen. However, it can't have been much fun for Amy, any of it, because he was never at home. First he was in prison, then at the wars, then at court. They were married for ten years and had no children, which says something, I think.'

'So not all that carnal, then?'

'It would seem not. So then we come to her death. She was living at Cumnor Place, which didn't belong to the Dudleys but was being rented for her by Dudley's friend, Anthony Forster, who's a suspect in the case. There's stuff about him in the church at Cumnor, apparently. I should tell you, by the way, that Cumnor Place, where she died, no longer exists, so we can't view the crime scene. Anyway, I'm sure you know about the circumstances of her death. It was a September Sunday and Amy Dudley gave all her household the day off to go to Abingdon fair. She wasn't alone, though. There were three ladies staying in the house – Forster's wife and a couple of others – who stayed behind. Their story was that she was sitting with them after dinner when she suddenly got up and left the room. She didn't return and they didn't go looking for her. When the servants got back from the fair, they found her lying at the foot of the stairs with a broken neck.'

'And the women weren't suspected?' he asked.

'No. Her husband was suspected, of course, but it's much more likely that Cecil – Lord Burghley – had her killed. He was desperate to halt Dudley's progress – he was a threat to his own influence with the queen – and he'd been spreading rumours for months about Dudley's plans to poison his wife so he could marry the queen. Obviously, if she then died, Dudley would be suspected and a marriage with the queen would be impossible. As it was, when Amy died Dudley ordered a thorough coroner's inquest and a verdict of "mischance" was recorded. Dudley didn't get to marry the queen, but he survived politically and became a Privy Councillor et cetera.'

'So, it's thought Cecil had her killed? Who by?'

'Possibly Anthony Forster. But there is also the possibility of suicide. She must have heard those rumours about his plans to marry the queen, and have known that her husband didn't want her – and she may have had breast cancer. There are several references to her having "a malady of the breast". Suicide makes sense of her sending everyone to the fair, obviously. Or it could actually have been an accident. Falls down stairs don't often kill people, apparently, unless they hit their heads on something hard. But breast cancer often spreads to the bones, so she may have had porous bones, and so the fall killed her.'

'Poor woman.' He considered Gina's account and then he said, 'If we think Marina's killer was really out to kill Glenys and was following the Amy Dudley story in some way, then he didn't do very well, did he? Because if her killer was Cecil, he set Dudley up as the prime suspect, whereas what we lack is a prime suspect in our case.'

She didn't answer, so he turned to look at her and found that she was looking back at him, very bright-eyed, her lips clamped firmly together. 'Is this a trap?' she said.

'What do you mean?'

'If I answer, will you put me out on the road, here in the wilds of Berkshire, and leave me to hitch home? I mean, it's not fair if you can talk about it and I can't.'

He glanced at her again. 'You didn't really think we were going to spend the day together and not talk about it. You didn't think that for a moment, did you?'

'No,' she said, and she was laughing at him, 'but I knew I wouldn't be the first to crack.'

'So?'

'So?'

'What do you think? Why hasn't anyone been set up as a suspect?'

'Hold on, not so fast. You have to absolve me from my promise first.'

'Fine.'

'No, that's not good enough. You have to say, "I absolve you from your promise not to talk about the Marina Carson case and I promise not to put you out on the road and leave you to hitch home." Go on.'

'Oh for heaven's sake.'

'You have to say it!' She was happy now, back in charge, laughing at him.

'OK. I absolve you from your promise not to talk about the Marina Carson case and I promise not to put you out on the road and leave you to hitch home.'

She gave a sigh of satisfaction. 'Good. Well, I'm not sure I have an answer to your question, but it seems to me that you –

the police, I mean – were expected to notice the Amy Dudley connection, so maybe it's a red herring somehow.'

'In that case, this is a wild goose chase, isn't it?'

'A wild herring chase.'

'What?'

'That's what Annie used to call it, "a wild herring chase." I think –' her voice sounded slightly odd but she cleared her throat and went on, '– I think there is a connection but it's being used to distract us – you, I mean. Sorry! I was thinking if Cecil directed all the suspicion onto Dudley, her husband, your killer is directing suspicion the other way – out of the circle of friends and family. The link with the show is designed to suggest an outsider, a crazed fan, so maybe you should be looking nearer to home. And there are two very unpleasant characters who run the Aphra Behn Theatre and seem to have open access to Charter Hall. Neil Cunningham and Alex Driver. They knew all about *Amy* because they worked on the original production. They were also lurking about near Charter Hall when I went there last weekend. And they'd have been able to find an actress to make the phone call for them. If you're looking for prime suspects, they'd be my first choice.'

'Not a bad answer, DC Gray.'

'Oh DS, please. Surely I'm worth DS?'

'Too insubordinate, I'm afraid. But tell me, what about motive?'

'I haven't worked one out. Perhaps they were blackmailing her and she was going to blow the gaff. Or she was blackmailing them. They strike me as people who would have murky secrets.'

'How do you know them?'

'I hired some costumes from them this week and they were extraordinarily rude.'

'Fancy dress party?'

'Ellie's school play.'

'And on that basis, you've decided they're murderers?'

'I think it's possible.'

Cumnor was asleep in the noonday sun. He parked the car and they sat on a bench on a small patch of green, where Gina unveiled the picnic. It was stylish, as he could have predicted. French bread, pâté, good cheeses, sticks of celery, grapes and plums, a piece of fruit cake. There was also just a half bottle of red wine "because of the driving and you being a policeman."

He wondered what people would make of the two of them as passers-by glanced their way. Did they look like a couple? Probably not. Probably they were making too much effort for that – too polite, trying too hard to be entertaining. It was a pleasure though, this companionship, a shared meal. It reminded him again that he had resolved to get a grip on his life and stop living like a hermit. Involuntarily, he said, 'I can't remember the last time I had a picnic.'

She put a hand on his arm and said, quite seriously, 'You really should get out more.'

At the church, he pushed open the heavy oak door and a figure seemed to loom at them from the darkness. To the right, behind the door, a sizeable statue stood on a three or four foot pedestal and the sun streaming in through the stained glass window behind turned it into a lowering shadow. Up close, it was instantly recognisable as Elizabeth I. All the iconography was there: the piled hair, the semi-circular ruff, the stiff, richly embroidered folds of the farthingale. The face was blander than usual, though, without its usual beaky watchfulness.

'Not much character in the face, is there?' he said.

Gina pointed to the inscription on the statue's base. *'Erected by Robert Dudley, Earl of Leicester, in compliment to his Royal Mistress,'* she read. 'Perhaps the compliment extended to getting the sculptor to shorten her nose. Oh look, there are the

Amy Dudley memorabilia, just beside the statue. That's a bit ironic, isn't it?'

It was a pathetically small collection; testimony to a life not much celebrated and a death not much mourned, he thought. There was no contemporary picture of her, only a Victorian artist's impression, all bows, ringlets and frills, and an expression of patient melancholy. Near it, the curator of this little collection had placed a picture of the queen, quite unlike the vapid statue. Here she was an ageing tyrant, grim and wilful. There were also a few letters in an impossibly cramped 16th century hand. Gina stopped suddenly and pointed to one of them. 'Oh look,' she said. 'Look at this one here.'

He looked. It was an earnest little note, written by Amy Dudley to a Mr Flowerdew about the sale of some wool from the sheep on the estate, and thought to be the last letter written by her before her death. There was a typewritten version of the letter beside it, and he read there Amy Dudley's apology for the delay in coming to a decision about the wool, explaining that she had not been able to discuss it with her husband, "he being troubled with weighty affairs and I not being altogether in quiet for his sudden departing."

'Isn't that the saddest picture?' Gina said. 'There she is, only twenty-eight. She's the Countess of Leicester but she hasn't got any status. She's trying to do her duty and run a household and an estate but she knows that her husband's attention is somewhere else entirely – knows that he's engaged in a desperate struggle to maintain his power and his favour with the queen. If Walter Scott's to be believed, his "sudden departing" would have been to his castle at Kenilworth, where he was planning to entertain the queen with such splendour that his favour with her would be assured. No wonder he hadn't got time to worry about the sheep!' She stopped, looked up at him and said, 'I have a certain fellow feeling. I used to be married to a man like that.'

'Really?' he asked cautiously. He wasn't sure if he was supposed to take this seriously.

'Yes. Did I tell you, he's a human rights lawyer? He was always away, defending people on death row, prosecuting villains at The Hague, standing up for the rights of the downtrodden generally, and when he came home, he wasn't at all interested in the sheep – or the state of the gutters in our case.'

'But you must have been proud of him, weren't you? It's a worthwhile thing to be doing.'

She looked away from him. 'The thing about Andrew is,' she said, 'he's all for humanity in general but he doesn't actually like people very much.' She laughed. 'But I don't think he ever wanted to kill me. And I had the children, which poor Amy didn't. And anyway I was a tough old bird, even when I was young.'

He decided to take a scenic route home and they stopped in Windsor for tea at a hotel. 'I fancy cakes on a tiered plate,' Gina said.

They didn't get the tiered plate, but they did get warm scones and clotted cream. After her second scone, Gina sat back with a little '*hah*' of contentment and said, 'I wonder what the rooms are like here.'

Scott, engaged in loading the last of the strawberry jam onto his scone, looked up, startled, and felt the blood rush into his face. He stared at her and saw her begin to colour too – he'd never seen her blush before.

'Oh, no,' she said, covering her mouth in confusion. 'I didn't mean – no, no, no. Sorry – just idle speculation.' She waved a hand around, as though batting his thoughts away. Then she smiled. 'I've got to go to work tomorrow,' she said. 'Haven't you?'

When he dropped her off at home, she said, 'Thank you for this, David. I'm afraid it won't have advanced your case but it saved me from a miserable day. I'm really grateful.' She leant over and he thought she was about to kiss him, but she put her hand on his and said, 'Good luck with the case. And do have a look at those two at the Aphra Behn.'

17

MONDAY 4ᵗʰ OCTOBER

'Tis not that time of moon with me to make one
in so skipping a dialogue

Yesterday was an odd day and I've woken this morning still
feeling a bit *bouleversée*. The French do have some good words,
and this is one of them. You couldn't say in English that you
felt *overturned*, but *bouleversée* gives me a vision of myself as a
stranded beetle, on my back and waving my little legs about.

Anyway, yesterday. It was my choice to leave before Annie
did. I don't think I was sulking; I just didn't want to participate
in all the hubbub of her departure when I didn't have a role to
play. So, I asked David to pick me up at ten, and he did,
looking really rather gorgeous in a beautiful soft suede jacket
and shades. I hoped someone in the street was noticing as I
sashayed out to the car. I wasn't so sure about my own outfit.
I did actually buy a new jacket for the occasion – ridiculous, I
know – and in the shop I thought its shade of turquoise was
cheerful and optimistic, but when I put it on yesterday it
looked a bit brash and I nearly lost my nerve and rummaged
in my wardrobe for something else, except that I know that
leads to a downward spiral of panicky indecision, so I stuck
with the turquoise.

When I went in to Annie's room to say goodbye, she was

still in bed, so kissing her felt like it did when she was little and got a good night kiss. I had dithered over a present for her. When Ellie went off to Manchester, I gave her a wad of cash and a tin of home-made flapjacks, but I was afraid Annie would laugh at the flapjacks and Andrew was bound to outgun me with quantities of cash, so I bought her a bag of rather fine undies – two bras, four pairs of pants, a nightie and several pairs of socks. 'An emergency store,' I said, 'for when you don't get round to doing your washing.'

I'm not sure, really, what the trip to Cumnor was about. It was a distraction for me and saved me from feeling humiliated, but I'm not sure what David thought it was. I think he enjoyed it, and he was good company, but it didn't advance his investigation one bit, I'm afraid. And then there was that stupid remark of mine about rooms at the hotel. What was I thinking of? I do like watching him blush, though. I would have kissed him goodbye when he dropped me off at home, but I thought after the rooms thing I'd better not. The question now is, was yesterday's outing a date? Does he think it was a date? If so, I asked him out, so now it's his turn to ask me. Will he? Watch this space.

Today, we are paying for yesterday's warmth with a misty morning and I cycle with caution into college. There I spend a pleasant enough morning. I move on to *Entertaining Mr Sloane* with my literature class and they are delightedly shocked at its irreverence and cynicism. Then I start one of the Chinese groups on short presentations and though their articulation makes them painfully hard to follow, they have compensated by producing impressive PowerPoint visuals. Finally, I have an open tutorial hour, which produces nothing much except one poor Chinese girl, new this term, who feels she's floundering. The one child policy puts such pressure on these students: everything is invested in them and there's the expectation that they'll support not only their parents, but both sets of grandparents in old age. Lili weeps a bit and tells me she rang her mother to tell her the work was too hard and she was afraid she was going to fail.

'What did she say?' I ask.

'She said, "Well, daughter, you'll just have to work harder."'

I tell her I'll talk to her other teachers and see if we can identify her specific problems. 'And then we'll put them right,' I say cheerfully. 'That's our job.'

I've just despatched her and I'm thinking about lunch when the phone rings. It's Janet, the principal's secretary. Can I "pop in" and see the principal, she asks, as soon as possible.

'Give me twenty minutes,' I say.

I nip over to the SCR and eat a quick sandwich. You never know what you'll get when you're summoned to Norman Street's office: on one occasion, I was treated to deli sandwiches; on another I got the sack. In fact, the time he sacked me was the last interview I had with him. That was two and a half years ago, and you'll realise that he changed his mind later because obviously I'm still here, but I am wary of this encounter, especially as I have no idea what it can be about.

I put on some lipstick and tame my hair a bit. I'm glad I decided to wear the turquoise jacket again; I feel it gives me added bounce. I go into Janet's office and she looks at me warily. Last time I was here, there was a lot of shouting and she may be worried that it's going to happen again, so I smile warmly at her and say in my sweetest voice, 'Reporting for duty, Janet.'

She looks even more alarmed, but she buzzes through to the principal and I am ushered in. Our principal is a red-faced man with sharp little eyes and a wide, sharky smile. He used to get red-faced only when angry, but lots of being angry plus a good deal of eating and drinking in the interests of the college seem to have made him permanently scarlet. Bets are being laid on how long it will take before he keels over. From this you will gather that I am not the only member of his staff who loathes him.

He ushers me in and asks how the Chinese students are doing. The deal I secured with a Chinese university for several dozen students was the reason why the principal unsacked me a couple of years ago. Since then they have kept my department – and the college, actually – afloat.

'They're fine,' I say. 'They get better each year because they're more prepared. Those who are here already warn the new ones what to expect, so they're not so shocked.'

'Why? What is there to shock them?' He's on the offensive already.

'Oh, the relative informality of the teaching for one thing. But more the fact that they're expected to have opinions or work out problems for themselves. One student said to me the thing she dreaded most was a seminar leader turning to her and saying, "And what do you think?" They're really not used to it.'

He has lost interest already, I see. This isn't what I've been summoned for. He paces about a bit and surveys the area of his empire he can see from his window. With his back to me, he says, 'I'm sorry to hear that you're not willing to serve our community, Gina.'

And suddenly I know what this is about. Bloody Marcus Bright. 'Community service?' I say. 'Don't I have to commit a crime before I get that? I haven't even had an ASBO yet.'

'Always ready with the clever answers, aren't you?' he says and comes across to loom over me. 'Local people need to feel that this college is at the heart of this community. They need to see us supporting local projects with our expertise. What better link could we make than with the town's oldest educational establishment?'

'By which you mean Marlbury Abbey School, I assume,

160

and I also assume that Marcus Bright has come to you complaining that I've refused to go and teach his sixth formers.'

'Bright, yes, that's the chap. Head of sixth form. Said he'd seen my article in *The Herald*. So I want to know why you've turned him down.'

'Well, I'll give you the same reason I gave him: because I don't regard Marlbury Abbey School as part of the community. It's not there to educate Marlbury children. The boys there come from all over the country – all over the world, in fact – air freighted in for the English public school experience. And the local parents who send their sons there do so precisely to remove them from the local community – to save them from contamination – no rubbing shoulders with Marlbury's grubby homegrown kids.'

He explodes. 'Well that's simply ridiculous. I've never heard such nonsense. That's just socialist tosh.'

'I'd be happy to give my services to any of the local state schools,' I say. 'Marlbury High, William Roper. I taught at William Roper for years. If they asked for me, I'd be quite willing to help out.'

'Yes, well they haven't asked for you,' he snarls, throwing himself into the chair behind his desk, 'but Marlbury Abbey have.'

'And I've turned them down. Apart from anything else, I wasn't sure my contract would allow me to be paid to work elsewhere on a working day.'

'They wouldn't pay you,' he says, shuffling papers in search of something. 'The college would bear the cost. You'd be seconded by us.'

'And I'd be relieved of some of my teaching here? It'd be difficult to find anyone to cover for me.'

He finds what he's looking for. 'I've been looking at your teaching timetable. On the light side, I would say. I don't think we need to relieve you of any teaching.'

'So when you say, "The college would bear the cost", you mean I'd do it for free?'

'Wednesday mornings,' he says, 'that's when these sessions would happen, and I see you're free most of the morning.

'Staff meeting,' I protest. 'That's when we have our weekly staff meeting.'

'Well, that's easily rearranged.'

'No! It's not.' I am shouting, I realise, and I think of Janet sitting next door. More quietly, I say, 'All my staff are timetabled with a free hour on Wednesday morning. There's no other time when we're all free.'

'I doubt anyone's teaching at six o'clock,' he smirks.

I get up. 'I'm sorry,' I say, 'but I won't do it.' I start to move towards the door; he bangs the desk; I think again of Janet.

'Come back here,' he roars. 'We're not finished.' In the interests of his blood pressure, I return to my seat. 'I want this done, Gina. *The Herald* always makes a spread of those boys setting off for Nepal. This year, I want our name linked to that. And I won't have any of my staff telling me they won't do what I've asked them to do. Take a look at your contract,' he says, leaning forward with all his sharky teeth on display. 'I think you'll find it says that you will "undertake such duties as the college authorities shall require." I am requiring you to do this and you're not in a position to say no.'

Unwisely, I laugh. 'But you can't require me to work somewhere else!' I hoot. 'Next thing we know, you'll be sending staff out to be lollipop ladies or pick up litter in the park.'

'OK.' He sits back in his seat. 'If that's your last word, I shall have to ask a member of your department to take on the work.'

And now he's got me. Why didn't I see that coming? I have been outmanoeuvred and he's laughing now. Because of course I can't let him do that. They won't be able to stand up to him and I can't let any one of them get forced into taking

162

this on just because I once spent a chilly, gropey May Morning in a punt with Marcus sodding Bright. Never gracious in defeat, I get up and head for the door.

'I can't allow you to victimise my staff,' I say over my shoulder as I go, 'so obviously, I'll do it.'

'Will you speak to Mr Bright or shall I?'

'Oh I will,' I call, as I swing through the door. 'You can count on it.'

I see Janet flinch as I let it slam behind me.

My last task of the day is to drive over to Surrey to collect my mother from the convalescent home where she has spent the past week. Ellie and Freda appear at the college gates at four o'clock and we set off. I've calmed down since lunch time. I rang Marcus Bright as soon as I got back to my office after seeing the principal. I intended to be cold and cutting but he was so bloody smug I ended up screaming at him. 'Underhand,' I shouted, 'cowardly and dishonest.' He changed tack and got all apologetic, but it was too late. It was 'against natural justice,' I yelled, that I should be forced to teach at his absurdly over-privileged school for nothing, and if he had any decency he would see that the school made a substantial donation to The William Roper School PTA funds. He agreed instantly but he is an untrustworthy creep and I shall believe it when I see the colour of his money. Anyway, I felt better when I came off the phone and went about my afternoon session in the language lab quite cheerfully.

Now, in the car, I have a bit of a conversation with Freda about her day (she mainly tells me about lunch) and then I ask Ellie, 'How about you? How was it being back?'

'Fine, really,' she says. 'I had a good rehearsal at lunch time and the kids seemed pleased to see me back. Someone in the office had crossed out Marina's name in the register and that gave me a bit of a wobble, but I was all right.'

So, we're all right, it seems, and I sit back and close my eyes in preparation for my mother. The traffic isn't bad and we make good time, so we end up eating our packed supper in the car park at the convalescent home (They eat early there, so my mother will already have had her meal). Our picnic is not as elegant as the one I provided yesterday – ham rolls, crisps, cartons of juice – but it does also include the remainder of the grapes, plums and fruit cake.

Replete, we go up to the front door of the once stately home and my mother is produced. She is looking a great deal better than she did in hospital and she is escorted not only by the matron but by a couple of nurses and a young man who carries her bags. She performs introductions as though she were hosting a cocktail party and they all address her as Dr Sidwell and tell me how wonderful she is. One of the nurses runs ahead with her camera and we pose at the front door with our medical entourage for all the world as though she were royalty. I am panicked at the thought of the problems she may have with re-entry to the all-too-real world of home *chez nous*.

Then Matron turns to me with the hint of a tear in her eye and says, 'She has been so delighted that you were all coming to collect her – daughter, granddaughter and great-granddaughter. It's lovely to see you all. We have so many lonely patients here.'

So here we are, a model family, and there I was thinking we were a shambles. Well, maybe what you see is a kind of truth. We are all here, after all, and Ellie and I have laboured to turn the dining room into a welcoming bedroom, lugging Annie's bed and dressing table downstairs just last night and adding flowers, books, and pictures by Freda. What is also true is that Freda and my mother are holding hands and Freda is hopping up and down with delight. So, for once, I just smile and don't tell Matron that she doesn't know the half of it.

My mother sits in the front on the way home and I sit in the back with Freda. We are all quite quiet, except for Freda, who feels we are in need of entertainment so keeps up a running commentary on what she can see in the rapidly deepening dusk: 'Car, car, nuvver car, lorry, bikishel, car, car' and so on.

When we get home, we put the old and the young to bed, Ellie tussling with Freda and I devoting myself to my mother, though she is even more resistant to help than Freda is. Eventually, Ellie and I sit down at the kitchen table with a glass of wine and Annie rings. She says she just wanted to say that the undies are lovely, and she tells me everything's great – brilliant – but her voice wobbles a bit and she sounds a long way away, so I take the risk of saying, 'It all gets better, you know' as we say our goodbyes and she doesn't bite my head off.

And so to bed.

18

WEDNESDAY 13ᵗʰ OCTOBER

And the rain it raineth every day

Life speeds up in the next couple of weeks, what with my mother, the sessions at Marlbury Abbey, two Chinese students running off to London, the measuring up of the *Twelfth Night* cast for their costumes and further dealings with the delightful Mr Driver. Ellie is dogged by directorial difficulties: in the space of a few days, Sir Andrew Aguecheek leaves school and gets a job in Curry's; The Count Orsino is made captain of the football team and the Lady Olivia misses so many after school rehearsals that one day Ellie leaves the cast under the care of Ben Biaggi, drives down to Olivia's home on the scary Eastgate estate and hauls her away from the television. 'Her mother's daughter after all,' my mother comments gnomically.

Meantime, in contrast, DCI Scott and his investigation seem to have gone into hibernation. I can glean no news of any progress: there is nothing in the local paper; Ellie hears nothing at school and though Eve and I achieve a *rapprochement* of sorts, she has no gossip she's willing to pass on either. I don't know whether David heeded my advice to turn his attention to Driver and Cunningham, but they're still down there at the theatre, charming as ever.

And David himself, you ask? Where is he? Your guess is as good as mine. Whatever he thought of our jaunt to Cumnor, he hasn't been moved to suggest a replay. He has been out of radio contact – and every other kind. I sent him a text, thanking him for the outing, and got a brief, polite reply. Since then, nothing. Like a teenager, I started to convince myself that he'd lost his phone, and hence my number. But he knows where I live, doesn't he? So that doesn't work. I have to conclude that he just doesn't like me, hard though that is to believe.

In other ways, however, life is surprisingly satisfactory. Eve seems to have forgiven me. We went out for a drink, had a big hug, said nothing about our falling-out and now seem to be all right, though I do have the feeling that I've been shown the yellow card. (Have I got that right? I really shouldn't use metaphors I don't understand). I also still have the feeling that there's something odd about Colin's behaviour that afternoon when Marina was killed, but I shall not open my lips so wide as a bristle may enter on that subject.

My mother has settled in well and is remarkably uncritical of my domestic arrangements. It's not surprising, I suppose: she was never keen on domesticity herself and is unmoved by dust along the picture rails, lime scale round the taps, cat fur on the carpets and general stickiness engendered by Freda. She doesn't even seem to mind that the contents of kitchen storage jars don't always coincide with their labels. Her only beef is with the garden, which is, admittedly, rampantly overgrown. I've never been a gardener and I have relied, over the years, on a series of weather-beaten men on bikes who turned up at random intervals and hacked, lopped, tugged and mowed the garden's most egregious excesses. Since the last one departed without warning, the forces of nature have had it all their own way. I do understand my mother's frustration at not being steady enough on her pins to go out and give the place a good seeing-to. As it is, the highlight of her day is supervising Freda's bed-time and they are developing an ever-extending routine involving stories, rhymes and games I didn't realise she knew. Were they part of my childhood and have I suppressed them in my conviction that I was a martyr to my mother's job? I don't know.

The only fly in my ointment – and it is a very large bluebottle – is my first session at Marlbury Abbey School. This is, in so many ways, worse even than I expected. It takes place some ten days after my being routed by the principal and it gets off to a bad start with the porter at the lodge gate.

The school backs onto the abbey and is hidden from the vulgar eyes by hefty stone walls. Above these, the abbey is visible, calm and grey; its ruined end, where Henry VIII knocked it about a bit, offers great stone window embrasures, open to the sky. Embedded in the thick wall is a large, studded oak door and inside that a small pedestrian entrance. I lean my bike against the wall and go inside. The brief interlude of good weather departed the day after the Cumnor trip and it has been raining ever since, so I have arrived this morning looking less than impressive in my wet weather gear.

'Good morning,' I say to the porter, dripping onto the lodge floor. 'I'm here to teach a sixth form group. Where can I leave my bike?'

He looks me up and down over the top of his glasses and says, 'Other entrance for the bike blocks.'

'What other entrance?'

'Minster entrance. Through the precincts, down Dark Entry.'

'Well, I haven't got time to go all round there now.'

He says nothing.

'OK,' I say, 'I'll just leave it outside chained to a gargoyle or something, shall I?'

In fact, I chain it to a lamppost, where it's probably an obstruction, and I return.

'And you are?' he asks.

'Gina Gray. Marlbury College.'

He runs his finger slowly down a printed page before him and shakes his head. 'No-one of that name here, madam,' he says. He is small, portly, dark-suited and moustached – ex-military or trying to look as if he is. I usually get on very well with support staff in educational establishments – porters, caretakers, cleaners, tea ladies – but I don't think I can be bothered with this chap. I am tempted to cycle back to college and tell the principal that Marlbury Abbey wouldn't let me in, but instead I say tersely, 'Mr Bright is expecting me.'

'Oh, well,' he says, 'why didn't you say so?' He picks up the phone and speaks. 'Morning, Mr Bright. I've got a lady for you here, sir, a Miss Gray.' He has noticed my naked ring finger and despises me accordingly.

Two minutes later, Marcus arrives, damp, breathless and effusively apologetic: so sorry – held up – problem with a boy – should have given my name to Bill et cetera. 'Mrs Gray will be coming in every Wednesday morning, Bill. She's very kindly agreed to teach a general studies course for us. Ginn – Gina, this is Bill – keeper of the gate and of everything else.'

Bill and I nod at each other with polite hostility. Like a dog, I think he can tell that I'm not a friend.

It is break time and Marcus guides me through into a quadrangle, where groups of boys, apparently oblivious of the rain in their absurd little-gentlemen frock coats and wing collars, are milling about. Weathered stone walls rise on all sides of the quad, and we duck into a doorway on the far side where I'm led first to Marcus's office, where I divest myself of dripping waterproofs, and then to a staff room quite unlike any other staff room I have encountered. Modelled on an Oxbridge common room, it is high-ceilinged and oak-panelled and exudes an air of maleness as tangible as cigar smoke. Most of the staff, including Marcus, are wearing gowns, though I notice one or two younger men who are not. The dominant impression is of begowned, male middle age. Just my kind of place.

Marcus offers me coffee, but where is the hot water urn with its permanent sediment of lime scale? Where are the institutional tins of instant coffee? Where is the array of battered mugs? Here, coffee is waiting in pots on electric hot plates, flanked by jugs of hot milk and garnished with biscuits. Marcus pours coffee into charming china cups and introduces me to the senior master.

'How do you do?' he says. 'I don't think much of these biscuits they're giving us now, Bright. You're on the SCR committee aren't you? Can't you do something about it?' Marcus undertakes to have a word and adds that he and I are old friends and that I was at St Hilda's. A faint gleam of interest comes into the senior master's eyes. 'Ah, "the wenches of St Hilda's." What was it we used to say about the women's colleges? "The women of Somerville, the ladies of Lady Margaret Hall, the chaps of St Hugh's, the wenches of St Hilda's." Do they still call them that, I wonder?'

'I should hope not,' I say, 'not now they're admitting men.'

Our coffee dispatched, Marcus leads me across the quad to the Hertford Room, where I am to teach. This turns out to be a small lecture room with a carpeted floor, panelled walls and a dais at one end. There are no desks but chairs with flaps on the arms for taking notes. A group of about twenty are sitting there – mainly boys with a little huddle of girls to one side. Although I saw a lot of boys in gowns outside, only one of these is wearing a gown. They rise in a body as we enter. Marcus performs introductions and leaves. The atmosphere changes: bodies slouch, legs are stretched out, chairs are tipped back.

I survey them. I've decided to start by revealing their ignorance to them. Everyone thinks they can teach English – after all, they speak it, don't they? – but it doesn't work like that. Learners want to know why things are right or wrong; they're not content just to parrot what a teacher tells them, especially if the teacher is only eighteen or nineteen years old. An inexperienced teacher without an arsenal of grammatical terms to reach for soon ends up digging a very deep hole and disappearing from sight. I do realise that revealing their ignorance to this lot is a high risk strategy, though. They don't look like people who will take that well. Still, never mind. I'm not aiming to please them, after all.

I hit them with the future tense. It's a bit like a conjuring trick, really. 'How do we form the future tense in English?' I ask them and they walk obligingly into my trap and tell me that we use "will". Then I ask them each to tell us about something they're planning to do at the weekend and, though there's a bit of smutty nudge-nudge-wink-wink stuff, they oblige again: someone is going home; someone else is going to write an essay; another's parents are visiting; another is going to buy a birthday present and so on. Not a "will" to be found. They're *going to* do things or they *are doing* things – present tense. 'So when,' I ask, 'do we use *will*?'

I am met by a sullen silence so I write on the whiteboard:

It will be windy tomorrow with heavy showers

Then I add,

You will meet a dark stranger and travel to foreign lands

And

That boy will end up in gaol

'Predictions,' I say. 'That's what we use *will* for. If I ask you, "What time does your train leave?" you'll answer, "10.55" or whatever – the scheduled time – but if I ask, "What time will your train leave?" you may well answer, "I don't know – your guess is as good as mine", because I seem to be asking for a prediction.'

They eye my sentences, less than impressed. There's a bit of shuffling and muttering. 'Or,' I say, 'what about these?'

> *I will be famous one day*
> *You will do as you're told*

'Volition,' I say, 'literally *willing* something to happen. And then, if we use the contracted form, we can add these:'

> *I'll give you a ring*
> *I'll pay you back tomorrow*
> *I'll love you forever*
> *I'll kill him*

'Statements about the future?' I ask. 'Or what?'

Silence. They don't want to play my game. Then one of the girls says, 'Promises. They're like promises – or threats.'

'Exactly. Promises and lies, the casual undertakings we make every day and hardly expect to keep to. When we're really confident about a future event, we talk about it in the present: "I leave tonight"; "I start my new job on Monday"; "I've got a French lesson this afternoon." Things that are scheduled, things we can count on, we talk about in the present. And different languages express the future in different ways, so some learners will find the English way of talking about the future incredibly difficult.'

Silence again. They are resentful. They don't want this to be difficult. This linguistic complexity doesn't fascinate or intrigue them; it depresses them, and they would like to blame me for making things more complicated than they need to be.

'As a matter of interest,' I ask, 'how many of you are modern linguists?'

No-one raises a hand.

'Classicists?' I ask.

No-one again.

'So I'd be right in thinking you're not people with a keen interest in language?'

They glance at one another and exchange the odd smirk. Then the boy in the gown says, 'I don't suppose Mr Bright explained to you how it works with general studies courses?'

'He told me you were all people who want to go out to Nepal in your gap year and teach English.'

I'm disconcerted by a burst of laughter. 'Wishful thinking on Bright Boy's part,' says one of them. 'Most of us haven't made any plans for gap years yet.'

'Except to get totally rat-arsed a lot.'

'And some surfing would be good.'

'And plenty of tottie.'

'So how come you chose this course?' I ask.

'Hobson's choice,' a dark, thin-faced boy says. 'The options go up and we sign for them: Oxbridge candidates, scholars and exhibitioners first, then prefects, then the rest of us. This was what was left.'

So this whole thing is a total con. I will strangle Marcus Bright. So help me, I will strangle him with my own two puny little hands. (Note, please, the *will* of volition.)

'Well,' I say, 'since you've been so frank with me, I'll be frank with you. I'm not getting paid for teaching you. My boss at Marlbury College has strong-armed me into giving my time and expertise free to this course on the understanding that you're all going to be doing your bit for the developing world. Now I'm apprised of the true situation, it's quite probable that you won't be seeing me again. Maybe you'll be able to spend the time playing snooker in the common room. But I feel honour bound to complete today's session, so here's a puzzle for you.' I write two columns of words on the white board:

milk	*egg*
anger	*tantrum*
rain	*snowflake*
applause	*prize*
toast	*sandwich*
furniture	*sofa*
money	*pound*

'What,' I ask, 'is the difference between the two columns?'

They are pretty unwilling to engage, but the girls have a go. The column on the left is 'more abstract,' they suggest. 'Milk, abstract?' I ask, but they have got a point and after a while I give them a clue. 'The indefinite article,' I say. 'Try the indefinite article.'

And then they get it. The words on the left can't have "a" or "an" put in front of them (except "toast", but that's as in a toast to the bride and groom, not as in breakfast food). These are uncountable nouns and they give foreigners a lot of trouble because they're not uncountable everywhere. I add for good measure that when talking of uncountable nouns the opposite of "more" is "less", but when speaking of countable nouns, its opposite is "fewer". They don't believe me, of course, because they hear "less" used wrongly all the time: in one hour on *The PM Programme*, I heard "less people", "less problems", "less trains", "less cars" and "less newspapers". It's become an old-fashioned distinction, but it happens to be an obsession of mine. A few years ago, a former pupil of mine at William Roper became the manager of our local Sainsbury's and the notices at the express tills were changed from "nine items or less" to "nine items or fewer". I wept with pride. By such small victories do I mitigate my defeats.

A bell rings and they leave. The boy in the gown is last to go, and now I look at him properly, I know who he is. He is a remarkably good-looking boy: tall and graceful with pale skin, blue eyes and dark hair and lashes. He also has an air of adult composure.

'Edmund,' I say. 'It is Edmund, isn't it?'

'Yes.' He's surprised but not flummoxed. He looks at me quite coolly with his mother's pale blue eyes.

'I notice you're wearing a gown, so I assume you're a scholar.'

'I'm a modern languages exhibitioner, yes.'

'But you didn't say so when I asked if there were any modern linguists.'

'No.'

'And you, presumably, did have a choice of general studies courses.'

'Yes.'

'And you chose this course because you're interested in language?'

'I chose it because I wanted to meet you.'

'Really?' I am startled and can't disguise it.

'My mother told me about you.' He is giving me a disconcertingly appraising look.

'I see. Well, we met under difficult circumstances.'

'So she said.'

Did I tell Glenys my name? I don't think I did. It was all so confusing, with Freda screaming and her brandishing her spade, and I was too busy swearing at her to introduce myself, as I recall. So, she got my name from Alex Driver or Neil Cunningham, no doubt. And then she thought it was worth telling Edmund about me. I am amazed to find that I have been the subject of such interest.

'Tell me,' I say, cleaning the white board to cover my confusion, 'the scholars first thing, does it apply to all aspects of school life?'

'Oh yes.' His smile is sardonic, adult. 'We know our own degrees.'

'*Macbeth*,' I say. 'Is yours one of those families where people are quoting Shakespeare all the time?'

'It is. But *Macbeth* especially. My mother was playing Lady M when Hector met her and he went to every performance, apparently. I think they both know every word.'

'I thought actors were superstitious about quoting from *Macbeth*.'

'It's only supposed to be bad luck if you quote it in a theatre. Anyway, it's quite old-fashioned to be superstitious about it now. Well, thank you for an interesting class. I hope you do come back next week.'

And he's gone, leaving me thinking about *Macbeth*. Renée Deakin said her hoax caller had quoted from Macbeth: "I don't want you battering at my peace", that's what she claimed she said. So either the caller was someone who had spent a lot of time with the family or Renée had picked the line up from Glenys and embroidered her account, or – or what?

Cycling back to college, I plot my revenge on Marcus Bright. My first instinct is to storm in to see the principal, tell him he's been had and suggest we abort the project. Then, in consideration of Janet's nerves, I decide that e-mailing him might be preferable. By the time I get into my office, however, I have a much better idea, because I know, if I'm honest, that telling Norman Street the truth will get me nowhere: he won't admit he's been conned and he won't give up on this as long as he thinks he can get us into that picture in *The Herald*. So, as snitching on Marcus isn't an option, I decide on blackmail instead.

I phone Marcus and make him an offer he can't refuse. I tell him that the boys have dished the dirt on his shabby little trick; he protests that his intentions had been honourable but that other general studies courses offer an edge for Oxbridge candidates; I say that's not my problem and I will continue to teach the course only if I receive the first cheque to the William Roper PTA the following week.

'£400 for this term,' I say. '£50 a session for eight sessions, and cheap at the price. A further cheque after Christmas if you want me to carry on. I assume you can find the funds for that?'

'We do have a visiting lecturer fund,' he says.

'What could be more appropriate?' I ask. 'Why didn't we think of that before?'

19

WEDNESDAY 27th OCTOBER

No more cakes and ale

I'm doing a lot better with my Marlbury Abbey class now I know where I stand, and I'm getting some female solidarity from the girls, who kept a low profile the first week but are now raising their heads above the parapet. They've actually been thinking. They came back last week with some questions about countable and uncountable nouns and they wanted to know what you should tell beginners about how to form the future tense. The boys looked lofty, of course, but we can live with that.

Marcus was as good as his word, too, and I got my cheque last week. Instead of ushering me into the common room, he took me over to the bursar's office. The bursar, balding and bearded like the middle-aged Shakespeare, was most gallant but demurred at my request to have the cheque made out to the PTA.

'If it's coming from the lectures fund, Marcus,' he said, 'we'll pay it to your charming lecturer. And you, dear lady, are at liberty to give the money to whomsoever you please.'

I had to admire the grammatical perfection of "to whomsoever" even as I bridled at "dear lady".

'Fine,' said Marcus. 'I'm sure we can trust Mrs Gray to do

the gentlemanly thing.' And they both laughed heartily. They don't actually care what I do with it.

I've also got Marcus to cough up for a set of copies of a good text book, *Beginning English*, so this week I distribute them. 'If you do go to Nepal,' I say, 'treat this as your bible and you won't go far wrong.' Just as I say this, a man in a dog collar comes into the room and they all leap to their feet. 'Carry on, chaps,' he says, and they subside into silent scrutiny of *Beginning English*. He takes me aside. 'Canon Aylmer,' he says, shaking my hand. 'Headmaster. Just thought I'd pop in and welcome you. Awfully good of you, this. How are you finding us?'

'Well –' I stammer. I've no idea how I'm going to continue, but it doesn't matter because he is a man who answers his own questions.

'Just like any other school really, aren't we?'

'I think that depends on what other school you have in mind, Canon,' I say.

He looks at me over his half moon glasses. 'Well yes, of course, some wouldn't... but young people are all the same underneath, wouldn't you say?'

'I'd say they're as different from one another as adults are.'

'Would you? Would you?' He casts an eye over my class. 'I don't think I know many of these chaps,' he says, and adds conspiratorially before he leaves, 'not some of our brightest sparks, I think.'

I've invited Eve and Colin to supper tonight. This is partly by way of apology and reconciliation and partly as cover for inviting David too. I know, I know. I've weakened and I shouldn't have. I convinced myself that he's just shy, and confused because I sort of dumped him once before, so I decided I'd invite him over – with Eve, Colin, Ellie and my mother, so it's perfectly harmless – and if he said no, then I'd know he really doesn't like me, and if he said yes, then I'd know he was just shy and I'd have given him an unmistakeable signal that I liked him and I really would wait then for him to make the next move. Well, he said yes, and I'm cooking goulash, which is one of my stand-bys, and I go into the health food shop next to the school for caraway seeds and smoked paprika.

The shop is called The Burnt Cake and I imagine it has catered for the stomachs of the Marlbury Abbey boys since the days when their monastic fare really did need eking out. Hot pies and ginger parkin, I imagine, were the order of the day. When my girls were small, it was a sweet shop, stocking every flavour of crisp from hedgehog to barbecued lobster and every chocolate bar in the galaxy. A Saturday treat was to buy liquorice here because it offered all sort of shapes including – wonder of wonders – skipping ropes, complete with sugar-beaded handles. About five years ago it reinvented itself as a health food shop, which must have pleased the boys' parents and saved them a fortune in dentists' bills. Out are the gaudy displays of chocolate bars and elaborate pyramids of bottled drinks; in are flapjacks and cereal bars, packets of nuts and dried fruit, wholemeal rolls and fruit loaves, sacks of grains and pulses, a wide assortment of spices and a shelf of batty "natural" remedies.

I find the spice shelves and the caraway seeds but, as the spices are arranged from top to bottom in alphabetical order, I have to crouch down to floor level to find the smoked paprika. When I'm down there, I notice a pair of unmistakeable Marlbury Abbey striped trousers and look up to see Edmund Carson standing at the end of the stack of shelves, turning over cereal bars. He hasn't seen me, I think. I wonder if he's allowed out of school during lesson time. Probably not, I'd guess, so I decide it's better to turn a blind eye. As I'm down there, looking at the relative strength of what's on offer – gentle warmth is what I'm after, not blowing their heads off – I hear some muttered conversation and I notice that a man has joined Edmund. He's an ordinary-looking man, in his thirties I suppose, wearing an anorak, and he looks incongruous beside Edmund in his fancy dress uniform. Edmund is tucking something away in a breast pocket and he draws from his side pocket a DVD box, instantly familiar for the vibrant pink rose visible inside. The man takes it, looks at it and turns it over just in time for me to see that it has a 6 stamped on the back. I'm pretty sure the one I saw at Charter Hall had a 4 on it, so I wonder what that can mean.

He puts it in his pocket and I stand up to find Edmund's eyes on me.

'Have you lost something?' he asks.

'Lost something?'

'You were down on the floor. I assumed you were looking for something.'

'Only smoked paprika,' I say. 'End of the alphabet.'

He is more composed than I am. How can that be when he's probably out of school illegally and I've spotted him selling off DVDs of his mother's show. Wouldn't any other teenager be embarrassed?

The man leaves and I say, 'I seem to see those DVDs everywhere. A bit of a cottage industry, is it?'

'Oh,' he laughs, 'yes. They can be ordered online but they're cheaper if bought direct, and I get paid commission.'

'I've seen the show,' I say, 'but I saw the understudy play Amy. I'd love a copy of the DVD if you can get me one.'

'Of course,' he says, 'I'd be delighted.'

Eve's daughter, Gwen, is serving in the shop (she's an artist who needs a day job to keep afloat.) I chat to her while she fills some pitta with hummus for me, and I take this away to eat at my desk while I deal with the day's e-mails. Then I google

DVDs of *Amy* to see what I get. Well, I get lots of hits on the show – ticket agencies, reviews and so on – but not a single site selling the DVDs online. So, I was right. It really is a cottage industry and Edmund, for all his Marlbury Abbey swagger, doesn't mind touting them around.

I didn't consider, when I cobbled this party together, that both Ellie and Colin might be embarrassed by David's presence, having recently been interrogated by him as witnesses/suspects in a murder case, and by the time I think of it, it's too late. Anyway, it's no more embarrassing for them than it is for me to eat dinner with Colin, who knows me inside out, so to speak.

It all goes rather well, in fact. We have to eat in the kitchen, since my mother is occupying the dining room, but that's all to the good as I don't feel the need to unearth the good china or make sure the glasses match. David shows surprising ease with Ellie and Colin; my mother enjoys a little rant at Colin about the state of the NHS; Ellie and Eve are very funny about their struggles to put on *Twelfth Night*; the goulash is almost as much of a triumph as Mrs Ramsay's *boeuf en daube* and we are all very cheerful. The Carson case isn't mentioned, but when my mother has gone to bed and Ellie says she's promised to meet Ben Biaggi to talk about music, the four of us settle down with glasses of brandy and Eve says, casually as you like, 'So, David, have you had any kind of breakthrough in finding Marina Carson's killer?'

I guess he's been prepared for this because he's quite cool.

'Police work's mainly slog. We're still working on the forensic evidence, and on witness statements. We shan't give up, but in the meantime we've got other serious cases to deal with.'

'More serious than the death of a child?' Eve asks.

I can't let her bully him – only I am allowed to do that – so

I step in. 'It's an odd thing, but I've found myself teaching Marina's brother.'

'The lovely Edmund?' Eve asks. 'He's not at the college now, is he?'

So I tell the tale of my press-ganging by Marcus Bright and Norman Street. I've had quite a bit to drink so it loses nothing in the telling and everyone has a good laugh at my expense. Eve says, 'Now I know the PTA has that money, I'll tap them for some new display boards.'

Colin asks, 'How does he seem – Edmund?'

'All right. You mean after what happened to his sister? All right.'

I turn to David. 'Did you talk to Edmund, during your investigation?'

'I didn't. One of my officers did. There was nothing he could tell us, as I recall. He was at school, and had been all week. I imagine as a boarder he's a bit detached from the rest of the family.'

'He's close to his mother,' I say. 'I've seen them together. And he's not even embarrassed about selling DVDs of her show.' I tell the story of this morning's encounter. 'And I saw a whole stack of the DVDs out at Charter Hall when I was there. I wonder how many they've sold. I'd love to go back and have a look.'

'The Carsons have moved back in,' David warns sharply. 'I wouldn't advise trespassing.'

'What puzzles me,' I say, pouring some more brandy, 'is why they're all so devoted to Glenys – Hector, Edmund, Renée the cleaner – and even those two shits at the Aphra Behn changed their tune with me when they thought I was a friend of Glenys's. From what I've heard, she seems a thoroughly selfish woman.'

Colin drains his glass and says, 'I don't think you can explain the power to inspire devotion, though in Glenys's case

I'm sure it's connected with her power as an actress – charisma if you like. As for selfish, I've got patients who are selfless wives and devoted mothers and their families just make more and more demands on them till they buckle under the strain. Talking of which, I've early surgery tomorrow.' He smiles at me. 'Thank you, kind hostess. That was a lovely meal.'

I smile back, but I'm startled to see, when I look into his face, something in his eyes that is very like despair. I look across at Eve, who is smiling serenely as she comes across to kiss me goodnight. When I look again at Colin, he seems all right. The occasional twinge of angst is an occupational hazard of daily contact with human misery, I suppose.

When they've gone and I'm loading the dishwasher, I pin down the little niggle that's running round my head. "Kind hostess," Colin called me. Not such an odd phrase, but not commonplace either, is it?

"This diamond he greets your wife withal,
By the name of most kind hostess."

That's the message Banquo brings from King Duncan to Macbeth, who, together with his kind hostess of a wife, is plotting to murder him in his bed. And why use those words to me? Was he conscious of what he was saying? Why turn me into Lady Macbeth as though I'm plotting against him? Why quote from *Macbeth* at all?

I go to bed and dream of blood.

20

WEDNESDAY 17th NOVEMBER

I have not seen such a firago

We had an early snowfall yesterday. *Snow in November!* Everyone professes to be amazed and astonished although actually we had snow in November only a couple of years ago. As ever, it has brought the town – indeed the whole country – to a standstill. The media love it: it's so much more fun than wars and the economy. Lovely snowy scenes adorn all the front pages and glitter from the television screen. Freda adores it and was out in the garden at eight o'clock this morning. My mother is under strict instructions to go nowhere. She doesn't like instructions, strict or otherwise, and I am suspicious of the apparent meekness with which she acquiesces. Is she planning to go out as soon as my back's turned, or does she really not feel very well? She has been here for six weeks now, and though she seems all right and is walking quite well, she hasn't mentioned going home. I need to find out how she's feeling, but asking my mother about her health is the most difficult thing in the world: she bamboozles me with medical terminology and speaks as though she was talking about someone else – a slightly irritating patient who happens to share her name; her defective alter ego. I must sit down with her and have a talk, but not today. Today my life is scheduled to be screwed up both by William Roper School and by Marlbury Abbey School, and now the snow is going to finish things off, because I daren't ride my bike.

Eve and I have arranged to go into the Aphra Behn first thing this morning, to pick up the *Twelfth Night* costumes. The production isn't on for another three weeks but having the costumes to rehearse in is a real bonus. You may ask yourself how I wrung this concession out of the delightful Mr Driver and I have to tell you that it was not my doing but Renée Deakin's. I bumped into her in town one day, as she was on her way to the theatre to pick up some costumes for Marlbury Operatic, weeks ahead of their production of *The King and I*. I moaned that we were only getting ours for a week, she said she would have a word, and bingo! Alex Driver, Renée said, was "quite a sweetie" when you got to know him. I wonder how long that takes. Anyway, I'm grateful to her, of course, but a bit of me is also unnerved by her palliness with the man who is still, in my mind, a possible killer.

I don my big winter coat, which I can't cycle in and which only comes out for snow; I wrap a hefty scarf round my neck and I put on a pair of flowered wellingtons, which I thought were charming when I bought them but now see are ridiculous on a woman of my age. I walk down to Eve's house, taking ages as I stumble and slither on the crunchy snow, and I'm frozen when I get there, despite coat and scarf.

'Ooh my ears,' I cry as Eve opens the door. 'I've got frozen ears.'

'You need a hat,' she says. 'Pick one off the hat stand.'

She has an old-fashioned curved beech hat stand in her hall, which has always carried an assortment of headgear that I thought purely decorative. Most of the hats are not actually much help in alleviating snowy ear syndrome, but I do find a splendid Russian-looking one – the sort that British politicians used to wear when visiting the Soviet Union. It is huge and furry and comes well down over my ears, threatening to cover my eyes as well. I look in the mirror, hoping I'll look like Liv Tyler in *Eugene Onegin* but finding I look more like a transsexual guardsman.

'Oh, that's Colin's,' Eve says. 'He bought it years ago, when we had a really bad winter, but he thought it encouraged his patients' fears about his 'red' tendencies. Wear it. It'll save your ears.'

Eve manoeuvres her car the short distance to the theatre and we go in through the stage door. We have an appointment but I'm unsurprised to find that Alex Driver is not waiting to receive us. The harassed ASM with the frizzy hair says she's not sure if he's in. She takes us to his office and looks inside but finds it empty. She suggests we go down to the costume store while she sees if she can track him down.

To give him his due, Alex Driver has left all our costumes hanging on a rail with a label on it reading *Gray*. Eve hasn't seen the boys' jackets before so while she's appraising them, I mumble something about just checking we've got the right fat suit and speed off to where I saw the boxes of DVDs before. They are not there. I look around but there is no sign of them. Thwarted, I rejoin Eve and we're debating how long we're prepared to wait when the little ASM comes in and says, breathlessly, 'Sorry, Alex has just rung. He can't get in from Upper Shepton. They haven't gritted the roads out there. He says take the costumes and sign this.'

She hands me a form, which I sign, thereby undertaking to return the costumes undamaged in one month's time, and Eve and I start gathering up armfuls to take out to the car. As we're returning for a second load, I say, 'You go on down, Eve. I'm just going to find a loo.'

And this is where my behaviour becomes difficult to excuse if we're following standards of strict propriety. I open the door of Alex Driver's office and I slip inside because, you see, when

I glanced in over the ASM's shoulder earlier, I thought I saw a large cardboard box very like the one I saw before, down below the stage, and if there's no longer one down there, then it's very likely to be up here. I really need to find out whether this one's got DVDs of *Amy* in it and, if so, what numbers they've got on their backs, because I can't make any sense of this number thing, and it's really bugging me.

I don't allow myself the luxury of looking round. Alex Driver may be safely snowed in, but the ASM might put her frizzy head in any time, so I make straight for the box, discover it is half full of DVDs, take one out, find a number five on its back and slip it into my coat pocket. Now that is the really inexcusable bit and I don't quite know why I do it, except that I'm more and more convinced that there's some sort of mystery about these DVDs and I'm going to have to watch one. (You may remember that Edmund Carson promised to get me one, but he hasn't yet delivered.) Anyway, however I spin it, this is theft; I am a thief, and I shall be punished for it, you'll be glad to hear.

When everything is in the car, Eve drives off to school and I walk round to Marlbury Abbey for my usual Wednesday morning stint. The central quadrangle of the school looks like a Victorian Christmas card. Boys in mufflers with rosy cheeks are sliding round it, tossing snowballs at each other and the ancient stone walls ring with their childish laughter. Or something like that. I could call it Dickensian, except school is never jolly in Dickens' world, is it? My hat elicits a certain amount of laughter as I make my way round to my classroom (I skip the coffee these days) but they are civilised enough not to throw snowballs at me.

My class arrives, affecting a languid disregard for the snow, and we get down to negatives and question tags. We take it for granted, I point out, that the negative tags, "isn't it?" and "doesn't it?" on the end of a question invite the answer "yes", while the positive tags, "is it?" and "does it?" invite "no", but that's actually quite counter-intuitive to a learner of English. We also explore the difficulties of negatives cancelling each other out in English (unless you live within the sound of Bow bells) and the time passes agreeably enough.

Edmund hangs around at the end of the lesson, as he often does, and watches me as I'm getting back into my wellies. 'Interesting stuff about negatives,' he says. 'I'm quite getting into this.'

'Enough to go to Nepal?' I ask, as I wrestle my feet into my boots.

'I don't think the parents would care for that,' he says. 'They tend to want me to be close at hand these days.'

'Oh yes,' I mumble, feeling I've been crass, 'yes, of course.'

'I'm sorry I haven't been able to get you that DVD,' he says. 'I've got a problem with supply at the moment.'

'Not to worry,' I say cheerfully, hardly thinking about what I'm saying as I button up my coat and wind my scarf around, 'I've got one.'

He lets out something between a shout and a laugh. 'You've got one?'

'Yes.' I reach into my pocket and produce it. 'Voilà.'

'Where did you get it?' The tone is casual but he's watching me intently. And what am I to say? *Stupid woman! Try thinking before you open your mouth*, I berate myself silently.

Aloud, I say, 'Oh, I – stumbled across it.'

'And what did you think of it?' He's still watching me, his eyes locked on mine.

'I haven't had a chance to watch it yet – I just got it this morning.' I'm just about to put it back in my pocket when he reaches out a hand.

'Do you mind if I have a look at it?' he asks. He takes it and turns it over – possibly to look at the number on the back, I surmise. 'I thought so,' he says. 'This'll be a pirate version.

Very poor quality. Why don't I keep this and get you a decent one?'

It's about to go into his pocket but I shoot out a hand for it. 'No!' I say rather more loudly that I mean to. 'I'm sure this'll be fine. If it's not, I'll let you know.' There's almost a tussle for a moment, then he lets go and I tuck it back, deep into my coat pocket.

'Fine,' he says. 'I'll see you later at this Question Time thing. Looking forward to it.' And he's gone.

I should explain about the Question Time thing: it's another of Marcus's brainwaves – a team of local worthies will answer questions on the state of the world put to them by members of an audience of sixth formers. It will take place at seven-thirty this evening and, as it's out of working hours, I shall get paid £100 for doing it, which will come in handy what with Christmas approaching and my having increasing numbers of mouths to feed. The other members of the panel are a cleric from the abbey, the editor of *The Marlbury Herald* and Neil Cunningham, director of the Aphra Behn Theatre. You may wonder what I am doing among these stalwarts of the Marlbury establishment and I did ask Marcus that very question. 'Oh, I'm sure you'll hold your own,' was all he said.

So, I'm to be there for my nuisance value – who better? I'm to be the grit in the oyster, the *balance* on the team. I'm the only left-wing feminist Marcus knows and for once I'm actually being invited to be stroppy. The trouble is, I'm so stroppy that I'm tempted to thwart Marcus by not being stroppy. I could play the little woman for the evening: I could smile, be self-deprecating and agree with everything the men say, couldn't I? Couldn't I? Well, actually, no.

I'm not thinking about this, though, as I trudge across town to the college with the snow getting in over the tops of my boots. I'm thinking about the DVD in my pocket and Edmund's reluctance to let me keep it; I'm thinking about one lot with fours on the back, one lot with fives and one lot with sixes; I'm thinking about the frustrating fact that I won't get a chance to look at this one till I get home late this evening, because we have a staff meeting at five (rescheduled because of my morning engagement at Marlbury Abbey) and then I've promised myself a pizza at Pizza Express before the Question Time thing (I was invited to have dinner with my fellow-performers but there is only so much a woman can take, so I declined).

Perhaps it's my wet socks, but I feel increasingly pissed off as the afternoon goes on. I'm snappy with my colleagues at the meeting and the walk in the biting wind afterwards puts me in a foul temper. Pizza Express, which has had the temerity to establish itself in a half-timbered building on the abbey's doorstep, feels empty and cheerless, and even a glass of wine with my pizza doesn't cheer me up. I eat the pizza too fast, order a cappuccino but then leave half of it because it's weedily weak and I stomp round to the abbey gateway, through the precincts, round by the cloisters and into the school quad.

My team-mates are drinking after-dinner coffee with Marcus in the common room when I arrive looking slightly demented, I imagine, in my outsize hat and flowery wellies. Once I have divested myself of these, I am introduced by Marcus as "our linguistics expert." Neil Cunningham appears not to recognise me; the others smile enthusiastically. We have a bit of nervous conversation about possible questions and all lament the fact that we haven't paid more attention to the news over the past week, though I suspect we've all been boning up like mad, and then Marcus ushers us out once more and we climb some steps to the school hall.

It's no surprise to find that the hall bears no resemblance to school halls I have known and every resemblance to an Oxford college hall, down to stained glass windows and portraits of benefactors – pale, male and stale – on the walls. The boys, and a scattering of girls, are already gathered and applaud politely as we file in, and seat ourselves on a high platform beneath an assortment of coats of arms. They applaud again as we are introduced.

Things kick off fairly sluggishly with a question about funding for the arts – is it less important than funding scientific research? My colleagues speak passionately of the benefits to humanity of artistic endeavour, though they fail to tackle the question of how these benefits can be calibrated against those of scientific endeavour, or whether all scientific research is of equal value, and I point this out, but only half-heartedly.

Then a portly boy in a gown stands up. He is one of those sixteen-year-olds who is already forty-two. He asks, in his plummy professor's voice, 'Does the team think that political correctness has gone mad?'

I'm called first on this one. I say, rather prosaically, that I think "political correctness" has become a catch-all term for a number of different areas in which government, local government, the police and other authorities are trying to manage changing attitudes in society – areas where attitudes that were once acceptable aren't any more – and shouldn't be. As far as the words people use are concerned – the names they call people or the epithets they use – I think of PC as standing for "polite" and "civilised".

'There's no excuse,' I say, 'for calling people by a name they don't like. We wouldn't do it to our friends and colleagues and we shouldn't do it to other people. We've no business using terms that people find demeaning, or making jokes about people's sexuality or skin colour or nationality or height – or hair colour, actually. Ginger-related insults still seem to be allowed.' I get a laugh and I go on, 'Personally, I don't see any harm in making jokes about people's religion. Those other things – race, gender, sexuality, physical appearance – are things people can't help – they don't choose them. We choose our religious beliefs and we should be prepared to defend them and to take criticism of them. I don't think saying, "You can't say that because it offends me" works in this context.'

My colleagues are not inclined to be analytical. They are determined to have fun. They all have their little anecdotes about hyper-pc imbecility: Birmingham City Council has renamed the Christmas season Winterval; actresses suddenly want to be called actors; a government booklet for nursery school teachers warns against playing musical chairs with the children because it encourages aggression; short people are being described as "vertically challenged"; a government minister is given a warning by police after using the term "nitty-gritty"; a teacher is prosecuted for putting sellotape over a girl's mouth "even though the girl thought it was funny". I signal to Marcus that I'd like to come back into the discussion, but I'm ignored.

The next question is clearly for me, but Marcus thinks it will be more fun to leave me till last 'Have women lost more than they've gained by claiming equality with men?' a girl asks.

The chaps witter on about the break-up of the family, the impossibility of "having it all" and the danger of men becoming redundant. The reverend gentleman bemoans the divorce rate and the loss of the little courtesies that were once shown to ladies; Neil Cunningham says small businesses won't employ women because maternity leave is such a problem (has he got trouble with the little ASM?); the editor does a little editorial on the horrors of laddettes. Then it's my turn. I take a deep breath and address the girls in the audience.

'I'm sorry,' I say, 'if the young woman who asked the question thinks we may have lost more than we've gained, but I have to tell you that we've still got a way to go and this is no time to be turning round. When you go out into the world of work, your male colleagues may or may not hold doors open for you but you'll only get real respect from them if you're earning the same as they are. Economic equality is the key, and we're a long way from having that. So don't let them tell you that it's all gone far enough when we're only half way there. That's the oldest trick in the book and we're not falling for it.' I don't make much impression. The applause that greets my words is merely polite and we move on.

"Is the English language going downhill?" is our next question, and I'm on first.

I'm prepared for this one because people tackle me about this all the time. "You're an English teacher," they say. "Doesn't it drive you mad when people say...?" and then they launch into their favourite linguistic prejudices. So I launch into my usual spiel. I say that language is organic, that it's a developing and evolving thing and you can't freeze it in a moment and say, "This is correct and will be for ever more." I point out how much the language has changed since Shakespeare was writing and that many things he wrote would be judged incorrect by modern standards of grammar. I tell them that modern English grammar was invented by 18th century grammarians who wanted English to be more like Latin, but that English isn't a Latin language and that's partly why there are always exceptions to every grammatical rule. On the other hand, I say, I hate sloppiness: I hate language being used carelessly or clumsily. I am outraged when people whose business is words – politicians and broadcasters – resort to tired catch phrases and empty clichés; I hate it when, given a glorious language with the largest, most finely-tuned vocabulary in the world, people restrict themselves to a tiny subset of words. 'Language change – being creative with language – is to be celebrated,' I conclude, 'but language abuse is a serious crime.'

And then my colleagues are off. Marcus fires the starting gun and they're galloping off in all directions on their individual hobby horses. They denounce dangling participles, greengrocers' apostrophes, split infinitives and "uninterested" confused with "disinterested". They deplore *re*search pronounced with the stress on the first syllable and all other Americanisms; they lament the death of "whom" and of the the subjunctive, and they hail text and e-mail messages as the harbingers of the end of civilisation as we know it.

Now, I could happily add to their list of horrors. I hate talk of amounts of people, as though people were an amorphous mass like milk or flour (it's the countable/uncountable problem again); I hate it when "may" gets used instead of "might" ("he may have died" means we don't know if he died or not, whereas "he might have died" means he didn't actually); I hate people screwing up our beautifully complex conditional forms; I hate mixed metaphors because it means people are reaching for metaphors without thinking about what they actually mean. On the other hand, I also know that everything I've said this evening about the inevitability of language change is true too, and I hold both attitudes in my head simultaneously. This evening, I'm so irritated by my colleagues' unthinking fuddy-duddiness – and indeed by the whole atmosphere in this absurdly grand hall with boys and masters sitting there in their gowns – that I raise a hand quite imperiously to Marcus and I enter the fray again.

'I simply don't believe that it really pains my colleagues to listen to an infinitive being split or to hear "flaunt" instead of "flout", or to buy their potatoes with an apostrophe in them, but they like to flag up their outrage because that shows that they know what's right, that they are members of an educated elite which believes it owns the language. Well, I have to tell them that they don't. They can hold on to the written language because they can stop people from passing exams if they don't conform to their rules, but the spoken language is utterly democratic. Every English speaker owns it and can use it as he or she chooses – provided they can make themselves understood to the people they want to understand them. Textspeak is a case in point. My colleagues here hate textspeak, but textspeak is only punning really – you have to be very alert to the possibilities of language to use it creatively. I use it. I enjoy it. But I'm nothing like as good at it as people who are texting all the time – which probably means people who don't have proper jobs. What the establishment hates is the fact that language change – both vocabulary and accent – happens mainly from the bottom up. It starts among the young and streetwise and it spreads rapidly up and out. It can't be stopped, and all of you are affected by it, however hard your teachers are trying to turn you into stormtroopers for the establishment. Spoken language is anarchic and that's why the middle-aged are frightened of it.'

And here we draw to a close. I don't hang about afterwards. I've done my bit, stirred things up, earned my money. I want to go home. I slither back to the common room and get back into snow gear. No-one comes with me; it seems they all have their outdoor gear with them. I finger the DVD in my pocket as I put my coat on. In fifteen minutes, I promise myself, I shall be sitting down with a pot of tea, wearing dry socks and watching this mystery disc. I wind my scarf round my neck and I pull Colin's hat down over my ears. Then I go out into the icy dark, cut through the streams of boys dispersing to their rooms and walk through to the cloisters. There are two figures ahead of me who are, I suspect, a couple of my fellow panellists, but I don't hurry to catch them up. Instead I phone Ellie, who is picking me up from outside the abbey.

'Are you out there?' I ask.

'Yup. Parked illegally just outside Pizza Express.'

'I'll be with you in two minutes.'

'How did it go?'

'I really couldn't say.'

As I break contact, I hesitate a bit. It really is forbiddingly dark through here. The only light filtering through comes from a pale, cloud-screened moon and I can no longer hear the footsteps of the pair ahead of me. I'm tempted to turn back, to ring Ellie and ask her to go round and meet me outside the school lodge, but that will take more time and I really don't want to be out any longer than I need to. I pull my scarf up higher and turn off into the little cut though to my left which is known, unappealingly, as Dark Entry.

I will never be able to recall exactly what happens next. There is neither fear nor pain – just the sound of running feet and an extraordinarily violent impact, which knocks the breath out of me before I hit the icy ground and lose contact with the world.

21

WEDNESDAY 17th NOVEMBER

20.50: CALL-OUT

Scott had just put a pizza in the microwave when his phone rang.

'Paula?' he said.

'I'm at Marlbury Abbey School, guv,' she said. 'We've got a situation. A possible assault. I would deal with it myself but the victim's asking for you.'

'What, me personally?'

'Yes. The thing is, it's Gina Gray.'

The microwave pinged and he turned it off automatically.

'What's happened to her?' His voice was as level as he could make it but it sounded odd to his ears, and probably to hers.

'A boy at the school found her unconscious in the abbey cloisters. She'd just left the school, apparently. He went for help and found Dr Fletcher, who called an ambulance. The daughter – the one we interviewed about the Carson case – turned up and called us. A patrol car attended and called the station. The duty sergeant called me. I've just got here. She's come round and she says she has to speak to you. Something about a DVD. She's not making a lot of sense.' She broke off and said something he couldn't hear, then came back. 'The ambulance is here now.'

'OK. Are the uniforms still there?'

'Yes.'

'Have you secured the crime scene?'

'Trouble is, we don't know if it is a crime scene. It's quite possible it was an accident.'

'What's Gina saying?'

'She says someone hit her.'

'Then I suggest we go with that. Tell the uniforms to secure the scene and wait for me. Is the ambulance still there? You go in the ambulance and stay with her. I'll get to the hospital as soon as I've talked to the witnesses.'

'OK. I'll see you later.'

She was about to ring off but he stopped her. 'Paula?'

'Yes?'

'Is she all right?'

'She seems OK. Shocked. A bit hysterical. OK, I think, but you never know with head injuries, do you?'

More snow was falling as he edged the car down his drive and along the ungritted roads of the estate. Once on the ring road, he picked up speed but had to slow to a crawl again in the narrow streets round the abbey. He took his car into the precincts and parked behind the patrol car, in which a uniformed policeman sat with the engine running.

'Why aren't you at the crime scene?' he demanded.

'We're taking shifts, sir. It's brass monkeys standing out there.'

He led Scott through the cloisters to where his colleague was pacing, barely visible in the intense dark, his feet ringing on the flagstones.

'What do we think happened?' Scott asked.

The PC shone his torch into a dark little alleyway. 'A Mrs Virginia Gray, sir. She was found in here by one of the boys at the school. Seems she'd had a blow to the head and there was a piece of scaffolding lying on the ground. There's scaffolding up the wall there, you can see. The boy went for help and brought a doctor back with him, and a Mr Bright, a teacher at the school. They moved her into the school and called an ambulance.'

'What time was this?'

The constable took out a notebook and shone the torch on it. 'About 8.40 p.m. they say.'

'Who called you?'

'The victim's daughter, Eleanor Gray.'

'How did she know what had happened?'

'She'd arranged to pick her mother up, apparently. She was parked outside the gates and when her mother didn't turn up, she came looking for her. She was pretty upset when she called. Said her mother had been attacked and everyone was trying to pretend it was an accident.'

'Everyone?'

'Mainly Mr Bright and the headmaster, I think, sir.'

'Where can I find Mr Bright?'

'This is his number, sir.' He tore a page out of the notebook.

'Good.'

He took the torch and shone it up the wall at the grid of scaffolding, then called DS Andy Finnegan. 'Andy? I'm sorry to get you out on a night like this but I'm down at the abbey. A woman appears to have been attacked in the cloisters here. Paula's gone to A&E with her; I'm going to start talking to witnesses. I need you to get SOCOs down here. It's pitch dark so they'll need floodlights. It needs to be done now. Can't wait till morning. Snow'll blow in and mess everything up. When you've got them sorted, come and join me on the interviews.'

'You're lucky,' he said to the PCs. 'As soon as the SOCOs turn up, you can take a break.'

He called the number he had been given. 'Mr Bright? DCI David Scott. Where can I find you?'

Marcus Bright came to meet him, carrying a torch. As they walked through the cloisters, the torch light bounced off a pile of scaffolding poles lying on the ground.

'Have those just been taken down or are they going up?' Scott asked

200

'They've just come down. They've been working on the stonework up there.' He flashed the torch upwards. 'They've only got the work in Dark Entry to do now.'

'Dark Entry?'

'Where the accident happened.'

'You think it was an accident?'

'What else?'

'The victim thinks otherwise.'

'The victim had a blow on the head. And she was always inclined to dramatise, I seem to recall.'

Scott looked at him sharply. 'You know her well?'

'We were childhood sweethearts, in a manner of speaking,' Marcus Bright said with a grin.

Too pleased with himself and too cheerful for the circumstances, Scott thought, and surprised himself by the intensity of his dislike of the man. He followed him to the headmaster's house, where they found Colin Fletcher sitting with Canon Aylmer. They were seated in leather armchairs either side of a log fire and a lad of seventeen or eighteen, in school uniform, was seated rather awkwardly on a sofa nearby. Marcus Bright ushered Scott in and said cheerfully, 'Here we are. All your witnesses gathered together, chief inspector.'

Canon Aylmer looked startled. 'Chief inspector? This is hardly a matter for a chief inspector, is it?'

Scott ignored the question and said, 'Actually, we prefer not to have our witnesses gathered together – it muddies the waters – but since you've all presumably discussed what happened, I'm happy to talk to you as a group. Tell me, first of all, what was Mrs Gray doing at the school? She was leaving here when she was hit, I understand.'

'She'd just been taking part in an in-house *Question Time* with the sixth form,' Marcus Bright said.

'And that finished when?'

'At eight-thirty.'

'Did you see her leave?'

'I didn't. I wanted a chance to thank her, but she must have nipped off pretty quickly. I thanked the others and saw them off the premises but I missed Gina.'

'Did the others leave by the same exit as she did?'

'The normal exit is out through the school lodge and Jeff Gould – the editor of *The Herald* – went out that way. I don't know why Gina was going the other way – especially in the dark. Dr Reeve was going back to the abbey so he went out through the cloisters, and the director of the theatre, Neil Cunningham, went with him because it's a short cut to the theatre.'

'And you don't know whether Mrs Gray left before or after them?'

'Oh, before I would think. I'd have seen her if she'd been after them.'

'Well, we can check with them whether they saw her.' Scott turned to the boy on the sofa. 'You're the boy who found Mrs Gray?'

The boy half rose, but Scott came and sat beside him.
'And you are?'

'Micklejohn, sir. Iain Micklejohn.'

'Micklejohn,' put in Canon Aylmer, 'is our head of school.' Noting Scott's look of puzzlement, he added kindly, 'Head boy.'

'I see. And how did you come to be in the cloisters, Iain?'

'I was walking through to the abbey. Dr Reeve had offered to hear my reading for the end of term service.'

'It's not the end of term yet, surely?'

'No. There's another two weeks but this'll be my first service as head of school and it's the part of the job that worries me most.' He was a fair boy with a freckled complexion and the colour rose to his face as he spoke.

'So, tell me what happened.'

'Well, I nearly tripped over her. I felt myself tread on something just as I turned into Dark Entry. I thought it was a

202

cat or something, but I realised it stretched right across the entry. It was really dark, so I knelt down to feel what it was and then I realised it was a person.'

'What did you do then.'

'Well, I spoke to her. Said some pretty stupid things – "Are you all right?" – you know. I thought it might be a drunk wandered in – they do sometimes sleep in the precincts – but I realised this person was – well I thought they might be dead, so I legged it back to school and found Mr Bright in his study, talking to Dr Fletcher.'

Scott turned to Colin Fletcher. 'And how did you come to be here?' he asked.

'I'd come to see a boy in the sick bay.'

'Wasn't it late for visit?'

'It was, but I was concerned about him. I rang and spoke to Matron at the end of my evening surgery and she wasn't quite happy about him, so I went home and had some dinner and then came round.'

'Fortunate coincidence,' Scott said. 'So, you and Mr Bright went with Iain here, and what did you find?'

'We found her lying just inside Dark Entry, face down, but she was just beginning to stir.'

'You had a torch with you?'

'Yes. Two. I turned her over and recognised her, of course.'

'Did she recognise you?'

'I – I don't think so.'

'Why the hesitation?'

Colin Fletcher looked acutely uncomfortable. 'I shone my medical torch on her eyes. I wanted to see how her pupils reacted. She looked at me and said, "Colin, why did you hit me?"'

Marcus Bright broke in, 'She was obviously quite confused. Didn't know where she –'

Scott interrupted. 'What did you do then?'

'Then Ellie – Eleanor – her daughter – turned up. She was

very upset, obviously. I thought we all needed to get inside. I'd sent Micklejohn to get a stretcher from the sick bay. He turned up with it and Marcus and I carried her through to the school. Marcus had alerted Canon Aylmer to what had happened, and he came to meet us and suggested we brought her in here.'

'And you called an ambulance?'

'I examined her again, properly. She'd suffered two head injuries – one, I assume, where the scaffolding hit her and one where she hit the ground. I didn't think the skull was fractured, but she did seem quite confused and I decided she ought to go to A&E.'

'You say she was confused. What did she say?'

'There was something about a DVD,' Marcus said. 'At least, I think that's what she was saying. 'It's not in my pocket,' she kept saying.

'Something she lost when she fell? Did anyone go and look for it?'

'Well, no. It didn't seem important. Her handbag was all right and her wallet was still in it. Her daughter picked that up, with her briefcase, and brought it back.'

'And the piece of scaffolding?'

'Was just lying there. We left it where it was.'

'Why did Eleanor call the police?'

Marcus Bright gave an expansive shrug. 'You'd have to ask her that.'

'Did she suggest that you should call us?'

Canon Aylmer, who had been watching in silence from his seat by the fire, said, 'She did. But there seemed no reason to do so. Mrs Gray wasn't mugged. Her bag was still there. It was a very unfortunate accident, but luckily Micklejohn stumbled on her very soon after it occurred and medical attention was at hand.' He smiled at Colin Fletcher.

'But Eleanor Gray was quite sure her mother had been attacked,' Scott said. 'Why did she think that?'

Colin Fletcher glanced at Canon Aylmer, then spoke. 'It was what Gina was saying,' he said. 'I told you she asked me why I hit her. Well, she asked several times why someone hit her.'

'What did she say exactly?'

'Just "Someone hit me. Why did someone hit me?"'

'But you didn't take it seriously?'

'Excuse me, sir.' It was Iain Micklejohn who spoke and he was addressing Canon Aylmer. 'May I say something?'

'Of course, Micklejohn, if you think it's relevant.'

'I do, sir.' He turned to Scott. 'I heard someone running. As I was walking towards Dark Entry, I heard someone running along the cloisters on the other side, towards the school. I noticed because it was odd at that time of night and I wondered if it was a boy who'd been out of school without permission and was trying to get back in before lights out. Then finding the lady and so on put it out of my head.'

Scott handed his notebook over to the boy and said, 'Draw me a sketch of the cloisters and show me where you were and where you heard someone running.'

The boy took the notebook and drew a rapid sketch.

'And this arrow on the right is the route you took,' Scott asked, 'and the one on the left is where you heard someone running?'

'Yes.'

'Thank you,' Scott said. 'You've been very helpful.' He looked round at the others. 'This was just preliminary,' he said. 'I shall need to talk to each of you again.'

Walking back to his car, he found that the SOCOs were already in place. 'Fast work,' he said to Andy Finnegan, who was standing watching them, stamping his feet against the cold. 'Anything obvious there?'

'Yes, guv. Take a look at this.' He handed Scott a soft, dark object in an evidence bag. Scott looked at it under the SOCOs' lights.

'What is it?' he asked.

'A hat. Fur. Russian-type thing. Definitely a man's, I'd say.'

'So possibly the attacker's?'

'I'd have thought so. Not likely someone just walking through there would have lost a hat and not noticed, is it?'

'No. Get it into forensics asap in the morning. Should be plenty of DNA on it. Anything else?'

'Only the piece of scaffolding.'

'Which won't have any prints on. You couldn't handle it without gloves in this temperature. They haven't found a DVD lying around, I suppose?'

'A DVD? No. Why?'

'I'm not sure. Get them to look at that scaffolding against the wall, will you – to see if there's anywhere a piece could have worked loose.'

'You think it could have been an accident?'

'Not really, no. The headmaster would like it to be an accident. Odd, really. If it was an accident, she could sue them. If it's a crime, they're off the hook.'

'A crime attracts more attention. Bad publicity.'

'I suppose. You get off now. Leave them to it. I'm going up to the hospital to talk to the victim.'

22

THURSDAY 18th NOVEMBER

She hath abjured the sight and company of men

They gave me something to make me sleep last night, so I wake this morning from complete unconsciousness, as though I'm coming up from the depths of the sea. I'm utterly nonplussed at first: the hard, high bed, the white walls, the icy white light filtering through the window blinds are a mystery. How did I come here? Then, piece by piece, the memory of yesterday comes back to me. It comes in freeze frames: Colin's face looming oddly above me; Ellie weeping in the torchlight; the ambulance men, cheery in their yellow jackets. It comes in sensations: the numbing coldness of the ground beneath me; the piercing light of Colin's probing torch; the unreality of a stretcher ride through the cloisters; Ellie's tears dripping warm on my cold face as I lie on some sort of sofa – where?

Anyway, it doesn't take me long to see that I'm in hospital and to remember how I got here. I must say it was an advantage to go to A&E with a police officer in tow. DS Powell breezed us through and I was scanned and put to bed in a room of my own in no time. (They don't like police officers hanging around the wards – it unnerves the other patients). I don't know what time Ellie left, but I do remember her ringing my mother and then passing the phone to me. 'Virginia,' my mother said, 'do exactly as you're told. You can't be too careful with head injuries. Anything odd – numbness, double vision, severe headache obviously – tell them immediately. I know you. Don't think you can tough it out.'

I choose to believe that, when translated, her words would equate, roughly, to: "I love you my darling daughter, and I'm really rather worried about you."

DS Powell hung around asking questions and I told her a bit, but I was really waiting to talk to David. I knew he would come, but I was unprepared for how comforted I would feel by his coming, and how – shamingly – I would weep with relief. I told him the whole DVD story – about the boxes at Charter Hall and the Aphra Behn, about Edmund and the numbers on the backs, and about my DVD going missing. It all sounded so improbable when I came out with it that I thought I was going to have to make a scene to get him to take me seriously, but it turned out that he'd already got a full-scale investigation under way – scene of crime officers scouring Dark Entry for clues and all the rest of it. And he told me what I could have told him – that my DVD was nowhere to be found.

'We have found a man's hat, though,' he said. 'Do you think your attacker was wearing a hat?'

I got really ratty because I was sick to death of being asked questions I couldn't answer. 'I DON'T KNOW!' I yelled. 'As I told your girlfriend, I didn't see anything. It was DARK. He was BEHIND ME!' Then a thought struck me. 'What sort of hat anyway?'

'A Russian sort of thing – black fur.'

And then I got hysterical. I started to laugh and I couldn't stop. 'My hat,' I gasped. 'No, Colin's... I was wearing... probably saved my life... like a helmet... funny... if he was the one who hit me.'

At this point, a nurse came in, told David off and stuck a needle in my arm, so that was the end of that.

Now, this morning, I'm desperate to go home. I tell anyone who will listen to me that I'm absolutely fine. There's a block on mobiles in here but I commission the ward phone and ring Gillian in the department office to tell her she'll need to cancel my morning classes but that I will definitely be in in the afternoon. However, my every enquiry about going home is met by the response that I must wait for the doctor to see me. It happens that the doctor, a harassed houseman of about sixteen, arrives at the same moment as my mother walks into the room.

'How did you get here?' I ask ungraciously.

'Ellie brought me. She's just parking.'

'But she should be at school.'

My mother gives me that special look of contained exasperation that I've been getting from her for nearly fifty years. Then she has a medical conversation with the doctor. They pay no attention to me – I am, after all, only the patient. I catch mention of "cerebral compression", "asymmetry" and "cerebro-spinal fluid", but it seems I don't have any of those because, in the end, the doctor says I can go as long as I "take it easy" and "follow medical advice."

Ellie arrives with some clothes for me, which is fortunate as it turns out that my others have been taken away for forensic examination. There is a level of unreality about all this which I can't quite cope with. On the one hand, I'm quite sure that I was deliberately mugged last night; on the other, I can't really believe that I'm the centre of a serious criminal investigation.

Anyway, I get dressed, feeling much more wobbly than I expected to, and I totter out on Ellie's arm. Back home, I put up the feeblest of resistance to being sent back to bed and Ellie leaves me with a tray of tea and toast and marmite, the paper and the morning post, promising to be back straight after school. My mother, who hasn't slept much, I suspect, goes off for a rest, telling me to call if I need anything.

'Don't be ridiculous,' I say. 'The last thing we need is you falling down the stairs.'

Left alone, I survey what Ellie has left for me. I eat the toast and marmite and drink the tea but I can't summon the energy to open the post, and *The Guardian* seems to demand more concentration than I can manage. Defeated, I ring Gillian again to say that I won't, after all, be in this afternoon, and then I sleep.

I wake alert and rattled, disentangling myself from jagged dreams in which I'm being interrogated under dazzling lights. The lights, I realise, are the bright square of window, outside which the snow is falling once again. I lie watching it fall, and let my whirling thoughts, as if by sympathetic magic, drift and settle. I start with the last words I spoke before I went to sleep, *The last thing we need is you falling down the stairs*. The words eddy and settle into the absolute conviction that my mugging and Marina Carson's murder are somehow linked. And the link is the DVDs. I don't know how it works but it does, somehow. The other link, of course, is blows to the head. Marina was hit with a golf club; I was hit by a piece of scaffolding, apparently. And I was nearly hit before. Glenys Summers tried to hit me with a spade. Three attacks, all with weapons that happened to be to hand. An attacker who doesn't come armed. But it's not one attacker, is it? Glenys Summers was in London when Marina died, and she was in London again last night, I assume, on stage, in front of thousands of people (though I should suggest to David that he checks up on that.)

So that doesn't work. I struggle to sit up and I reach for my bag on the floor beside me. I root around and find an old envelope and a pen. Then I write:

Where was GS last night?
Other suspects
Neil Cunningham (on the spot)

Colin Fletcher (why there?)
Edmund Carson (DVD)

Neil Cunningham is on the list because he's always been on
the list as far as Marina's murder is concerned – largely because
he has free access to Charter Hall and I don't like him – and
because he could so easily have followed me last night. Could
he have known I had the DVD? Could he have spied on me?
Could there be CCTV in Alex Driver's office? Then Colin. I'm
fond of Colin and I love Eve, but I have to add Colin, whether
I like it or not, because I've never been satisfied with his story
about what he was doing the afternoon Marina was killed,
and because it just seems too odd that he was ostensibly
visiting a sick boy at eight-thirty in the evening, and because I
remember there was something odd about his face when he
was bending over me with his torch out there in Dark Entry.
And Edmund? Well, he's the real suspect, isn't he? If I was
mugged for the DVD, he's the one who knew I had it and who
didn't want me to have it. Motive and opportunity, and he'd
have walked through the cloisters in the past few days, so he
knew the means was to hand. But he's just a boy, and David's
sure he couldn't have killed his sister, and what could possibly
be on that damned DVD that was worth nearly killing me for?

Enough. This is getting me nowhere. I put the envelope and
the pen back in my bag. Distraction. I need to think about
something else. I put on my glasses and I pick up *The Guardian*.
And then I see it. Not the whole thing – that's going to take a
while longer – but I know what's on the DVDs and I see,
dimly, how Marina fits in. That's the bit I'd left out of the
equation, and I'm sure the police have too. My friend Hannah,
half way across the world, had the key to it, though. I feel sick
and sweaty and what I mostly want to do is to shut this half-
knowledge away in a box, to say feebly that I'm not strong
enough to think about this now and to take a couple of the

211

sleeping pills the hospital gave me to put myself into a dreamless sleep. The part of me that doesn't want to do that, however, the reckless, stubborn, stupid part, has me swinging myself out of bed to totter on my marshmallow legs into Annie's room, where my computer has a temporary home. There I boot up and trawl back through screeds of e-mails in my in-box, noting in a detached sort of way that my hand on the mouse is as shaky as an old drunk's. I find Hannah's answer to my query about Marina. *Why would a child's VRQ and reading scores go backwards?* I asked, and she came up with several possibilities, but it is point two that rivets me as it sits on the screen in front of me:

2) An emotional trauma could have set her back too, but you would expect her to make up lost ground eventually (unless the trauma is on-going, of course).

And so it begins to fit. I make it back to bed and I call David. 'David,' I say, 'can you come and see me?'

'Gina? Are you all right? Are you still in hospital?'

'No. I'm home. I think I understand why I was mugged, David. I think I know why Marina was killed. But it's complicated and I don't understand it all. Can you come round?'

'Gina, are you sure you're not –'

'David, my head is perfectly clear. I know what I know.'

'I'm just about to go into a meeting. I'll come round straight after that?'

'How long?'

'An hour or so. Try and rest.'

Easier said than done. I feel hot and shivery, as though I'm running a temperature, and I have a moment of self-doubt. Could I be feeling so preternaturally lucid because I'm actually delirious? I do the things you're supposed to do to calm down, taking deep breaths and visualising mountain streams, but I lack conviction. I can't calm down till I've talked to David. I picture him walking into the room and then I'm horrified at the thought of what he'll find. I am, I realise, hot, smelly and unkempt. And when was the last time I cleaned my teeth?

I throw back the duvet and climb out of bed again, heading for the bathroom, where I look in the mirror and find a mad woman looking back at me, her hair wild; bruising discolouring one side her face; her cheeks feverish, scarlet circles, and above them, her bloodshot eyes staring at me in crazed alarm.

'You have to get a grip,' I say aloud to my wild alter ego.

I clean my teeth; I wash, I press a cold, wet flannel to my cheeks; I comb anti-frizz lotion into my hair; I clean my teeth again; I dump my sweaty pyjamas in the laundry basket; I return to my room and put on a nightdress – not glamorous but cool, at least. The bed has grown cool in my absence, too, and I crawl back into it gratefully, switch on Radio 4 and compose myself to wait.

It's a classic Radio 4 programme: some foreign correspondent reporting from a place I've never heard of. I've begun to get mildly interested in it when I realise that, behind the radio voice I can hear movement downstairs. My mother, presumably. I turn the radio off so I can hear if she starts to mount the stairs and can rush out and stop her. But it's not her step. It's a man's step, firm and purposeful. David already? Has he cried off his meeting? Did I not hear the doorbell? Has my mother let him in? The feet start up the stairs. 'David?' I call tentatively. There's no answer but the feet keep coming. The door opens and Colin Fletcher comes into the room.

I scream. It's only a small scream – somewhere between a gasp and a squeak, really – but Colin knows it was a scream. 'Sorry if I startled you,' he says. 'Eve asked me to bring you some flowers.'

I look for the flowers, but his hands are empty. 'I didn't

213

hear the bell,' I say, my voice claggy in my throat. 'Did my mother let you in?'

'No.' He's looking shifty. 'I didn't want to disturb you so I went round the back. I could see through the French windows that she was asleep, so I tried the kitchen door and it wasn't locked. I left the flowers there and I just wanted to see how you are.'

He comes into the room and stands at the foot of the bed, looking at me. I look back and I am convinced that he has come to kill me. I don't believe his story about the back door being unlocked. I'm not neurotic about security but I don't leave doors unlocked. He's got in, just as he got into Charter Hall, and he's going to finish off what he failed to finish off when he hit me yesterday. I eye the distance between the bed and the door. Could I distract him and then make a dash for the bathroom and lock myself in? No chance, not in my present state. My knees would collapse under me. David. I'll ring David. My hand goes to the phone by the bed. 'Excuse me, Colin,' I say, and my voice sounds clogged with catarrh again. 'I just need to make a phone c –'

He comes to the side of the bed and sits down. 'It's just a flying visit,' he says. 'I just wanted a quick look at you.' He takes hold of the hand that is reaching for the phone and feels my pulse. 'Mm,' he says, looking intently into my face, 'that's going hell for leather. I think I should give you a sedative.'

So that's how he's going to do it. He's going to inject me with something.

'It's all right,' I squeak. 'I'm fine.'

'You don't look fine. Let's have a look at the bumps.' He gets closer, taking my head between his hands. I seem to be having trouble remembering how to breathe and I wonder if he can feel the vibrations of my thudding heart. 'Doesn't look too bad,' he says, and then he smiles. 'I'm awfully glad you had my hat on. It may just have saved your life.' Then he gets

214

up. 'You're sure you don't want something to calm you down?'

I shake my head. I don't trust my voice.

'Well, take it easy,' he says. 'You've had a nasty shock.' And he's gone. I hear him open the front door and close it behind him; I listen to his footsteps on the path; I hear his car start up and drive away. I lie back, limp and helpless, and let weak, invalid tears of relief trickle down my face.

Relief and shame. Shame rushes in on me in a hot wave. What the hell possessed me to cast Colin as a sinister killer? Colin, who saw the girls through nappy rash and colic, earaches and tonsillitis, chicken pox and measles? Colin, who is married to my best friend, who stood at the end of my bed wearing a tweed jacket identical to all the others he has worn for the past twenty years? I'm appalled at myself, and horrified at the thought that Colin, that kind, funny, gentle man, must have read my fear of him in my eyes. How am I ever going to face him again?

I'm right about the rest of it, though. All right, Colin doesn't belong on my suspects list, but I'm right about the core of it, I'm certain, and when David turns up I pour it all out to him. Actually, he has some trouble getting in. Ironically, where Colin had no trouble effecting an entrance, David the cop is stalled at the front door by my mother who, terrier-like, is guarding the entrance. I hear their altercation in fragments:

'… asked me to call,' says David.

'… can't be disturbed,' says my mother.

'… sounded quite urgent,' says David.

'… needs to rest,' says my mother.

'… just for a few minutes,' says David.

'… has to follow medical advice,' says my mother.

Terrified that he'll allow himself to be sent away, I have to haul myself out of bed yet again, to stand at the top of the stairs in my nightie and tell my mother, forcefully, to lay off. She makes an elaborate pantomime of washing her hands of me and shuffles off to her room; I go back to bed and when David comes in bearing a little bunch of freesias, I launch in.

'The DVDs,' I say. 'If someone was prepared to half-kill me to get my copy back, there's got to be something really incriminating on it – and that doesn't mean a crap musical. It's got to be criminal, and that means it's got to be porn. More than that, I think – David, I think it's child porn – it's paedophile stuff.'

David starts to break in. 'Don't stop me,' I say, 'or I shall lose my courage. It was this that made me realise.' I point to an item in the paper about the arrest of members of a French paedophile ring. 'I told you there was a puzzle about Marina Carson – about her attainment scores going down while she was away in Switzerland. My friend who's a child psychiatrist says emotional trauma while she was away could have done that – but that her attainment should have picked up when she got back *unless the trauma is ongoing.* I think she was abused while they were away. I think she was made to pose for porn DVDs and I think it carried on after they got back. The DVDs all have different numbers on the back – I've seen four, five and six – so they must be different – a series. Obviously, it can't just be Marina on them – there must be other children as well – but I think she'd finally had enough and someone was afraid she was going to blow the whistle, and so they killed her.'

David sits down in the chair by the window and puts his head in his hands. Then he looks up. 'I don't need to point out, do I, that this is pure guesswork?' he asks. 'And the autopsy on Marina found no evidence of sexual abuse.' I open my mouth to protest. 'But,' he adds, 'if we take a look at one of those DVDs we'll know if you're right, won't we?'

I stare at him. I felt so sure my intuition was right and I so wanted him to take me seriously, but now he's sitting here not telling me I'm talking rubbish and, perversely, I don't want him to. I want him to tell me that I'm talking utter nonsense and he can prove it, that by a horribly unlucky chance Marina interrupted a burglary, that no-one has been abused – not Marina, not any other child, that Marlbury is just the safe, dull little town it makes itself out to be and all is hunky-dory.

We're silent, avoiding each other's eye. The pictures in my head are dark and inchoate, but he must really know, mustn't he?

'I can only guess at what we're talking about here,' I say. 'But you must have seen this sort of stuff, presumably, in the line of duty?' He nods. 'So what is it like?'

He looks away. 'It's vile,' he says, 'in a way I can't begin to describe.'

'I realise that,' I say, more brusquely than I intend, 'but what I mean is, couldn't she have been made to do things that wouldn't have hurt her physically- that wouldn't show up in an autopsy? You know what I mean. I don't have to spell it out, do I? Maybe -' this comes as a new thought, '- they made her be an abuser.'

We sit and look at each other. 'It's possible,' he says. He gets up and goes over to the window, watching the snow falling. 'Paedophile images are disseminated online,' he says. 'I've never come across them being sold on DVD.

I would like to say, 'Yes, of course, it was a silly idea, forget it', and then I could pack it up and not have to think about it any more and spend the afternoon reading *Little Women*, my book of refuge when all else fails. Instead, I say reluctantly, 'But it would be quite clever, wouldn't it? If you access porn on line, the police can always find it on your hard disc; a DVD is much easier to hide or destroy. The problem would be distribution, if you were going to sell actual discs, but Edmund and those two at the Aphra Behn may have found a way to do it.'

'So in your scenario, it's just the three of them, is it? And

Edmund would be the link with Switzerland? A boy of what – fifteen – when they came back?'

'He's very adult for his age. Unnervingly, actually. His parents could be in it too, I suppose. But if Glenys was involved, then why would Marina have been so protective of her? She obviously saw her as vulnerable. In fact, supposing Driver and Cunningham got Marina to do what they wanted and keep quiet by threatening harm to Glenys. Perhaps they were deliberately working on Glenys's nerves – making her jumpy – and making Marina feel that she had to keep her safe.'

'They could have made the DVDs at the theatre, but more likely they'd have done it at Charter Hall. We found a sort of studio – nothing sinister in it, just a few cameras and some lighting. Hector Carson said it was Edmund's. His passion, he said.'

'So if they were filming there, they'd have needed to keep Glenys scared – make sure she didn't come exploring and find out what they were doing.'

David has stood up and is standing with his back to me, watching the snow falling.

'Adults and children,' he says, without turning round.

'Sorry?'

He turns. 'The neighbours saw adults and children being ferried up and down the river in the Carsons' boat. We assumed they were running an illicit business, but not this kind.'

'So you think I'm right?'

'I think there are grounds for investigating. Cunningham and Driver could have got hold of the children. Child actors are often models as well, aren't they? Cunningham and Driver will have access to all the child modelling agencies, and we know some of them are a front for paedophiles. They'd ferry them up to Charter Hall, put the fear of God into them to keep them quiet and send them home with a nice pay packet. As far as the parents were concerned, it would have been just a modelling assignment.'

Swallowing the bile I feel rising in my throat, I say, 'So all you've got to do is search their offices – there'll be lists – maybe mailing lists of clients – ' I stop as I see the look on his face. 'Well, I expect you know what to do,' I finish lamely.

'I expect I do,' he says.

'Sorry. But there is just one more thing.'

'What?'

'I've got a picture in my head. Something Eve said when we were first talking about Marina. She said Hector spent most of his time with Glenys when she was in the clinic and there was a housekeeper and her husband to keep an eye on the children. I don't know why, but I pictured something sinister: a big, dark house, frightened children, a mean-faced couple, something Dickensian. Maybe that's where it started, in the house. You could try and find the couple. You could ask –'

'Gina. This may be an inspiration on your part and it may not. I'm taking it seriously. Just leave it with me.'

'All right. Fine. I'll leave it to you.'

'Good. I think you should sleep now. You don't look well.'

'I'm all right.'

I listen to him going down the stairs and I can't let him go without saying one more thing. 'David,' I call. 'You really have to get hold of one of those DVDs.'

'No, really?' he calls. 'I didn't think I'd bother.'

And he slams the front door behind him.

23

FRIDAY 19ᵗʰ NOVEMBER

Most provident in peril

'I HAVE to go to this meeting. I'm forty-seven years old. I make my own decisions.'

I am yelling at my mother and my daughter, who have joined forces to keep me chained to my bed. 'It's an examiners' meeting,' I say in a tone that is battling to be reasonable. 'We have things to discuss. Arrangements for orals, for one thing. They were a disaster last time. I have to be there. I have things to say.' I catch a glance between the two of them. 'And don't look at each other like that!' I yell. 'There is a world out there where my opinions are actually valued – in contrast to here, where everything I say is automatically dismissed as nonsense.'

My mother pounces. 'Well, now you are talking nonsense, Virginia,' she says. 'If you want to convince us that you are actually feeling better, you'd be wise not to talk such wild rubbish.'

How does she do it? How does she manage even now to turn me into a raging adolescent? 'I'm not discussing this any more,' I say as coolly as I can manage. 'I have a meeting to go to.' I stamp upstairs, my head ringing.

I don't, in fact, feel at all well. I slept badly, tormented by dreams. The outhouse studio at Charter Hall turned into a horror movie, with mirrors, trap doors and dungeons, and the child I had to save, but never could because I was a helpless, crawling creature, was not Marina, of course, but Freda – Freda sometimes with her own face and sometimes with Annie's. And the person I blamed was not the abuser, who was nowhere to be found. No, the person I raged at, voiceless and struggling for breath, the person who should have been protecting the child but was looking the other way, was my mother. I woke once, struggling for breath, and was puzzled to find that my face was wet with tears.

Well, it doesn't take an oneirologist to interpret all this and I'm not proud of what it says about the state of my subconscious, so I'd sooner get out and shake off the miasma that my night-time horrors have left behind. Besides, I can walk about today without danger of falling over and though I feel a bit shaky and sick, a nasty dream is hardly good grounds for crying off a meeting.

The meeting actually is important; it's about the Cambridge exams and I owe it to my students to be there. It's happening out at Dungate, on the coast, where there's a profusion of language schools occupying, for the most part, abandoned hotels. The Cambridge exams happen here in one of the better-preserved hotels, which offers its "conference room" for the occasion, and fills it with wobbly folding tables and chairs (one of the issues I want to talk about). I'm not going into college this morning; I'm simply going to take the train out to Dungate, go to The Wellington School of English to talk and eat sandwiches with my fellow English teachers, and then return to Marlbury. It's hardly a taxing day, and the alternative is to stay at home wondering how David's investigation is going and whether he'll let me know if he finds anything and whether, in truth, I want to know if he does.

There are problems about my going out anywhere, though: I have bruises all over my face and my warm outdoor clothes have all been taken away for forensic examination. I can't do much to conceal the bruises, which are now an angry purple and seem only to glow more vividly under a film of foundation. I try wearing a silk scarf over my head and tying it under my chin, which does something for the bruises but makes me look like the queen at a point-to-point, so I decide I'd rather look like a victim of domestic violence and take it off. Instead I bundle my hair, which is filthy but can't be washed because of my head wounds, into a velvet hat, which I bought to wear to a wedding a couple of years ago, and, since my winter coat has been taken into custody, I dig out from the spare room cupboard a fake fur coat, which dates from the 1980's when they were all the rage. *Fun furs* they were called, though I'm not sure in what exactly the fun resided. Were we supposed to have fun in them – more, say, that in cashmere? Was the fur itself having fun at our expense, the acrilan having a laugh at those of us foolish enough to think it was genuine animal? Or was it the little furry creatures who had been saved from being turned into coats who were having the fun? Whatever the case, I wrap myself in its fun-imbued warmth, add a pair of après-ski boots, a relic of a long-ago school ski trip, and thus quaintly accoutred I depart, in a taxi, for the station.

Dungate was a popular resort up till the 1960's, and its sea front is thickly lined with substantial Victorian villas. A relatively short train ride from London, it thrived as a watering place with its pier and pleasure gardens and little theatre, but since the advent of package deals to foreign parts with guaranteed extra sun, it has suffered a sad decline. The villas have become care homes, hostels, half-way houses and private language schools. The pier is haunted by wraiths: sad foreign students, homesick and chilled to the heart by the brisk east wind, mingle with down and outs who once, as children, had a happy holiday here and have washed up on this coast in a muddle of alcoholic nostalgia.

It is breathtakingly cold here this morning and The Wellington School of English seems to be economising on its heating bills. The sandwiches are from Marks and Spencer's, but I'm still feeling sick and can't enjoy them. My colleagues are all too polite to ask me who socked me on the jaw but it may be a tacit sympathy vote that allows me to get my way over the thorny questions of wobbly desks and waiting areas for oral exams. Our students have enough to contend with without having to write at desks which wobble about and threaten to collapse. It's particularly hard for those students – Chinese, Japanese, Thai, Greek, Arab – who are writing in a new script, and they regularly get docked marks for poor handwriting. A letter must be sent to the exam board, I urge, demanding decent desks. As for the orals, students waiting for their turn sit outside the exam room and can hear everything examiner and student say through the thin partition wall. This can be a blessing in enabling them to prepare or a curse in sending them into a spiral of panic.

'Either way, it's NOT RIGHT,' I trumpet, and I go on, with increasing stridency, to insist that the hotel must be tackled and told to provide a proper waiting room.

Trivial issues, you may think, and I suspect my colleagues think so too, but for some reason, this morning, they seem matters of critical importance to me. The others gaze at me in puzzlement and I see myself in their eyes, not just the usual scruffy, pushy Gina, but a woman turned slightly alarming by her stridency, her battered face and her evident closeness to tears.

I leave the meeting in plenty of time to catch the 2.53 train, since the ice is frozen solid on the pavements here and the slithering stumble to the station isn't to be undertaken in a hurry. The train is dirty and chilly, as they always are on this line, and it stops constantly, but I sit on it passively, noting, as I always do, the succession of unmistakeably Saxon place names along the way: Washam and Culham, Little Felling and Church Ritton, Elmcote and Eastcote, Ladyfield and Shepton Halt. I hear *Shepton Halt* several times before it occurs to me that it would be possible for me to get off the train when we get there, go round to Charter Hall to pick up one of their DVDs and be back in Marlbury on the next train.

I'm worried that David won't give priority to getting hold of a DVD, that he'll start asking questions and putting the wind up those slime-balls at the theatre, and they'll dump the DVDs in the river or somewhere before we can get hold of one. I should have faith in him, I know, and I do, really, but I can't bear the thought that they might get away. Also, I would like to get a look at this studio David talked about. I want to see it because I think I can deal better with the images which danced in my head all night if I've got a real life image to keep them at bay. As we approach Shepton Halt, I remember something I saw in yesterday's local paper: there was a picture of Glenys Summers and the announcement that she would be switching on Marlbury's Christmas lights today. What time? I can't remember and I need to know. I can't risk bumping into her again. I call my mother.

'Virginia?' she asks. 'What's happened?'

'Nothing's happened. I'm fine. I just want to know what time the Christmas lights are being switched on.'

'Why?'

'Oh, you know, congestion in town and so on. I'm wondering whether to take a taxi from the station or if it's better to walk.' (When did I become such a smooth liar?) 'Could you have a look in the local paper for me? It's in the recycling probably, but it'll be near the top.'

She is away for ages and Shepton Halt is approaching. I'm just deciding I'll get out come what may when she is back on the line, a little breathless. 'Four o'clock at the clock tower,' she says.

'Excellent. I'll be home soon after five, I should think. And don't worry, I'm absolutely fine.'

The steps up to the bridge at Shepton Halt are icy and I'm negotiating them with care when a thought occurs to me. The train I've just got off is the London train. Anyone getting the London train from here has to cross the bridge to get to it. How did Glenys get over here with a sprained ankle on that fateful afternoon when her daughter died? Her ankle was too bad for her to drive, so Colin drove her. Presumably he helped her over the bridge too. I have an absurd but arresting image of him picking the little woman up and carrying her over the bridge.

No-one has swept the drive at Charter Hall. There are tyre marks but no footprints in the virgin snow, I notice. The house looks secretive, shuttered and, under a sky that's now metallic grey, deeply unwelcoming. I crunch up the drive as fast as I can and head round the side of the house. To my right are the stables where I saw the DVDs, and I dodge inside. Initially, I think I've lost my bearings and gone to the wrong place because it looks quite different: the stalls are all there but they are completely empty. I run up and down, looking hopelessly into each as though I can conjure back the stacks of boxes. I was right: the police have screwed up and the whole lot are now at the bottom of the river. Or were they moved weeks ago? Were they moved on the day I saw them, even, a few days after Marina's death? Was that what Cunningham and Driver were arguing about in the Morgan that afternoon? Whatever is the case, this has been a fool's errand and now I'm facing forty minutes standing around on a freezing platform waiting for the next train.

I might, at least, be able to get a look at the studio. I emerge from the stables to look around and see that, over to my left, in contrast to the untouched drive, the snow has been trodden underfoot. I walk over to have a look. I was a rotten girl guide and failed to win my tracking badge but even I can see that someone has walked between the outhouse here and the river bank several times.

'White man he go that way,' I murmur and I walk towards the little quay where – and I don't know why I should be surprised by this – I find the blue boat, bobbing innocently on the water, packed with what looks, at first sight, like the contents of a rather naff pre-teen girl's bedroom. There is a Little Miss Sunshine duvet, a pink, fluffy rug rolled up, a rocking horse, a heap of furry animals and what looks like a folded backcloth. As it dawns on me what this is, I think I'm going to vomit. Saliva rushes into my mouth and I lean over, preparing to throw up, but I am stopped in mid-heave by something more alarming: the sound of someone walking up the drive towards me through the snow.

Well, of course they are. If I can follow footprints in the snow, so can they. Cunningham and Driver. David, no doubt, rattled their cages this morning and they've been here to destroy the evidence, and what a bonus! Here's nosey parker Gina Gray, who inconveniently survived being knocked on the head the other night, presenting herself for another pop. What will they do with me? Knock me out and dump me in the freezing river, I assume.

I turn round and head for the outhouse to my right, slithering and half running but keeping my feet, as much as I can, in the tracks that are already there. I find myself in a genuine theatre store, the acceptable face, one might say, of the Aphra Behn presence at Charter Hall. There are flats stacked against the walls, a chandelier and a full moon hanging from hooks in the roof, a leafless tree, a throne and a painted screen in the middle of the space, with a welter of chairs and stools filling the rest of it. I edge in, looking for a hiding place, sweating in spite of the cold, holding my breath, desperate not to knock anything over.

Slowly, slowly, I edge my way round the tree, the throne, the chairs, aiming for a door standing ajar at the far end. As I go, I'm straining my ears for the sound of those footsteps in the snow and I think whoever it is has followed my tracks into the stables, which gives me a couple of minutes but not more – it doesn't take long to search empty stables. Forcing myself to breathe slowly, I edge my way through the door into the room beyond.

It's darker in here and I have to stand still, listening to the bouncy thumping of my heart, until I can look around. It's a smallish room, maybe ten feet square, and it has nothing in it but a tall cupboard – locked, as I soon discover. I've got no doubt that this is the studio. *This is where it happened*, I think, and with the thought come images which threaten again to have me throwing up. *Don't be so bloody wet, woman*, I mouth silently and I home in on a second door, which stands next to the cupboard. I don't want to open this door. I'm rattled enough by this time to be panicked at the thought of what I might find there. What do I imagine? Well, anything, really. If this were television, there'd be a child tied up in there, or even a body. Is it ridiculous to think that's what I might find? Just how vile is this business I've stumbled on? I have no idea.

I don't like the fact that there's a key in the lock. I turn it, listening intently for any movement inside. Nothing. I push the door open a few inches and cold air rushes in on me. There's no room, no cupboard, no horrors beyond, just the world outside and the back door of Charter Hall facing me and a lit window beside it. Through the window, I can see someone moving about, someone standing at a sink, washing up. Renée Deakin. Without thinking, I rush across and hammer on the back door. All I can think of is that in there, in that bright kitchen with Renée, I'm bound to be safe. When the door opens, I almost fall inside.

Renée stares at me, puzzlement and alarm written almost

comically on her face. She reminds me of an Edwardian manual for actors I saw once, which gave examples of appropriate facial expressions for different emotions – grief, joy, anger, surprise et cetera – all ludicrously overplayed. I take a deep, wobbly breath and laugh unconvincingly. 'I'm so sorry, Renée,' I say. 'I must have given you an awful shock banging on the door like that. Someone chased me up the drive –'

I see her face close in disbelief. I'm afraid she thinks I'm mad and I remember what odd clothes I'm wearing – the red hat, the fur coat, the après-ski boots. With sudden inspiration, I say, 'Boys! Throwing snowballs. Nasty ones, packed hard.' Her face relaxes infinitesimally but I know she needs more. 'I was coming to see Glenys,' I say, and then I can think of nothing more. Inspiration fails my figuring brain. I can come up with no reason, no reason at all, why I should be visiting Glenys Summers whom, as far as Renée knows, I've never met.

'Glenys is in Marlbury,' she says. 'She's switching on the Christmas lights.'

'Of course she is,' I cry. 'How stupid of me.' I'm no longer watching Renée's face, though, because I've seen another one, at the window, pale against the gathering gloom outside. Neil Cunningham. 'You seem to have another visitor,' I say.

She glances at the window. 'Oh, it's Neil. They've been moving some props to take down to the theatre, for the pantomime.'

Neil Cunningham's face moves away from the window and then there's a light tapping at the door. As Renée goes to open it, I back further into the room, towards a knife block which stands near the cooker. He doesn't come in, though. He stands outside but his voice comes through clearly. 'Renée darling, I'm off. Taking the boat. I'll be back with it tomorrow. Thank you for the lovely cuppa earlier. Warmed the cockles it did.'

'You're very welcome, Neil. You know it's always a pleasure to see you.' Renée's voice sounds different – breathy, stagey, the vowels over-careful. 'I'd offer you another cup but you should get going before you're frozen in.' She gives a little gurgle of laughter.

'Oh yes, Captain Shackleton, that's me,' he says, and she gurgles again.

'Bye!'

'Bye!'

She closes the door. 'He's such a charmer,' she says. 'He always calls me *darling* like that. I don't care so much for Alex but Neil always goes out of his way to be pleasant.' She fills the kettle, switches it on and goes back to the sink.

Wasn't there something odd and contrived about that conversation? Wasn't Neil Cunningham really sending a message to me? Telling me he was going, that it was safe for me to leave, when all the time there'll be someone else out there in the winter evening, waiting for me? I look at my watch. It's a quarter past four. If I don't leave soon, I'll miss the train and then I'll be stuck for an hour waiting for the next train, prey to anyone who's after me, if not to hypothermia. My only chance of safety is to leave with Renée. They can't attack me while I'm walking down the drive with her, can they? Unless –

A wave of sweaty terror sweeps over me. Suppose she's in this with them. You'd need a woman around, wouldn't you, if you were luring children out here? Someone to deal with the model agencies and reassure parents? She's star-struck enough, isn't she, to do what Neil tells her? Or Glenys tells her. Could she – and the thought makes me sit down suddenly on a kitchen chair because my legs feel as though they might go – could she be the person who killed Marina? She didn't have much of an alibi, did she? What did she say? That she drove by that afternoon on her way to pick up the boys, but didn't call in because the doctor's car was there. But she could easily have been there earlier, couldn't she? The police wouldn't have checked out her alibi all that carefully because they'd no reason to suspect her. And she could have been the woman who made the call from the phone box in the morning – called her own number and left a message on the answer phone, which she wiped later.

I hear the sound of an outboard motor starting up. The boat's leaving. She turns to look at me, drying her hands on her apron. 'Would you like a cup of tea?' she says. 'You don't look very well, if you don't mind me saying. Very pale. I hardly recognised you when you came in the door. Have you had flu or something?'

Her tone is reassuringly normal, but then it would be, wouldn't it, if she's a clever killer? I don't know what to think and I'm so tired now that I can't go on making the effort. I've used up all my energy getting here and if I'm in a trap, then I am. I undo my coat, lean back in my chair and close my eyes.

'Thank you, Renée,' I say. 'I'd love a cup of tea, if you don't mind. As a matter of fact, I'm not feeling wonderful. I haven't had flu or anything but I did have a rather nasty experience the other night.' I prise my eyes open so I can watch her face. 'I was mugged. Someone hit me over the head as I was walking through the abbey cloisters in the dark. They didn't steal my bag though – only a DVD I had with me – a DVD of *Amy*, actually. Luckily, I was wearing a big, thick fur hat, otherwise I'd still be in hospital, I should think – or dead.'

There is unfeigned shock on her face, I'm sure of that. She certainly didn't know about this, even if she is working with them, and if she's so shocked by the idea of my being mugged, can she possibly be the person who hit Marina over the head? I don't know. My head feels so fuzzy I have to stop thinking. I take my tea, which is bracingly strong, and put some sugar into it. Renée watches me with the disapproval of a woman for whom calorie counting is a basic tenet of existence. She sits at the table and chats about her boys, and I murmur agreement, admiration, sympathy, surprise. I let myself relax. This is only a temporary reprieve, I know. There's still the walk to the station to be negotiated, but I'm glad of this respite at least.

Eventually, Renée says, 'Well, I must be getting going. My husband will be home with the boys.' I wonder if I can ask her for a lift to the station, but as she's putting her coat on she says, 'I didn't bring the car today. I didn't fancy the roads round here, so I walked.'

That's it then. We walk down the drive together, she chatting inconsequentially, I alert to every stir and breath. At the end of the drive, she says, 'You take care of yourself, now,' and she turns to the left and walks away, leaving me to turn right and face the terrible shadows in the lane ahead. And then, before I've gone more than a few yards, there's a sweep of headlights and a crunch of wheels and a car squeals to a halt beside me. I can't run. I've no strength for running, but as the driver's door opens and someone gets out, I close my eyes, open my mouth and prepare to scream my head off.

'Get in the car,' a man's voice says.

24

FRIDAY 19th NOVEMBER

08.30: OPERATION

'The first step is the DVD,' Scott said. 'Everything else follows from that. If we can't get hold of one then we've no grounds for search warrants.'

It was eight-thirty in the morning. He and Andy Finnegan had just parked behind the Aphra Behn Theatre; Steve Boxer and DC Sean Lytton were drawing up beside them; a squad car was parked in the boatyard next door; Paula Powell and Sarah Shepherd had gone to Marlbury Abbey School to talk to Edmund Carson.

'There's a light on,' Finnegan said. 'Someone got in there early.'

'Let's see who it is.'

The stage door had a key pad on it but there was a bell beside it, which Finnegan leaned on. There was a light patter of feet from inside and the door opened to reveal a young woman, no more than five feet tall, wearing dungarees and carrying a large bunch of keys on her belt. She peered at them through small steel-rimmed glasses; they flashed their warrant cards.

'Detective Chief Inspector David Scott. We'd like to talk to Neil Cunningham or Alex Driver.'

'They're – they're not in yet.'

'When do you expect them?'

'Alex is usually in by nine, Neil a bit later.'

'Fine. We'll wait outside then.'

Scott turned away and then turned back. 'There is just one thing you can probably help us with,' he said, pleasantly. 'We're wanting to get hold of a DVD of the stage show, *Amy*. I believe it was recorded here and you have some copies.'

'Well, I don't know if I can –'

'It is quite important,' Scott said, taking a step over the threshold. 'It's in relation to a serious assault that took place two days ago in the abbey cloisters. A DVD like that was one of the items stolen. It's important that we get hold of another – for comparison.'

Andy Finnegan pushed in past the girl. 'Where do you keep them?' he asked. 'Down here is it?' He set off down the passage with the girl in pursuit.

'I think I've seen them in Alex's office,' she was saying, 'but – well – OK, it's the one on the left at the end there.'

Scott followed and she unlocked the door with one of the keys at her waist. Inside, the office was tidy – pathologically so, Scott thought. The desk was empty but for a phone, a clean memo pad and a neatly-stacked in-tray; books and files stood upright on shelves; a cafetière and two mugs stood, clean and shiny, on a small table; a filing cabinet was topped by a single, glossy plant. The only item in the room that seemed even slightly out of place was a large cardboard box, standing behind the desk, under the window.

'In here, are they?' said Finnegan and thrust a hand into the box. 'Thanks very much,' he said, pocketing a DVD. 'Do you want a receipt?'

'Oh no, I expect it's all ri –'

'I think we'll give you one,' Scott said, and he sat at the desk and wrote briefly on the memo pad. 'Mr Driver will see that when he gets in.'

Outside the stage door, Scott said, 'Let's have it then, Andy. I'm going straight back to look at it. You and Boxer wait for Cunningham and Driver. When they arrive, take one each. Keep them pinned down in their offices till you hear from me. Keep them talking. Ask Cunningham again about the evening of the mugging and see how much you can rattle Driver about the DVDs. If this DVD's as incriminating as we think, once they know we've got it, they'll be desperate to get away. Don't let them.'

Back at the station, he headed for the room occupied by Marlbury's small vice squad. Only Sanjay Gupta was in there. 'Mind if I watch something in here, Sanjay?' Scott asked.

'Be my guest. Want me to join you?'

'I don't know. I'm taking a punt. It may just be a naff musical.'

'Sounds fun.'

Scott slipped the disc into the DVD player and they sat and watched for a few minutes. It was odd, Scott thought, that it felt less embarrassing to be watching with another officer than it would have been to watch it alone. After a while, he pressed pause. 'There's no doubt what it is, is there?'

'No. I've seen a lot worse. This is pretty soft as these things go, but no-one's going to be able claim it's just a home movie.'

'How do you stand it, Sanjay, week in, week out? Doesn't it get to you?'

'The day it doesn't get to me I'll apply for a transfer. If I didn't feel outraged I couldn't do the job.'

Scott stood up. 'Well, I've got a call to make. I guess the fall-out from this will be coming your way.'

'We'll be waiting.'

Back in his office, Scott called Andy Finnegan. 'Andy? Where are you?'

'I'm talking to Mr Driver.'

'Good. Bring him in.'

'Really?'

'Really. Have you got Lytton with you?'

'Yup.'

'OK. What about Cunningham?'

'No sign yet.'

'Right. I'll talk to Steve.'

To Steve Boxer he said, 'Wait for Neil Cunningham. You'll see him coming – he drives a very distinctive car – a Morgan. Call for back-up from the squad car and arrest him as soon as he gets out of his car.'

'I take it the DVD was the goods then, guv?'

'Oh yes.'

He had hardly put his phone down when Paula called. 'What's the story?' she asked.

'It's porn. Paedophile, as we thought. How did you do with Edmund?'

'Not well. He denies everything. Agrees that he has sold DVDs but insists that they were legit – a recording of *Amy*. Says Gina must have got hold of a rogue one from somewhere – nothing to do with him.'

'Was he able to show you genuine *Amy* DVDs?'

'He was awfully sorry but he's fresh out of them. Went like hot cakes, apparently. Do you want me to bring him in and confront him with the stuff on the DVD? See if we can shake something out of him?'

'Not yet. He's a minor – we need to go carefully. Stay with him, though. I'm sending someone over with a search warrant. Keep him there and give his room a good going over. I'll ring the headmaster and tell him what's happening.'

Canon Aylmer was predictably resistant to the prospect of a police search. 'Really, Chief Inspector, I hardly think – all this has already been most disruptive. Mr Bright has had to leave a class to sit in *in loco parentis* on your officers' interrogation of the Carson boy.'

'Crime is disruptive, I'm afraid.'

'But surely this search can be done on a more unofficial basis.'

'There's no such thing as an unofficial search, sir. I'm sure you'll understand that we have to follow procedure.'

'And what exactly do you expect to find?'

'I can't say exactly, but the search is in connection with the distribution of pornographic material.'

'Oh, well.' Canon Aylmer gave a little laugh of relief. 'If it's top shelf magazines you're looking for, I don't know why you're picking on Edmund Carson. I'm afraid you'd find them under a lot of the beds. Adolescent boys, you know.'

'It's a good deal more serious than that, sir. We're talking about the distribution of obscene images of children. I wouldn't be wasting my officers' time on anything trivial.'

'All the same, I'm not sure I can give permission without –'

'With respect, Canon, I don't need your permission. I'm informing you as a matter of courtesy. One of my officers will be arriving with a search warrant in the next half hour.'

He called the duty sergeant to get search warrants issued for the school and for the theatre, then he looked at his watch. Not yet ten. The next step was to talk to the Carsons and he wanted to take Sarah Shepherd with him. He made himself a cup of coffee and stood drinking it, looking out of his office window, waiting for Finnegan and Lytton to return with Alex Driver. When he saw them arrive, he went down to greet them. Driver was handed over to the duty sergeant and Scott took his officers on one side. 'It'll do him good to sweat for a bit,' he said. 'Andy, I need you to go back to the theatre for a search. Top to bottom. You know what you're looking for. Take one of the guys in the squad car in with you. Sean, I'll drop you off at The Abbey School. You can help Paula with the search of Edmund Carson's room. I'm picking up Sarah Shepherd and taking her out to Charter Hall with me.'

The temperature had risen under a weak, struggling sun, and the roads were slushy as they drove out to Lower Shepton. In the unswept drive of Charter Hall, however, snow still lay thick. Scott rang the doorbell and clattered the heavy, wrought-iron knocker, but got no reply. Ten-thirty, he knew, was early for Glenys Summers. He led the way round the side of the house, glancing into outhouses as he went, feeling the snow begin to leak in through the seams of his shoes. The little blue boat, he noted, was missing from its place by the landing stage.

They found Hector Carson in his lair, dressed in a huge coat with a moth-eaten fur collar. The room was cold enough to send their breaths spiralling up in steamy clouds, despite the pungent smell emanating from a calor gas heater near the desk. Hector Carson gazed at them, mild and perplexed.

'Was I expecting you?' he asked.

'No, sir. Detective Chief Inspector David Scott. You remember me?'

'Oh. Yes,' Carson said unconvincingly.

'And this is PC Sarah Shepherd. She was your family liaison officer – after your daughter's death.'

Light came into Hector Carson's eyes. 'Do you have some news?'

'I'm afraid not. We're here on a different – though probably related – matter, regarding your son, Edmund.'

'Edmund? Has something happened to Edmund?'

'No. Edmund is quite all right, but – you haven't had a phone call from the school, then?'

'I don't answer the telephone, I'm afraid. I find it such a distraction.'

'I see. Mr Carson, I'd really like to talk to you and your wife together about this. Do you think we could go into the house?'

'Well,' he said gazing about him vaguely, 'what time is it?'

'10.45.'

'Oh, that's a little early for Glenys, I'm afraid. Her beauty sleep, you know…'

'Perhaps just this morning you could wake her? This is quite important.'

'But nothing has happened to Edmund?'

'No.'

'Well, we can go indoors and see.'

He led the way, not round the side of the house to the front door but between some outbuildings to the kitchen door, which he opened, ushering them into a large, hardly modernised, Edwardian kitchen, where the remains of a solitary breakfast still lay on the table. Leaving them there, he went into the interior of the house and they heard his heavy tread on the stairs.

From force of habit, they looked around, opening drawers and cupboards, glancing at postcards stuck to the fridge. Scott was amused to see that Sarah Shepherd also checked the bread bin and the freezer, favourite emergency hiding places, but theirs was not in the nature of a real search. Scott had a warrant in his pocket but he wasn't ready to use it yet.

Hector Carson returned, looking anxious, and said his wife would be down soon. He waved vaguely to chairs and the three of them sat round the table, contemplating the remains of Hector's breakfast, which he seemed to have no will to clear away. They sat in silence: Scott did not want to say any more until Glenys appeared and neither Sarah nor Hector came up with any small talk. Thus they were when Glenys appeared in the doorway. She was wearing a towelling dressing gown and slippers but she had stopped to put make-up on, Scott thought – nothing excessive, just enough to give her the dewy complexion of a younger woman.

'What's this? A wake?' she asked. 'Haven't you offered our guests a cup of coffee, Hector?'

'No, really.' Scott put up a hand to forestall her. 'We're fine.'

'Well,' she said, 'I think I'll have one. Hector darling, would you mind?' He stood up and she took his chair. 'Now, Chief Inspector, what's all this about?'

'This morning, Mrs Carson –'

'Glenys, please!'

' – two of my officers, one of whom was PC Shepherd here, interviewed your son Edmund in his room at Marlbury Abbey School with regard to the selling and distribution of obscene images of children. We believe that he has been selling DVDs containing pornographic material.'

She was neither shocked nor amazed, and she was too shrewd and too canny an actress, he thought, to attempt to feign shock and amazement. Instead, she looked at him very steadily, opened her eyes wide and said, 'And what does Edmund say about that?'

Scott ignored the question. 'I understand,' he said, 'that DVDs of your stage show, *Amy*, are being stored in one of the outhouses here.'

'And who told you that?'

'We conducted a thorough search here, Mrs Carson, after your daughter's death.'

'I see. Well, you know more than I do. I never go into the outhouses. I've made one of them available to the Aphra Behn Theatre, and what Hector and the children do with the rest of them is up to them.'

'But you know of the existence of these DVDs? You remember the recording being made?'

'I do, vaguely. It wasn't a big deal. Only two cameras, as I recall.'

'Have you ever watched the recording?'

'Now why would I want to do that?'

'What about you, Mr Carson?' Scott asked.

Hector Carson looked round from mopping up some spilled coffee and said, 'I'm sorry?'

'Oh do come and sit down, Hector,' his wife said. 'Forget about the coffee. Have you seen any DVDs of *Amy* around anywhere?'

'Aah,' he said, 'I don't –'

'You won't get anything from my husband, Chief Inspector,' she said. 'He's not of this world, I'm afraid.'

'Would you mind if we had a look for the DVDs?'

'Be my guest, though I don't quite see how they connect to this alleged crime of my son's.'

'We believe that the DVDs he has been selling are packaged as DVDs of *Amy*.'

'And what makes you think they're not of *Amy*?'

'We've watched one of them.'

If she was shocked now, she showed it only by the slightest flush.

'And you obtained this one from Edmund?'

'Tell me,' Scott said, waving her question away, 'when *Amy* was recorded, who made the recording?'

She hesitated for a moment. 'Neil arranged it, I suppose. I really didn't take an interest.'

Scott stood up. 'Thank you,' he said. 'There's just one more thing before we go outside to look round. You had a housekeeper when you were away in Switzerland. Can you tell me her name?'

'What on earth does she have to do with anything?'

'It's one of a number of leads we're following to a paedophile ring we think Edmund may have been drawn into.'

'Oh really, this just gets more and more ridiculous.'

'The name of the housekeeper, Mrs Carson?'

She looked at her husband and then back at Scott. 'I was very sick while we were away. That's why we went. I was in a clinic for most of the time. Hector made all the domestic arrangements. I suppose I knew he'd found a housekeeper, but I have no idea of her name.'

'Mr Carson?'

'The housekeeper you employed in Gimmelwald, Hector. I don't suppose for a moment you can remember her name?'

'Name? Oh no. It was some time ago. So much has happened, you see, and...'

He trailed off. Scott stood up. 'Never mind. But it does mean, I'm afraid, that I shall have to bring in a team of officers to go through all the papers in the house until we find her name and address. We do try not to create too much chaos, but I can't guarantee that the papers in your study won't get mixed up quite a bit.'

Animation sprang into Hector Carson's face. 'No, no!' he said, struggling to his feet and toppling his chair over. 'I really can't have that. There is years of research in my room – years. If my notes are disturbed, I shall never...'

'I understand that, sir. So if you could find us the name and address yourself, you'd save everyone a lot of trouble. I suggest PC Shepherd goes over to your study with you to help you find what we need. Meanwhile, I'll take a look round outside.'

He glanced back as he walked away from the house and saw Glenys Summers standing at the kitchen window, watching him, her face inscrutable.

His search yielded nothing: the stables where Gina had, presumably, seen the boxes of DVDs, were empty. Other outhouses held theatrical paraphernalia, some stacks of mildewed books and several rusty bicycles, together with the assortment of useless and broken objects that accumulates where there is no will to throw them away. He returned to the car, switched on the engine to get the heating going and waited for Sarah.

She appeared five minutes later, triumphant. 'Not a problem at all,' she said. 'It turns out he kept a diary while they were in Switzerland. Said he couldn't get on with his writing so he kept a diary instead. I could just get the name, but I thought you might want to take the diary away.'

'You thought right.'

Armed with his search warrant, he commandeered the six volumes of Hector Carson's Swiss journal. Carson tore at his wild hair and protested tearfully; Scott was impressed by the way Sarah soothed him but found himself with little sympathy for the man. They piled the books in the car and departed.

Back at the station, Scott learned that Neil Cunningham had still not turned up at the theatre and that officers sent to his home had found it empty. Boxes of papers were being brought in from the search of the theatre; the Carsons' boat had been seen moored near the scene dock; Edmund Carson's room and common room locker were as clean as a whistle.

Scott took Paula with him to see Alex Driver. When he looked in through the spy glass of the interview room door, he saw that he was pacing the room with the contained, neurotic energy you see in caged cats. Offered coffee and a cigarette, he took both. Questioned about the DVDs in his office, he insisted, initially, that, as far as he knew, they were recordings of *Amy* and that whatever the police claimed to have found was planted evidence. Told that all the DVDs in the box contained criminal material, he suggested that boxes had been switched without his knowledge.

'Where did the box come from?' Scott asked.

'It was cluttering up the under-stage space,' he said, drawing on his cigarette in a way Scott found irritatingly Noel Coward. 'Neil wasn't happy with it down there so I brought it up and gave it a temporary home.'

'And who put it under the stage in the first place? That would be your responsibility, I imagine?'

'Oh yes, I put it there.'

'And where did it come from?'

'From the person who made the video, I assume. It just

turned up one day. I think Lynette – our ASM – must have taken delivery of it.'

'What did you plan to do with the DVDs?'

'Oh the whole thing was a cock-up. Neil assumed The Duchess of York's management would sell them and take a cut, but they didn't want them because it wasn't filmed there, so they became a white elephant. I thought we might be able to get rid of them during the panto season – sell them in the foyer.'

'Were you present at the recording of the show?'

Driver took a sip of his coffee and grimaced theatrically. 'I was in and out.'

'And can you tell me who was doing the recording?'

'Doing the recording? Yes, it was Glenys's son – Edmund Carson.'

'You're sure of that?'

'Quite sure.'

'Wasn't it odd not to use a professional?'

'According to his mother, he's a gifted amateur, and Neil likes to save money. He arranged it. It was up to him.'

'Mr Driver,' Scott said, 'we have a box full of pornographic material taken from your office, and my officers are removing from the Aphra Behn Theatre material which is very likely to incriminate you. Would you like to start again? Wouldn't you like to forget this pathetically unconvincing tale you've been telling me and try telling the truth?'

Driver stubbed out his cigarette. 'Thanks for the fag,' he said, 'but you can take the so-called coffee away. Rat's piss might be preferable.'

'We'll be keeping you in custody over the weekend,' Scott said, with a glance at the duty solicitor, who had sat silent throughout the interview, 'so you'll have the opportunity to see if you prefer the tea.'

He ate lunch in the canteen with Paula, who was quiet and

distant. That suited Scott, who wanted a chance to think. Afterwards, he took Hector Carson's journal up to his office and started to read it. The early stuff was tedious – obsessive detail about the travel arrangements for the journey out – and he found the whole thing irritating in its self-conscious style and its air of portentousness, but he persisted and began to build up a picture of the life the family had lived in Grimmelwald. Gina had been right in her supposition that no-one had been paying much attention to the children. Hector wrote of endless days at the clinic, soothing, cajoling, distracting. Glenys, at least in the early months, seemed to have been always on the point of discharging herself and Hector had appointed himself as her loving gaoler. Of Edmund and Marina he found barely a mention, though he scanned forward into the record of the second year of their exile. He found the name he was looking for, though. The housekeeper who had had charge of these two lost children was a Mme Ducret, Martine Ducret, and her husband was Armand Ducret.

He looked at his watch and was surprised to find that it was already four o'clock. He needed Boxer back to track down the Ducrets. It was unlikely that Cunningham was going to turn up at the theatre now. He called Boxer. 'Come back in, Steve.' He said. 'And stand the others down. I've got a job for you.'

Unable to settle to anything else while the evidence was still coming in, he decided to phone Gina. It was, after all, only fair to let her know that her hunch held true thus far. He called her home number and, after a delay, was answered by her mother. 'Virginia's not here,' she said, 'and I really don't know where she is. I tried to keep her at home, but she insisted on going to a meeting out on the coast – Dungate, she said, I think. She phoned some time ago to say she was on the train, but she said she wouldn't be home till after five, so I can't think where she's gone to now.'

'What time did she call?'

'About three-thirty.'

'I see. Thank you.'

So where was she? She'd worried him yesterday: there was something hectic about her. She'd escaped from the house on some pretext and taken a train – where? He knew where. Of course he did. She couldn't trust him to do his bloody job, could she? He'd made a joke of it when she called out to him to make sure he got hold of a DVD, but she was serious. She really thought it was all up to her. Well, she hadn't gone to the theatre in search of a DVD, so there was only one other place she could have gone.

He got in the car and drove out to Lower Shepton. It was growing dark and the snow was hardening on the country road, so he had to take his time, cursing as he went. Driving through the village, he noticed a sign to the station and turned off. It was possible that she was there, waiting for the train back. He climbed the steps onto the bridge and scanned the handful of passengers on the far platform, waiting for the Marlbury train. There was no sign of Gina.

Back in the car, he drove towards Charter Hall. There were no pavements here but he scanned the sides of the road. Approaching the house, he saw two women emerge and part. One started to walk towards him – an odd-looking figure in a red hat and a long fur coat. When did you see a woman in a fur coat these days? Then the beam of his headlight caught her face, eyes shut against the light, mouth open, and he braked hard. Getting out, he looked across at her.

'Get in the car,' he said.

She opened her eyes. 'David? What the hell are you doing here?'

'Ditto?' he asked grimly, taking her arm none too gently and pushing her into the passenger seat.

'Where are you taking me?' she asked.

He ignored her, turning the car and setting off at a speed he knew was too fast for the state of the road. He had no intention of talking to her; he was too angry to trust himself. In the end, though, it was her uncharacteristic silence that made him glance at her. She was leaning back against the headrest with her eyes closed and he could see the glinting snail trail of a tear running down her bruised cheek.

'What happened?' he asked.

'Nothing. It's all right. I just spooked myself, that's all,' she said, but she didn't open her eyes. 'I just wanted to get another DVD. I knew they'd get rid of them as soon as you –'

'I know what you thought. You thought I was stupid.'

'No! It was just – anyway I was right. They'd all gone.'

'Yes.'

'So, did you get hold of one?'

'Yes.'

'You did?'

'Yes.'

'And?'

'And you were right. That's what I called to tell you.'

'So, what –'

'We've made an arrest.'

She opened her eyes. 'Who?'

'I'm not telling you anything more, Gina. You're out of control.'

'Well, it's not Neil Cunningham, I know that. I've just seen him, getting rid of – of the evidence.'

'What evidence?' His voice was sharp.

'Some of the stuff you saw on the video, I should think.' He could hear tears threatening. 'The contents of a child's bedroom. He took it away in the boat.'

'Right.'

'Glad to be of service.'

She had been shocked and scared but she was putting on a

good show, he had to admit, and as she climbed out of the car he watched her gather the last shreds of bravado about her. 'Thank you for the lift,' she said. 'So much quicker and more comfortable than the train.'

He watched her as she stumbled up the path and fumbled for her door key. As he rolled down the car window to call out a futile injunction to keep out of things from now on, the door flew open, a voice said, 'Where have you been, for God's sake?' and she seemed to topple headlong into the house.

25

08.00: INFORMATION

'I've got them,' Steve Boxer said. 'Armand and M-M-Martine Ducret.'

He had something good, Scott knew. The stammer was the way Steve betrayed excitement.

'And?' he asked.

'And they're both in Swiss prisons.'

'For?'

'He for a sexual assault on a minor and taking pornographic images of children – seven years; she for the procurement of minors for indecent purposes and the distribution of pornographic images of children – five years.'

'When were they convicted?'

'Last year.'

'Get me all the details you can, Steve. Names and addresses of the children involved, if possible.'

'Could be difficult. The Swiss are hot on protecting witnesses.'

'See what you can do.'

He looked round the room. 'What else have we got?'

'We've got Neil Cunningham in custody,' Andy Finnegan said, with studied casualness.

'Good work, Andy. How did you find him?'

'I thought he might try to get into the theatre during the night, to see what we'd taken. I put a couple of men on patrol. They spotted him round the back just after five this morning. It was still dark, but he triggered a security light.'

'What was he doing?'

'Mooring the Carsons' boat.'

'Anything in it?'

'Practically nothing.'

'There was stuff in it when it left Charter Hall yesterday.' To Andy Finnegan's questioning glance, he added, 'He was seen by a witness.'

'So he delivered it to somewhere else on his way?'

'More likely ditched it in the river.'

'What kind of stuff was it?'

'Nursery stuff.'

'That figures. I said the boat was practically empty. There was a doll. Cabbage Patch Kid sort of thing. One that got away, I guess.'

'What did you find at the theatre?'

'Plenty, potentially. Files of agents' photos of kids and mailing lists of addresses too far afield to be theatre-goers in Marlbury.'

'Good. Now comes the crap job, Andy. I need you to watch that DVD all the way through and look for matches with the kids in those agents' brochures. Did anyone check the DVDs in the box? Do they all have the same number on them?'

'I checked,' Paula said. 'There are fives on the top and sixes underneath.'

'Then you'll need to watch one of each. Paula, how do you feel? Are you up for joining Andy on that?'

She gave him a long look. 'Course I am.'

'Good. Anything else?'

'Prints,' Paula said. 'Edmund's prints are on the DVDs. We took a sample of ten and his prints are on all of them.'

'On the discs themselves?'

'Discs and cases both.'

'So the chances are he packaged them up. Right, we'll bring him in. I'll do it. Sean, you come with me. They'll have Saturday morning lessons at The Abbey, so he'll still be there. The headmaster's bound to kick up a fuss so I'd better be there. Arresting him will bring the Carsons in, I imagine, but that's no bad thing. Andy, before you start on the DVDs, pass those mailing lists onto Vice. Get them to run checks on all those names. Paula, I want searches of Driver's and Cunningham's houses right away.'

Canon Aylmer did not, in fact, kick up a fuss. When Scott phoned him, he quickly abandoned bluster and accepted the inevitable, grateful for the suggestion that he summon Edmund to his study so that he could be removed discreetly. Edmund was pale and watchful, but seemed unsurprised at their arrival. When offered the chance to phone his parents, he declined; when offered the choice of the duty solicitor or the family solicitor, he opted for the duty solicitor. The duty sergeant phoned his parents anyway. The phone went unanswered and he left a message.

Back at the station, Scott went to interview Neil Cunningham. He'd been thinking hard, on the way back from Marlbury Abbey School, about Cunningham's behaviour. Why hadn't he and Driver moved faster to destroy evidence? Why were the DVDs still there yesterday? Why hadn't the photos and mailing lists been shredded? Once they knew Gina had a DVD, they must have known it was all up, mustn't they? Mugging her and taking the DVD back was a desperate act but it could only buy them a bit of time. Stealing only the DVD and none of her other belongings had been an amateurish mistake, only drawing attention to its significance. But they had taken no action, and Cunningham's first concern had been to destroy evidence from Charter Hall. Could it be that they hadn't realised that they were in the frame? Edmund knew that Gina had seen the DVDs at Charter Hall. When she turned up with one, he would naturally have assumed that she'd got it from there and he'd have passed the information on to Driver and Cunningham. Their priority, then, had been to get rid of the DVDs at Charter Hall and the evidence that filming had gone on there.

He left Edmund Carson with the duty sergeant and went to the interview room where Neil Cunningham was waiting for him. It must have come as a shock to Cunningham to find that, while he was busy cleaning up Charter Hall, the police had been taking sacks full of evidence away from his office, but there was no evidence of shock now. He sat back in his chair, hands loosely clasped on the table in front of him, an expression of amused alertness on his tanned face. His silver-grey hair was smooth, his clothes unruffled. A casual observer would have taken him for interviewer rather than interviewee. Unlike Alex Driver, he had rejected the offer of a solicitor. Scott fought down rising fury. Who did these people think they were, Driver, Cunningham, the Carsons, with their undentable confidence, their teflon-coated detachment, their amused superiority?

He switched on the tape, introduced himself and Sean Lytton and got started. 'Mr Cunningham,' he said brusquely, laying out on the table photocopies of the brochures and mailing lists taken from his office, 'these are copies of items taken from the desk in your office at the Aphra Behn Theatre. As you can see, they are model agencies' brochures showing pictures of children, and mailing lists with addresses in this country and continental Europe. Can you tell me the purpose of these items?'

Cunningham smiled. 'I run a theatre, Chief Inspector Scott. Agents send me pictures of their clients – and we have to maintain contact with our audience base.'

'Don't play games with us, Mr Cunningham. It's a waste of everybody's time. Only a handful of the addresses on these mailing lists are local. These are not potential audience members.'

'You'd be surprised how far our fame spreads.'

'And the photographs?'

'As I say, agents send them – of adults as well as children.'

'Why do you say that?'

'What?'

'Why are you at pains to suggest that you have photos of adults as well as children?'

'Oh, please. Now who's playing games? I'm not stupid. I know what you're after. If I'm brought in here in a dawn raid and questioned about photographs of children, I can work out what general area we're talking about. Though I have to say I'm not sure where the mailing lists fit in. Am I supposed to be engaged in selling children by mail order?'

'In effect, yes.'

'Really?'

'What do you know about DVDs, apparently recordings of the show, *Amy*, being stored at your theatre?'

'I've seen them around.'

'Have you watched one?'

'No.'

'But you organised the recording?'

'I believe Alex Driver, my stage manager, did that.'

'Glenys Summers says you did it.'

'Why have you been talking to Glenys? I really would advise you not to go to Glenys for your information, Chief Inspector. She's not reliable.'

'But it was Edmund Carson who made the recording?'

'Edmund? No, I don't think so. Why Edmund? He's only a boy.'

'I was informed that Edmund did it.'

'Well you were informed wrong. I've told you, leave Glenys and her family out of this.'

'Were you present when the recording was made?'

'No.'

'So you don't actually know who made it?'

'I'd know if I'd paid a schoolboy to do it.'

'Who did you pay?'

'I really don't recall. It was months ago. You have all my records now. No doubt you'll be able to find out.'

'Further stocks of these DVDs were being stored at Charter Hall until a short time ago. Why would that be?'

'I have no idea. Christmas presents, perhaps.'

'If I told you that I've watched one of the DVDs found at your theatre and it contains pornographic material designed for paedophiles, you would be amazed, I suppose?'

Neil Cunningham leaned back in his chair. 'I would be amazed,' he said.

'What did you mean when you said that Glenys Summers was unreliable?'

'I meant leave her out of all this. It's all Glenys can do to get herself on stage every night. Leave her alone.'

'I'm interested that you're so anxious to protect her, Mr Cunningham. What did you do with the material you removed from Charter Hall yesterday afternoon?'

He saw the manicured hands on the table opposite him clench, momentarily, into fists. 'What material?'

'You tell me.'

'I don't know what you're talking about.'

Scott leaned forward. 'I'm talking about a boat-load of soft toys, bedding and nursery furniture. You were seen going up river from Charter Hall yesterday afternoon in a motor boat belonging to the Carson family, with a load of that description. Shortly after five this morning, you moored the boat behind the Aphra Behn Theatre. It was empty except for one item. Would you like to tell me what you did with the rest?'

'This is sheer fantasy. I know quite well who has told you this story and it's utter nonsense.'

'Do you deny that you brought the boat up to the theatre?'

'Of course not.'

'And what did you do with it between leaving Charter Hall around 4pm and arriving at the theatre at 5am this morning?'

'I moored it at the bottom of my garden –'

'– Which is just outside Marlbury. We know. I have officers there searching the premises at this moment.'

'And you really expect to find a stash of fluffy toys there?'

'No, I don't. I assume that you ditched your load in the river as soon as it was dark – all except this.' He placed on the table an evidence bag containing a rag doll. 'I'm quite prepared to drag the river between here and Lower Shepton, but I'd far sooner you told me where you dumped the stuff. We have enough evidence now to charge you with possession of indecent images of children; by Monday, when you appear before a magistrate, I expect to add further charges. Co-operating with us is really your only option at this point.'

'I think I'd like my solicitor here at this point. I take it that's all right?'

'That's all right, but if you're thinking of applying for bail, I should tell you we shall oppose it. We have good reason to believe that you would attempt to intimidate witnesses. We'll pick up where we left off when your solicitor arrives.'

Scott and Lytton got themselves coffee from a machine and Scott tried ringing Charter Hall again. There was still no reply. 'We'll go and see him anyway,' Scott said. As they were walking to interview room two, his phone started ringing. He checked the caller ID: Gina. He switched it off.

They found Edmund in animated conversation with the

duty solicitor, a young woman Scott had not met before. She introduced herself as Laleh Shahidi and asked if Edmund's parents had been contacted. Edmund intervened. 'There's no need, Laleh – I can call you Laleh, can't I? I don't want to worry them. You may not know, but my sister was killed only a few weeks ago.' He shot a reproachful glance at Scott. 'I really don't want them bothered with this nonsense.'

'If that's your client's decision,' Scott said to Laleh Shahidi, 'then I'd like to get started.' She gave a little gesture of reluctant agreement and he turned to Edmund. 'I understand you've been selling DVDs of your mother's show, *Amy*.'

'Then you understand wrong. I haven't.'

'You were seen selling one. You offered to get one for one of your teachers.'

'Oh, her!' He gave Scott a disconcertingly adult look and Scott felt himself begin to flush. 'She wanted one and she seemed to be so into it, I said I'd get her one. That doesn't mean I sell them.'

'We removed a box of DVDs, packaged as the recording of the show, from the Aphra Behn Theatre yesterday. Your fingerprints were all over them – both the packaging and the discs themselves.'

'I don't deny packing them up. Doesn't mean I sell them.'

'If you don't make any money out of them, why pack them up?'

'Just doing my bit. And I get paid for the hours I put in.'

'Did you make the recording?'

'What?'

'Was it you who filmed the show?'

'No, of course not.'

'But you are keen on photography and film? You have a studio, don't you, at home?'

'If you can call it a studio. It's just an old pigsty, actually.'

'If you didn't film it, who did?'

'How should I know?'

'Alex Driver says you filmed it.'

'Alex Driver would.'

'What's that supposed to mean?'

'You can't trust Driver, Chief Inspector. You can't believe a word he says.'

'Not a good person to go into business with then, is he?'

'I wasn't aware that I had.'

'Your mother says Neil Cunningham arranged the filming; Cunningham says he left it all to Alex Driver; Driver says you were the cameraman; you say you know nothing about it. You've not done very well at co-ordinating your stories, have you?'

'Why all this fuss about who did the filming anyway?'

'Because there never was a film, was there? It was a fiction – just a cover for what you were really filming, and selling.'

Edmund leaned back in his chair. 'This is fascinating,' he drawled. 'Do go on.'

'It will come as no surprise to you to hear that when we watched these so-called show DVDs, we found instead footage of indecent and obscene acts involving young children. In other words, pornography designed for paedophiles.'

'Really?' Edmund tipped his chair back on two legs. 'How extraordinary.'

'We know that Alex Driver and Neil Cunningham were involved in this too. We have incriminating material from the theatre and we have them both in custody. Now we have you, too, and my next step will be to arrest your parents.'

'I've told you – leave my parents out of this.'

'No, I don't think I will. Boxes of those DVDs were stored at your home. I don't believe for a moment that they didn't know they were there. In fact, everything points to them being the instigators of this nasty little business. I think it's time they told me the truth.'

'LEAVE them OUT of this!' Edmund was leaning forward, all his affected languor gone, the colour hot in his pale face. 'It was mine, OK? I thought of it, I brought in Alex and Neil, I did the filming. The recruiting – using the model agencies – the boat – everything – it was me. I'm the mastermind.'

'And did you also try to kill Mrs Gray?'

'No!' He laughed. 'I'm not owning up to that.'

'Only it's obvious that she was attacked because she knew too much and had a copy of the DVD, and Driver and Cunningham both have cast iron alibis.'

'How convenient.'

'Isn't it? Driver was back stage at the theatre – actually "on the desk", we're told – and Cunningham left the school after the debate with a canon from the abbey and went into his house in the precincts for a glass of whisky. Unless the canon was also part of your enterprise?'

'I'm afraid not.'

'So that leaves just you. You knew Mrs Gray had the disc – in fact you tried to get it off her – you were at the debate and could easily have followed her. You knew there was scaffolding conveniently lying around in the cloisters. You say you went to your room afterwards but nobody saw you go. An unanswerable case, I would say.'

'Really, Chief Inspector,' Laleh Shahidi broke in, 'it's no such thing. It's purely circumstantial. My client –'

'Your client can speak for himself, Laleh. I didn't do it, Chief Inspector, and just to save you time I'll give you a bit of help. Why don't you talk to Bright Boy?'

'Bright boy?'

'Mr Marcus Bright, our esteemed head of sixth form.'

'How is he involved in this?'

'He's involved like the pervy little creep he is. It was pure luck that I realised he'd be interested. Oh, he's only a punter – doesn't do the business side – but it's made it much easier for me to do business, knowing he wasn't going to come crashing down on me. And I could always get an *exeat* from old Bright Boy if I wanted to do an afternoon's filming.' He stopped. 'Look, I really don't want to talk about this any more.' He turned to the solicitor for support.

'My client requests a break,' she said.

'Five more minutes,' Scott said, 'and then that'll do for now.' He turned to Edmund. 'How could you be sure the children wouldn't tell their parents what had been going on?'

'I've been there. I know how it goes. You know it's wrong, but you think you're the one who'll get into trouble. Grown-ups can't be wrong, can they? Besides, they all want to be stars, these kids. Tell them they'll never get another gig if they spill the beans and they'll keep their mouths shut. And we paid them. Their parents pocketed what the agencies paid; we slipped the kids some cash for their trouble.'

'Are you sure Marcus Bright attacked Gina Gray?'

'Well, I didn't see him do it, if that's what you mean. Really, you people expect everything on a plate don't you? All I can tell you is he was in a complete funk when I told him she'd got a DVD – career in ruins etc – and I saw him follow her into the cloisters. Make of that what you will.'

You had to admire his coolness, Scott admitted. He was like his mother in that.

'Just now, when I asked you why the children didn't talk, you said you'd been there. What did you mean,' he asked.

Edmund gave him a sour little smile. 'You went to police college, didn't you, Chief Inspector? Didn't they tell you that the abused become abusers?'

'Are you telling me you were abused?'

'Sounds like it, doesn't it? Oh, not by my parents.' He held up a warning arm. 'Don't get that idea. Not by them.'

'But by the people who were supposed to be looking after you when you were in Switzerland. M. and Mme. Ducret?'

'How do you know about them?'

'We're the police. We know a lot.'

'And you guess the rest.'

'Sometimes. They filmed you, I suppose, you and your sister? And made a lot of money out of it. So when you came back to the UK, you thought you'd have a go at it.'

'I wanted to go to a good school.'

'You were paying your school fees? And you expect me to believe that your parents weren't involved?'

'I told them I'd got a scholarship. Well, I have, actually, but it only covers tuition fees. I wanted to be a boarder, so I needed to find the rest.'

'And what about your sister?'

'What about her?'

'What was her part in all this?'

'She was no use. She got freaked by what happened to her in Switzerland. She couldn't handle it.'

'But she knew about it, didn't she? What happened? Did she come back early from school one day – one of those days when she was worried about her mother – and find it going on?'

Edmund said nothing. His animation had left him. He sat slumped in his chair. Scott continued, 'So you decided she had to be silenced, did you? Your own sister, a little girl of thirteen?'

Edmund roused himself. 'I didn't do it. You know I didn't. I was in class.'

'Yes, you were. So who did kill her? Was that Marcus Bright too?'

Edmund looked at him for a long time. 'I don't know,' he said.

Marcus Bright started by blustering, soon declined into whining and quickly petered out in a welter of tearful confession. Yes, he had attacked Gina Gray, but he hadn't meant to do her any harm He'd just wanted the DVD back. He had a headship in his sights and he couldn't allow her to wreck it all. Not that he had been involved in the making of the DVDs or the selling of them – he'd just watched them, only watched them. It was a weakness, he knew, but it was pretty harmless stuff, really – he doubted the children involved thought anything was wrong. It didn't make him a worse teacher, did it, that he liked these things? He had never touched a child in his care, and never would. Was it fair that his life should be wrecked because of this one weakness? When Scott pointed out that that he'd comprehensively wrecked it now by getting charged with GBH, he managed a smile. 'It's always the cover-up, isn't it?' he said.

He had an alibi for the afternoon of Marina's murder, though: he had been teaching and twenty-two GCSE History students could vouch for him. He had given them a test that afternoon, and their dated answers in their exercise books testified to it. So who had killed her? They had everything else: the DVDs, the mailing lists, the confessions. They could prosecute the four of them – Carson, Cunningham, Driver and Bright – and be pretty sure of convictions. But they still didn't have the killer.

26

SATURDAY 20ᵗʰ NOVEMBER

Daylight and champaign discovers not more

I am woken by the unprecedented arrival of Annie bearing a mug of tea. As I struggle out of the frowsty cocoon of my drugged sleep, I ask, 'What's wrong? Why are you here?'

'I came to see YOU. Ellie said you'd been nearly killed. I came to see you and you weren't here and Granny didn't know where you were and we were frantic, and then you came home and fainted all over us.'

'Fainted? Did I?'

'Don't you remember?'

In a way, I do. Only I would have thought it had been a dream. I do remember lying somewhere and they were all looking down at me: Annie, Ellie, my mother, even Freda. 'Was I out for long?' I ask.

'No. I thought you were dying but Granny was very imperious. She said, "Open your eyes, Virginia" and you did.'

'There's no saying no to Granny.'

'And then she took charge and we got you into bed and she gave you a sleeping tablet and I hope you had a good night's sleep.'

'I did.' I sip my tea. 'I feel ready for anything this morning.'

This is not true. I feel rather peculiar, actually, but I can't possibly spend the day under the iron tutelage of Annie and my mother. 'What time is it?' I ask, groping for my watch and my glasses, neither of which I can find.

'Nearly ten o'clock. We let you sleep. We've been up for hours. We're going to the supermarket. You're to stay there. Granny'll be here if you need anything.'

'I'll need to come with you,' I protest.

'No you won't. You're not going anywhere, especially not in those clothes you were wearing yesterday. How could you, Ma? You looked like some random bag lady.'

'They took my clothes for forensic whatever...'

'Anyway, Granny's put us in charge. We're shopping and we're cooking.'

'You – cooking?'

'El can cook. You're not to think about anything. Granny says you need a complete rest.'

I drink some more tea. 'OK,' I say.

'There is just a question of the money for the shopping, though,' she says. 'Neither El or I are up to financing it.'

'Pass me my bag.'

I hand over my debit card and my PIN number and she leaves. I lie with my tea, listening to the sounds of the house – the shouting, the running up and down stairs, the cries of protest from Freda, my mother's stick on the tiles in the hall – and I try not to think about yesterday. I try not to think at all.

Ellie arrives with a plate of toast and marmite, another mug of tea and *The Guardian*. She announces that they're off. 'Don't try to go anywhere,' she says. 'Granny's guarding the door.'

The toast and marmite is good and I find that I'm rather hungry, which I take to be a good sign. Fainting! Oh really, how pathetic. How could I have done that? I finger the bump on my head. It's going down. No more excuses for being weedy. I pick up the paper and glance at the headlines, but I can't seem to engage with the news. I turn to the futoshiki puzzle – one of the pleasures of the Saturday paper – but I can't even get started. And the quiz looks unfathomable. Have I suffered brain damage? Will I ever function properly again?

I abandon distraction and allow myself to think about what I really want to think about. What do the police know? Who has David arrested? Why won't he tell me what's going on? Does he know who attacked me? Does he know who killed Marina Carson? How can I make him tell me?

I go to the bathroom and clean my teeth. On my way back, I glance in at the chaos of Annie's room and my computer sitting primly in the corner. I could, I think, just check my e-mails. That would feel like normal life without being too taxing. I delete a lot of spam and surf some trivia before deciding to send a message to Hannah. I realise that I never even let her know that Marina got killed, let alone that her diagnosis has helped the police to net a child porn syndicate (at least, I assume it has, and that David will tell me so in his own good time). I trawl back to have a look at her original message before writing mine, and that's when I see the link she sent me to Glenys Summers' fan site.

I click on the link, and there she is, quite a bit younger-looking than I've seen her recently, and winsome as buttercups and daisies. I read the text:

Glenys Summers is one of the best-loved actresses in the UK. Born in Cardiff, the youngest of three daughters of a postman, she started her theatrical career at the age of twelve, working in pantomime and summer shows. She starred in several television series in her teens, but her first adult role was as pretty, tragic Dora in *Oh Mr Copperfield*, the film musical that was to make her name in the wider world. Many other film musicals followed, including *Princess Anastasia*, *The White Cliffs of Dover* and *Queen for a Day*. A period of ill-health forced her into retirement at the height of her career but she made a triumphant return to show business in 2009, when director Neil Cunningham persuaded her to take the title role in *Amy* – her first major stage role.

Amy opened in the West End at the Duchess of York's Theatre in November 2009 and is still enjoying a sell-out run. Get tickets if you can!

Glenys lives near the small market town of Marlbury and says that her main hobby is country life. She was married to designer, Justin Chaput, but they divorced in 1998. In 2000 she married the well-known writer Hector Carson. They have one son. Their daughter recently died tragically, but Glenys says that work is the best cure for a broken heart and has gone on with the show.

I sit and consider this. I note the omissions and euphemisms – no date of birth and "a period of ill-health" – but what really strikes me are the dates. Surely they must be wrong? I google Hector Carson to check, and find not a fan site but a brief Wikipedia entry:

Hector Gordon Carson (born Edinburgh 1948) is best known as the author of *The Trilogy of Corisande*, a series of epic novels drawing on folk tales and Arthurian legend, first published in 1978. His subsequent work was not as well received, though his volume of poems, *Minstrel Boy*, was nominated for the Rupert Brooke Award in 1984.

In 1990, he married the painter, Janice Halwood, with whom he had one daughter (born 1997). Halwood died of cancer in 1998. In 2000, Carson married the actress, Glenys Summers.

I gaze at the screen; I flick back to the Glenys Summers site; I write down some dates; I consider them; I go back to my room and I call David Scott. He doesn't answer. I am returning to my computer when my mother, on the alert, calls from the bottom of the stairs, 'What are you doing, Virginia? Go back to bed.'

'Just going to the loo,' I lie.

'What, again?'

'Am I being rationed now?' I shout, and return to bed.

The "complete rest" my mother prescribed is out of the question, though. How can I rest when I've got this half-thought running round in my head? Because it is only a half-thought. It just changes the landscape a bit, so that what I thought before – and feared – seems more possible. I knew why and now I think I know who. What I don't know is how, and that's what David has got to work out. I phone again, and again ten minutes later. His phone remains switched off. What is he doing?

I lie and fret and from somewhere, unbidden, comes a picture of Annie's room as it was when I was in there just now. What was wrong with it? No bed. There was no bed in it. Just a sleeping bag on the floor. Because Annie's bed is downstairs in my mother's room. Her first visit home from university and she has to sleep on the floor and I haven't even asked her how things are going. Come to think of it, wasn't she looking thinner? And when was the last time I asked Ellie about school or about her play? And Freda? Panic grips me. Where is Freda? I haven't heard her downstairs? Did they take her with them or has my mother nodded off and left her to wander off God knows where? Useless. I'm a useless, stupid woman, obsessed with the death of someone else's daughter and thoughtless about my own. I'm hauling myself out of bed again to go in search of Freda when I hear the front door open and Ellie and Annie returning with the shopping.

I strain my ears for sounds of Freda and when they come running upstairs, bright-eyed and shiny-cheeked with the cold, to present me with a yard-long till-receipt I scream, 'Freda! Where's Freda? What's happened to her?'

The stop dead and stare at me, their smiles frozen. Then they exchange a look. 'She's downstairs, Ma. In the kitchen,' Ellie says.

'Well she shouldn't be left alone in the kitchen,' I yell. 'There are knives in the kitchen and bleach and she might turn the cooker on and –'

Ellie starts to say something but Annie gets in first. 'For fuck's sake, Ma, get a grip. She's unpacking the shopping and Granny's with her. Dr Fletcher left a prescription for some sedatives for you and we got it made up. I'm going to give you one.'

My phone rings and I grab it. 'David?' I say. 'What the hell have you been doing?'

The girls roll their eyes and depart.

'I've been working,' he says tersely. 'How can I help you?'

'I think I know who killed her, David. In fact, I'm sure I do.'

There is a silence. It's a silence with a suppressed sigh in it, I can tell. Finally he says, 'Listen, Gina. You had a lucky intuition and it's been helpful and we're working on it. But what's not helpful – what is, in fact, in danger of derailing the whole case and sabotaging a prosecution – is you deciding to conduct a one-woman investigation of your own. I assume you're off work and have nothing to do but sit around having bright ideas, but for heaven's sake just watch day-time TV or something.'

'Don't you dare be so bloody patronising. Well, all right. All right. Fine. If you don't want to hear what I've got to say, fine. But I'm entitled to information from you. I've been the victim of an assault. If you've charged anyone with that, I'm entitled to know. I'm entitled to know if you've found out who mugged me because then I'll know if I can feel safe.'

Now he sighs out loud. 'We have charged someone with the attack on you. We got a confession, in fact. And you are entitled to know who it is.'

'Which of them was it? Driver or Cunningham?'

'Neither.'

'So Edmund then?'

'No.'

'So who on earth –'

' Marcus Bright.'

'Marcus Bright? No! Why?'

'He was a customer. He knew if the DVD got to us the whole thing would come out. Said he didn't mean to do you any harm. He was just saving his skin.'

I'm actually deeply rattled by this news. When someone you thought of as annoying but harmless turns out to be thoroughly vicious in thought and deed, the world tilts on its axis a bit, but I'm not letting David know I'm shaken or he'll be telling me to have a nice cup of tea and a lie-down. So, I say, 'Marcus Bright! Well I always knew he was a sleaze ball. And that would explain why he was a bit half-hearted in that punt.'

'What punt?'

'Never mind. A long time ago and in another country. And besides the wench is dead.'

'Gina, are you all right?'

'Yes. Perfectly. So, is Marcus the person you told me you'd arrested yesterday?'

'No. We've got Driver, Cunningham and Edmund Carson. Now you'd better tell me about this idea of yours.'

'Not if you're just humouring me. I'm serious about this, David, and if you're not then I'll shut up and you can work it out for yourselves. I expect you'll get there eventually, and since I don't think it's a serial killer we're talking about, I suppose it doesn't matter if it takes you weeks to plod your way there.'

And then I hang up because I can feel my voice beginning to wobble and I'm absolutely not going to cry.

My phone rings almost immediately. 'You can't refuse to give information to the police, you know,' he says quietly.

I feel exhausted now. There was a kind of excitement in my discovery but that's gone and I'm just weary with the weight of the miserable truth.

'Well,' I say, 'You need to look at a couple of websites. You ought to look at the information yourself – raw, as I did. I don't want to interpret it for you. Let's see if you come to the same conclusion as I did.'

'So what are these web sites?'

'One is www.glenys-summers.com – it's a fan site. The other is Hector Carson's Wikipedia entry – you can google him. Look at the dates and call me back if you think it's worth it.'

I lie back and close my eyes. Annie appears with my lunch on a tray. 'Covent Garden soup and garlic bread,' she says, putting it down on the bed with a flourish. The soup is an alarming dark red. It looks like a bowl of blood.

'This soup?' I enquire tentatively.

'Beetroot,' she says.

'I have supped full of horrors.'

'What?'

My phone rings again. Annie snatches it up. 'Hello? No, this is her daughter. Who's that? Oh, Chief Inspector. No, I'm sorry, she can't talk to you any more. She's supposed to be having complete rest. Medical orders.' I have my hand stretched out for the phone and am hissing furiously at her to *give it to me*, but she gives me a teasing grin. 'She may be well enough to talk to you tomorrow,' she says. 'I'll tell her –'

'ANNIE,' I shout. 'This isn't a joke. Give me that sodding phone or I swear I will throw this bowl of soup at you.'

She hesitates. Then she tosses the phone onto the bed and sweeps out.

'David?'

'Gina? Are you –'

'I'm ALL RIGHT,' I yell. I take a deep breath. 'What did you think?'

There is a pause. I wait.

'The only interpretation –' he stops.

'Yes?'

'The only interpretation shouldn't necessarily mean anything as far as we're concerned, only you said something yesterday, as you were getting out of the car.'

'Did I? I wasn't really myself. I don't remember what I said.'

'Well, you said, "Thanks for the lift. It's so much quicker by car" – or something like that.'

'Oh, I see.'

'Do you? And then there are the steps.'

'The what?'

'The steps – over the bridge at Shepton Halt. Didn't you notice them?'

'Yes. I imagined Colin Fletcher carrying Glenys up them.'

'Which is possible. But the alternative is –'

'They were never there.'

'Exactly. You know him, Gina. What do you think? Could he have done it?'

'I really want to say no. His wife is my best friend; he's been our doctor for ever and ever. I've always thought he was a nice man – a good man, in fact. But –'

'But?'

'But, to be honest, I've never believed his story about what he did that afternoon. It didn't add up.'

'No. Well, I'm going to have to talk to him. Look after yourself. Bye.'

'David,' I say, just as he's about to click off.

'Yes?'

'Let me know.'

'Yes.'

I push my lunch away, wondering if, among all the other horrors, the world is about to come crashing down on Eve Fletcher's head. Well, I'm not staying here in bed, at any rate. There's a chance that David will call round after he's talked to Colin and I can't talk to him in bed again. Anyway, I need to be doing something and I need suddenly, urgently, to feel clean. I gather up a random assortment of clothes and head for the bathroom, where I run a deep bath, clean my teeth twice, wash my hair with great care, massaging gently round the tender bits, soak and scrub myself and clean my teeth over again.

I expect to find at least one of my gaolers outside the door, ready to pounce, but there's nobody there. I listen. From downstairs I hear rhythmic roaring and the sound of a man working himself up into hysteria. This can only mean that there is a football match on and the girls are engrossed. Mother, presumably, is taking a nap. My bath has exhausted me and I don't want to do any more thinking. The prospect of thinking is like the prospect of food when you're already full up, but when I sit down in the chair by the window in my room, to wait for David, my head refuses to empty. Instead, a whole new idea comes unbidden and takes root.

When the doorbell rings, I'm on the alert for it and I get to the door just before Ellie, Annie and Freda come straggling out of the sitting room. David hesitates on the doorstep as the girls loom threateningly behind me. I take hold of his arm.

'Come in,' I say. 'We'll go in the kitchen.'

I drag him down the hall, neatly side-stepping my mother, who emerges from her room, and I shut the kitchen door firmly behind us. We stand and look at each other. He looks pale and tired and – what? Sad, I suppose. Before he can ask me again if I'm all right, I say, 'You look dreadful. Would you like some tea?'

'Aren't you supposed to be doing nothing?'

'Making tea doesn't count.'

We sit at the kitchen table with mugs of tea and a new box of chocolate biscuits, purchased by the girls, which neither of us wants, and I ask, 'Did you see him?'

'Yes.'

'And?'

'And he denies everything. He drove Glenys to Shepton Halt, went on to his surgery – where he was seen, by the way – to do some paperwork, went back to Charter Hall to leave a message for Marina, found her dead.'

'Did you ask him about the steps?'

'Yes, and it shook him. That's how I know he's lying. I don't think he's ever been to Shepton Halt. Why would he? He didn't even know there were steps there, I reckon. But he's no fool. He rallied quickly enough. "Oh yes, the steps. Glenys did need a bit of help, but the ankle wasn't too bad really – only a bit of a sprain," he said.'

'Did you ask him about the DVDs?'

'Yes. He said he didn't know anything about them and I think he's telling the truth.'

'But that doesn't make any sense, does it? What would his motive have been?'

'I don't know.'

'So are you going to talk to her?'

'He's probably spoken to her already. She'll be fore-armed. And I've got nothing on her. Yes, you saw the DVDs at Charter Hall, but there's only your word for it and Edmund will swear she wasn't involved. So will Neil Cunningham.'

'What is it about all these men? Why do they all fall under her spell?'

'The mixture of vulnerability and knowingness. Like Marilyn Monroe, only without the figure.'

'Wasn't the figure the point?'

271

'Not altogether.'

'Well, I'm not under the spell and I've had an idea. It's a bit off the wall and your knee-jerk reaction will be to say no, but I think it could work, so please just hear me out.' He is watching me warily and I know I sound – and look – manic. I can feel that my cheeks are scarlet and I know my untended hair has dried into a wild frizz. I take a breath and pitch my voice low. 'I was thinking about evidence,' I say slowly, calmly. 'Now what I'm proposing is something a police officer couldn't do because it would be illegal, but I was thinking teachers – especially English teachers – often know more about kids' home lives than parents imagine. Children are always being asked to write about what they did at the weekend, or in the holidays. Sometimes they're even asked to keep a diary...' I go on, and he listens to me and doesn't interrupt except once, when I've nearly finished.

'You're not suggesting sending Ellie, surely? That's –'

'Of course I'm not,' I say. 'What sort of mother do you take me for? I'm suggesting sending me.'

27

SUNDAY 21st NOVEMBER

Nature with a beauteous wall
Doth oft close in pollution

I look at my watch. It is exactly 12.30pm. 12.30 on a November Sunday, when any right-minded woman with two daughters, a granddaughter and a mother staying in her house would be in her kitchen, listening to *The Food Programme* and peeling vegetables for lunch. Instead, I'm sitting in the back of an unmarked police car in the lane near the gates of Charter Hall with David Scott and Paula Powell. In another car, just up the lane, sit two more plain clothes police officers. Paula Powell is fastening a monitoring device to my bra. David is looking out of the window.

To be honest, I never really expected to be here. I came up with the idea and I was all prepared for a fight with David about putting it into action but I didn't really think he'd agree to it. And then, when he had agreed, I thought the posse at home would refuse to let me go, but David arrived on the doorstep at eleven-thirty, greeted the girls, patted Freda on the head, smiled charmingly at my mother and said, 'I'm afraid I shall need Gina for a couple of hours. Police business. I'm not arresting her, don't worry. I shall return her safe and sound. Got everything Gina?' And that was that.

So, here I am, and I really wish I wasn't. I feel sick and I want to blame David for the fact that I'm here, but when he asks if I'm sure I'll be OK I say, 'Of course I will,' so fiercely that Paula Powell gives me a startled look. David just says, 'Right then. We'll be listening to everything and we'll be communicating with you. Make sure you keep your earpiece in and if I give you instructions, follow them.'

Though the snow is melting in the town, here it still lies in mounds down the drive. The house looks bleak and lifeless and I have a sneaky moment of hope that Glenys may not be there. Hector is in his writing room, I know. Another policeman is in position at the back of the house and relayed this information to David while I was in the car. I wish I was better dressed for the scene ahead. A good costume does give one confidence but the police still have my coat and I know that Glenys will clock my fake fur as tawdry in a moment. Under police instructions, I'm wearing a baggy cardigan underneath too, to hide my equipment (no, please, this is not a *double entendre*) but I have eschewed the après-ski boots, and the wet slush is already soaking through my shoes. I reach the front door, take a deep breath and a firm hold on my briefcase and ring the bell.

It is answered quite rapidly, and there she stands in jeans and a huge, baggy sweater which makes her look tinier than ever. The blue eyes blaze open and narrow again. 'Why are you here?'

I smile brightly. 'You remember me?' I ask. 'Gina Gray. I was here before.'

'I know who you are. I asked why you're here.'

I brandish my briefcase. 'I've brought a few more things of Marina's.'

'What are they to do with you? I thought you taught at Marlbury Abbey.'

'An errand for my daughter. She's busy with the William Roper School play. I'm sure you know how it is.'

'All right. I'll take them.'

She puts out a hand, but I move the case out of her reach. 'The thing is, there are some things here which I really feel we need to talk about.'

'There is nothing I need to talk to you about. You didn't teach Marina. You can leave the books and go.'

'If I go, Mrs Carson, I shall have to take the books with me, and I'm afraid I shall take them to the police station.'

'What do you mean? What the hell are you talking about? What are the police going to do with them?'

'I think they're going to work out why Marina was killed. Do you think I could come in?'

The sitting room we go into is scuffed and shabby but grand in its proportions and pretensions, with carved cornices, swagged curtains and a chipped chandelier. A window in a deep recess faces down the drive, while french windows look out over the garden at the side. Glenys has obviously been enjoying her Sunday morning. There is a fire burning in the grate and a coffee cup and an empty cafetière are sitting on a small table by a cushion-strewn sofa. Pieces of *The Mail on Sunday* lie scattered around the floor. It's a surprisingly domestic scene, though her husband and children are, of course, missing from it.

She gestures me to the sofa while she takes an upright chair by the fire. I sink inelegantly among the sagging springs. *First move to you, Glenys.*

'Well?' she says.

'Well,' I say.

Unable to sit erect and look commanding, I decide to affect nonchalance. I take off my coat and sling it over the back of my sofa, I nestle my briefcase beside me, I lean back on my cushions. 'I've been taking a look through these books,' I say, 'and there are one or two things I feel you ought to know about. In Marina's English book in particular.'

275

She gives a derisive little snort. 'I can't imagine what you found there. The child could barely write.'

'So you did know about her problems with school work, did you? Only I gather the school had some difficulty communicating with you and Marina's father.'

She shrugs. My right ear suddenly crackles into life. 'Don't get side-tracked,' David's voice says. 'Stick to the point. Don't give her thinking time.' I want to respond, but that's obviously not the idea. 'Marina's standard of English wasn't high,' I say, 'but what she wrote is perfectly comprehensible. Perhaps she made more effort with this because it interested her. They were asked to write a diary, you see –'

'Fucking teachers,' she explodes. 'Sticking their noses in. Trying to spice up their dreary old lives. Like peeping Toms is what they are.' I hear the Welshness seeping back into her careful elocution. She stops abruptly, and then goes on in a changed tone. 'Anyway, I can't imagine what Marina can have had to write about that would be remotely interesting. She led the dullest possible little life. I was always trying to get her to go out like other girls of her age but all she wanted to do was hang around the house.'

'Yes, I imagine that was what caused the problem.'

'Problem?'

'She was around here at odd times – unexpected times – coming home from school in the middle of the day, for example. In the end she knew too much about what was going on here.'

She laughs. 'Going on here? Nothing goes on here. The arse end of nowhere this is.'

There's the Welshness again. I'm beginning to recognise it as a sign that she's rattled. But it doesn't last, and I must say I do admire her ability to switch tones. "Turning on a sixpence" I believe it's called in the acting world. Suddenly she appears to relax. Now she is all amused indifference. 'Well,' she says, rummaging around behind some videos and DVDs that stand on a shelf above the television and producing a bottle, 'I think I'll have a drink while I hear about the exciting goings-on at Charter Hall. Really, I had no idea the girl had so much imagination. Do you want one?'

'NO!' David's voice buzzes furiously in my ear. 'You don't. You need to keep sharp.'

Oh really? I never thought of that. Thanks for the vote of confidence, David.

'No thank you,' I say, and add primly, 'I don't drink whisky in the morning.'

'Really?' She leaves the room and returns with two glasses. 'Brought you one just in case,' she says. She pours the whisky into her glass with elaborate care, swirls it round, takes a good swig then sits down and says, 'Now, tell me this story. You do realise, by the way, that it is just a story, don't you? It must have crossed your mind that it's – well, probably not made up, but copied from something she'd read, I imagine.'

'I don't think Marina was up to reading anything as adult as this,' I say, 'and it doesn't read like something she's copied. There's so much left out, you see – so much she dared not write for fear of putting you in danger.'

I think this is the moment to produce exhibit A. I take the exercise book out of my bag, the unused book which I got from Ellie yesterday and spent the evening *distressing*. I've written MARINA CARSON with some twiddles on the front and I've added a few doodles on the cover – cats and flowers. Inside, I've filled about ten blotched pages. It wouldn't bear close inspection – it's more like a stage prop – but it's good enough to brandish from a distance.

'At first,' I say, flicking a few pages, 'I think she wasn't quite sure what writing a diary entailed. She writes a bit about the family – interesting in its own way but not what her teacher intended, I should think. One worrying thing – 'I flick through a page or two '– she says she lived in Switzerland for a year and "very bad things" happened to her and her brother there. I suppose you must know what she means?'

She drains her glass and goes to refill it. 'I really don't' she says, with her back turned to me. 'Very bad things were happening to me too.'

'Right. Only then she gets the hang of the diary business – or maybe it was the first time she felt she had anything worth writing about – and she describes a day when she went home early from school. She writes that she always knew when your nerves were bad and you might do "something silly". She worried about you.'

She gives a derisive hoot of laughter. 'Oh *my nerves*, my precious *nerves*. There's nothing the matter with my nerves – what did you say your name was? Jean?'

'Gina.'

'Well, Gina, there's nothing the matter with my nerves. Nerves of steel I've got. I like a drink, that's all. I'm a drunk. I've been pretty much on the wagon while I'm doing this show – you know about my show?'

'Yes, I've seen it – with your understudy.'

'Poor you. Well, I've fallen off only a few times, but the child got herself in a state about it. Thought I'd lose the part and we'd have no money. She wasn't bright but even she could see that her father wasn't bringing home any bacon.'

'And maybe she was afraid you might take her off to Switzerland again, where something very bad happened to her,' I say.

She looks at me and takes a swallow of her drink. 'Maybe,' she says.

David crackles in again. 'Get on with it. You're losing momentum. Surprise her.'

'Anyway,' I say, opening up the book, 'Marina wrote that she came home early one day. "*Mummy's friends from the theatre were doing something wrong. There were some children there with them and it was wrong. My brother was there too and I wanted to tell Mummy about it but he said it was a deadly secret and I must swear not to tell anyone, not even Mummy because it would upset her and make her ill."*

'So she went and wrote it all down. Marvellous!'

'I suppose she thought that wasn't telling anyone. After all, diaries are private, aren't they?'

'Well, it's all nonsense of course, anyway. God knows where she's picked up this stuff from. Off the internet, I suppose.'

'You don't know about Edmund then?'

'What about Edmund?'

'He's been arrested – yesterday – to do with child pornography, I gather.'

She slams her glass down on the floor beside her, where it keels over and whisky trickles out in a brown stream onto the carpet. 'Why wasn't I told? He's only a boy. They've no right to arrest him without telling his parents.' She stops and looks at me. 'How do you know, anyway?'

'I teach at Marlbury Abbey School. I believe the police tried to contact you yesterday. And so did the school.'

'Well, I was at the theatre and Hector doesn't answer the fucking phone. I'm going to the police station now. I'll pay his bail or whatever and bring him home. They can't possibly have any evidence against him. This is all nonsense. This story of hers must have got round and no-one has the sense to see that it's just a child's horror story.'

'The police have got evidence against Edmund. There's –' David nearly bursts my ear drum. 'You're not a police officer. Don't know too much.'

'Well,' I backtrack. 'I think there's some sort of evidence – fingerprints on DVDs was what I heard.'

She jumps to her feet. 'I'm going to the police station now. Where are my car keys?' She takes a step and treads on her glass. 'Fucking thing,' she says, kicking the broken glass under the chair. 'Car keys. Where are my fucking car keys?'

'You're not in a fit state to drive,' I say. 'If you get breathalysed you'll just be in more trouble. And the roads are icy. I'll drive you to the police station – when we've finished this conversation.'

'I don't want to finish the conversation. I want to see my son.'

'And so you shall,' I say implacably, 'when we've just sorted a few things out.'

I put the exercise book down on the coffee table in front of me and pat it gently. She finds the glass she brought in for me and half fills it. She takes two good swallows and sits down.

'So the situation was,' I say, 'that Marina had seen something going on – your friends and your son making porn DVDs involving children, I guess.'

'You guess. Guessing is what it is. It's all guesswork this – guesswork and her lies.'

'It's a bit more than a guess, in fact. I've seen one of the DVDs.'

Her eyes do that extraordinary thing that they do, blazing open for a moment, a very bright blue, and then closing to slits, much like a cat's. 'You've what?'

'I came across one. Well, they're all over the place, dressed up as recordings of your show. Here in your stables, down at the theatre. I even saw one in The Burnt Cake one day. Edmund was selling it. Anyway, it was pretty nasty stuff. I'm not surprised Edmund didn't want you to know about it.' She slurps her whisky and says nothing. 'So there was a dilemma,' I continue. 'A thirteen-year-old girl knows about the business and can't be trusted to keep quiet for long, even if she has been threatened. What's to be done? Answer – kill her. Silencing her was the only safe move. But now I have a problem with the story: who killed her?'

'Remember you don't know about the alibis,' David hisses.

'Your friends from the theatre?' I continue. 'Did I mention that they've been arrested as well? Or Edmund? Well, you'd like to think that a boy wouldn't kill his own sister. The chaps at the theatre I've met and they seem nasty enough for anything, but there's someone else who keeps coming into my head. I read the newspaper reports about Marina's death at the time and there was one person whose behaviour that afternoon didn't seem to make any sense.'

'And who was that?' she asks, looking at me over the rim of her glass.

'Dr Fletcher,' I say.

I watch her very closely but she hardly flickers. She just takes a swig and says, 'Colin?'

'Yes. I know Colin well. His wife's a great friend of mine and he's been our GP for years, but I couldn't make any sense of what he did that afternoon.'

'And why is that?'

'Well, piecing it together from the papers and from talking to Eve, it seems that around lunchtime he came out here to see you – and that's odd in itself because GPs don't go out to patients any more, do they? Not to young women with sprained ankles they've already treated?'

'Colin is an old friend.'

'I think he must be more than that, but we'll come to that later. Let's take it, for the moment, that he came out to see the ankle – or maybe to take a look at your nerves – then what did he do? He drove you to the station, went back to his surgery and then drove out here again, where he broke into the house, found Marina dead and called the police. Now, why did he come back? What was that about?'

'We hadn't left a message for her. He thought she'd be worried if she got home and found me gone.'

'But he's a doctor. He's not your private physician, he's not

281

a chauffeur, he's not a nanny and he's not Marina's father, yet he was behaving like all of those, apparently. I know Colin, and he's pretty brisk when he's in doctor mode. I just can't see him driving round the countryside on errands in the middle of a working day.'

'Perhaps you don't know him as well as you thought you did.'

'That's what I started to think. I asked myself what I would think of his behaviour if I didn't know him and think he was a nice man. And I thought, supposing he was part of this child pornography thing – very shocking, of course, a family doctor, a father and grandfather, but supposing he was – then he'd be desperate to keep it secret, wouldn't he? If Edmund told him that Marina knew, he'd have a choice between killing her and losing everything.'

She's watching me intently, all the affected indifference gone. 'Go on.'

'Well, at first I thought you must have summoned him to tell him that Marina knew, and – '

She raises a hand in protest. 'Don't bring me into this. I knew nothing about it – if there was anything to know. I just wanted stronger painkillers for the ankle.'

'OK. But you asked him to drive you to the station, so he knew the house would be empty. He went back to work and returned at about four, expecting Marina back from school at the usual time. She was already there of course, and he killed her, and then called the police. Or so I thought, but that doesn't work because he'd be the prime suspect if the police arrived and found her newly dead. So, he must have killed her earlier – between taking you to the station and going back to Marlbury. But then why did he go back later?'

'Perhaps he'd left something incriminating behind.'

'Yes, I thought that. Maybe he wanted to clean away any possible fingerprints. It was dangerous, though, because it brought him into the frame, got him involved.'

She sits for a long time, swirling her drink round, her feet tucked up under her in her chair. 'I knew there was something odd,' she says finally, in little more than a whisper. 'Alex and Neil were so secretive about what they were doing when they were here. And I did think I could hear a child's voice sometimes out at the back there. But people came and went, you know, from the theatre – stage hands and so on – and I never dreamt... as for Edmund being involved, it's nonsense, I'm sure. Alex and Neil are trying to save their own skins by blaming him. A boy! How could they do it?'

'And Colin Fletcher?'

'He was very strange that day. Very jumpy. He leapt at the idea of taking me to the station. Now I see why. I can hardly believe it. Colin. You never really know people, do you?'

I allow a good ten seconds of silence and then I give her a little round of applause. 'A great performance,' I say. 'One of your best.'

'What do you mean?'

'And you would happily let him take the rap, wouldn't you?'

'What the hell are you talking about? You're the one who –'

'Yes, I was, wasn't I? I was interested to find out just how rotten you are.'

'Excuse me?'

'No, I don't think I will. If Colin Fletcher killed Marina, you were in on it too. What my account left out was your phone call to Renée Deakin. Because it was your phone call, wasn't it? Whoever made that call did it to make sure the house would be empty when Marina came home, but there was no point in getting rid of Renée if you were there, was there? The caller had to know that you weren't going to be there either, and the only person who knew that was you.'

She has uncoiled from her chair and has her feet on the

ground. She is watching me with a kind of feline intensity. She is still clutching her glass but she has stopped drinking.

'Actually,' I continue, 'I was pretty sure that it was you who made the call all along. Ever since Renée told me what you'd actually said. It was that quote from *Macbeth* that did it – about battering at your peace. It put paid to the bungled burglary theory, anyway. Burglars' accomplices don't quote Macbeth, but you do, don't you? Your whole family. Edmund told me so. You put on a dark wig, nipped down to the phone box, called Renée, faking a cold to make it more plausible when you denied it later, and the coast was clear for you. You'd prepared the ground well: you'd done a leap from the stairs – which needed a bit of courage, I must admit – so you could persuade the police that it was you the killer had been out to get, and you'd given Marina whatever the signals were that would make her think you might go on a binge, so you could be pretty sure she'd come home at lunch time. I'm not sure what you fixed with Colin. Did he know what you were planning to do? Did you plan it between you, or was it an inspiration of yours to call him out so he could give you an alibi?'

I pause. I'm not really expecting her to answer but I'm feeling rather sick. I don't want to have to tell this bit of the story. She says nothing – just goes on watching me – so I have no option but to carry on. 'Well, anyway, I don't know exactly what happened that afternoon, but I guess it went something like this – do stop me if I'm wrong. You heard Marina's key in the lock and you waited upstairs in your bedroom. Marina came in and looked around for you downstairs. She couldn't find you so she went up to try your bedroom, and there you were, too nervous to go downstairs on your "broken" ankle. 'Just give me a hand, darling,' you said. 'Let me lean on you.' Then you put a hand on her shoulder and limped to the top of the stairs. And then you got yourself in position and gave her a good, hard push. You're a strong woman – I remember the way you wielded that spade. She was off guard, off balance, and down she went, top to bottom, onto the stone floor. And then you went down, took a golf club out of Edmund's bag and hit her hard on the head. That's the bit I don't understand. She was dead. The fall killed her. You must have seen that. Why did you need to smash her head in?'

For the first time, she peels her gaze away from me and looks down into her glass. She mutters something I can't hear. I can feel David holding his breath on the other end of my wire. 'I'm sorry,' I say, 'I didn't hear you.'

She still doesn't look at me but concentrates on swirling the drink round in her glass. The she says, quietly but clearly, 'I couldn't stand her twitching.'

'Wait,' David's voice is whispering. 'Don't say anything. Give her space.' I wait. She speaks again, angry this time. 'Her body – twitching – arms and legs like a big spider. I had to stop it. I had to make her still.' I go on saying nothing. I don't think I could speak if I wanted to. Finally, she drains her glass, reaches for the bottle and says, as she pours a glass full, 'And now you're going to say, *How could you? Your own daughter!*'

My voice, as I answer, comes out cracked, as though I've breathed in lungfuls of plaster dust. 'No, I'm not,' I rasp out, 'because she wasn't your daughter, was she?' She doesn't answer – just takes a swig from her glass. 'Marina was three years old when you married her father. You had a son, Hector was a widower with a little daughter. It was good publicity for you. Bury the drink and drugs rumours, underplay the rackety first marriage, hype up the family-life-in-the-country image. And it worked well. You made a perfect instant family – except I suppose it wasn't perfect, was it?'

She slumps back in her chair and talks to me with her eyes closed. 'I don't like babies. I don't like their mess and their clinginess and their whingeing. Edmund wasn't bad. He got used to the way I lived. I could leave him with anyone and he'd just get on with it. And he was such a beautiful child. Everyone admired him. A little star. And then I got landed with Marina – a clingy, whingeing little thing, always pulling at my clothes, mauling me about. And her father encouraged it, always picking her up and plonking her on my lap. *There we are! Go to Mummy then!* And there she'd sit, yattering away and peeing on me – it took her forever to get toilet-trained.' Then she looks at me. 'Oh don't sit there looking so pi. You want to try bringing up someone else's kid.'

'She had no mother,' I say. 'Her mother died. It's the worst thing that could happen to a tiny child.'

She laughs. 'Oh no. Worse is getting the wicked stepmother, isn't it?'

'Keep calm', David murmurs. 'Don't lose it.'

'Tell me,' I say – and my voice is admirably steady – 'did you know the children were being abused when you were in Switzerland? Because that was what happened, wasn't it? The "very bad things" that Marina wrote about?'

'Of course I didn't. If I'd thought anyone was harming Edmund, I'd – their bloody father was supposed to be looking after them.'

'But Edmund told you about it eventually, I suppose. He's a bright boy – very mature. He wasn't prepared to be a victim. He saw a business opportunity and when you all came back to England and money was tight, you and he hatched a plan for a nasty little business. And you knew a couple of nasty little men who could help you. A perfect set up: you provide the premises, they have the contacts with the child model agencies. And distribution? Does Edmund manage that?'

She says nothing. I feel exhausted. I'm on the last lap now but my legs are going from under me. 'Then,' I say, 'Edmund told you that Marina knew what was going on and you decided you'd have to kill her. But you couldn't do it all on your own. You needed an alibi, and who better to give you one than Dr Colin Fletcher, respected local GP?' I give her a moment but she doesn't respond. 'You're going to have to help me out a bit here,' I say, 'but I guess you rang Colin Fletcher just before you expected Marina home. You knew when to expect her – coming home at lunch time was what she did when she saw one of your "states" coming on. You told him something terrible had happened and asked him to come right away. I'm sure you put on a good performance. And when he arrived, did you tell him what you'd done?'

Her eyes open in genuine amusement. She throws back her head and laughs. 'What? Dr bleeding-heart Fletcher? I loved your story, by the way, making him into a murderer, but you're quite right – that won't wash. No, I couldn't risk telling him, not even with the way things were.'

I'm not sure what she means by this but I decide not to pursue it. Instead, I ask, 'So, what did you tell him?'

'You're so clever, you tell me.'

'Well, I suppose you told him it happened while you were – what – out in the garden? You came in and found her there. You were distraught, terrified. You didn't know if it was an accident or murder and if it was murder then the killers might still be in the house, so you called Colin. Most people call the police. How did you explain calling Colin?'

'*My nerves,*' she says.

'Of course. Your nerves. You couldn't possibly deal with it all – not after the terrible shock you'd had, and the grief – we mustn't forget the grief. Being interviewed by the police would be more than you could handle. It would drive you over the edge again, and this time you might not recover. Am I right?'

She looks at me. She's bleary from the whisky now, not as sharp as before. 'More or less.'

'And then you asked him to drive you to Marlbury – not Shepton Halt – to catch the train to London. It takes less than fifteen minutes from here to Marlbury on a clear road, but it takes twenty-five on the train because it's on a single track and it stops at all the piddling little stations on the way. If you made a quick getaway, you could get the 1.58 train from Marlbury and be safely in London when Marina's body was found. And, of course, if the police thought you'd got on the train at 1.33 at Shepton Halt, then they'd assume that you'd had to leave the house before Marina got home.'

She sits up straighter in her chair and looks at me again, more sharply this time, more focussed. 'How do you know all this – about the train times and all? I don't believe you're just some teacher. Who are you? Are you police?'

'I told you, I'm a friend of Eve Fletcher's. She told me about Colin driving you – only she thought he'd taken you to Shepton Halt, of course. I'm also a big train traveller. I know how inconvenient the steps are at these little two-platform stations and I thought how awkward it would have been for you at Shepton Halt with your sprained ankle. You know, it's funny how these things strike you.'

'Hilarious,' she says sourly. 'Finished are you, now?'

'Almost. Just one more question. I assume Colin lied to the police and perverted the course of justice and whatever else they decide to throw at him because he's your lover. Am I right?'

She twists her mouth in a grimace. 'My lover? Oh please! He's in love with me – of course he is – but that's not quite the same thing. I've let him go to bed with me once or twice, mind, but it was no fun. He was always overcome with guilt about his fat wife. Mostly what he wanted was to hang around me, panting with doggy devotion.'

'It sounds as though he had the same problem as Marina. Pity you couldn't push him down the stairs.'

'That's a sharp little tongue you've got in your head. I bet you're a bitch in the classroom.' She sloshes some more whisky into her glass. 'What I don't understand,' she says, 'is why

Colin had to come back here and "find" her. We'd agreed we'd leave her for Hector to find.'

'And you can't understand why he didn't do that?'

'No. It got him involved when he didn't need to be.'

'Then you don't understand him. He's a good man. A decent man. He agreed to protect you but he was never going to leave a dead child lying in an empty house for her father to find. He couldn't do that. Only someone without an ounce of humanity could.'

'Only someone like me.'

'That's enough,' David hisses. 'We've got enough. Get yourself out of there.'

'Well, on that note,' I say, 'I think I'll be going.'

I stretch out my hand for the exercise book, which is lying on the coffee table between us, but she is too quick for me in spite of the whisky. She snatches it up and, in a single movement, throws it into the fire. There one corner catches and it arches up and falls out onto the hearth. She jumps up, seizes it and hurls it straight at me. I don't register, for a moment, what's happening: I just have an extraordinary sensation of heat and a searing pain down my neck, and in my hands as I try to beat it away. As it falls to the ground, I stamp on it but the flames lick up and start to ignite the edges of my skirt. At the same time I realise that sparks are smouldering on my cardigan and there is the pungent smell of burning hair. I run to the French windows, yank them open, rush out into the garden and throw myself face down into the snow.

Feet come running towards me and I look up to see the policeman who has been stationed at the back of the house. I realise that I have summoned him. I have summoned him with my screaming. I think I've been screaming ever since the missile hit me. Now footsteps approach the other way. I roll over to see David round the front of the house, at a run, followed by a posse of policemen.

'Put the fire out and search the house,' he shouts, and stops to look at me, lying on my back in the snow.

'Are you all right?' he asks.

'I'm cool,' I say, and I start to giggle helplessly.

He pulls me to my feet and shakes me quite hard.

'What happened?'

'She set fire to me.'

He takes a look at the side of my neck where my hair caught fire. 'We'll get you to A&E as soon as we can,' he says. 'You're soaking. You need to get warm. Have you got a coat?'

We go back into the sitting room, where the fire has been quenched, though there's a lot of smoke. I'm shaking violently and I look round helplessly for my coat. David says, 'I need to take the recording equipment off you. It won't do it any good to get wet. Do you mind?' And without waiting for an answer, he has his hands up under my shirt and is detaching the stuff.

'This is very romantic,' I say, and the giggling starts up again. His mouth tightens into a very thin line, but he takes off his coat and puts it round me. It is warm with his body heat and the comfort of it steadies me. I wrap it closely round me and subside onto the sofa, where I hiccup a bit and concentrate on not shaking.

Then we hear, through the open windows, an unmistakeable sound – the sound of a motor boat starting up. With a curse, David rushes off round to the back of the house. He returns, still swearing. The policemen who have been searching the house come in, drawn by the sound of the boat. David turns on the young DC who had been stationed at the back.

'Well?' he asks, with dangerous calm.

'Sorry sir. I came running when this lady screamed and then I thought I'd be more use helping the search.'

'And how wrong you were. You've just lost us our killer.'

'Yes, sir.'

'It was my fault,' I say. 'I shouldn't have screamed.' David opens his mouth to say something and then seems to change his mind. 'If it's any help,' I say, 'I think she's wearing a fun fur coat.'

Paula takes me back to the car, where she digs out a first aid box and puts a sort of dressing on my neck. She then takes me to A&E again, and she's very kind really. I go a bit wobbly and hysterical before we get to the hospital and she takes it in her stride. She even tells me I did bloody well. She's a nice girl.

At A&E, they're disconcerted to have me in again so soon. They treat the burns all right, and say they're not too bad and the snow treatment was a good idea. The also give me painkillers and antibiotics and say I can go home later. I have the sense, though, that I have triggered some automatic alert by getting attacked twice in a week and they want to get Social Services on my case. It's quite touching really. In the end, Paula manages to convince them that the police have things in hand and they let me go.

As Paula drives me home, I'm dreading the outrage and recriminations that will be waiting for me, but I arrive to find the house in empty darkness. There are two notes for me on the hall table. One is from Annie, saying she has returned to Oxford since she doesn't seem to be needed; the other is from Ellie, saying she has gone to see Ben Biaggi, taking Freda with her. My mother, I assume, is having a nap. I creep up the stairs to my room, strip off my clothes and clamber gratefully into bed.

The painkillers send me to sleep in spite of everything and it's some time later that I awake in deep darkness to the sound of my door opening. My mother appears. I struggle to a sitting position. 'Don't go on at me,' I say. 'Just don't go on at me. I couldn't help it and it's not as bad as it looks.'

'David Scott's been round,' she says. 'Gave me an

explanation of sorts. Said you were quite a heroine.' And she bends over and kisses me on my forehead. It is so unexpected that it knocks the stuffing out of me. My breath rises in my chest in a great sob and the next moment she is sitting on my bed and I am weeping in her arms like the child I don't remember being.

Later again, Eve rings.

'Eve,' I say, 'are you all right?'

'Yes, I'm all right. They've arrested Colin. But that won't surprise you.'

'I –'

'It was you, wasn't it?'

'I don't –'

'It's all right. I've talked to Michael Fairbrother, our solicitor. He sat in on Colin's interview with the police. That taped evidence – the conversation with Glenys – that was you, wasn't it?'

'Yes. I am sorry, Eve.'

'Don't be.' I can hear that she's crying, but she goes on. 'You know, I've always wanted to believe that people were basically good. That they could be foolish or frightened or unhappy and that could make them hurt other people, but I never believed in wickedness and I never met anyone I thought was wicked. Except her.'

'Did Michael say anything about – about her and Colin?'

'The police don't seem very interested in that. I knew about it, of course, from years back, that he was in love with her. There was nothing to be done about it. I just hated to see her make him unhappy.'

'They haven't caught her, I suppose?'

'Not yet.'

'But they will, surely.'

'I wouldn't be so sure. She'll be good at disguising herself.'

'She's wearing my coat.'

'Well, there you are. She's got money, contacts and the ability to get more or less any man to do what she wants. I should think she's well on her way to a country where there's plenty of cheap drink and no extradition treaty with the UK.'

'But it'll be so unfair if Colin gets prosecuted and she doesn't. I'll just have ruined things for you and she'll get away with it.'

'Oh don't give yourself airs, darling. You haven't ruined anything. There are several people who come higher on my list of who's to blame than you do – and I'm one of them. Give yourself a break, why don't you? And get some sleep. You'll feel better in the morning.'

28

THURSDAY 25th NOVEMBER

08.00: AFTERMATH

The headline screamed from the front page of the *Marlbury Gazette*. Not litter in the town centre, not parking charges, not wheelie bin protests, not the controversial sculpture on the roundabout, not vandalism, not a mere smash and grab in the High Street, but a five-star juicy scandal such as a local paper editor can only dream of. Scott read the report as he waited for the kettle to boil:

THEATRE CHIEF ON CHILD PORN CHARGES

Neil Cunningham, director of Marlbury's Aphra Behn Theatre, appeared at Marlbury Magistrates' Court on Tuesday to answer charges of producing, possessing and disseminating indecent images of children. During the three-minute hearing, Cunningham, aged 52, spoke only to confirm his name and address and to enter a plea of not guilty. Appearing alongside him on the same charges were Alexander Graham Driver, aged 38, stage manager of the Aphra Behn Theatre, and a seventeen-year-old boy. Applications for bail by all three were rejected and they were remanded in custody.

Neil Cunningham is a widely respected theatre director

who has boosted the Aphra Behn's flagging audiences in recent years with a string of popular plays and musicals. Friends said yesterday that they were astonished at the news of his arrest. A spokeswoman said that the theatre's programme would continue as planned over Christmas and New Year. The theatre board will hold an emergency meeting on Friday.

A surprisingly accurate account for a local paper – for any paper – Scott thought as he sat down with his coffee. No embellishments, no speculation. He turned the page and his eye was caught by another headline.

LOCAL WRITER FOUND DROWNED

Local writer, Hector Carson, was found dead in his car in the River Mar in the early hours of Wednesday morning. The car was brought to the surface by firemen after neighbours spotted it in the river near Mr Carson's home, Charter Hall, in Lower Shepton. The police have revealed that Mr Carson left a note and foul play is not suspected.

When Mr Carson's 13-year-old daughter, Marina, died at the family home in tragic circumstances in September, the police launched a murder inquiry, but no arrests have been made.

It is understood that Mr Carson had spent much of the previous two days helping the police with their inquiries into the disappearance of his wife, the actress Glenys Summers. She has not been seen since she left home on Sunday afternoon in the family's motor launch. The police are very anxious to trace her and would be glad to hear from anyone who saw her on Sunday afternoon or since.

Mr Carson leaves a 17-year-old son, Edmund, who is a pupil at Marlbury Abbey School.

Might acute readers make the link between Hector's 17-year-old son and the 17-year-old boy in court? Were they intended to? Probably. Someone had got the story but was playing by the rules. But they were less likely to make the link with the story on page five. This story was accompanied by a smudgy photo, presumably culled from the *Gazette's* archive, of a rather younger Gina seen with some students at a college open day. Scott read:

ATTACK ON LECTURER

Mrs Virginia Gray, Head of the English Language Department at Marlbury College, suffered head injuries last week when she was attacked while walking through the Minster cloisters. Mrs Gray, aged 47, had been attending a function at Marlbury Abbey School and was on her way home. She was taken to hospital and received treatment, but was later released. A 48-year-old man has been arrested and is helping the police with their inquiries.

On the facing page was an equally blurred picture of Colin Fletcher beside the headline:

TRIBUTES TO LOCAL GP

Tributes have been pouring in to Dr Colin Fletcher, who surprised his colleagues and patients by announcing his retirement this week. Dr Fletcher, aged 58, has been a partner in the Cromwell House practice for thirty years.

Born in Marlbury, he attended the Abbey School before studying medicine at St Thomas's Hospital. Patients paid tribute to Dr Fletcher's kindness and thoroughness. Asked about his plans for his retirement, he said he would be spending more time reading and writing, and seeing his grandchildren.

Dr Fletcher's wife, Eve, is a teacher at William Roper School. They have four daughters, Laura, Georgia, Gwen and Vanessa, and six grandchildren.

Finally, near the back, among pictures of school sports teams and fêtes, he saw a leggy blonde surrounded by group of sheepish teenagers in self-conscious poses.

FUN WITH THE BARD

Pupils at William Roper School will be tackling Shakespeare for the first time when they perform *Twelfth Night* next week. The school's drama teacher, Eleanor Gray, promises that the production will be "fast and fun". 'I've cut quite a bit and we really work at moving it along, so no-one should get bored,' she says. A pupil, Shaun Adams, who plays the Duke Orsino, says Shakespeare's language is 'weird but you get used to it.'

Audiences will have the chance to see what they think of it next week, Wednesday to Saturday, at 7.30 in the school hall. Tickets are available from the school office at £7.00 (£4.00 concessions).

His phone rang. 'Why do you always ring me when I'm having breakfast?' he asked.

'I like to catch you unawares.'

'Why?'

'Otherwise you fob me off.'

'You know you're all over *The Gazette*, I suppose?'

'Oh God. What does it say?'

'Read it.'

'I never look at it. I can't stand it. It reminds me that I live in a provincial town.'

'And you don't notice the rest of the time?'

'I rise above it. Tell me what it says.'

'Read it yourself. You've heard about Hector Carson, I suppose?'

'No? What?'

'He's dead. Drove his car into the river.'

'Did he know about Glenys?'

'Not till we told him.'

'Do you feel bad?'

'I'm a policeman. I feel bad about murderers getting away.'

'No sightings of her then?'

'Disappeared into thin air.'

'A mistress of disguise more like. Your chaps who are looking for her do realise she'll be disguising herself, I suppose?'

'They do, Gina, yes.'

'So what are you doing to find her?'

Deep breath, he told himself. Glenys had, after all, set fire to her. 'We're doing what we do,' he said mildly, and then added, 'we find it pretty effective in most cases, but if you've got any better id–'

'Sorry,' she said.

'What?'

'Sorry. I didn't mean to imply, you know, that –'

'Are you all right?' he asked.

'Yes, fine – all things considered. Why?'

'You said *sorry*. I've never heard you apologise. I didn't think you could do it.'

'What do you mean? I apologise. I'm always apologising. I spend my life saying *sorry*. I don't know how you can say – why are you laughing?'

'Sorry,' he said.

29

WEDNESDAY 1st DECEMBER

Then come kiss me sweet and twenty

I told Ellie that Glenys had killed Marina – told her the whole ugly story, in fact, before it leaked out in dribs and drabs and caught her unawares. I was worried about how she would cope but I reckoned without the resilience of the young. She wept, of course, and I found her down in the kitchen at three in the morning making tea with brandy in it, but she had a play to put on and there is no-one more single-minded than a director with a first night looming. I, on the other hand, have been pathetic. I was signed off work for two weeks and I've drooped around the house, prone to sudden tears and looking like death warmed up. I've caught my mother looking at me sometimes: she's worried about me; I'm quite worried about myself.

Anyway, I have to pull myself together today. It is the first performance of *Twelfth Night* and we are all attending: I, my mother, Annie and, it is rumoured, Andrew. Only Freda is staying at home, with Eve's daughter, Gwen, to baby-sit. I wish we'd asked someone else. She arrives early and I feel quite uncomfortable with her. Colin was charged on Monday with obstructing the police by giving false information. He got off, more or less, with a suspended sentence but it's big news in *The Gazette* this morning. Gwen looks pale and miserable. I'm not sure if she's also reproachful, but I feel reproached anyway, so I announce that I'm off to the school to see if there's anything I can do to help and leave Annie to dish up a Sainsbury's fish pie and drive her grandmother along later.

It's before six when I arrive at William Roper and the front doors are locked. Later, no doubt, spruce, handpicked children will be standing in the foyer, taking tickets, selling programmes and ushering parents to seats, but for the moment all is dark and unwelcoming. I wheel my bike round the side and spot someone emerging from a side door. As a security light comes on I see that it's Renée Deakin. 'Renée!' I call and she turns towards me, her face pinched against the cold. She looks, in the bluish light, closed and wary and quite a lot older. 'How are you?' I ask as I hurry towards her.

'I've just been giving a hand with the refreshments for tonight,' she says, which isn't an answer to my question. 'A friend of mine's on the PTA.'

'I was sorry to hear about Hector,' I say.

She looks at me, dull-eyed. 'It's her I worry about. Glenys. I'm so afraid she's done the same as him.'

Not on your life.

'Oh I shouldn't worry about that,' I say. 'She's pretty tough, isn't she?'

'No, she's not!' She startles me with her vehemence. 'She's that fragile, nobody realises. She needs looking after. I don't know how she'll manage with Hector gone and Edmund – you know –'

'Do you have any idea where she might have gone?'

She gives a sharp laugh. 'I was just going to ask you the same. You're friendly with that chief inspector, aren't you? Don't you know anything?'

What I know, Renée, will break your heart.

'No,' I say. 'I don't know anything.'

I go in through the side door and make my way, via the kitchen and the canteen, towards the hall. As I'm walking past the backstage area, I hear hammering and I stick my head in, in case it's Ellie having some last-minute panic. What I see is Eve, up a ladder, nailing fronds of paper ivy to a flat representing a nicely distressed, old stone wall. I'm about to withdraw when she says, 'Hello Gina,' without turning her head.

'Eyes in the back of your head?'

'Years of practice.'

She climbs down the ladder and turns to survey me. 'Nice hair,' she says. 'Makes you look thinner.' Which makes me notice that she looks thinner. Her face has lost its plump bloom; she looks literally deflated. It's undersold, I think, the grief diet, though I did hear a woman in Marks and Spencer's the other day say to her friend, 'The great thing about my divorce was I went down two dress sizes.'

'Thank you,' I say.

I should probably explain about the hair. You will recall that Glenys set fire to it with a flaming missile, so I presented myself at the hairdresser's with an unconvincing story about a candle going out of control and asked Tracey to do her best to even it up. Well, Tracey's best was to cut most of it off. I was briefly traumatised. I thought it was going to make me look fatter. I've always thought I needed the big hair to balance the bosom, but actually it gives me a longer neck and I quite like it. Admittedly, the neck is under wraps at the moment, as it's pretty scabby. I didn't fancy wearing my coat when the police finally returned it to me, so I donated it to the hospice shop and splashed out on a new one with a high collar, above which only the tip of my scorched ear is visible.

'How's Colin?' I ask.

'Oh, you know, relieved I suppose, but humiliated. Today's *Gazette* has hit him hard.'

'And he's definitely going to retire?'

'Oh, yes. We can't stay here now. We'll take ourselves off.'

She sits down on a faux stone bench and I join her.

'Where?'

'Well, as it happens, Laura and her husband have bought a smallholding in Donegal. Martin wants to raise rare breeds and Laura thinks she can start up a craft centre. It may all fall flat on its face, of course, but we're thinking we might go over and join them. We can look after the children, at least, even if we're not much good for anything else.'

'It could be lovely.'

'Yes, it could.' She puts a hand on my arm. 'I'm not coming round to watch tonight, sweetheart. Cowardly, I know, but I can't quite face all those eyes. I've told Ellie I'll stay back here and cope with emergencies. Then she can watch from the front.'

'OK.' I stand up and drop a kiss on the top of her head. 'I'll talk to you soon,' I say. 'Tell Colin –'

'What?'

'I don't know. Tell him I hope – ' I'm saved from continuing by my phone ringing. 'Sorry. I'd better –' I fish it out of my bag.

'Gina?'

'David?'

'I thought you'd like to know we've got her.'

'Glenys?'

'Yes.'

'Where? How?'

'Where is somewhere unpronounceable on the west coast of Wales. How – she phoned Edmund.'

'And you were bugging his phone?'

'We've got his phone.'

'Are you allowed to do that?'

'No, but we thought we'd do it anyway. What do you think?'

'I just thought –'

'That possession of a mobile phone is a fundamental human right? I don't think so.'

'You'd think she'd have realised that you'd be monitoring his calls.'

'I'd think that maybe she loves him.'

'Her Achilles' heel.'

'Something like that.'

'Well.'

'As you say. Well.'

I put my phone away and turn to speak to Eve, but the bench is empty.

In the hall, Ellie has reserved a half row for us. Eight seats. By my calculations, there are only five of us. Who else is she expecting? Annie and my mother are the first to arrive, Annie performing her role of solicitous granddaughter with serious attention. Andrew arrives, not at the last minute for once and bringing Lavender with him. She is gazing about her in some bewilderment and it occurs to me that this may be the first time she has been inside a state school, but it is good of her to come and I greet her with enthusiasm. At the last minute, Ellie slips into a seat at the far end of the row, with a dark-haired chap, who must be Ben Biaggi, beside her. There is a spare seat on the end of the row next to me and I hope no-one will sit in it because the heating is on in here and I shall have to take my coat off and I don't want to frighten anyone with the state of my neck.

No-one has arrived by the time the houselights go down and I sit back and try to relax. I'm on tenterhooks through the first two scenes but it comes alive with Sir Toby, Maria and Sir Andrew, who are full of bounce and get the audience going beautifully, so I'm just beginning to enjoy myself when someone slips into the seat beside me. I decide not to worry about the view of my crusty neck since it's pretty dark, but I sneak a glance to see what sort of a person it is and find that it's David.

Ellie doesn't allow any flagging between scenes but I seize a moment when one lot of actors is speeding off and another arriving to hiss, 'What are you doing here?'

'Ellie asked me,' he says.

It's after the interval that something odd starts to happen to me. I come over all emotional. I am overwhelmed by the sheer effort these children are making, the seriousness of their endeavour. I know them well, these flaky adolescents with their attention deficit, their whims and moods, their chaotic home lives and unimagined futures. And my Ellie has cajoled and coerced them, bullied and flattered, and they have turned up to rehearsals week after week, and now they are acting their hearts out, navigating the language like tightrope walkers, performing as if for their very lives. I wipe away a tear or two and feel David turn to give me a glance.

And now we're at the reunion scene and I'm at it again. Viola and Sebastian, orphans, shipwrecked brother and sister, have found one another and we all watch, hushed, as they stand, eyes locked, and allow themselves to believe that it's true. Marina Carson has been in my mind all evening. I assume Hector named her after Shakespeare's Marina, from *Pericles*, another lost heroine like Viola, like Perdita, like Imogen. No reunions for Hector's Marina, though, no miraculous return from the dead, no loving brother to take her in his arms.

Then it's all over. Feste, a black boy with a husky, raw-edged voice, sings his final song:

'A great while ago the world began
With a hey ho, the wind and the rain,
But that's all one, our play is done,
And we'll strive to please you every day.'

The audience explodes into applause; the cast troops on, messily, unsmiling, slightly stunned, it seems, by what they have just done. Friends whoop and cheer, a few enthusiastic parents jump to their feet, the actors bow out of sync and, finally, break into smiles. As they shuffle off, I push my way along the row to hug Ellie. I shake hands with Ben Biaggi, give Andrew a *see what she can do* look, receive a fragrant embrace from Lavender, hug Annie, kiss the top of my mother's head, and then, because you have to fight back against the wind and the rain, I take hold of David and I kiss him.

A Note

For those who are interested, all chapter heading quotes are taken from *Twelfth Night* as follows:

CHAPTER 1:
And what's her history? (Act 2, Scene 4)

CHAPTER 2:
He was a bachelor then. (Act 1, Scene 2)

CHAPTER 4:
Youth's a stuff will not endure (Act 2, Scene 3)

CHAPTER 7:
Bring your hand to the buttery bar and let it drink (Act 1, Scene 3)

CHAPTER 8:
O had I but followed the arts! (Act 1, Scene 3)

CHAPTER 11:
If she be so abandoned to her sorrow
As it is spoke, she never will admit me (Act 1, Scene 4)

CHAPTER 13:
The rudeness that hath appeared in me
Have I learnt from my entertainment (Act 1, Scene 5)

CHAPTER 15:
For I myself am best
When least in company (Act 1, Scene 4)

CHAPTER 17:
'Tis not that time of moon with me
to make one in so skipping a dialogue (Act 1, Scene 5)

CHAPTER 18:
And the rain it raineth every day (Act 5, Scene 1)

CHAPTER 19:
No more cakes and ale (Act 2, Scene 3)

CHAPTER 20:
I have not seen such a firago (Act 3, Scene 4)

CHAPTER 22:
She hath abjured the sight
And company of men (Act 1, Scene 2)

CHAPTER 23:
Most provident in peril (Act 1, Scene 2)

CHAPTER 26:
Daylight and champaign discovers not more (Act 2, Scene 5)

CHAPTER 27:
Nature with a beauteous wall
Doth oft close in pollution (Act 1, Scene 2)

CHAPTER 29:
Then come kiss me sweet and twenty (Act 2, Scene 3)